Ori studied her. Ilanit was dressed to the nines, wear-ing something similar to what she'd worn for her bat-mitzvah party. A blue tee shirt, its collar cut, a gaudy blouse revealing thin shoulders, another peroxided streak in her hair, lipstick, purple tights hugging narrow hips and legs like two twigs, and fingernails gleaming with the polish from yesterday.

Ori looked at the yard: a curtain of lace on which were embroidered elaborate movements and light and shadow of distant lands, of a marketplace and its hub-bub. Where had that come to her from? She didn't know, just as she didn't know how she'd pluck up the courage to cross the meter of no man's land between the steps and the party, even with Ilanit's help. And with that thought her skin started burning. She clenched her fist so as not to scratch or touch it.

Sunburnt
faces

Sunburnt faces

SHIMON ADAF

TRANSLATED FROM THE HEBREW BY
MARGALIT RODGERS AND ANTHONY BERRIS

2013

Jacket art by Christopher Roberts.
Book design by Pedro Marques.
Text set in Garamond.
Titles set in Gill Sans and Commons.

Printed in England by the T.J. International
on Vancouver Cream Bookwove 80 gsm stock.

PS Publishing Ltd
Grosvenor House
1 New Road
Hornsea, HU18 1PG
England
E-mail: editor@pspublishing.co.uk
Visit our website at www.pspublishing.co.uk

CONTENTS

Sunburnt Faces

Introduction

LAVIE TIDHAR

LET ME START WITH SOMETHING of a bold claim: Shimon Adaf is the best writer of the fantastic working today. My one regret is that the rest of his books are not yet translated, and my joy is that *Sunburnt Faces* is, and that you can finally read it.

Adaf is a writer who breaks boundaries, who gives new life to tired forms, a playful, inventive, dedicated, serious novelist, with a poet's sensitivity and an editor's acute eye. He had been all those things, and more, in a remarkable literary career. He is the sort of writer one aspires to imitate, that one learns from by the very act of reading him.

Sunburnt Faces is, overtly, a realist novel. And yet, covertly, it is at the same time a meditation on Wonderland and the nature of fantasy itself. Adaf's fascination as a novelist is with the moment of coming-of-age, the painful transition from confusing childhood to no less confusing adult life. That moment recurs and is explored again and again in his work.

Sunburnt Faces is, I think, one of his most accessible books, and I still remember sitting up until three o'clock in the morning, on a hot and humid Tel Aviv night, unable to put the book down. Adaf is the sort of writer who can transform your life.

Shimon Adaf was born in 1972 in the small town of Sderot, in the Negev desert in Israel, and less than a mile from Gaza City. His parents came from Morocco, and like other immigrants were settled in the remote town. "It took me twenty years to love / this hole in the middle of nowhere," he wrote in his first poetry collection, *Icarus' Monologue*, "only places bereft of love are entitled to absolute love." His family were religious; Adaf himself studied at a yeshiva, a bright student expected, I imagine, to eventually become a rabbi of some renown. Some of his childhood experience and his gradual move away from orthodoxy into secularism is described in fictional terms in his 2011 novel *Mox Nox.*

Sderot, in its various guises, recurs throughout his novels, but Adaf began publishing as a poet, and a poet of some renown. To date he has published three collections of poetry, and in 2010 he won the prestigious Amichai Prize for his third collection.

His talent is easy to envy but the man himself is disarmingly self-effacing, with a sharp intellect behind the scruffy exterior. Where Western writers often write with the expectation of financial reward Adaf writes for art, choosing to make a living in a variety of jobs in order not to compromise his values.

He moved to Tel Aviv in 1994 and has lived in the city ever since. He played in a rock band and wrote lyrics for many of their songs. Many others of his songs and poems have been recorded by some of the leading musicians in Israel. In 2000 he became the editor of one of Israel's largest publishers, Keter: the youngest editor ever to hold that role. He has had a major influence as an editor on a new generation of writers, several exploring the fantastic in their works.

He wrote his first novel while at the Iowa Writers Workshop in the US. *One Mile and Two Days Before Sunset* was published in 2004, an unusual detective novel partially set in the vibrant rock scene of 1990s Tel Aviv, and whose hero is a devout reader of science fiction.

Already with this first book Adaf was displaying the hallmarks that would come to define his work: the interest in high and low culture, in the classics on the one hand and pulp science fiction on the other, the in-depth characterisation and the interest in coming of age and childhood's end, and most of all the beautiful writing: all are present here.

In 2007 Adaf published *The Buried Heart*, an ambitious – and, needless to say, unusual! – Young Adult fantasy based on Jewish legend and mythology. This was his first, full-on foray into the fantastic, and it was followed in 2008 by *Sunburnt Faces*.

By now, Adaf had quit editing in order to focus on his writing and, later, became a lecturer in Creative Writing, teaching several courses, including one on science fiction, at Ben Gurion University in the Negev desert. Considering he had, for a time, worked in a second-hand bookshop on first arriving in Tel Aviv, I think it is fair to say he has pretty much run the gamut of jobs in the book trade.

In 2010, Adaf published *Kfor* (Frost), to my mind his masterpiece. It is a hugely ambitious novel, describing a Tel Aviv some five hundred years in the future, and combining a detective mystery, poetry, science fiction and metafiction with astonishingly beautiful writing. It is a triumph.

It is also, as it eventually became clear, the first in a loose trilogy of novels Adaf has called *The Rose of Judea*. It was followed by *Mox Nox*, which combines the autobiographical story of a boy growing up in a remote town and his rebellion against his strict father and religious upbringing, with the story of an author (perhaps the same boy, grown up) in seemingly-contemporary Tel Aviv. This being an Adaf novel, of course, nothing is as straightforward as it seems, and the novel offers sudden, startling flashes into an alternative history, a weird historical conspiracy and eventually a ghost story a-la *The Turn of the Screw*. I rather feel Israeli reviewers simply did not know what to make of it, choosing to simply ignore the fantastical elements and treat it as a realist novel. Yet it ended up the surprise-winner of the 2013 Sapir Prize – the most prestigious literary award in Israel, modelled after the Booker and worth some £30,000.

I am proud to count Shimon as a friend, and even prouder to be able to present to you *Sunburnt Faces*, his first novel to be available in an English translation. May it be the first of many, and mat you love it as much as I did.

Lavie Tidhar

London
2013

For my sister Aviva
Who loved and fell silent

But when the calling
Of my only true name
Whirred toward me,
I started,
It stuck into me
Like a harpoon,
And I could
Not avoid it.
In a whisper
I call
To myself
With my
Own name,
And frighten
Myself with it,
As if the name
Came up to me
From far outside me,
From a time in which I was still
Without form.

Peter Weiss, *Leavetaking*
(trans. E. B. Garside, Alastair Hamilton
and Christopher Levenson)

ONE

Bat-Mitzvah

SHE WAS AWAKENED by the yowling of cats in heat and in the dim weightiness of stirring consciousness. She carried on listening, but it gradually faded, threads of a dream dwindling into the vast silence of the night. Yet she sat up in bed and cocked an ear, feeling for echoes and refractions. Nothing. Some of the lightening darkness filtered into the room through the almost completely closed slats of the shutter on the only window; darkness mingling with deeper darkness. Apart from that—a hush. You could drown in the density of the silence. It had been one of those nights in which summer breaks through the thickness of winter. Only two weeks ago they had celebrated the New Year of Trees at school, and the sword of the first *hamsin* heat wave had already struck Netivot. It had taken nature by surprise, albeit with exemplary precision as it did every year in March. The sound of the insects coming from the wild vegetation of early summer, from the nauseating blossom of the acacia and oleander, from the provocative eruption of the honeysuckle. The bees with their menacing buzzing and the cicadas and their sawing, the bothersome rustling. The constantly stimulated air still waited, cheated by the feeble movement of the seasons' clock. It had not rained. The dissonance of the clouds as they collided in their passing, and the whipping of the water, from the hesitant, shy drops of November to the assaults of the December and January hailstorms—the night

7

was clean of all these, innocent of the orchestras of winter and summer. She recognized its deep, scorched smell and inhaled it until her throat became dry.

She threw off the light summer quilt and put both feet onto the floor; putting them down all at once, ready, but not at all prepared for the chill of the tiles that flowed through them, up her body to her shoulders. Then she shivered. She hugged her shoulders mechanically and rubbed them, concentrating momentarily on the focal points of the heat beneath her hands and feeling how thin her arms were. She was almost twelve but relatively small for her age. It seemed that childhood still lingered in her, was slow to leave, evaporate, as it had from her classmates—especially Gvinush of whom her big brother said, when visiting her classroom to see how she was managing on her first day in junior high, "*Ya varadi*. She's grown a pair of real grapefruits there!"

In the space of a single summer Asher Elhayani had turned from a skinny kid into a clumsy youth. His limbs had lengthened and his voice deepened. Black bristles sprouted haphazardly on his chin and Adam's apple, which had become prominent and bobbed up and down when he swallowed his saliva between sentences. But despite the new-found confidence instilled by his new body he blushed as he said it, and she replied with a smile, "*Ya varadi*. What a beetroot you've become!"

Asher was right, of course. The other girls in the class whispered among themselves during recesses about "the pair of grapefruits". Ever since fourth grade, when Gvinush had sent her away shamefaced from a party in her house, they hadn't exchanged a word. Gvinush's real name was Rimona, but because of her yellow hair and pale skin she had been dubbed, since first grade, "Yellow Cheese", or the Hebrew abbreviation of the nickname, "Gvinush". In any event, that's what they called her behind her back. None of the kids ever called her that to her face. They were scared of her, perhaps because of her coloring—one kid, she doesn't remember who, once whispered that "My father said she's anemic", and burst into hysterical giggling—or perhaps because of her domineering temperament or loud voice or her race towards puberty in which her body collaborated and made everyone around her feel somewhat rebuked, childish.

Her throat had become even drier and she had to get to the kitchen. Without putting on her slippers she stood up, went to the door of her room, opened it carefully, and with even greater care went out. All week her father had been on nightshift at the factory and she knew how angry he got if his sleep was disturbed the following week when he was on the day shift, which was a week of complete fatigue and explosive anger.

Only the rustle of her nightgown, which she insisted on wearing on the wintry summer nights since she was eight, her mother's nightgown with the lace hem that gently scratched her shins, and the sleeves in which her hands were lost, only it broke the silence. And perhaps the touch of the flesh of her feet as it was softly squeezed on the tiles. The water spurting from the kitchen faucet was louder than the pounding of the blood in her ears and she quickly turned it off and opened the fridge. She would have to slake her thirst with freezing water and then she wouldn't be able to go back to sleep.

She was wide awake now and stared into the fridge. The cats, she thought after a few moments of standing doing nothing. Was it only a dream? And if not, maybe she'd find them in the yard. From the top shelf she pulled out a box with the leftovers of last night's chicken and slowly slid open the screen door giving onto the yard.

In the yard her eyes roved over the corrugated iron walls of the shed her father had built, the jumble of scrap metal, the bundle of metal piping that was the frame of the collapsible *sukkah*, the pair of gas cylinders, the lines from which clothes hung in colorful confusion in the still air. The bitter orange tree bent under the burden of the golden fruit left to rot on its branches, the mulberry tree with its broad, dusty leaves, its pink balls of blossom the size of her clenched fists hanging among them. It seemed that from the corner of her eye she could see elusive figures, perhaps the silhouettes of cats, under cover of the yard's still shadows. But when she quickly turned her head she didn't see anything. She opened the box, waved it in the air, sending out the aroma of chicken. No cat came. The dark sky curved above her, trapping her and the yard under a black bell jar sown with cracks and flaws: the stars gleaming metallically and indifferently. There was silence everywhere. Again she inhaled it, the power of the summer blaze whose closeness made her skin crawl, and went back inside.

She moved through the rooms, imagining that this big, emptied house that had been bought with the money left to her mother by her parents, is an enchanted nocturnal palace—enchanted by a thousand-year-old sleeping spell—that might be broken by the force of her movement. She opened the door of her elder sister Ofra's room, and peeped in. Soft breathing swallowed by the walls. She moved on to the door of Asher's room, her brother, two years her senior, who could fall asleep anytime, anywhere. He was on the youth bed he'd bought with his earnings from a summer job selling watermelons, his head between two pillows, the whistling exhalations from his mouth muted by them. In the aquarium, which he'd bought with the remaining money, black-striped goldfish slowly cut through the water making gentle waves, bubbling silently. Only the heating element buzzed, disrupting the melody of their movement. She closed the door.

And then, with a daring that only foolishness or boredom could have sparked in her, she went to the door of her parent's bedroom and opened it a crack. Her parents were asleep in their separate beds in a huge room. Her father was sprawled like a dead man on their double marital bed. Her mother was in a single bed nearby, shifting in a dream, mumbling, her hands pushing away something that only her eyes could see. Her heart fell. It's all right, she wanted to tell her. She wanted to go over and catch her mother's arms, bring them back to their place at the sides of her body or lay them folded on her chest. She wanted to whisper, *it's all right.* Instead she closed the door and went to the living room.

In the living room she absentmindedly stroked the faded embroidered upholstery of the armchair and looked around. Her glance fell on the TV set. Yes, the TV set. *I wonder if there's anything on at this hour.* She leant over the big-bellied, brown set and pressed the "ON" button. The piercingly high note that burst from the loudspeaker in the set's side startled her and she pressed the volume button continuously until the high-pitched scream diminished.

On the screen, on the only channel they could get—she'd heard from her classmates that with an outdoor aerial you could pick up Middle East Television—flickered a card divided into colored cubes surrounding a circle at whose center were numbers, a digital clock. It showed 03:25. What could she do until morning, she wondered.

She sank her small body into the armchair and rubbed her cheek against its rough upholstery. The changing numbers of the seconds, followed by the minutes, drew her gaze. She stared at them. Slowly, the presence of all the things around her was erased, the couches and the tapestries on the walls, the family photographs and the small rug that marked the center of the living room, the sturdy square table with its glass bowl— webbed with tiny slate veins—filled with plastic fruit. Only the ugly TV, the clock and its figures, remained imprisoned in her gaze. And then God spoke to her from the TV set.

How could she describe His voice?

If every molecule in the living room air was gifted with human consciousness, and each molecule could experience the power of all emotions from the moment of birth to death, and then screamed from the burden of this, or sighed, or bellowed, or lost its voice, or roared with the pain of happiness, or moaned, or groaned with the happiness of pain, or broke into sobs, or shouted for joy, or wept, and the passion of all these sounds was woven into a single syllable, perhaps then it would be possible to begin to describe the richness, the dimensions of the voice.

It came from everywhere in the room. From the minuscule structures of her roaring blood and the DNA helices spiraling in the cell nucleus, from the deposits in the veins and from the fine fatty stalactites trapped in her hair. Her body was a mouth and lips for the voice and the walls also shouted the bitter, wonderful sound, and the cherry-wood sideboard, and from behind its doors, among the bottles as translucent as sapphire, her father's arrack stormed to give voice to the glory of God, and both the pure and impure uttered the words. And yet, the voice that was plucking out her eyes and slicing her skin with ten thousand razors was coming from the TV set.

And God said to her, "Rise, Ori, my light, for your light has come."

And He let her fall from her life, although she hadn't realized that she was at such a great height.

And she fell.

———

What woke her first? The blow of her body hitting the arm of the chair in the living room, or her mother's hand shaking and pulling her up from the nothingness and the fall? She heard her mother say something as she bent over her, but the words sounded as if they were muffled by water, or perhaps the impenetrable silence of the night. But a bright morning was flooding the outside and shafts of hard light slanted through the window in the eastern wall of the living room and struck her eyelids. She knew they were shut. She opened them to her mother's dark face, it was creased with concern, her brown eyes were ready to weep and the corners of her mouth were down-turned. Again her mother spoke, but the syllables broke up on their way to her brain. She tried to focus her thoughts, something important had happened. What? She'd woken up in her bed and . . . She needed to clear her throat, it was dry, as if dust and rust had accumulated there, and her voice was hoarse as she asked tiredly, "What . . . what happened to the cats?"

Her mother's look of concern was replaced by an expression of wonderment, the skin of her face loosened and softened, wrinkles around her eyes fell away, the her lips pursed as if to say something.

"What happened to the cats?" she asked again.

"God be praised, God be praised," her mother shouted as she struck her chest hard and burst into cries of joy. She rolled her tongue between her lips, tried to imitate the other women of the neighborhood who would ululate at the ritual bath, at engagement immersions, at weddings and in the women's section of the synagogue before raining candies on the heads of the congregation.

"What's happened?" asked Ofra as she shuffled into the living room from the kitchen. "Who's died this time? Ima, I've told you a thousand times, stop showing us up with that stupid yelling."

Their mother, who usually silenced her older daughter with the words, "You and your brother and sister, you have no respect for anything, not tradition, not your parents, nothing. You have no fear in your heart," ignored her and quickly left the living room.

Ofra looked at her, turned the palm of her hand left and right questioningly.

"I've no idea. All I did was ask what happened to the cats," she shrugged as she spoke.

Ofra looked at her in amazement.

"You're talking?" she asked. "I don't believe it! I'm dying to see Abba's face when he hears you. When did you start talking again? You were fooling us, right? Admit it. I bet Asher his aquarium that you were just pretending."

"I . . . what . . . " she started to reply—and the world, over which a band of white light stretched in her consciousness, rose from its ruins, fell back into place around her, and her memory hit her.

———

Two months earlier she had come home from school, her body shaking. Blood dripped from a cut on her temple, it was smeared across her face and had stained her dress, endowing her with a terrifying appearance. From that moment until this morning she had not spoken.

Before her eyes flashed the image of her mother who had come running from the living room firing questions, her father's body tense with anger, the look on Ofra's and Asher's faces, and the whispering around her from that day on. In the emergency room they told her parents that nothing was wrong, just a superficial cut on the temple that would heal quickly thanks to her young age. Her father took the doctor who had examined her aside. He asked her something in an insistent whisper. She guessed what he'd asked, and the doctor's nodding head had provided a satisfactory answer. She saw her father's relief.

They left her alone for a day. But when she didn't speak next day either, they began pleading. She wanted to tell them that she didn't know and didn't remember, but her vocal cords were paralyzed. She had forgotten how to speak. The words formed in her mind but she no longer knew how to control the muscles of her mouth and lips to utter them, she no longer remembered how her voice should sound.

They took her for tests. They went through the concrete, neon-illuminated labyrinth of the Soroka Hospital in Beer-sheba. Blood tests. A throat swab—maybe it's a virus. The audiology lab—perhaps she's gone deaf. X-rays.

"There's nothing physiologically or physically wrong. We believe it's psychological." The doctors pronounced.

"So what are you actually saying?" her father bellowed at the doctor who gave them the test results, "What? That my daughter's mad?"

Her frightened mother knocked three times on the wood of the doctor's desk.

"God help us," she said.

"No, but we do need a psychologist's expert opinion so we know how to treat her, or to decide whether she needs treatment at all," the doctor said nervously.

She listened to the conversation. They talked about her in the third person in her presence. It made no difference to her. The words, cold and remote, sailed through the space in her skull from temple to temple.

———

The school counselor referred her to a psychologist who visited Netivot once a week. After the heavy rain that had drowned the week of Hannukah, the air became clearer. On the way to the psychologist her nostrils were assailed by the intoxicating smell of mud. On every patch of ground her eyes spotted different birds, buntings, warblers, sparrows. They were no longer a bunch of gray, tweeting feathers to her; each was unique, individual distinct from individual, species distinct from species. Without words that disguise the differences between one thing and another, the world is perceived more clearly. Even though it sometimes seems that the opposite might be true. Language makes distinctions only up to a point, then it becomes too general, too vague, it lacks precision. On the operating table a dull scalpel is likely to kill.

After a month of muteness she felt that even the voice in her brain, which had incessantly whispered thoughts and suggested things to say, had gone. A different way of seeing matured within her and she was able to differentiate between the birds; the beadiness of the eyes, the width of beaks, the hues and luster of the feathers.

In a wooden building, that a decade earlier had been a classroom in the elementary school, she sat facing the psychologist, a short round-faced man. His green eyes and flaring nostrils gave him the appearance of a lemur. She noticed the hairs on his knuckles. He smiled a lot, apologetically or because he was embarrassed? She didn't know. On the desks that remained in the room most of the green Formica tops were cracked. There were initials carved into the desk at which they sat, declarations of love, obscenities. With her fingers she felt the underside of the desk; they encountered the roughness of the chipboard, lumps of dried chewing gum. Where are the mouths that chewed the gum, the hands that carved into the Formica? For some reason a scene from a movie came to her head—prisoners trying to dig a tunnel to freedom with a spoon.

The psychologist asked her to assemble jigsaws of varying degrees of difficulty and she immersed herself in them. She put them together with ease. When she noticed that he was following her actions, she slowed down and feigned deliberation, and only then slid the pieces into place. The pictures were simple. One glance was enough to understand the pieces: lines and surfaces, shapes and color. He asked her to draw her house and her parents and her school, and she did. Detailed, precise drawings. All the birds she remembered, all the differences that distinguished one bird from another. The psychologist looked at the drawings with interest.

At the next session he again asked her to draw her family. She drew a great tit and a thrush she'd seen on a nature program on TV. Then she added the tired rose bushes she passed on the way to school, the red sepals sliding into rotting purple. Her sister had once picked a whole bunch of them, soaked them in a bath filled with water and immersed her body. The next morning Ofra woke up itching all over, her skin covered with a rash.

She drew the hedge carefully tended by her father to hide their yard from the neighbors. The climbing hedge had round leaves with red veins that emerged from the leaf stem; the tendrils were brown, knotty.

During the fourth session he asked her a direct question about that afternoon, and she wrote with a blue crayon, *I don't remember. Dontremember! Don't. Remember.*

"Mr. and Mrs. Elhayani, you've got a very intelligent daughter. But we're not getting anywhere. I've thought about trying hypnosis," the psychologist told her parents at the end of the session.

Her mother yelled at him that they didn't need his idolatry in Netivot, thank God, they've got the Baba Sali, and she dragged her out by the arm.

———

All this while, as she wandered among her recollections, she looked at Ofra in embarrassment.

"You're not starting your tricks again. Say something," Ofra said.

The words pulled her thoughts away from the Baba Sali's waiting room, where her mother sat beside her gripping her hand and her father impatiently paced the noisy room, chewing on his extinguished cigarette butt; they pulled her away from the tumult of the women laboring over the kneading of couscous, the old men stricken with cataracts, the feverish children.

"Something," she said softly to Ofra.

"Ima's probably gone to tell all the neighbors," said Ofra with a smile.

Their mother came back into the living room a short while later, and Ofra couldn't restrain herself and repeated her gibe.

"You probably went to tell all the neighbors."

"Tell me, Ofra, where's your brain? I've got far more important things to do. I called your father at the factory and Mama Elhayani to tell them I was right, that we're having the bat-mitzvah party as planned." Their mother leant over the armchair where she'd fallen and stroked her hair. "*Jinn*, sweetie, I knew we shouldn't cancel the party."

Yes, the bat-mitzvah. When they returned frustrated from the Baba Sali and it was clear that the amulet bound around her neck with a blue lace, and the blessed water with which she had been sprinkled, and his trembling hands, scrawny with age, covering her head during the prayer he had uttered, would not help, her mother informed her father, "I'm going to talk to your mother."

"Why? What good can she do?" her father said tiredly. He had been working double shifts to make up the hours he'd missed when they'd taken her for tests.

"She's helping me plan the bat-mitzvah. The girl will be twelve in two months time."

"What bat-mitzvah are you on about, Sylvia, are you out of your mind? First let's see that the girl's well."

"Ya'akov, she needs a purpose," she said, shaking her head.

She knew that her mother meant herself more than her. And indeed, until that morning her mother had diligently focused on the party. It was as if she had lost all her usual efficiency and decisiveness. They said at the senior citizens' day center where she worked that she was absentminded and sometimes forgot to check that the clothing of the old people in her care was dry and that they'd eaten their lunch. She spent hours planning with their grandmother, Mama Elhayani, who was not exactly renowned for her lucidity. She wasted days on end on the guest list, adding names and erasing others. One morning she consulted Ofra about inviting some distant uncles from her father's side.

"Oh, come on, Ima, who are you kidding? Like since your wedding you haven't kept an organized record of who came to every celebration and what present they brought? I still remember you taking it out before Asher's bar-mitzvah and you saw they hadn't invited you to their eldest daughter's wedding. So why are you suddenly playing the innocent?" Ofra grumbled.

"You come from your father's side of the family. Always digging, looking for a fight. You and him—a copy," her mother replied in a hurt tone.

Ofra snorted contemptuously and waved her hands.

"We've heard, we've heard you." And that afternoon, when their father got home from work, Ofra told him, "Abba, Ima's driving us crazy with the bat-mitzvah. Who needs it?"

Her father stared at his wife but didn't say a word.

———

Her mother's hand stroked her face, "So what do you say, *jinn*?"

And she, embarrassed by the uproar surrounding the bat-mitzvah and in a vain effort to conceal her resolve, said in a pampered tone, "I don't want a party, Ima. Nobody from my class will come. They're not speaking to me."

"Or more to the point, you're not speaking to them." Ofra laughed.

"Ima," Asher called from his room, "make me a cup of coffee."

"Get up and make it yourself and stop playing the tough guy like your friends," Ofra replied.

"You'd better shut up," Asher said as he came into the living room, "before I tell Abba what . . . " He stopped what he was saying when he saw Ofra and their mother standing beside her. "What's wrong?" he asked, alarmed.

"There's nothing wrong," she answered him. They all followed his amazed look, and then his sigh of relief, how he struggled to hide it as his Adam's apple bobbed up and down.

"I knew you'd start talking again sometime." he said with exaggerated toughness.

"*Yalla, yalla,*" said Ofra and the three of them burst out laughing.

As their laughter subsided, Asher said, red-faced, "So if you're talking again, maybe you'll talk to Rimona Peretz, you know that . . . " and he fell silent.

"The fact that I'm talking doesn't mean I'll speak to that pest."

"It'll be interesting to see how your nerdy school friends react," said Ofra.

Their mother slapped the arm of chair. "I've got an idea," she said, "an excellent idea."

———

In the end the bat-mitzvah party was a modest affair. Her mother didn't make anyone privy to her decisions, not even her. Her age-old determination burst forth again and she invited all her classmates, boys and girls alike, and also the kids from elementary school who'd gone on to the town's other junior high. She thought about the ploys her mother used. With any person and in any given situation she always knew which emotions would get her what she wanted—like when she haggled in the market. This time she'd probably played on pity and guilt.

The day her voice came back she didn't go to school. Next day she discovered that the rumor of the miracle that had happened to the mute had spread. Everybody knew. Boys and girls she didn't know came up to her at recess and said, "Come on, say something," and laughed. She spoke only rarely. She had become used to her tongue being frozen against her palate, and the clumsy thoughts that moved like a flock of sheep in her brain. In school her girlfriends kept their distance. She wondered if they were scared of her, if her brief muteness had left scars on her arms and legs, on some visible part of her skin. Even Ilanit, her best friend, who in the first days of her silence had tried to encourage her to speak, just gave her a forced, crooked smile and mumbled a feeble hello.

The still air was awash with fragrances. Now she had her voice back she did not distinguish between them, and only the dense fabric they wove around her made her restless, created expectation. She observed the guests as they arrived, carrying presents. Gvinush was among them too. Her upper body was covered with an embroidered strapless blouse, which not only accentuated her breasts but also revealed a thin line of transparent hairs running between them. She found she was unable to tear her eyes away from her. "Gross," she heard a familiar voice whispering in her ear, "what a slut." She turned her head to look. Yes. It was Ilanit. With uncharacteristic audaciousness she had peroxided a streak in her hair. Circular, black and white plastic earrings hung from her earlobes to her shoulders and matched the zebra blouse she was wearing, and her wide collar left one of her narrow shoulders bare. Her lips glistened

21

redly. How come she hadn't noticed until now? She really is a young woman.

"So what do you say?" Ilanit asked.

"I don't know. It's a good party, right?"

Asher, who had been busy clearing the yard—"of all the crap Abba's been collecting for years"—had strung a chain of fairy lights from the bitter orange to the mulberry tree. He had untied the knots of the clotheslines and adorned the posts bereft of their lines with tiny, flickering lights, the whole thing designed by their mother. At the party he had volunteered his services as a DJ; from one friend he obtained a big tape deck, and from another a collection of hits.

The yard was filled with the voice of Sandra, and Ilanit joined in, mangling both music and lyrics. "In the hill of the night," she screeched. "Yo, that song's the end." She started going wild, dancing with complete abandon as she went on singing. By the time Sandra was replaced by Cyndi Lauper's "Girls Just Wanna Have Fun", all the boys and girls in the yard were caught up in the fever of their clumsy dancing, unintentionally splitting into couples, and when Wham's "Careless Whisper" came blaring from the speakers, the random couples became fixed, girl in the arms of boy, trapped in the web of spring's whisper. She stood at the side, her head on Asher's shoulder, and watched them.

———

Only Ilanit stayed with her after the party was over. Her father went to bed early; a morning shift awaited him. And while Ofra, who had gone out with her friends and was now back, and their mother collected up the leftovers and the disposable plates and cups from the yard, she and Ilanit sat in her room and opened the presents. Ilanit's self-possession was fine by her. At first she'd feared that Ilanit would mistakenly think that their old closeness had been reestablished and she'd ask unnecessary questions. But Ilanit didn't ask. Her fingers untied ribbons and were swallowed up in red and purple gift wrapping decorated with hearts and silver stars.

"I saw you dancing a slow dance with Noam Ohana," she said.

"Yes," Ilanit replied, taking her eyes from the pile of greeting cards she had removed from the presents and was sorting, "he stuck to me the whole evening, right from when I started dancing." She coiled the end of a peroxided lock of hair around a finger, "And you," she asked, "why weren't you dancing?"

"I was too excited," she replied. "What do you think of Noam?"

"He's okay. Nice. Why do you ask?"

Two days earlier she had returned the classroom during recess. Noam was standing on a desk, his back to her, surrounded by the rest of the boys who were completely focused on him. They had not noticed her in the doorway. His shorts were round his knees and his underpants were also down, revealing his buttocks.

"Look," he said, "I've started to grow hair."

The boys' eyes were riveted to his groin. She fled, filled in disgust. That pervert, she said to herself, trembling. She felt he had unintentionally dirtied her.

"Look, I've started to grow hair."

She wanted to tell Ilanit, but just the memory nauseated her. And also the fact that it was one of many troublesome incidents she'd experienced over the last month. At the Purim party in the school gym she'd felt a tingling on the back of her neck and reluctantly turned her head. The principal, Yoram Tuitto, was standing behind the crowd of students, leaning against the wall and picking his nose undisturbed. After taking his finger from his nose, he wiped it on his pants leg and then plunged his hand into a plate of cakes. She tried not to think

23

about the other instances that seared her, and the words that popped into her mind: foulness, defilement.

"I was only asking," she told Ilanit, "I think . . . "

"Oh, come on," Ilanit protested, and added, "tell me, your brother Asher, has he asked about me?"

She bowed her head and smiled to herself, discovering fresh interest in the presents.

"What a cheek," said Ilanit a few moments later. She waved a piece of paper, "She didn't even buy a card, that Gvinush. Listen, 'Mazal Tov from Rimona'. That's all. Not to who. Nothing." She picked up Gvinush's present and felt it. "I wonder what it is. Probably something old."

"Open it," she told her.

"No, it's your present," Ilanit replied.

She sighed and opened the brown paper wrapping. Inside was an Alice band. A simple, pink plastic Alice band decorated with tiny butterflies shining in green and gold. Sparks of light leapt from them as Ilanit took it from her and examined it. "That tightfisted Kamtza Bat Kamtza," she said, "you can buy these for a shekel each from Knafo in the market. It's really insulting. That's what she's trying to do, insult you."

She shrugged.

"Don't just shrug," Ilanit protested, "you've got to get back at her. She's got no shame. Listen to me, Flory . . . "

She looked at Ilanit with sudden anger. It flickered in her eyes, she could actually feel them burning, flashing at her friend who fell silent. And in the gravest tone a twelve-year-old girl could muster she said, "Ilanit, don't call me Flory or Flora or Florence any more. D'you hear me? From now on my name is Ori, Ori Elhayani."

TWO

Books

DURING THE PASSOVER VACATION, two weeks after the bat-mitzvah, the love of reading was born in Ori. The love of writing followed close behind, like twins bursting from the womb with the hand of one grasping the heel of the other.

Now she demanded from everyone who knew her by her old name to call her Ori.

On the morning after the party, still red-eyed, Ori asked Elisheva Zikri, her literature and Bible studies teacher, if she would allow her to speak to the class. Uncharacteristically, Elisheva agreed with a silent, vigorous nod. Perhaps this was because a vestige of last night's solemnity still encircled Ori. Its aura, a kind of filmy gossamer spread all over her body and lightly shook the limbs and the flesh too delicate to see. Ori's eyes, despite their redness, gleamed like those of someone whose demands must be met.

That morning she selected her clothes with care. She had got up early, while Summer Time darkened the world, and hurried to the bathroom. A soft spring brightness began to protest against the impermeability of the windowpane, against the yellow tyranny of the incandescent light bulb. The pail, from the corner between the toilet bowl and the wall, she turned upside down on the floor. It rocked slightly as she got onto it. She looked into the mirror. Her hair, which didn't need straightening or blow-drying, fell over her face in straight lines, a curtain

25

of black plastic cords. Her eyes were half-closed with sleep and networked with burst capillaries, but still huge in her angular face. She studied her recurring image in the reflected depth of the brown pupils, the wall inlaid with blue ceramic tiles curving around the reflection of her body. Something was breaking up the proportions of her features. Her fringe. Yesterday afternoon, when the hairdresser's scissor blades stopped their snipping, she had known that this fringe wasn't right. It was too long, actually touching her eyebrows, spreading to the sides like two halves of a curtain locked in an embrace trying to hide her high forehead. It doesn't work, she thought. She got down from the upturned pail and it fell and lay on its side, crumpled from her weight. She'd have to think of something else. In the kitchen she climbed onto the work surface and from the top shelf took her mother's sewing box and removed a pair of scissors. From the living room she took the wood and cane stool her father used as a footrest when he watched TV. She went back to the bathroom. The stool was steadier than the pail beneath her feet. Very good. She would need steadiness. She combed her fringe with strong strokes, forcing apart the springiness imposed on it by the round brush and the hairdresser's skilful hand. It fell down over her face, straight. With the fingers of her left hand she divided it into locks, wound one around her finger and pulled it tight. She started cutting with the scissors in her right hand.

The result was less impressive than she'd hoped, but still satisfactory. She had cut the fringe almost to its roots and its length was even across her forehead. She gathered up the hair that had fallen into the sink and remembered her mother's warnings. Hair and nail clippings must not be left anywhere in the house; if a pregnant woman steps on a nail clipping she will abort her fetus, and should a single hair from her head find its way into the hands of the neighbors, they will be able to cast a shadow over her fate with one of their curses. She wrapped the hair in a piece of toilet paper and twisted it into a ball. She dropped it into the toilet bowl, flushed it, scrubbed the sink, and then took a shower.

She returned to her room with very light steps. From her closet she took a blue blouse with a petal-shaped roll collar embroidered with red and purple flowers. The blouse's sleeves were puffed at the shoulder and narrow at the wrist. Its buttons gleamed like ivory in the light flooding the room through the shutter slats. She put it on and smoothed the material over her body. She then put on a faded denim skirt that hung to her knees. On seeing herself in the closet's full-length mirror she thought something else was needed. She went to Ofra's room. Her sister, who was still tossing and turning in a struggle against wakefulness from the depths of sleep, did not see her. Ori quickly chose a belt from her sister's collection. She had had her eye on this particular one for a long time. It was long and of thick white leather, its big metal buckle fastened it loosely around her waist, the end falling between her thighs. Yes. Now, with the light pearl colored Converse All Star sneakers, the striped socks with their white and purple hoops and the Alice band Gvinush had given her, she looked perfect. A radiance like an electric eye leapt from its reflection and flickered through her body. Like Wonder Woman's sash, she thought.

"What's this, Flory, my love, why are you dressed up like Goldilocks?" Her mother said as she was about to leave for school.

Ofra, now up and staring over the rim of her cup of instant coffee, added, "Pccch, tell me, what's with the blouse, have you gone Yemenite?"

In class she assertively faced the astonished and silent stares—only Gvinush chuckled to herself—and said confidently, "From now on I'm asking you to call me Ori. Not Flora or Flory."

"What?" said Gvinush, and started laughing. But nobody laughed with her. Silence thickened the air in the classroom and quieted the brief, coarse laughter.

"Flora," Elisheva said embarrassedly, you can't be serious. I mean, changing your name . . . is a serious matter. I don't know . . . "

"Please, don't call me Flora anymore," fixing her with a look. "That's the last time I'll answer when I'm called by that name."

"Go to your desk," Elisheva said, the permanent anger slowly filtering back into her voice and eyes. "We've no more time to waste today."

Ori began striding towards her desk, which two weeks after she found her voice again was still reserved solely for her, with no one to share it with, not even Ilanit.

"You're getting more screwed up by the day. It was better when you didn't talk." The words spoken loud enough for everyone in the room to hear as she passed Gvinush's desk.

"What right have you to say anything, you piece of stinking yellow cheese?" She said to Gvinush, amazed by the violence that took over her voice, the toughness that straightened her back and the pleasure she got from the words.

Gvinush was angry and blood quickly rushed to her face, turning it a deep, poppy red, it spread like a rash, making her cheeks ugly.

Ori tore the pink Alice band from her hair and waved it above her head.

"Look at what this cheapskate gave me for a bat-mitzvah present," she yelled. The paper butterflies on the band made twisting, flashing tracks as they sliced the air. Then she grasped the band at both ends and bent it until a crack was heard, as weak as the soft cry of a body whose pulsing has ceased. In a class of silent students holding their breath it resounded like a thunderclap. She threw the two halves down in the middle of the desk between Gvinush and her slave, Aliza Edri.

"Who needs your presents anyway, eh?" she added, drunk with her sudden, imprudent triumph. Had Elisheva not grasped her elbow and led her to her desk, she would surely have stood longer at Gvinush's desk and drowned her with her thoughts.

———

"You've got some guts putting her in her place like that in front of the whole class," Ilanit told her at recess. "Now she'll be in your face all the time."

"You're the one who told me to get her back," she replied indifferently.

"Yes, but . . . Ori?" she said, pronouncing the name hesitantly, as a question, making both of them feel its strangeness. Then she said it again, this time with greater assurance, "Ori, I didn't really mean you to do anything," and she laughed.

"What time does the school library open?" Ori asked.

"I don't know. I think the librarian's off sick today."

"Oof, that Elisheva. What's the point of reading a book by that one . . . what's her name?"

"Galila Ron-Feder. And don't knock her. She writes well," Ilanit said. Ori snorted derisively. "No," Ilanit grumbled, "what's that for? What's happening to you lately? I cried at the end of *To Myself*."

"Is that the one they made us read in fourth grade? What's to cry about in it? The kid in the book is my brother Asher and your brother Reuven. It's about us, don't you get it? What, you get up in the morning, look at your family and cry?"

"Tell me, your brother Asher, has he asked about me?"

Ori turned away to look at the dusty soccer field from which the boys from the senior classes had ejected her classmates. A group of girls led by Gvinush commandeered one side of the paved basketball court. Two of them, Keren and Sima, held a rope that they began twirling as the others formed a line.

Gvinush went first, shouting "one" as she jumped, and was followed by Aliza and Zimra, "two, three, four", and so on. One by one the girls were 'out' at different numbers as they caught their feet in the rope and stumbled. At the end of this short qualification process the only two remaining were—wonder of wonders—Gvinush and Aliza. Keren and Sima reversed the direction of the rope, twirling it anticlockwise, which complicates skipping because you have to jump into the ovoid space made by the rope as it touches the ground, not at its zenith in the air. Ori knew that Gvinush was good at this. The two girls began jumping alternately, into the rope's arc and then out again. *"L'examere, la pipat la mer."*—what do the words mean, what language are they singing in—*"la pipat la bouche, la quadée de cabouche"*—Here the song took on a human guise— "A man got on a horse and yelled: January, February . . ." and on "July" the rope caught Aliza's ankles and she fell to the ground with a thump. The sweaty Gvinush yelled in triumph, ignoring the eighth and ninth grade boys who had gathered round and were elbowing each other in the ribs and laughing. She could guess what kind of jokes accompanied the nudges. *What a repulsive sight*, Ori thought, *what luck that Asher isn't here*, and quickly turned her head to a sight that really turned her stomach. Unseen by most of the kids on the basketball court, leaning against the wall of the gym, was Noam Ohana, his hand deep in his groin, feeling, touching.

"Gross," she said, and averted her eyes.

"Yes," Ilanit replied, "that Gvinush's got no shame. She'll do anything to attract attention."

"Let's get out of here," Ori said. She took Ilanit's hand and pulled her after her, "maybe we'll find the library open and be first for that book that Elisheva told us to read."

Ilanit freed her hand. "No, I want to stay in the sun a bit longer."

Ori didn't look at her. She stared at the ground. That way she wouldn't see what she was forbidden to look at. She ascribed the burning anger in her throat to Elisheva's announcement. Why did they have to invite Galila Ron-Feder? She remembered that she'd refused to write her book report about *To Myself* and had been given a written reprimand by the teacher. And now Elisheva and her nonsense. At the beginning of the literature lesson, which had been combined with Bible studies, Elisheva had excitedly informed them, her usually hoarse voice now clear, that the author Galila Ron-Feder would be visiting the school two and a half weeks after their return from the Passover vacation, and so they had to read her book, *In Light and Hiding: The Story of Ze'ev Jabotinsky.* "A moving book that relates our history, a book that will help us understand where we came from and what we're doing here," Elisheva said. "Prepare questions at home and we'll answer them during the lesson. I don't want you sitting in front of her like dummies."

Halfway to the library she slowed down. Although she had escaped from the filth surrounding Noam and the boys from the senior classes, her path was leading her towards something no less welcome. Ori didn't like reading, the books the elementary school teachers fed them with made her gorge rise. Except for Ofra, nobody in her family was a reader. And it had even taken Ofra some time to get to books. At first her sister had immersed herself in photo magazines, 'cine-novels', which Persian Rosa, their soldier neighbor lent her; Rosa bought them at the Tel Aviv Central Bus Station in Neveh Sha'anan, so she said. Ofra diligently read the stories accompanying the photographs and had even shown Ori some of them. Ofra lost herself in them and didn't answer her mother's calls, neglected her chores, the washing of dishes and floors. When she did her household duties at all she did them carelessly, so that her mother had to do everything over again, drawing a finger over the skirting boards and windowsills and lifting it up to the light to see the amount of dust. Close to last Passover, their mother gave up the fight over the household chores and brought in their father. That evening Ofra found three cine-novels torn into pieces in the middle of her room; it seemed that a lot of rage had gone into ripping them apart. She cried quietly into the night. Only Ori, in her shallow, restless sleep, heard her choked sobbing.

Afterwards Ofra chose to disappear. One day Ori followed her, so she knew where Ofra went. Ofra had found her private place on the lawn behind the municipal library where she read real, thick books whose pages had yellowed from standing so long on the library shelves. One summer's day their mother sent her out to look for Ofra and she covered the seven hundred meters from their neighborhood to the library in a risk ten minutes of walking. He sister was sitting on the mottled brown grass leaning against the trunk of a wasted poplar, her knees drawn up to her chest and on them a book. Ofra raised her eyes in a veiled look, and Ori knelt beside her.

"Ima . . . Ima's looking for you," she said.

"Tell her you don't know where I am," Ofra replied, immersing herself in her book again.

After a minute or two, once she realized that Ofra wouldn't return home, she got up and started back to their house, more slowly this time. She'd only gone a short distance when she realized that another question was gnawing at her. She turned on her heel and said, "Tell me, Ofra, are books really all that interesting?"

A rare thoughtful expression spread over Ofra's face, she who was always ready to blow up, to react without thinking. It seemed that she was formulating a reply, laboring over a complex explanation. Ori could actually see Ofra's thoughts colliding with one another and then sliding into place; now the explanation would make its way to her mouth and slip out. There, the saliva was being swallowed, the vocal cords tensing . . . but no. Ofra changed her mind at the last moment. She clenched her lips angrily and blurted out, "You'll never understand. Now get lost."

"I'll tell Ima on you, you'll see," she shouted at Ofra and started running, fleeing from there.

The school library was open after all. As Ori passed through the door she saw new books displayed on three wide metal stands, painted in dark, concrete-colored varnish, behind them were another ten or eleven sets of shelves of the same material. The floor was carpeted with dark blue felt and the whole space was flooded with neon lighting. To the right of the door was a counter, and a dark-skinned, timid girl, glasses wobbling on her aquiline nose, an eleventh or twelfth grader, was sitting behind it. She nodded to Ori with a pleasant smile.

Embarrassed, Ori turned to look at the books on display. Hard, rectangular surfaces, each tightly covered with a layer of shiny plastic. Untouched by human hand. She moved slightly closer, dragging her feet, and inspected the titles.

"They're new books," the library girl called.

Ori nods vigorously. She wonders what she's doing here? After all, she's got no interest in books. She'll just take that stupid book and go, so she won't go back into class after recess empty-handed. There were illustrations on some of the covers, books apparently meant for the junior classes—the kids from the adjacent elementary school also used the library. One of the illustrated covers at the end of the second row on the left-hand stand caught her eye. A girl sitting on a wood throne that looked as if it sprouted from the ground and encircled her body.

Her frowning black eyes stared straight ahead, her arms folded across her chest. An object hung from her sash. A magnifying glass, Ori thought. Her skirt appeared to be woven from leaves and a translucent nimbus hung over her shoulders. Towering above her was a giant, muscular, brown creature, molded from soil and clay, and from its thick, wild locks sprang a pair of tapering horns—ram's horns, she thought. Pelts draped its body, and its eyes, two slanting red slits, flashed, giving its face a baleful appearance. But no threat was apparent in the creature itself. Its right hand grasped a sword and its body inclined to the left, towards the girl, protecting her.

"Like it?" asked the librarian girl from behind her.

Ori realized that she'd been immersed in the picture and its detail for a few minutes, and the pulsing of her blood had heightened, blocking out noise.

"No," came her quick denial, "I was just looking."

"Okay," the girl replied, "looking is fine."

"Have you by any chance got Galila Ron-Feder's *In Light and Hiding*?"

"Yes, we've got twelve copies. They came yesterday. A gift from the council, I think."

"And how many can I take?"

"What are you, seventh grade?"

Ori nodded.

"Then you can have one, for two weeks. But if you take it today you can keep it until after the Passover vacation. Hold on a minute."

She moved past Ori and disappeared between the bookshelves. Ori went back to gazing at the book cover. "Ariella the Fairy Detective", she slowly read the title. She liked the sound of it. Now she also understood what the translucent nimbus hovering over the shoulders of the girl in the picture was—wings. "By Prospero Juno" she read. Not Israeli, she thought, maybe Italian or something. Her eyes moved back to the book's title, *Ariella the Fairy Detective*. She reached out and with a finger touched the drawing of the magnifying glass hanging by a cord from the girl's sash. An electric spark detonated at the tip of her finger. She screamed in amazement and pulled her finger away.

"What's the matter?" came the librarian's demanding voice from the far end of the library.

"Nothing," Ori replied loudly, and immediately lowered her voice to a whisper, even though there was nobody else in the library but her, "I'm sorry."

She put her finger back onto the cover and traced the outline of the wooden throne, and despite the plastic covering separating her finger from the book, she could feel the rough, rich texture of the wood and inhale its deep fragrance, a smell of decomposition, the scorching of the sun, the dimness of the soil and the promise of new growth inherent in every waning. She recalled the long winter days when she looked from her window at the shimmering firmament, waiting for a break in the evening clouds. Waiting for a ray of light whose gold was already touched by the purple bruise of the sunset and which dimmed the closer it came to the earth's surface. Although she didn't yet know it, it was the transformation that drew her attention, the alternation, the realization that from the moment of birth all things are marked to die. Then as they extinguish something new blossoms in them and they are transformed into something different. The memory filled her with excitement and she picked up the book and opened it at the first chapter, 'An Unfortunate Accident', and began reading. 'Ariella had always felt that she lacked something, something she couldn't give a name to.' She caught her breath when she reached the period at the end of the sentence, and she went back to the beginning. 'Ariella had always felt . . . ' she began

reading again, but this time, with no surprise knowledge awaiting her, her eyes raced across the page and the words began
piling up and competing for her attention.

"Here's the book you wanted." The librarian's soft whisper
and outstretched, tempting hand startled her.

Ori slammed the book shut and the air from between its
pages sighed in protest. "Ah," she said, "I . . . I think I'll take
this one instead," and held it out to the librarian. Then, still
embarrassed, she added, "Do you know if it's any good?"

"It looks a bit childish," the librarian replied, "*In Light and
Hiding* is more serious. It's . . . "

"No," Ori said more decisively than she felt, "I'll take this
one."

"Okay," the librarian said with pronounced reluctance,
drawing out the second syllable between her stretched lips, "it's
up to you. Let's open you a reader's card. This is your first time
in the library, right?"

———

Recess was almost over when she left the library and dragged her
feet back to class along the paved path. On both sides, behind a
low, blue metal fence, were margosa trees whose purple blossom,
an open lacework of tiny petals, had begun to flower. She felt
that they were inclining towards her as she walked—or perhaps
they were whispering to one another—their tops intertwined
until they formed a shady corridor through which she passed.
The opening sentence of the book echoed in her head, and the
burden of the short, sharp *hamsinim* of April—the heat that
fused the fronds into a dense, taut net—was removed from her.

The bell urging the return to the classroom raised the treetops upright, sending the margosas back to being the simple, rough-barked trees whose dirty-yellow fruit, hanging in

bunches, was only good for the children to play their war games with. She walked faster and got to class at the last minute. As she passed Ilanit's desk, Ilanit asked her if she'd found the book and whether there were still any copies left in the library. "Yes," she replied brusquely, "I found it. But I didn't take it. I don't feel like reading." And with that the desire vanished from her and the words she'd read in the book evaporated.

Five days later her mother fell ill. There were some early signs, but that vigorous woman refused to submit to them. She was in the middle of making the house kosher for Passover and to complete it she'd taken time off from her job at the day center. She moved from one room to another in the big house, taking clothes from closets and dusting each shelf in turn, replacing winter clothes with summer ones, piling up laundry, putting away the down quilts. Like a woman laying a snare for birds, she spread the contents of the house out in the yard to tempt the sun's rays. She refolded everything and scrubbed the walls—this year her father had decided not to whitewash them as he had in previous years. Ah, scrubbing the walls! There was no doubt that it was the source of the calamity. Sylvia decided to use paracetamol to fight the flu virus that had infected her. They would subdue the fever that had made her unwell. Even the world's greatest strategist and wiliest chess player make mistakes, so did her mother in her fight against the illness. From her arduouis scrubbing of the walls with a mixture of water and chemicals, toxic fumes from the cleaning agents, and bending her back her temperature soared.

"It will go down in a few hours," she said as she started vomiting. "It's all right, it'll pass. In any case, Ofra has been disappearing for long periods over the last few months, and who'll make the house kosher?"

This should have set alarm bells ringing and forced her to admit that it was the fever talking. That she should give up on a quarrel with her eldest daughter? Whoever heard of such a thing? Then she collapsed. Asher came home from school and found her on the living room floor, helplessly cursing her traitorous body.

"Asher," she said—or so she told anyone who listened, those moments were clear and etched on her memory—"be an angel and help me up. I've only got the living room walls left to do."

Asher led his mother to the couch and told her to stay there. He called his father at the factory and he, fuming at his feeble, sickly family who lacked resourcefulness, stormed into the house. When he saw his wife, smiling weakly, her almond eyes unfocused, barely managing to sip some water, anger was replaced by panic.

Towards evening they were driven to the hospital in Beersheba by Persian Rosa's father, the carpet merchant. There were rolled-up carpets in the trunk of his long, white van, and there were also some on the back seat, which had been folded for this purpose. Asher and Ofra squeezed in beside him in the front, Ori lay on the carpets in the back and her head bounced and jolted with each bump in the road. On the way Persian Rosa's father asked them questions, how they'd manage on Seder night and what the doctors had said. Politely, Asher started to answer, but his words dissolved into stammering. Ofra, too, didn't know the answers. They parted at the entrance to Soroka Hospital, he promising to come back in two hours as he drove off to his business in the city center.

Nausea flooded Ori as the three of them walked through the wide glass doors. She had been in this hospital before. More than once. Not as a visitor, not of her own free will, but as a patient, and she had been wheeled through the corridors in search of hope. Now, she felt that the city behind the glass doors was cut off. She was in another kingdom, the land of death and corruption of the flesh. She had never before sensed how this destruction was concealed in each of the body's smells—in the stench of urine and the sourness of sweat. How it was concealed in the surfeit of carbon dioxide emitted from the lungs and blood of the elderly people hobbling down the corridor, in the children with dressings over their injuries, in the young men in casts and the gangrenous girls. There were many beds standing against the walls near the internal medicine wards and on each of them a patient with a unique stench sprawled.

She wanted to retreat, to flee the place where flesh had such a powerful hold and such paltry dominion, but Ofra, who sensed her flinching, pulled her by the arm to the information desk. A mustachioed fleshy man looked at them through the glass and Asher inquired, "Sylvia Elhayani?"

They clustered around the bed. She and Ofra ignored the other five women patients in the ward, the green plastic curtain hanging lifelessly from its stainless steel rail, the IV stand with its small plastic bag that sent fluid through a transparent, twisting tube that disappeared into their mother's arm. But not Asher. In the next bed was an old woman who didn't stop groaning and complaining about her illness to a younger woman, her daughter perhaps, in an accent that made Asher laugh, especially when she said: "Oy, Dvora'leh, it hoits so much."

"Everything's fine," their mother soothed them, and as usual her voice was assertive. "It's just pneumonia." In both lungs, because she didn't take care of herself and the inflammation spread from the infected lung to the healthy one. Yes, the doctor was surprised when she was admitted in that condition. What, didn't she feel she had difficulty breathing? Hadn't she checked her temperature? Pneumonia's rare at this time of year, did they have pets at home? No. She explained at length about making the house kosher for Passover and its importance. She didn't gloss over a single detail. Yes, he listened to her, she saw how his

39

face showed his amazement. These poor people without roots, they don't know anything. It all seems like idolatry to them. And I'm sure his wife doesn't do anything at home, that's why he was so surprised by all her efforts. And yes, she told him, and when she told them she smiled slyly, her eldest daughter helps her, only now she's in eleventh grade and she's got a lot of exams. And they shouldn't worry, they're giving her antibiotics through the tube and if the tests are all right they'll discharge her in a few days, she'll have enough time to prepare for the festival, she's already planning how she'll manage to do more . . .

Their father, who was sitting on a chair by the wall, a short distance from their mother's bed, remained silent the whole time. A withdrawn, constricted, tense silence. The whole room was drawn into him, as if he were its nucleus and the surrounding walls a cloud of electrons, a haze of possibilities and probabilities.

"I'm not finished with you yet," was the first sentence he uttered; it was unconnected with the conversation taking place. Without directly addressing any of them by name or leaning towards them, by a gesture or motioning with his chin, the four of them knew he was talking to Ofra. Ofra looked straight at him, challenging, but coughed violently. In her surprise she had swallowed the gum she was chewing. Asher banged her on the back until she managed to cough the gum out in a brilliant arc that ended on the bed of the old lady groaning "Dvora'leh, Dvora'leh".

Dvora'leh got up angrily as the gum hit the side of the bed, and cut off the flow of the old lady's complaints. One fleeting glance at the family facing her was enough. An expression of disgust came over her face. She took away from them and spat at her groaning mother, "Barbarians. Animals. Why were they brought here at all?" And the mother repeated, "Oy, Dvora'leh, it hoits," and added a few more words in their language.

This time Asher didn't laugh and Ori could imagine why.

Even in her suffering their mother was capable of one of her caustic looks. The tenseness of her mouth and the hardening of her eyes hinted at disappointment and despair—all her efforts to instill good manners in her children had come to naught.

Ori didn't want to see if she was right. Her look was drawn backwards; again that itch at the back of the neck, the fine hairs bristling, the different nature that permeated and rose within her, which she had learnt to obey involuntarily.

A doctor was standing in the doorway. Despite his white coat and his coming from the brightly lit corridor into the dimness of the room, by his blade-thin figure, his tense stance, she knew whose emissary he was. With a slow movement of his head he summoned Dvora'leh. She tore herself from her place, leaving behind her mother's soft groaning and her own harsh opinion, and went over to him to hear what her heart had long predicted.

"All you do is cause trouble," their father told Ofra. "Tomorrow morning you're going to carry on with what your mother didn't manage. She'll tell you what to do, and how. Asher, you're in charge of the shopping."

"What about me?" Ori asked. She tried to imbue her voice with a demanding tone but only a squeak came out, "I want to help too."

"You'll help as much as you can," her mother said sharply, leaving no room for doubt that it was she who had drawn up the new work arrangements. "But you've got to rest. I'm not sure you've recovered."

"But . . ."

"No buts," her father said, cutting her short.

———

She thought about calling Ilanit's house and asking for the number of her aunt and uncle in Beit Shemesh where she'd gone for the entire Passover vacation. It was morning and she had to talk to somebody.

Last night their father had come home from the hospital and right away started getting ready for his night shift. She's going to be all right, he again told them, but Ori's anxiety, a slow-moving rodent gnawing away in her chest, did not ease. While their mother was imprisoned in that castle, where the body and its approaching end was, she had no faith in words, in consolation.

As the light flared in her room she leapt out of bed and went to offer her help to Ofra, who was laboring over the remaining wall with a sponge and water that stung the eyes. Ofra looked at her with a hard expression, a stare of pride Ori knew from their parents' faces. If she had been sentenced to this labor, this existence, she would welcome it, make it hers out of choice. Until the day arrived when she would join the army—that was the permanent threat she declaimed whenever she'd had enough of their parents' tyranny—and then she'd be free of them, and afterwards, when she had completed her service, she would sail away, go to Tel Aviv, to Hollywood. Her face would never again be seen in Netivot. Should anyone wish to see her, they would have to go to the community center cinema where her face would look out at them from the screen. But on this occasion she didn't say anything and just waved her hand dismissively. "You heard what Ima said," she muttered and went back to scrubbing the wall.

Ori went to the phone but could not summon up the courage lift the receiver. What would she say to Ilanit? That her mother was in hospital? What could Ilanit do, feel sorry for her? And why would she ask Ilanit's parents for her phone number? Had Ilanit wanted to keep in touch during the vacation she would have given her the number herself. How strange it was to be having these thoughts, to suddenly feel this quailing. Everything that had so far come naturally now needed justification and clarification, intricate excuses. Without warning, speaking to one of Ilanit's parents had become a barrier, a river whose foaming, turbulent current drove her back. Why had she thought about a river?

She trudged back to her room, her body fatigued from inactivity. And as she fell back onto her unmade bed her eyes lit upon the abandoned book. It had lain on the shelf in her room for a week. Each morning it waited for her—the light filtering through the slats danced and flared on the creases in its plastic cover. Ariella's glance came to her from the depths of the cover, not losing its weight, its erudition, but the urge to open the book had vanished shortly after she borrowed it. She studied the cover illustration once more, and this time it was not the girl's penetrating look that drew her to it, but the malevolent glint on the face of the wild creature protecting her. Again her curiosity was piqued and she opened the book.

———

Evening fell without her noticing it sliding around her, stealing in from the window, and afterwards—the silent softness of its movement. When she closed the book it was already a *fait accompli*, Netivot was once more in the hands of darkness. In the last chapters she felt her vision dimming and the print blurring. She got up and absently switched on the light, her eyes not leaving the page for a second, and went back to bed. Now she was lying there with her arms outstretched, panting, the book dropped onto the rug at the foot of the bed. Warmth floated through her body as if caressing her with innumerable hands, with feathers and fine satin, and her skin was like pure silk. She thought about the story with wonderment, attempting to hunt down its core in the waves of pleasure that shivered her flesh.

Ariella, the book's heroine, was her age—twelve—and lived with her parents in London. One day a calamity overtakes her.

Her parents are killed in a horrendous crash on the Underground and the stunned Ariella is sent to live in a village with her paternal grandmother whom she has never met. She had once heard her parents talking about the old shrew, that's what they called her, as they discussed her opposition to their marriage. When Ariella reaches her grandmother's home she learns from personal experience that not for nothing was she called 'the old shrew'. Her grandmother treats her cruelly and exacts her revenge on the girl for her father turning his back on her, she insults and humiliates her and orders her to do horrid, purposeless jobs.

One night, when the despairing Ariella is weeping bitterly into her pillow, a creature made of moonlight and tin appears in her room and leads her to an ancient oak tree. There he begs her to return to the City of Tempest and help them; he has been searching for her twelve years, a dozen years of darkness and destruction. Ariella declines, saying it is a case of mistaken identity. She is not the girl he's looking for. She has never heard of the City of Tempest. The creature asks her to dig under the oak's roots when the first glimmer of dawn appears in the sky. Ariella stays awake all night, leaning against the tree's trunk.

When the first band of light gleams in the sky, she puts her hand into the space that has appeared between the roots and takes out a parchment scroll. The scroll contains directions for getting to the City of Tempest. But she still hesitates. She goes back to her grandmother's house, and her grandmother, displeased with her for leaving the house without permission, mercilessly vents her anger on her. At the day's end, as twilight merges with the golden air of summer, Ariella decides to try the transporting spell. She succeeds in casting it and wakes up in a cave, inside a vast crystal bead, completely frozen.

A crowd of creatures, who look like children at a masquerade, surrounds her. As she inspects her body she sees that she, too, is in costume: close-fitting trousers of shiny scales cover her legs. She is wearing a blouse of the same scaly material. Her arms are very white and wings are stuck to her shoulders. Her head, when she feels it, is adorned with a diadem. The creatures rejoice at her awakening. They think she is another Ariella, their seer and revelator. The City of Tempest was stricken by a spell, they tell her, diminishing something from all things. The spell had cast a twelve-year slumber on her. But now she has awakened she could discover its source, for this is her role—she is their fairy detective, the patron of riddles—to expose the instigator of their troubles and restore matters to their original state. She tries telling them that she's not who they think she is, but when she opens her mouth to protest and explain, she realizes that all the creatures can hear when she talks about her grandmother's house and London, is a meaningless twittering.

They lead her from the cave to her chambers to rest, and there, in the mirror, the truth is revealed: she is not in costume. Her soul and consciousness reside in a new body, the body of a fairy. The wings sprout from her body and the diadem on her head is made of a dozen precious stones set into her brow, endowing her with the wisdom of the Urim and Thummim. In the hope that as soon as she gets to the bottom of the matter she will also discover how to get back to England, she sets off to investigate.

Four border countries encircle the City of Tempest, the Kingdoms of the Seasons: Spring, Summer, Autumn and Winter. And there is a fifth kingdom, Napoli of Darkness, of which all creatures have heard but to which none knows the way.

In the Kingdom of Summer, the first border country she travels to, she meets Pereh, an ugly, powerful, horned creature. She saves him from the king's soldiers and certain death. But they are both captured and taken to the King of Summer's court to stand trial, and there she discovers the first clues in solving the riddle. The spell was part of a longstanding conflict between the Kingdom of Summer and the Kingdom of Spring and with the identity of their young, haunted, tormented kings, who had been born on exactly the same day. With the help of Pereh, who has become her right-hand man and confidant, she escapes from her imprisonment in the Kingdom of Summer and ends up in the Kingdom of Spring where she finds the key to the mystery.

After restoring matters to their former state in the City of Tempest and the Kingdoms of Summer and Spring, and digesting the knowledge that she no longer has a home to go back to, Ariella decides to remain in the City of Tempest and devote herself to her vocation as a fairy detective.

Ori turned the story over in her mind, following the threads of the plot, their crossings and relationships. Not even Ofra's call that supper was ready, and the puzzled look Asher gave her from the doorway when he came to see where she was, could budge her from her thoughts.

In particular she thought about the Kingdom of Spring and the paragraphs describing how Ariella crossed the thick beech forest that led there, and the signs of spring abounding in summer's domain: the warm light, an ocean of molten honey, brightening and becoming flakes of shaded gold, a latticework of amber, and the broad-leafed, thick-trunked beeches, massive trees rising from the mist of forgotten times, casting an enchanted silence on the forest as if they were nourished by sleep and dreams. What connection has that with April here, the lull in the heatwave's rule, which has only gone underground in order to return and reveal itself in its old, full splendor, with the nettles and the thistles, and ricinus dried-up in the noonday sun?

That's where she wanted to be, with Ariella, where each of the seasons is always at its height, where the colorful City of Tempest borrows from them whenever it wishes.

After half an hour she picked up the book lying at her bedside. She began wondering. The mystery of the spell had been solved, but the story itself, the story of Ariella and Pereh, had not ended.

She turned the book over and for the first time read the back cover. It was the first volume in a series of seven by the British author, Prospero Juno, about the adventures of Ariella and Pereh and the mysteries they investigated. *Seven books!* she thought joyfully. *Seven!* she almost sang aloud. She'd go right downstairs and ask Ofra if they were in the municipal library. She repeated the author's name, Prospero Juno, and the titles of his other books— only three were mentioned on the back cover. She'd remember them by heart. The simple idea of writing their names on a piece of paper did not come to her naturally

Just as she didn't like reading books, she abhorred the trouble involved in writing. In first grade, after they'd learnt all the letters of the alphabet, she'd seen how the fever of writing had infected all her friends. They scribbled on every empty and available surface, filled their notebooks densely with their names, the names of their brothers and sisters and parents. They began sending notes full of mistakes to one another, and doodling on the blackboard with chalk during recess. She avoided this, even though her handwriting, first in block letters and then in grownup ones, was good and legible. She only wrote her homework and class assignments, but in brief and to the point. She didn't have the desire, the passion was not ignited in her, neither distractedly nor intentionally at first, to write of the world as it passed and dwindled.

In fourth grade her friends began collecting stationery sets and trading them, and after that they began writing to other girls in distant towns. Gvinush even corresponded with some girl from a kibbutz in the north of Israel and with a girl from Kiryat Shemona whose house had been destroyed by a Katyusha rocket. As usual she got carried away. She was so enthusiastic about letter writing that she hadn't been able to restrain herself and had sent a heartrending and totally untruthful letter to the children's TV program, "Loop the Loop", in which she said that her father was out of work and they had no food for the Sabbath. The presenter, Dalik, read it out with tears in his eyes. Next day she was punished at school. The principal, Rivka Dadon, who every now and again would kick the knees of children who dozed during morning prayers, held a special school assembly in the gym and brought Gvinush onto the wooden stage at the front. "Now," she reprimanded her in front of everyone, "because of your lying we'll have a stigma. Even so the government and the media say that we whine and whine for no reason, that we shout all day that they owe us, and lie."

Gvinush apologized with such humility that anyone who knew her knew that she didn't mean a word of it, or of what she wrote in the letter of apology they made her write to "Loop the Loop". Dalik, it emerged afterwards, refused to read it on air. That day Ori went to see Gvinush, back then they were still bosom pals, to buck her up. But Gvinush wasn't in, she'd gone out somewhere with her father. Her mother showed Ori to her Gvinush's and asked her to wait there. She'll be back in ten minutes, she promised.

She quickly got bored waiting and began inspecting the room, which she knew well, and yet because she was alone, dimensions were revealed in it that she'd missed before. The poster of singer Ofra Haza now seemed repulsive, and the one of singer Adam was horrifying. The room was a mess of revolting bric-a-brac, and the tumult of colors disturbed her. She began poking around the drawers of the pinkish Formica covered dressing table which was fixed to the bed and had worked copper handles. A "toilette" is what Gvinush called the complex structure of her double bed, the two chests of drawers and long oval mirror. The middle drawer contained a notebook whose cover bore a photograph of Farrah Fawcett. On her forehead was written "Diary", and on her beautifully coiffed hair was "Rimona Peretz" on one side, and "Top Secret" on the other.

Ori opened the notebook at random and there a surprise awaited her. Rimona had written about her: "Dear Diary, I wanted to say that today I noaticed that Flora is starting to be ugley. Her nose is big!!!!"—she felt her nose angrily. What is she talking about?—and went on reading. The next paragraph made her blood boil. "But Asher her brother isn't ugley. He's a hunk like Amar from Amar Akbar Anthony." Under this was a heart pierced by an arrow. On the feathering was written "Rimona" and on the point—"Asher Elhayani". In the middle was written: "For Ever and Ever Amen".

She turned the page. Here, too, there appeared at the top the touching salutation "Dear Diary" followed by a story that had happened in class and was connected with Ilanit. Ori didn't manage to read it because the sound of distant merriment accompanied by low, resentful grumbling told her that Gvinush and her father had come home. She put the notebook back.

The next day she went back to Rimona's house and on some pretext or another went into her room to wait for her. Again she read the diary. After that for a whole month, she finagled invitations from Rimona and plotted to get there early; or she arranged to meet in the center of town, by the kiosk, and went instead to her room and the hidden diary, to the confessions, the dreams and the words of longing and desire.

One day, when Ori completely sure of her skill in deceit and the power of her plotting, she totally immersed herself in a juicy excerpt that had just been written and compared the noble attributes of Adam Carrington from "Dynasty" with those of her brother Asher. She heard heavy footfalls but their sound came no closer, but oddly, they sounded close all the time, as if someone by the door was stamping. She closed the notebook and stuffed it into the middle drawer. As she straightened up Rimona came in, her facial muscles trembling from the effort of appearing calm and friendly. They chatted aimlessly for a while and then Ori went home with a gnawing feeling of impending disaster. At the end of a three-day silence Rimona invited her to a party at her house in two weeks time. Thinking back, and knowing Rimona's scheming nature, her lust for vengeance, she should have suspected something and declined, but she accepted the invitation. From the day of the party, every time she had to write something her insides turned over. At first she'd think of the words that Gvinush had almost certainly used in her diary to describe the insults she'd heaped on her, and the final act of humiliation. Afterwards, all that remained was the mechanical flinching, the horror associated with forming the letters.

But on that exciting April evening, under the window opened to the richness and profundity of the stars, under the seeming threat of the slivered moon, on her bed in her room, breathing deeply and silently chuckling to herself, a buried and hidden urge rose in Ori. She got up, went into Ofra's room and in her satchel found an empty notebook. After going back to her own room she opened it and copied the book's concluding sentence: "'Whether I like it or not,' Ariella told Pereh, 'this is my home,' and betwixt the boughs dusty birds obscured the embers with their song." The final words had a curious ring to them more than they had meaning. She underlined them and wrote in the margin, "Need to find out what these words mean." Then she straightened up and stretched. She was suddenly aware of a strong desire for something sweet, of a nauseating constriction in her body, the racing sugar in the veins. Before she left the room she glanced at the book in its place on the chest of drawers. She had no doubt that tomorrow she would again read it from the beginning.

THREE

Nature

SYLVIA ELHAYANI WAS DISCHARGED from hospital on Passover Eve, and the three of them—Ori, Asher and Ofra—stood on the verandah of the house facing the street. They were close to the rail and arranged from right to left by age, and looked at their father supporting their mother as she hobbled frailly up the asphalt path, her face gray and sunken.

"She doesn't look so good." Ofra stated the obvious in a choked voice.

The doctor had insisted that she stay in hospital for another day for observation and diagnosis, but their father insisted that his wife would spend Seder night with her family and that being with them would "help her more than a thousand medicines." Asher was present at the conversation between their father and the doctor and had reported on it to Ofra when he'd got back from the hospital the previous evening.

Ori had just finished the third of the Ariella books. She had found all of them in the municipal library, where she'd gone with Ofra two days after their mother had been admitted to hospital. All seven were arranged on a shelf, as if they were waiting for her. When she opened them and looked at the cards in their plastic pockets stuck to the inside cover, she discovered that nobody had ever taken them out. Logical, she thought, for she, too, had come across them by chance.

She borrowed the second volume, the third and fourth, and devoured them—a book in two days. When Ariella's adventures in the third book, in which she solved the mystery of the frozen lakes in the north of the Kingdom of Winter, came to an end Ori wanted to go back to the sentences that had most struck her. She wanted to copy them into the notebook she'd started with the first volume—to extract whole paragraphs that were hers alone—some of the notebook's pages were already crammed with them. Then she would stretch out on her bed, feel the warmth climbing from her belly to her face. How wonderful to be alive in the spring that by day terrifies the world with its uproar and in the evening is a black art of renewal, that makes darkness light and bitter sweet.

She was not allowed the time to stretch out on her bed. She heard sounds coming up from the kitchen and knew that Ofra and Asher were swapping secrets. For a moment she thought about whether to listen or go back to her fantasies, to the pleasurable reconstruction of the book in her mind's eye. But the power of the story's influence was broken, and she found herself increasingly captivated by her siblings' voices. She left her room and listened to them, until Ofra saw her and gestured her to join them.

"You've turned into a real bookworm," Asher said.

"It's better than when you were just a worm," Ofra added with unexpected affection. Ori smiled at her sister. She was unable to bear a grudge against Ofra for long, even though sometimes there was pure malevolence in her sister's actions and words.

On the day Ori had announced her change of name in class, Elisheva had stopped Ofra in the corridor and asked her what this decision meant and whether her parents knew of it. The surprised Ofra, who'd never missed an opportunity for causing trouble, hurried to their mother with the news.

Reconstructing the rumor's route to her mother was not beyond Ori's ability; it was enough for her to see her mother's face as her lips spat the new name, and the malicious, cunning smile spreading around her sister's mouth. Yet Ori was adamant. In the face of her mother's cutting look, she said, "It's my new name. I wanted to tell you and Abba about it this evening when he gets home from work."

"*Ewa*, Flora, *b'shaltiah*, you've gone too far" her mother said angrily, "changing your name, and to a boy's name as well. We only change a name if somebody's dying. Is that what you wish for yourself?"

"I don't like the name you gave me," Ori replied.

"What's wrong with it, eh? Tell me. It's a good name," her mother went on in the same scorching tone, and she felt defeated. But it was Ofra who unwittingly came to her rescue.

"Its just *tsumi*, attention-grabbing," she said.

That word, "*tsumi*", uprooted Ori from her fear, cleansed her of any stabbing guilt and sorrow that came from within her. She had been named after her maternal grandmother who had died before she was born, and her reply was harsher than she'd intended.

"It's a name of ancient Moroccans," she said, and was answered by Ofra's laugh, a mocking, torturing laugh that scratched the ears. She turned to her sister.

"What do want of me?" she asked. "Why are you bullying me?"

"Listen, cool it, understand? Why do I need Elisheva on my case with all your nonsense?" Ofra said harshly.

Their mother's rage did not abate until early evening. Ofra left her no doubt in deciding how to tell her husband.

"Abba, have you heard about the latest bee in Flora's bonnet? She's changed her name to Ori." Ofra gaily yelled

Their father had just appeared in the doorway and their mother looked at him, her mouth tightly closed, and nodded.

He sighed. This was not what he'd planned for the evening. He studied Ori as she got up from the couch and stood facing him resolutely, her arms folded.

"What now?" he asked.

"I wanted to tell you about it this evening. But Ofra makes a big deal out of everything."

"And this isn't a big deal?"

"No. It's my personal business. I can't go on any longer with this name."

"And why is Ori any better?" he asked, surprising her.

She'd expected a tidal wave of black rage that would inundate the room and smash any opposition she had thought out, the dams and dikes she'd built, the convoluted arguments, the ways of evading her mother's artifices, to dull the blow, until her father would say, "There's no point in arguing, this one's got a head as hard as her mother's," and leave the issue unresolved and pending. But instead a spark lit up his face and she grasped that glimmer forming in his eyes.

"It's a better name," she said

"Ya'akov, I've sworn on my life today, it's not going to happen." their surprised mother said.

"Sylvia, I told you when she was born. She's chosen it herself," their father replied, to which the mother responded,

"Ya'akov, it's my mother's name. My mother's!"

"And much good she did us."

"My parents made amends for their mistake, Ya'akov. And I'm sure my mother persuaded my father. Because if it had been up to him . . . You know it, it's my way of remembering her."

"The child chose the name herself," their father repeated.

"But Mama Elhayani is still alive," whispered their mother.

This was a battle of wills that Ori failed to make sense of, it was taking place in a different arena, between her father and mother, and she had no part in it even though it was about her.

But Ofra understood. Because when her father nodded and spread his hands in submission and asked, "What's for supper?" and followed his wife into the kitchen, Ofra moved closer to Ori and whispered, "You stupid jerk, look what you've done."

"What? What have I done?" Ori protested.

"Mama Elhayani's name's Zohara," Ofra replied, "and now you've got them fighting. Because when you were born they argued over which grandma you'd be named after."

That night, when all the wrath and obduracy proved useless and Sylvia realized she was in a rare situation in which her husband was not taking her side in the constant battle she waged against her children, she tried persuading Ori to change her mind, at least for her mother, of blessed memory, so she said three times, 'of blessed memory'.

"Ima, I'm not doing it because of Grandma." Ori was steadfast in her refusal, even though she buried some of her compassion.

"So for who?" Her mother asked.

"For me," she replied and closed her eyes.

She didn't speak to Ofra for three days afterwards, but addressed her in the third person, through Asher.

"Tell her she shouldn't go into my room without permission."

At first Ofra laughed.

"Who are you trying to impress, eh?" She asked.

When Ori didn't reply it was Asher's turn.

"Ori, stop being so spoiled." He accepted her new name without question, without any particular surprise.

By the next day Ori could no longer maintain the boycott she had imposed on her sister, and in the morning even found an excuse to ask her if she would lend her the pearl earrings she'd bought before Purim.

"You think? You're too young for them, and if I find you've been touching my Rimmel one more time, you're dead." Ofra answered her quite naturally.

Later Ofra loaned her the earrings when she dressed herself up for their mother's return. Ori stood on the verandah happily touching her earlobes to make sure the earrings were in place. Afterwards, when she saw her mother's bowed posture, she fingered them again, nervously.

As her mother and father approached the house and their mother saw her waiting children, Ori watched Sylvia pull herself out of the cloud of ash covering her limbs. She straightened up, her gait became more severe and measured.

It's all right in the hospital where everyone is worn out and in pain, but her children should see her weakness at home? When she greeted them on the verandah and ceremoniously kissed all three on both cheeks, only Ori's breathing broke into a sob, and it was a choked call buried in her mother's chest.

"What's wrong, *jinn?* Nothing's happened." She took Ori into her arms and even then their mother's posture did not bend.

As she entered the house she studiously eyed Ofra's work, the cleanliness of the floors and walls. She checked the pots to see if Mama Elhayani's dishes were a success, looking at their color, whether paprika and saffron oil were glinting in them. She managed to obtain these things by the skin of her teeth every Passover, because yellow-golden turmeric is not kosher for Passover. She inhaled the spicy aromas deeply, and then opened the refrigerator. Only when she was satisfied, even though here and there she'd made a comment to Ofra, and Ofra had hissed back "Ingrate," even in the face of her father's darkening expression, did she slump onto the couch.

"Do me a favor, sweetie, get me a glass of water," she said to Ori.

As if on a prearranged signal their father took the pharmacy bag from Sylvia's purse. Taking one of the antibiotic pills the doctor had prescribed he placed it into the palm of her hand,

and she swallowed it and drank the water Ori had quickly brought, leaving a trail of drops behind her.

"Have you brought the *haroseth* from Rabbi Danino?" She asked Asher.

"Don't worry, Ima" Asher said, "everything's fixed," then added as he saw their father going towards the door, "Don't you trust me, Abba?"

"Tell me, what are you talking about, have you gone paranoid like Ofra? I'm going to bring Mama Elhayani," their father replied.

Ofra said, "What? She's coming to us for Seder this year? I thought that Georgette . . . " Their mother cut her short.

"No, she's not going to Georgette's. We should be together this year."

Then their father left.

That was a sign, one of the first. And she should have seen it, even though it was brief, fading away into the late air like a wisp of smoke from an ember and vanishing in the chain of events. Because that Seder Night was the happiest festival eve she remembered, and even Mama Elhayani's ramblings—which every now and again interrupted the reading of the *Hagga-dah*—and her hurt, infantile reaction when one of them gently reproved her, "Grandma, not now," did not blight its splendor.

She and Asher and Ofra read the *Haggadah* in stirring harmony and it brought them so close that they were even breathing in unison. But no, it wasn't the harmony that was wonderful, but the fact that Ofra and Asher joined in the reading. For each year Ofra ignored the *Haggadah* open in front of her at the first page and stared dully at the white, plastic-covered tablecloth and the wineglasses and the covered tray and the package of matzos.

Asher would try and make them laugh with his responses to their father's determined and droning reading. Their father's voice would rise on the words "By your blood you shall live", and Asher would challenge him with "Yeah. Sure. Why not." His father would whisper in feigned alarm, "The time has come to recite the Morning Prayer," and Asher would yawn hugely and say, "*Yalla*, bring in the pillow."

Only Ori, who had also not been following the text, was carried away on the tortuous rising and falling of the singing. More than anything she liked the singing of "*Bivhilu*"—'In haste we left Egypt'—when their father raised the covered bowl over their heads and circled it above them, according to age.

"That's it, Ofra, tonight Abba's settling accounts with you. Oops, he's dropped it." Asher would say when it was Ofra's turn.

And Ofra would reply, "We've heard you, retard."

Tonight, nothing of all this. The three of them were united in their resolve and stuck to the text. Ori had never before noticed how beautiful the words were and how heavy they lay on her tongue, falling from her lips to an unfamiliar depth.

As they sang "*Bivhilu*" a kind of awe hung in the air.

When their father burst into song, he opened the circle of blessing with his wife, only then did he move on to Mama Elhayani, his mother, who giggled at her distorted reflection in the bottom of the tray.

Their mother tried to accompany his singing this evening with Moroccan trills of joy, but her tongue betrayed her and she started coughing. Ofra came out from under the tray's canopy that had reached her and slapped her mother's back, saying, "Ima, maybe you should take it easy," and poured her a glass of water, and then went back under the stainless steel ceiling and said seriously, "Abba, from the beginning."

Their grandmother, whose lucidity was suddenly restored, rolled her tongue in her mouth, and between lips cracked at the edges, her uvula a-tremor, emitted the Moroccan trills somewhat coarsely and their mother smiled.

The day of the festival itself was also filled with enjoyment. Their father and two other families in the street slaughtered a sheep and a goat together.

Asher, to whom the task was assigned, got up early on Passover morning and prepared the wood. He lit it with a flame he took from the memorial candle in the kitchen, and fanned it to a slow burn until the embers glowed. This year they had decided not to use electricity, even though the custom of using electrical appliances on festival days that did not fall on the Sabbath had taken root amongst all the North African immigrants since their arrival in Israel.

Ori went out into the yard to keep him company, bringing with her the fourth volume of Ariella stories, and Ofra, who had got home late from a party, also came out to inspect Asher's work. Her eyes were swollen with sleep and her hair disheveled and squashed, and she yelled orders at him until the wind changed and the smoke drove the girls back into the house.

Ori was already half dreaming as she went inside, the Ariella books had bemused her. Her thoughts trickled, elusive. As she went in her mother asked for a glass of tea and she placed the book on the table that Ofra had begun laying and went into the kitchen. There she took the guttering memorial candle and lit the gas. The heat of the flame that ignited immediately hit her face and she recoiled and hurried to put the kettle on. She looked at it and its peeling red coating, and the web of cracks spreading over it was transformed into a scene of the sky over the Kingdom of Autumn. It was just as she'd imagined it, deep magenta, in a permanent sunset splitting the gathering cirrus clouds. She was lost, together with Ariella and Pereh in the crystal corridors darkened by the colors of the setting sun. Only the hiss of the angry steam erupting from the kettle's spout, like a hiss for the fly that is in the uttermost part of the rivers of Egypt and for the bee that is in the land of Assyria, shattered her reverie and she regained her composure and turned off the gas.

———

She saw Ilanit by chance on the intermediate days of the festival week. The librarian at the municipal library—who told an insipid joke when Ofra led Ori to the desk and asked to open a reader's card for her—had told her that the library would be open for one day during the intermediate days, and only until noon. She walked quickly so as not to be late, in case the wonderful, the menacing had occurred, and another child had been captivated by the Ariella books and stolen them from her. She let her feet take the shortcut without remembering that it would take her along Gvinush's street. Only as she approached the house at the bottom of the hill, which was lower than the road and was accessed by going down a stairway and crossing a small, paved front yard, did she realize she'd made a mistake.

She scanned the front of the house, the dusty square shutters and the graying tiled roof. Then she saw the two of them sitting on plastic chairs, sipping some sort of drink and having a lively conversation. Gvinush was wearing shorts and a brief tee shirt with a picture of Lee Majors. As she spoke her whole body was animated, her arms waving, her hair every which way. Ilanit wore her new best clothes, a mustard tee shirt, embroidered around the coarsely cut neckline, and patched and patterned jeans, nodded at Gvinush, answering with a few short words, laughing.

Ori froze. She didn't have the strength to cope with Ilanit's embarrassment when she gave her a beaten, guilty look, and Gvinush's teasing giggles. Maybe if she walked away quietly . . . but no. Ilanit put her glass beside her chair and stood up as if getting ready to leave. No! Where could she hide from her? She turned her head and saw a patch of shadow on the opposite sidewalk. What cast it the shadow? The sun was almost at its zenith and the light fell like velvet. The tall cypresses at the sides of the street, the house fronts, were wrapped and immersed in light, but there was a patch of shadow on the sidewalk, dense and gloomy. She hurried across the road, stood inside the shadow, and at that moment Ilanit came up the steps from Gvinush's house, turned left and walked up the street. Although it seemed to Ori that Ilanit's eyes had met hers, she didn't notice, she didn't react.

Ori continued on her way to the library, her steps heavier, the footfalls echoing on the asphalt. She felt a pang of hurt because of Ilanit's betrayal. She hadn't called to tell Ori she was back. The whole neighborhood—including Ilanit's gossip-mongering mother—knew Ori's mother was sick and about her hospitalization. Ilanit could have called. Ori wanted to scream in anger, to utter the most terrible words she knew, but they weren't in her. Instead she felt the bristling on her neck intensify and gave herself up to it. She walked in the direction it told her to walk, to a small wadi. There, the wild bougainvilleas grew uninhibited, their bells opened red and serrated and sent out stamen tongues. There too the oleander blossom cascaded downward. And there she saw Noam Ohana killing a kitten. The fingers of his right hand were clenched around the skull, and the tiny body gripped in his left hand protested with spasmodic muscle movements. Its mewing filled the air. How its screams had not been heard outside the wadi, how they had not been heard from one end of Netivot to the other, how the warblers on the oleander were not startled from their perches, she did not know. Noam twisted his hands in opposite directions as if wringing out a floorcloth and the kitten was silent, its body barely twitching. Stunned, silently, Ori turned and left. The nausea she'd felt on seeing Noam killing the kitten had gone and only a sweet cleanliness surrounded her as she floated on drunken air currents. But when she saw the library, its lawns radiant around the poplars, the nausea returned and she ran through the door and downstairs to the toilet as the bile rose in her throat.

In the days that followed Ori hardly left the house. When she was not reading she kept her mother company. Day by day Sylvia gradually returned to her former self, as did her domination of the home.

"Why are you sitting here like an old woman," she scolded Ori, "get out, go for a walk, what have you got to do here? Why don't you go to Ilanit's?. . . What's going on, have you caught the reading bug as well, just don't become *m'hinda*, stubborn, like Ofra. I'm away from home for a few days and the whole world's turned upside down. Before you were a *dawara*, a stayout, we couldn't keep you inside for a minute." On the days she was in a slightly better mood, when the pain in her sides had lessened, her words were kinder. "*Jinn*, girls who hide themselves at home, nothing comes of them. Believe me, I also . . . " and here she fell silent. Ori tried to guess the conclusion of the sentence, what the words she couldn't bring herself to utter.

Her mother couldn't bring herself to use Ori's new name and called her "*jinn*". Sometimes, in revolt against her defeat in the battle of wills with her daughter, she'd call her by her old name, drawing it out and enunciating it hesitantly as if in an effort to bring it up out of her memory.

She'd sat at home, Ori thought, *never*. It didn't fit in with the other stories. Their mother, an adventurous and lively young girl, had left her parents' home in Tiberias at nineteen and followed her husband, who she'd met at a bus stop two years earlier when he was a rookie soldier, and had come to Netivot with him. They'd set up house and their mother became pregnant and gave birth their eldest daughter. Maybe she'd ask Ofra—she'd certainly know what their mother meant.

Ori was reluctant to go out, she'd go back to her room after telling her mother, "Don't worry about me, Ima, you just take care of yourself." After a few hours of continuous reading she'd come out of her room again and maybe go into the yard.

She noticed that Asher, too, even though he spent little time in the house, had got into the habit of checking on their mother now and again as she stood in the kitchen or lay on the couch, or stared uninterestedly at reruns of "Lace" or "The Thorn Birds", or eagerly watched the two hundred millionth rerun of "Hasamba and the Horse Thieves." Once, when Ori left her room and he didn't notice she was there, she saw him wiping his eyes, they were red when he removed his hand.

———

When Levi Bonni, the science teacher who was just known to everyone as "Bonni", came into the classroom, a black outline encircling his body caught Ori's eye, and her heart missed a beat. He put his faded yellowish leather briefcase on his desk with a slap, adjusted his glasses, and said with a bitterness that Ori was sure had escaped no one, excepting perhaps Gvinush, who was doodling in her notebook, and her neighbor Aliza who was giggling over the doodles, "I'm sure you're all very happy to come back from vacation directly to a science lesson."

She agreed with him. There was no lesson worse than science to open their return from the Passover vacation. Bonni, with the glasses he constantly touched protectively and the untidy beard he didn't bother grooming, made them uneasy. He maintained this distance. It was unlike that observed by most of the teachers, whose attitude was a blend of contempt and fear that their young charges would exploit any closeness. Bonni's distance told them: you don't want to know me and I have no interest in getting to know you more than I have to. The exception to this rule was Sigal Danino.

Bonni impatiently called the roll and the clouded outline of his body again captured Ori's attention. When he got to Sigal Danino's name he stopped momentarily and looked at her. Despite her fatness, the frayed collar of her school blouse and her denim skirt showing years of wear, she sat there upright and proud.

He didn't waste any time. He'd barely finished the roll call and was already writing the formulae of uniform motion on the board. In the first half of the year they had studied elementary biology, and from then to the end of the year they would be learning elementary physics, so Bonni told them. He accompanied his writing with explanations.

"As I'm sure you remember, when we talk about constant speed, distance equals speed multiplied by time, speed equals distance divided by time, the time required by a body to move at a certain speed is obtained by dividing distance by speed." He turned to the class, "That's the basis. But now we'll move on to a more complex form of motion. Who knows what it is?"

Sigal Danino called out, "Motion at a variable speed."

"Put your hand up, Sigal," he told her gently, "I don't allow calling out in my class," and to the class he said, "Sigal's right."

He turned his back to the board and Ori knew where the trouble would come from. She looked at Gvinush, who whispered to Sigal and Sigal turned to her. Gvinush laid a finger on her eyebrows, and Sigal, whose eyebrows almost met at the bridge of her nose, turned away apathetically.

"Copy the formulae into your notebooks, you'll be getting them in the test," Bonni said as he swiftly circled the new formulae he'd just written down. Ori copied them into her notebook:

$V = a \cdot t$
$S = \frac{1}{2} a \cdot t^2$

"You already know what the letters 'V', 'S' and 'T' mean from the previous formulae. Right, Rimona? Would you like to refresh everyone's memory?"

"Why're you picking on me," Gvinush replied, "what've I done to you? Ask Ophir Shriki, he knows it all."

"But I asked you," Bonni said.

"Something to do with motion," said Gvinush.

"That's a five-point deduction from your grade. You should start paying attention, young lady."

"All right, all right," Gvinush said.

"Does anybody have the answer?"

Only Sigal put her hand up, but Gvinush fired a reproachful look at her and she lowered it.

"Anybody else except Sigal?" Bonni asked. "What about you, Ophir?"

"Speed, distance and time," Ophir blurted reluctantly. It's beneath his dignity to answer unchallenging questions, Ori thought.

"Very good. And what about the letter 'A'?" he asked, "Who knows?"

Sigal put her hand up eagerly, and Bonni smiled at her. "Yes, Sigal."

"It means that the motion of a body depends on whether it's alive or dead."

"Very true," Bonni confirmed and his voice became dulled, serious. "'A' means 'animation', that is, life. If the body is animate, it moves differently than if it's inanimate."

Ori looked for Ophir Shriki's face. Without her being able to pinpoint the reason, it seemed to her that what Bonni had just said was total nonsense. It was unthinkable that Ophir would let Bonni's explanation float over their heads without protest. A strange expression distorted Ophir's features, a kind of stubborn hesitancy. He also felt that Bonni was talking nonsense, but he didn't know the correct answer for certain, she thought, so he was struggling with himself not to challenge Bonni's explanation, although his body straightened and his nose twitched and he shifted in his seat.

"No way," Ori said sharply. And she saw how Bonni slowly and thoughtfully turned his eyes on her as if bringing them back from a distance.

"Yes way", he said.

"But . . . " she started again, and Bonni tut-tutted with displeasure. Ophir didn't need any more. He stood up and called out, "How can you measure if a body is animate or inanimate?"

"What do you mean?" Bonni replied, turning towards him heavily.

Ophir smiled weakly. "Instead of the letter in the equation there should be a figure, right? You said so yourself, and the figure shows a quantity of something. So how do you measure the quantity of . . . "

"Of life," Ori interrupted.

"But an inanimate body is heavier than an animate one," said Sigal in Bonni's defense, and he backed her words with a nod. "When my little sister's asleep, for instance, I can't pick her up, but when she's awake she's lighter. And when my father tripped over a stone in the street a couple of days ago, two people couldn't lift him."

"He should go on a diet," Gvinush interjected. Her shadow Aliza Edri started laughing. "And your sister, your whole family are blimps."

"Rimona!" Bonni shouted, "Hold your tongue!"

"But what's it got to do with weight?" Ophir demanded, deaf as usual to any exchange that deviated from the subject that had fired his interest. "Weight isn't mass."

"It is if it's like in the Danino family, masses of fat," added Gvinush.

Aliza Edri's laughter infected the other girls including Ilanit, Ori noted to herself in disgust.

"How dare you!" Bonni sprayed at her angrily. "Leave the room this minute, go to the principal's office."

"Just you wait and see what's coming to you, *d'boza*, fatso," Gvinush whispered to Sigal on her way out, and Sigal, so used to being hit, scrunched up in her seat trying to hide.

"So I don't understand," Ophir went on, still on his feet and his voice excited, "how can you measure the quantity of life."

"Sigal is right," Bonni said affectionately, and Sigal's face lit up a little, "living bodies have a soul and it uplifts them, makes them aspire upward, away from their inanimate nature. Flesh is just an outer skin. The more spiritual people are, the lighter they are. In India and China there are monks capable of levitation."

Ophir stammered a protest but it was drowned out in the hubbub that followed. Gvinush hadn't gone to the principal's office as she'd been told but had gone outside and circled the building. Her face was looking in at them from the window. She puffed out her cheeks and held out her arms as if circling them around a huge belly. The girls burst out laughing and Bonni's face flushed with anger. He went to the window and gestured for her to come back inside, and Gvinush—Ori couldn't believe her eyes—put her forefinger to her temple and twirled it. Bonni flew into a rage, his whole body showing anger. He began banging on the window with the flat of his hand. Once, twice, and the glass cracked. Ori heard him panting, entranced she studied his rigid back. He turned, clenched both hands and strode from the classroom to the boys' shouts of delight and applause. Ori looked through the cracked window to see Gvinush running towards the school gate.

"That Gvinush's a real maniac, eh?" Ilanit said to her as they walked home from school that day, and in her voice Ori heard the sound of envy. Throughout the day she'd ignored her.

When Bonni marched out of the room and left the noisy class to its own devices, she'd taken out the fifth Ariella book, put her hands over her ears and focused on the pages. She lost herself in the Kingdom of Spring, along the pathways crisscrossing the eastern edge of the realm that passed over the suspension bridges crossing the small lakes. It seemed that they stretched onward, until they ended by touching the points of the stars glinting in the azure of the sky.

At recess she escaped to the limestone hill on the far side of the soccer field and found a niche to rest in as she read. She thought nobody knew where she was, but Ophir Shriki found her, he was also a loner and knew all the school's hiding places.

"I never knew you were like that," he said as his shadow fell on her.

"Like what?" she asked.

"A reader."

"Ah," she said and waved him away.

Ilanit didn't seek her company during classes, but as she went through the school gate on her way home she heard her calling her name. She stopped and waited, and Ilanit walked faster and as she approached.

"Ori, what's happening?" She asked.

"Nothing," Ori replied.

Ilanit twisted the peroxided streak in her hair around her finger.

"You're acting a bit weird . . . " she said hesitantly.

"Why didn't you come to my house or call in the vacation?"

"I was at my relatives in Beit Shemesh, I told you I was going."

"I thought you were coming back in the middle of the vacation."

"No, of course not, I stayed till the Mimouna celebration the day after Passover. My aunt makes . . ."

"But my mother was sick, why didn't you call?"

"I don't know," Ilanit replied, "I . . ." and she fell silent.

"All right," Ori said.

"Want to come to my house?"

"I can't, I'm going right to the library. I want to exchange books."

"Since when do you go to the library?" Ilanit asked in surprise. Ori shrugged.

"So maybe this evening?" Ilanit said.

"I want to stay with my mother—my father's working days this week—so I think I'll stay home."

"Whatever," Ilanit replied somewhat grumpily, then she added, "what a maniac that Gvinush is, eh?"

"I'm going this way," Ori said, pointing in the opposite direction to where they lived.

"But that's the long way round, why don't you . . ."

"It's the way I like," she interrupted Ilanit impatiently, and turned away.

"Wait a minute," Ilanit called after her, "what's with your mother?"

"She's all right now," she replied without turning her head.

Her mother was indeed well again. She could say so with certainty because that morning Ori had asked her to sign the consent form for the annual school trip that was late this year, after Shavuot, and her mother had refused with an emphatic shake of her head, "No, you're still weak."

"I'm fine, Ima," she told her, and Ofra, who was passing the kitchen door, couldn't resist the temptation and said, "Why are you mollycoddling her? She's only making out that she's so small and fragile. And anyway, didn't you go on at her all through the vacation to get out of the house?"

"You mind your own business." Their mother shouted.

"Then you stop making a big deal out of everything. *Yalla*, what can happen, she'll get a scratch. Get sunstroke, get drunk, won't sleep at night, some boy'll make a pass at her, her eyes'll be opened a bit. What can possibly happen on a school trip?" Ofra replied.

"You," their mother said, "I pity the husband you catch."

"Trust me," Ofra said, "every morning he'll thank God that I married him."

Their mother nodded and made a decision.

"We'll see what Abba thinks this evening and then decide."

Ori knew that she'd heard the final refusal.

As she approached the library she saw that Ophir Shriki had got there before her. He was sitting in one of the black leather couches in the empty lobby and alternately tapping each knee-cap with his right hand.

"I passed you on my bike and you didn't even notice me," he said as Ori reached the door.

She nodded and looked at him. A short skinny boy, some-what sweaty, his troubled blue eyes darting here and there in their sockets as if he wanted to absorb everything he saw, to swallow the real. He had a permanent tic. Every so often he'd twitch his nose to the right and sometimes, when he realized what he was doing and regained control of his nose, his eyes blinked and he'd rub the fingers of his right hand against each other as if rolling an invisible piece of cloth between them. He had a military haircut, clipped almost to his scalp.

"What d'you want?" she asked.

"I came to check out the crap Bonni told us."

"Who cares," she dismissed him summarily and started walking towards the children's book desk.

"It's actually interesting," he said as he fell in step beside her.
"Don't you have to go to the reading room?"
"Yeah, but I wanted to ask . . . "
"What?" she asked shortly as she turned to him, anger in her eyes.
"Nothing," he replied, alarmed. "See you in class." And he fled.

All week she avoided Ilanit and her feelers. She also tried to avoid Ophir, but he popped up suddenly everywhere she went. He waved to her from his desk in class and followed her during recess. Once he passed by her home as if by chance. Sigal Danino also fell into the habit of asking her things. The two most despised kids in class laid siege to her, and all she wanted was to escape, to vanish. They were skilled in ambush and foray, just as Ori had perfected her maneuvers to avoid Ilanit: she didn't make eye contact, part of her was aware of her presence all the time, while the other plotted to drive her out of her reach.

There was something vulgar about this entire dance of intrigue that had been forced upon her, she suddenly felt entangled in this human net, there were knots that must be tied, threads to be unraveled. When had she become enmeshed in it, and had she been snared voluntarily? These questions were of no importance because she was already writhing in the net and the waves of sweat she dripped into it only caused her to sweat more. She found that she escaped Ilanit only to fall into the hands of Ophir and Sigal.

A week after that lesson, which the kids rehashed over and over, together with accounts of Gvinush's admirable insolence, the science lesson was cancelled due to the Holocaust Remembrance Day ceremony. It took place during the morning and dragged out until the end of recess because of glitches in the sound system, the lateness of the teacher who compered the ceremony and mistakes made by the singers and readers. She and her classmates had to go from the schoolyard to the gym for their physical education lesson. On the way there Ophir stuck to her right side, whistling the Partisan Anthem, and Sigal Danino marched on her left. Without warning, in a low voice and with a pain that hurt Ori even though she'd sealed herself off, Sigal said, "I hate PE. I hate Judy."

Ah, Judy. She and her husband Josh, American Jews and physical education teachers, had come as far as Netivot to build up the slack bodies of the North African immigrants, with their terrible nutritional habits, the amount of cholesterol they consumed from regular meat barbecues and the natural tendency towards idleness they had brought with them from the lands of blazing heat.

Judy was completely dedicated to physical perfection and looked like a painstaking copy of Olivia Newton-John from the clip of "Let's Get Physical" that had been broadcast on the hit parade. She was a long-legged peroxide blonde, although her ankles were thickening a bit, with long muscles and nice hips that were slightly broader than those of her idol, Valdani, and which attracted fat cells. Judy clearly favored her pretty girl students who would grow into magnificent young women, and had no compassion for the ugly and rejected. Ori, with her child's inhibited body, confused Judy. She was nimble and supple, but not feminine. Because Judy didn't know how to catalogue Ori she dismissed her and didn't consider her when picking sides.

"Well, you're smaller than the rest of the girls. Real petite," she told Ori when she rejected her and chose Gvinush and Aliza to lead the volleyball teams.

Ori preferred to attribute 'small' to her age because she was the youngest in the class, even though she'd been born in April. Until the age of four, so family lore had it, she'd developed rapidly and was mainly known for her quick tongue and incessant chattering. They didn't hesitate to accept her into a preschool kindergarten with children almost a year older. Afterwards things changed

"You fooled everybody. Up until you turned four you were a right little rascal and that's why they were so quick to take you into kindergarten, but afterwards, when you'd got what you wanted, being with the big kids, you became as stupid as a donkey." Ofra had once said.

By contrast, Sigal Danino couldn't be acquitted due to lack of evidence. Her fatness overshadowed whatever beauty she possessed and was the main target for Judy's mocking barbs—her protégées, Gvinush and Aliza, followed her lead.

"You've just got to ignore her," Ori told Sigal.

"In your dreams," Ophir said.

"What do you know about anything?"

"Because Josh is her husband. So it's obvious."

"What about Josh?" Sigal inquired.

The tremor his name and presence caused in all the girls, and the aura of 'from America', hadn't escaped her.

"There's something strange about them. Something that doesn't fit."

"What?" Ori asked.

Ophir didn't bother to reply. He left them with a blink and went to the basketball court for his own PE lesson.

———

At the Remembrance Day ceremony where they handed out lapel stickers with the traditional picture of the helichrysum flower, known in Hebrew as 'Blood of the Maccabees', an eighth-grade kid she didn't know said, "Bees' Blood again." This malapropism, which might have been intentional, was adopted by his classmates and passed on to the seventh grade. They shouted 'Bees' Blood' at one another and giggled. A tidal wave of low, muted murmurings rose from them until the principal cut them short. Shouting through a megaphone in his powerful, grating voice he told everyone to get ready for the siren that would signal the opening of the ceremony.

In the ceremony Aliza Edri went on stage to sing 'We're From the Same Village'. She sang in the affected tone and exaggerated enunciation that the music teacher loved so much. She began too high, in a tremolo seemingly expressive of clear, strong singing, but at the opening of the chorus, when the score climbed up the scale, her voice hoarsened and broke and she cleared her throat in embarrassment and fell silent. Into that silent lull Gvinush blurted out, "Bees' Blood," and this new coinage rang around the yard and laughter erupted from the ranks of the seventh-grade students.

The principal, who was the first to recover from the shock, leapt onto the stage angrily, shoved Aliza away from the microphone, put the megaphone to his lips and commanded them, "Silence!" But the damage had been done. Except for Ori and Sigal not one seventh-grade student stood to attention, as they had been ordered, filled with awe. They stole glances at each other and giggled behind their hands. When the ceremony was over they merrily left the yard to go straight into a science lesson, which following its cancellation the previous week had been pushed into the PE slot. Ori saw Sigal's smug walk and Ophir's eyes flashing with tension and excitement as they both drew up beside her.

Bonni was a few minutes late and the class was in uproar. One of the boys, Tiran Vanunu, sprayed fruit juice over Noam Ohana's white shirt, and Noam got him in a chokehold and forced him to the floor.

"You'll eat dirt, you shit, you hear?" he shouted as he tightened his grip, and the other boys gathered round.

The action came to Ori through a screen of fog. She forced herself not to look. She felt as if a steel rod was implanted into the back of her neck, her head was bent over her desk. Now, she told herself, Bonni will come in enveloped in his black aura. I mustn't look at him. I mustn't. But either she couldn't restrain herself or her eyes had a will of their own. When Bonni finally came in, with his graying beard and his yellow leather briefcase, he cut off the boys' uproar by slamming the door, and she stole a glance. The darkness had almost swallowed his figure.

He ran through the roll, put the register on his desk and folded his arms. He stood in silence for a long moment and then said restrainedly, "Can anyone . . . " but the sentence was cut off. Like a sprinter making a false start and haring down the track Ophir shouted from his desk at the back, "Sir, I checked the equation you taught us and 'A' isn't whether the body is animate or inanimate, it stands for 'acceleration'."

"Who gave you permission to speak?" Bonni asked in a restrained voice, which now bore a menacing tone.

"But, sir, I went to the library and read everything about Newton's Laws . . . "

"Newton's Laws," Bonni repeated, tapping his glasses lens with a finger. "So all of a sudden somebody's read up all of Newton's Laws. Very good, so thanks to Ophir Shriki the end-of-year exam will now include additional material, Newton's Three Laws of Motion."

Ophir ignored the waves of resentment that flooded the room, Noam Ohana's promise to make him eat the pages of his notebook and the storm clouds gathering around Bonni. Ori, too, tried to stop him and warn him through clenched teeth, but Ophir couldn't be stopped as he forged ahead.

"Okay, but this time teach us properly," he said.

"Your shouting won't do you any good. Open your books," Bonni commanded, the anger in his posture and movements suppressing the murmurs in the room.

"Ophir, dictate to them."

Ophir eagerly complied.

"The First Law: A body continues to maintain its state of rest or of uniform motion unless acted upon by an external unbalanced force. The Second Law . . . "

"Hold it," Gvinush cut him off, "slower."

"The Second Law," Ophir went on, accentuating the words, "the net force on an object is equal to the mass of the object multiplied by its acceleration. The Third Law: To every action there is an equal and opposite reaction."

"Very good," Bonni said. "And now can anybody, except Ophir, explain? Rimona, what about you?"

"How would I know, it all sounds like *t'harwid*, crap, to me."

Sigal raised her hand hesitantly and Bonni gestured to her with his chin.

"Yes, Sigal," he said.

Sigal bowed her head when she saw his expression. Ori studied the mixture of sorrow and compassion in Bonni's face, he knew how the scales would tip for Sigal and that he was unable to tell her.

"I think," she said, staring into her notebook, "that the body doesn't want to change. Let's say if someone's thin, then he's got to make an effort not to be thin. And he also can't understand someone who isn't, who can't be."

"Rubbish," Ophir said before Bonni digested her answer, "it's not that kind of body."

"So what body could it be?" Bonni asked.

"What d'you mean?"

"We're talking about physics and we don't know that we're talking about ourselves," Bonni replied.

Ophir twisted his nose and his jaws moved in a counter-clockwise rotary chewing movement.

"What's that got to do with anything?" he asked. "If you've got an object, right, and it's stationary, it won't start moving on its own, will it? You've got to exert force to make it move. That's what the law's about."

"And a human body," Sigal argued, "can move on its own, no?"

"But it's not about that," he persisted.

"Look," Bonni said, "the First Law of Motion has been refuted. Life is against it. The very existence of life refutes it. There are countries where the dead refuse to die. They stay with you, in the arteries, in memories, and no force you exert on them will erase them or stop their movement."

Ophir didn't respond; he waited for a question. But Bonni went on lecturing.

"And the Third Law, action and reaction. When a person dies, what reaction is there to that action?"

"Maybe that a baby is born," Sigal whispered.

"But a baby is new life. It's not what was. It's an action that has one direction. All reality says no to these dried-up laws."

"But I read that modern science is based on these laws, that's what it said," Ophir said, but feebly.

"Science has nothing to say about life," Bonni said and his voice choked.

"Then why are you teaching us this stuff at all?" Ori asked suddenly.

"So you know what to watch out for," Bonni replied, and again his eyes filled with sadness and distance as he looked at her. "But it seems to me that you know already, Ori, you're already discovering the limitations of blood."

"Bees' Blood," Gvinush said automatically in a hollow voice.

Bonni stiffened. "What did you say?" he hissed.

"Nothing," Gvinush replied.

"*What,*" Bonni repeated, his voice rising, "*did you,*" he thundered, "*say?*"

"What?" Gvinush said archly, "Stop making a big deal out of every word I say."

Bonni covered the distance between them in long strides. "How dare you!" he shouted, and banged on the desk.

"*Sma'alla*, God help us," Aliza Edri said, clapping a hand to her chest.

"Don't think I didn't hear you at the ceremony earlier," Bonni said, and as he leant towards her the wildness of his movements was clearly evident. "Your filthy joke. Who are you to dare mock the soldiers who gave their lives so you could live your pitiful life?"

Gvinush's normally pale face became even more pallid. Shouts of protest came from the direction of the boys, but they were weak and unassertive. Bonni ignored them.

"You have no respect for anything," he said. "Now, everyone move your desks against the wall and arrange your chairs in a circle in the middle of the room."

He pushed the teacher's desk against the door, blocking it. Then he sat down on it and waited. Not one student moved.

"I said," he shouted, "arrange your chairs in a circle." His shout quickly sent them to do as he had told them. The task was completed within five minutes. The circle of chairs stood in the middle of the room and the students, Ori among them, crowded onto them.

Bonni brought his own chair into the circle and stood behind it, outside the circle. He moved stiffly, it seemed to Ori, who'd already seen her father on the verge of an outburst as he contained a terrible anger. *You've got to freeze*, she thought, *and if you must move, then warily.*

, "Sir, why . . . " Sigal said in a low voice, but he cut her off with a gesture without looking at her.

"You," he said, "have been given the best of everything. And what do you do with it? You laugh. How fortunate you are to be at your age and free of worries. But instead of your good fortune making you sensitive to the suffering of others, you mock them. The death of others is easy for you, you laugh and make fun of it."

"But, sir, we didn't . . . " Noam tried to say, but Bonni shut him up with a glare.

"You didn't what?" he demanded, "What? You didn't laugh at the ceremony? I saw you, each and every one of you. You may have fooled Principal Tuitto, that overgrown dummy, but not me. Not me . . . Perhaps you're so impervious and focused on yourselves that you've got no idea about it. Perhaps it's your evil—you were born stained with evil, you're immersed in it, and it crawls out at every opportunity . . . "

Not one peep cleaved the silence his words left behind them. Bonni heaved a deep sigh and looked at the ceiling. He began mumbling, meaningless syllables. In the jumble of vague sounds it seemed to Ori that she heard the name 'Itzik' and the word 'forgiveness'.

"Sir . . . " Sigal said again, but his expression was fixed when he turned towards her.

"I had a brother," he suddenly said, emerging from his mumblings and looking towards the window.

What was he looking for? The school gate could be seen from here and closer than still were the senior class workshops, a woodwork and metalwork shop, and the sloped structure of the bomb shelter that a kid, evidently from the elementary school, was sliding down in a rectangular cardboard box.

"I had a soldier brother. He was born when my parents were already old. Fourteen years younger than me. His name was Itzik. We, my sister and I, called him Itzik. In the army they called him Tzachi. That's what he wanted. Tzachi. Four years ago I went to have Friday night dinner with my parents. There was me, my sister and my parents. My mother served my father with the fish starter. That's how he is. Without fish for the first course, it's not Sabbath Eve. I hate fish, but my father . . . And then, as she was serving, my mother dropped the plate. My sister, who was sitting with her back to her, jumped up. And I hurried to her as well. Only my father remained seated. 'That's it,' my mother said, 'Yitzhak's finished, he's gone,' and she started crying. I said, 'Ima, what are you talking about?' and she replied, 'That's it. It's over.' When I turned round I saw my father holding his head in his hands, his shoulders shaking. Next day we were informed that Itzik had fallen in Lebanon."

He spoke quietly, emotionlessly, and Ori saw Sigal rising from her chair, wanting to get up and go to him. She quickly shook her head and Sigal sat down. Bonni said, "Since then, every year on this day, Remembrance Day, I stand at the ceremony in the military cemetery, and here in this school, and I feel that boiling water is being poured over my head. But in my legs a frozen shiver begins, and the heat of the water and the coldness of the shiver meet here," he pointed to his navel, "and I don't hear the siren, only the sound of my mother's plate shattering on the floor, and I know that all this can't go on much longer."

He removed his glasses and wiped their lenses with his shirttail.

"Sir, forgive us," Sigal said, "no one meant anything."

"Yes, yes," the children began competing and supporting her in a rising murmur.

Their power of movement was restored and they shifted in their seats, and Ori felt she could again breathe freely. Then, Gvinush's giggle exploded into the sea of agreement. Ori knew that giggle, it was a giggle of distress. Once, when they were in kindergarten, she'd seen a boy hitting Gvinush, and Gvinush reacted by giggling, a giggle that only increased the rate of the boy's blows, the fists and kicks. All they got out of Gvinush was a louder giggle, more urgent, defiant. If the teacher hadn't come out and grabbed the violent child Gvinush might have been beaten senseless. And that's how Gvinush was giggling now, delicate uncontrolled crystals of laughter. Ori expected a calamity, an outburst, but Bonni's shoulders suddenly slumped and he started crying brokenly; bitter, dry weeping.

"I loved him," Bonni said when his weeping abated and he was able to speak. "And since then, because that love has nowhere to be channeled to, it goes out to the world. I love everyone, I love until my heart is about to explode in my chest, and I cry when I'm at home alone, and through the window I see the day outside changing into evening and the children going home from the street, I cry because of my love for them, children I barely know, and all the more so with you. Even you, Rimona, I love and forgive you, even though you're hard, as hard as stone, and you put all your energy into making the lives of people weaker than yourself a misery. I love you and forgive . . . "

He moved towards Gvinush and she jumped up and ran to the far wall, alternately giggling and screaming, "Mama, get that madman away from me!"

Her call for help fell on deaf ears. The boys sat there stunned. Had there been something violent, threatening, in Bonni's gestures or demeanor, they could have responded with violence of their own. But the teacher was moving laxly and crying. What could they do to a weeping man?

Gvinush's face was terror-stricken when she realized that nobody was coming to her aid. Between her giggles she yelled, "Don't come near me, you hear? You don't know what my father and brothers will do to you if you touch me."

"Why, why are you being like this?" Bonni asked timidly, "I don't want to harm you. Give me your hand. Hold it out."

He closed in on her, and now there was pleading in her giggling, "Get away from me, you maniac, Imaaaaa!"

Ori could restrain herself no longer and didn't know from where she summoned the strength to act. She stood up and interposed herself between Bonni and Gvinush.

"Sir," she said, "she's very scared. She knows you love her, but she's scared."

Her words got through to him, she saw. The lenses of his glasses were damp, but a spark of recognition reignited in the depths of the eyes they protected.

"You understand me, don't you, Ori?" He said to her, and she nodded.

He turned on his heel and went back to the chair he'd put in the opening of the circle. His knees were trembling and he collapsed onto it.

"You look at me," he said, his voice shaking and the corners of his mouth twitching, and some spittle appeared on his lips as he spat out his words. "And you see an adult, who for you is an indistinct creature you don't understand. For you, perhaps, I'm a ludicrous old man, maybe that's what you call me behind my back, maybe you even use worse names than that. But one day, when you get to my age, you'll understand that all this time you were young. People grow old slowly, their soul always lags behind their body. The more the body is destroyed, the more they want. That's why I'm not worried about your distant future, but I do worry about you now and about what will happen to you in the coming years, about what kind of people you'll become, what you'll believe in. When we were young, I and my generation were always looking for something to idolize, which opinions and beliefs we should have. But you, you'll be living in a different time and you'll ask yourselves what not to idolize, what shouldn't be idolized, and I'm telling you, don't idolize death and don't idolize love. You were born on soil teeming with blood and death, and you're growing up in a time that wants to force you to love according to its needs . . . And death and love, the temptation to idolize one or the other is great, and you're already becoming habituated to them. I've seen terrible phantoms rising from this land, and you'll see them too. But you, let the dead bury the dead and live, and don't worship love, which is the most dangerous of worships, don't let yourselves become slaves to love . . . Love life, not love . . . Don't reject life . . . Love every flower, every bird, every stone in its flight, this is my hope for you . . . " His words became a stammer and the enunciation was difficult to understand, as if leaden weights were pressing on his lips. He fell silent and glanced at Ori again. "But you, Ori, you know all that, don't you?" he said as if pleading, tiredly. "The people that walked in darkness have seen a great light: they that dwelt in the land of the shadow of death, upon them hath the light shined."

His last words sent a shudder down Ori's lower back and she wanted to move closer to him, to understand more, but his head began shaking on his neck and his hands waved, a spasm shook his entire being and the spittle on his lips thickened and was flecked with blood—perhaps he'd bitten his tongue—and immediately, just as the seizure had begun, it ended all at once and he sprawled in the chair, his eyes closed and weeping. His body was still.

Gvinush was the first to realize that the siege had been lifted and she ran to the closed door, pushed the desk blocking it aside, opened it wide, ran out into the corridor and yelled, "Help! Bonni's gone crazy!"

She was followed by the whole class, but not for long, for with their movement out of the room, a few moments after Gvinush's yelling, there began a counter-movement, a crowding inside from the adjacent classrooms.

Ori didn't manage to rouse Bonni with her shouts. Sigal, who had rushed to him, stayed beside him, tried to stop his muscles jumping by holding his shoulders gently and urgently whispering to him, failed too.

In the doorway, above the heads of the curious students, appeared the bent figure of the janitor, whitened with age, and the fleshy, smug figure of the principal. As they approached him, Bonni's hand, limp on his chair, fluttered across Ori's hand. She leant over him. His eyes opened to a slit and tiny pink bubbles of saliva still oozed from the corners of his mouth as he mumbled to her weakly, "Woe is me, for I am a man of unclean lips, and I dwell in the midst of a people of unclean lips."

FOUR

Hair

SHE ALMOST MANAGED TO SKIP the meeting with Galila Ron-Feder, but Ilanit called her. Why? They hadn't seen each other for a few days and that morning—when Elisheva told them that the meeting would be in the gym because at the last minute the principal had tacked the 8ᵗʰ grade onto them because he intended to make a speech in the presence of the famous writer who was visiting their school—she hadn't caught sight of Ilanit. She lagged behind the students flocking to the gym and on the concrete pathway that passed close by the synagogue, she bounded towards the entrance, walked up the steps and waited at the top by the wooden doors—beneath the arch bearing the legend 'This is the gate of the Lord into which the righteous shall enter'—until the noise of the of students abated. Then she went back down and inspected the gym door, which had just been closed. She turned to leave and had taken a few steps when she was struck from behind by Ilanit's voice.

"Ori, where are you going?"

Embarrassed, she turned towards the voice and now the gym door was open and Ilanit was waving to her from it.

"Ori, come on, everybody's waiting for you," she called.

Ori knew she had no choice. She trudged towards Ilanit who grabbed her arm and led her to the seat she'd kept beside her in the last rows of chairs that striped the green parquet floor with white.

"I saved you a good seat at the back," Ilanit whispered.

Most of class were sitting there, at the back of the hall, even Sigal who had a zeal for attentiveness and summarizing was sitting a row in front of them, smiling, her notebook open on her lap, and she turned her head as Ori took her seat.

"Well, did you read the book in the end?" Ilanit asked with her urgent curiosity, as if they hadn't been on the outs. "Is that why you went to the library that day?"

Ori nodded. She *had* read the book, not because Elisheva has asked her to, but because of Ofra. She was coming to the end of the Ariella books. She was reading them too quickly. One evening the previous week she was filled with anxiety—what if her pleasure came to an end with the conclusion of the series—and she hurried to Ofra's room before she'd even digested the thought. Ofra was playing "Total Eclipse of the Heart" at full volume on the tape recorder one of her friends had given her. Wearing a towel on her head, face to the ceiling and eyes closed, she mouthed the words of the song. Ori stood in the doorway not daring to go inside, until on the line 'and I need you more tonight' Ofra opened her eyes and saw her. She hit the stop button on the machine.

"What d'you want?" she asked, not allowing silence to again well up in the room.

"I wanted to ask . . . but maybe I'll come back some other time," Ori said.

"Come on, stop playing the spoilt brat. Your tricks might work on Ima and Asher but not on me. What did you want?"

"The books I'm reading . . . what if when I finish them . . . what if I don't . . . "

"There's no such thing," Ofra replied, "it's like a bug."

"But . . . "

"No buts. Tomorrow you're coming to the library with me and you'll see."

Ofra kept her promise. Next day she was waiting at the school gate. They walked in silence side by side. The words were stopped up between them. Ori thought about the meaning of the words 'stopped up'. For the first time in her life she could see it: the words dwelt inside her and inside Ofra like clear glass balls, and thick, cloudy, grayish smoke burst from the heart of the balls and sealed them.

"Well say something." Ofra said about a quarter of the way there.

"What?"

"I don't know. Something. Your silence is bugging me."

And Ori said the first thing that came into her mind. "What's the story with Ima and Abba, I mean, how did they meet, was Ima really . . . ?"

"What's Ima told you?"

"That it's not good for girls to sit at home and that she knows . . . but what does she know?"

"Ah, *that* story."

"What? What? Tell me."

"What'll you give me for it?"

"What d'you mean?"

"You've got to give me something in exchange. Maybe you'll let me read the notebook you're writing."

"No, no way," Ori protested automatically and stopped. And then she thought, How does that scorpion know I'm writing, nothing gets past her.

Ofra walked on, then stopped, and called to Ori.

"If you want a story, you'll have to pay."

"Then I'll tell you something instead."

"Pchhh," Ofra replied and waved her hand as if brushing away a fly, "what could you possibly know that I don't." Despite the casualness she tried to give her words, Ori could see that her curiosity had been piqued.

"So, what d'you say?"

"Okaaaaay," Ofra said, widening her mouth and drawing the syllable out, "but only if you tell me something good."

"I saw Asher crying," Ori said quickly, knowing that if she waited a second and thought about the words that had come from her tongue, she would regret them and swallow them before they became sound. And yet, as the words passed her lips she felt she was disclosing a secret that had been entrusted to her. "Because of Ima", she added quickly to take the sting out of the words.

"No way," Ofra said, her eyes sparkling. "When did you see it?"

"In the Passover vacation. He didn't notice that I'd seen. I was by the door."

"You're a snake in the grass, you are, I've always said we've got to watch out for you."

"It wasn't on purpose."

"Asher crying? Have you noticed that he stopped asking you about Rimona Peretz about two weeks ago?"

"About Gvinush? What's she got to do with it?" Ori asked and immediately thought, it's true. He hasn't asked about her since the bat-mitzvah.

"Nothing at all," said Ofra in a more thoughtful tone than usual.

"Now it's your turn," Ori demanded.

"Okay," Ofra began reluctantly, "Ima and Abba met when Abba was in the army. He was living here in the immigrant transit camp near Netivot and Ima lived in Tiberias. Abba was a cook at some base in the north and one day, when he was going home on leave, he met Ima, who was still a girl, at a bus stop. She was waiting for her brother who was also supposed to be coming home for the weekend."

Ofra fell silent and Ori felt cheated. "That's it?" she asked unbelievingly.

"No," Ofra replied, "that's the background. Because Abba was engaged to someone in Netivot and Ima was a shy girl, very close to her family, and she hardly ever left the house."

"Ima?"

"Yes, yes, Ima."

"So how . . . ? And what . . . ?"

"If you stop interrupting all the time with your stupid questions, maybe you'll understand."

"Why d'you get so annoyed about everything?"

"Because you've got a talent for annoying people. Ever since your bat-mitzvah you've been stuck-up."

"Ofra . . ."

"Anyway," Ofra continued with Ori scowling at her, "Ima took a shine to Abba, and because she was so naïve she told her mother who right away kicked up a fuss and forbade Ima to leave the house until she found out who this boy was. And when she heard he was engaged she freaked out and yelled that Ima was shaming the family by wanting to go out with a married man."

"But Abba wasn't married."

"Do you want to hear the story or not?" Ofra shot her an angry look.

"Yes," Ori whispered, crestfallen.

"Well, in brief," Ofra said, "Ima was depressed for about a month, she said she was seeing black around her eyes. Say she'd be looking at you, she'd see you but everything around you'd be dark. She stopped eating and she was nauseous and dizzy all the time. What I haven't told you is that Abba took a shine to Ima as well, and the next time he left the base he went looking for her in Tiberias. He knew her name so he found her in a snap. Tiberias is like Netivot. They all live up each other's ass."

Here Ofra burst into sudden loud laughter and Ori waited vainly for it to subside.

"Well?" she finally demanded.

"Abba was out of luck that day. Ima's father and brother dropped on him like a ton of bricks and beat the shit out of him and told him not to dare show his face in Tiberias."

Ori gasped.

"Yes, yes. Why d'you think we're not in touch with Ima's side of the family?"

"Because of that?"

"Not only. Next day Ima plucked up courage, grabbed her things and left home. To Abba's parents' house. She hitchhiked. She was in luck. The moment Mama Elhayani saw her coming into their house she said to Abba, 'That's your wife'. And Abba called off his engagement and got engaged to Ima."

Ofra fell silent for a moment and Ori mulled over the story.

"Just a minute," she said, "how come Ima's parents left her and Abba some money?"

"Ima was surprised by that too. Maybe they changed their mind about what they'd done to her. Grandpa on Ima's side died first, he had liver cancer they didn't catch in time. And her mother died a year later, a bit before you were born. And that's it. She left Ima all the money they had on condition she'd buy a house with it. And that's what Ima and Abba did."

"How d'you know all this?"

"Look, here's the library already. That's how it goes when you chat, time passes quicker." Ofra said, not bothering to answer Ori's question.

They took the three steps to the entrance and in the lobby they passed the librarian from the adult lending library on her way to the rest room and she shot them a smile.

"When you go in, I want you to choose the book you least want to read, okay?" Ofra said.

"Why?"

"If I tell you, the experiment won't work."

Ori nodded and went into the children's section. She knew which book was the last one in the world she wanted to read—Galila Ron-Feder's *In Light and Hiding*. She found it easily and went back to Ofra who was waiting impatiently for the librarian to return to the adult section.

"Here, I found it," she told Ofra.

"Great," Ofra replied, "when you've finished it, come and talk to me."

"But Ofra, it's a book . . . " she started to complain, but Ofra cut her short.

"You don't have to, you know."

Ori nodded again, knowing she had to resign herself to her fate.

She felt that the book was forced upon her, the book whose reading seemed to her like chewing a stale wafer; chocolate-covered. Although its deep color brightened and dimmed, it held a promise of sweetness, the wafer was still bitten and chewed like a piece of cardboard.

The pages stuck in her throat, boluses of cellulose, but she persevered with her reading and on Saturday afternoon, when she was almost at the end, she took her eyes from the book and peeped through the window slats of her room. Her father was sitting in the yard, sipping a cup of coffee. These were his moments of grace when he could still enjoy the tranquility of their home before leaving for his evening shift. She saw his nape tense and his hand touch the corner of his mouth. For more than six months now he hadn't smoked on the Sabbath. Close to the end of the Sabbath day, when his desire was at it's height, he'd chew on a toothpick, now and then holding it between his fingers and taking an imaginary puff. She tried to look away from him in case he sensed her watching, shattering the peace he had earned by hard labor, but she couldn't tear her eyes from him, because what Ofra had told her was fresh in her memory. She tried to imagine her father as a younger man, attractive, his eyes filled with love. Something of this was still evident when he looked at their mother.

He spoke Ori's name without turning his head, the syllables shooting from his tongue still filled with happiness. Then he added, "Come here."

She went. She pushed open the screen door that kept the bugs, that had begun gathering as March expired, from the house, and went out to him.

He patted the plastic chair at his side.

"So," he said, "I heard there's trouble at school."

Despite the casualness in his words, a small feeling of alarm sparked inside her, a spreading flame. She began examining her actions, what had she done lately that might have aroused his anger? Until he went on—had he sensed her body tensing beside him?—"Your mother told me your science teacher went crazy."

"Ah," she smiled at him, "I'd already forgotten."

"What happened exactly?"

"Why?"

"Too many things are happening here lately."

"What do you mean?"

"Nothing. I was just saying."

"I think that Bonni's been crazy for a long time. It didn't happen suddenly."

"Still," her father said, "still."

She'd thought about this herself, but hadn't imagined that somebody else had noticed the damage, which is what she called the disruption. Something was disrupted, she knew it. Her entire body was in turmoil and weighted with its presence. Of all her family, only Asher, despite his shows of toughness, was perhaps sufficiently sensitive to grasp the deterioration that had begun in the world. Her father was hardly at home, when he wasn't overcome by the force of his anger he was indifferent and remote, a passing guest.

"What's happening?" she asked.

"First you," he answered, and her heart missed a beat.

"Me?" she protested, and said quietly, "What's it got to do with me?"

But her father didn't answer.

"Then your mother. And now your teacher. It's too much."

"But I'm all right," she said, "and so's Ima, she's better."

"She's got to go back for a checkup. She should have gone on Thursday, but she didn't. She found something else to do. You and her are the same."

"I wish I was like her."

"You're both the same. You don't listen. You've got to have everything your own way. You don't compromise on anything. That's why she took your changing your name so hard."

Ori was silent. Then she said, "But Ima's all right, isn't she?"

"We'll know when we get the test results."

The wind came up and its chill intensified the clarity of the air. A dark cloud of gnats buzzed on the mulberry tree. The lawn spread over the bare soil, which had more bald patches than grass, had started to dry up at its edges, summer had emerged from the depths of the earth and was already cracking the surface. This is Netivot, the town where the heat crawls up from the depths.

Her father put his arm around her.

"You're all skin and bones," he said, squeezing her shoulder as if to illustrate his words. He looked down at her and she saw the black stubble on his cheeks, sown between the wrinkles that had begun making furrows around his mouth and eyes when he frowned. Although he hadn't had a cigarette since last night, he was still shrouded in the smell of tobacco, sharp and delicate at the same time, consuming her breathing. His lips tightened. A tooth was missing from his upper jaw. "It'll be all right," he finished.

She knew that this was his way of dismissing her from his embrace, from the stooping and protective heaviness.

"I've got to get back to my book. I've got to finish it for tomorrow, for the meeting with the author." She stood up as she spoke.

He gave her a wan hint of a smile and she turned her back on him and went back to her room.

That evening Ofra came to her room and asked, "Well, have you read it?"

She nodded, a strange, perverse nod. Her head was heavy from reading and she felt she had to force her neck to stay upright. It hadn't been like that with the Ariella books. Perhaps because throughout this book she had remained outside, wanting to get in and being pushed out by the force of events that did not excite her.

"And what do you think?"

"I don't know. This book's only part one. And I wouldn't want to read part two. I wouldn't want to read another book like it."

"And reading in general?"

"Yes, I'm already missing it."

"I told you so," Ofra said triumphantly, "it's like a bug. If a book you didn't like hasn't killed your desire, it means you're hooked."

Ori didn't answer.

"So, what now?" Ofra added.

"Nothing," Ori replied.

"Disappointed?"

"No, it's not that."

"Then what?"

"I don't know, maybe it's nothing. All of a sudden I'm sad. I don't know, I feel like crying."

She hadn't realized that her thoughts had benumbed her so much. On the contrary, the author's words sailing through the space of the gym were hawsers and anchors that held her where she was, stopping her from sailing away. The author said something about the importance of her book, especially at this time when the younger generation was losing all contact with its historical and national origins, and about the essentialness of heritage . . . Here the thread broke.

When her consciousness returned and focused, the author's words seemed so horribly familiar and Ori realized that she was reading from her book. She read in a voice filled with vim and vigor, but not enough to mesmerize Ori, and again she was benumbed until she was awoken by Ilanit's whisper.

"Ori, you're away!"

A cold object was pressed into the palm of her right hand. Mechanically she opened her hand and gripped it.

"Osez." Ilanit whispered.

Ori looked at the object. A pair of scissors. She returned Ilanit a surprised look.

"Osez", Ilanit whispered again.

"But what?" Ori wanted to know, too loudly, because Sigal turned round and silenced her with a reproving 'Shhh'.

With her chin Ilanit gestured towards Sigal, whose brown curly hair cascaded dense and knotted onto her shoulders.

"No," Ori said.

"But I said 'Osez'," Ilanit replied.

That stupid game. Ori was sure that they'd got rid of it. They hadn't played it since fifth grade, but before that they'd played it all the time. The rules were simple. If one of them made the other hold an object in her hand and immediately said 'Osez' before she could reply 'Passez', the one holding the object had to fulfill a task imposed on her by the other. They challenged one another with ever more daring assignments until in fifth grade Ori made Ilanit put thumbtacks on Gvinush's chair. Somebody snitched, because with unprecedented speed Gvinush found out who was responsible and dragged the weeping and shouting Ilanit back and forth by her hair across the soccer field for an entire recess. Afterwards they stopped playing the game, for always, Ori thought, until it came back from some depth of friendship. Ori knew that she was now forced to pick up the gauntlet, which in their joint history far outweighed the weak protest of common sense.

"D'accord," she blurted the word of submission and added, even though she knew full well what Ilanit's request would be, "What do I have I to do?"

Ilanit gently twisted around a finger a lock of Ori's hair that covered her ear, and whispered, "I command you to cut off a piece of Sigal's hair."

Ori shook her head in refusal, but sentence had been passed, and she bent over the back of Sigal's chair, holding the scissors in the trembling fingers of her left hand, and with the right selected a lock of hair, taking care not to pull it, not to break Sigal's tense concentration, and with a swift snip cut off the end of the lock.

But Sigal felt her hair being stolen and yelled "Aiee," then turned round. When she saw the shocked Ori with her hands full of scissors and hair, she paled and her eyes—which Ori only now noticed were beautiful, gold-flecked and honey colored, with long lashes covering their slant—half closed. She got up and ran outside to the accompaniment of the fading words of the author, who was unaware of what caused the disturbance. Perhaps she thought that her high-flown confession—how wonderful it is for her to be here, in Netivot, a town so far from the center of the country, and how sure she is that hers is a true mission, for here, in this township, the people undoubtedly know less about the exemplary figures who had sacrificed themselves so that they, all of us, would have a home—is a somewhat out of place exaggeration.

———

Ilanit took the lock of hair without stating what she intended to do with it, but Ori didn't care. Sigal's eyes had lost their gleam and were seared onto her own retinas as she left the gym, head bowed, at the end of the lecture. Not one of their classmates demanded satisfaction for Sigal, nor were their thoughts troubled by the question of why she had got up and fled from the gym. Except for Ophir Shriki, who stopped by her and said, "I thought you were nicer than that," and then nodded, or perhaps it was just one of his tics, and went on his way.

Osez, passez, d'accord, osez passez d'accord, osez passez d'accord, the insistent whisper whirled around in Ori's lowered head, and she almost bumped into Asher. She saw a pair of skinny shins that sprouted black fuzz, a pair of white Pama sneakers, tight-fitting socks. A basketball bounced on the ground and rolled, and two strong arms stopped her, and she raised her eyes.

"Wow, girl, look where you're going," Asher said, with a smile in his thickening, breaking voice; when her eyes looked at him—what had he seen in them—he added, "Ori, is everything okay?" and his Adam's apple bobbed up and down.

She nodded.

"You've shot up," she said, and the movement of her head strained her neck muscles. "When did that happen?"

Truly, it seemed Asher was growing by a few centimeters every day and he'd soon be as tall as their father.

He laughed. His eyes flashed at her. Gaiety rose from him and washed over her, and she wanted to be close to him, immerse herself in his cheerfulness, but his hands held her in place, at the usual, safe distance.

"At long last you're noticing what's going on around you," he said, "you've been a real space cadet lately."

She smiled at him with difficulty and swallowed her saliva.

"Are you okay?" he asked again.

"Yes, everything's great," she said.

"I've got to run," he told her, "I've got PE." His eyes were drawn to the basketball that had rolled and come to a stop in the bushes by the synagogue door. "I promised Ima I'd help her with the shopping today because Abba's on evenings. Tell her I'll be late, I've got basketball practice."

"What practice?" she asked, "Is it something new?"

"Yes. Josh wants to get a basketball team together. Hapoel Netivot or something. He held tryouts and I'm in the squad."

"But Asher, does Abba know?"

"No. I haven't told Ima and Abba. Today's the first practice."

She grimaced. She had evidently grimaced because Asher said, "Stop that thing with your mouth. I'm almost fifteen, I don't have to ask permission for everything I do."

He strode to the ball and pulled it out of the bushes, spun it in the air and caught it on his right arm rolling it across his chest and then onto his left arm, before he caught it in both hands, smiled at her and walked away.

She watched him as he walked, tall and thin. No, not exactly thin anymore; something of the man's weightiness that filled their father's swaying gait was already there, his limbs moving and resting. His muscles were already coarser, no longer the childish smoothness but a new suppleness. As he disappeared into the gym she felt the momentary happiness dissipating, to be replaced by the memory of the locked pupils of Sigal's eyes, and the words.

Osez, passez, d'accord, osez passez d'accord, osez passez d'accord, she wrote over and over again in her notebook when she got home and took it from under her mattress, the hiding place she'd found following her talk with Ofra. She wasn't prepared for anyone to see its secrets. Osez, passez, d'accord, osez passez d'accord, osezpassezd'accord, the words dripped from the previous paragraphs, lines she had taken from those she had copied from the Ariella books, from words that had pierced her flesh. She leafed back, scanned the paragraphs, perhaps she'd find consolation, what were they, these written words. They were undefined: not poetry, some sort of thoughts, unclear confidences, confused. As if adding a further twist to the tangle, the line before 'osez passez d'accord' contained Bonni's words, before the janitor dragged him out of the classroom, limbs limp and expression blank. "Woe is me, for I am a man of unclean lips, and I dwell in the midst of a people of unclean lips."

"Ori, phone," Her mother called from the living room, her call ending with a thin cough. The coughing had returned, even though she was on her feet, was well. She had returned to her job at the senior citizens' day center and to her housework as if she'd never been ill at all. Only a wheeze and a passing pallor like a fleeting expression of insult were left as signs of her weakness.

Ori came out of her room. Her mother was standing in the living room holding the phone like a torch. She didn't meet her eyes. In general, she had hardly spoken with her mother since she'd refused to let her go on the school trip and had voiced her arguments to her husband that same evening, and he had shaken his head and said, "You're not going."

"Hello?" she said, putting the receiver to her ear.

"It was a laugh today," Ilanit said. "Where did you go afterwards?"

"I didn't feel well so I went home."

"What's the matter?"

"Nothing, just a stomach ache."

"And now?"

"It's better."

"You should have seen what went on afterwards."

"And Sigal?" Something vague and heavy hit her in the chest as she spoke the name.

"Don't know. I didn't see her all day."

"Why did you make me do it?" she asked.

She didn't hear Ilanit's reply. A stabbing at the base of her nape took her out of the conversation and she turned her head quickly. She dropped the phone and ran down the hallway to the kitchen where her mother was sitting on a chair, choking and banging her chest with a clenched fist, her breathing cut by half, a whistling jet of air. She's suffocating, Ori thought, and her body reacted with a will of its own. She ran around the chair, stood behind her mother, and pounded her back open-handed, the way she'd seen her do it on numerous occasions to Asher, who tended to eat too quickly and make jokes at the same time.

The pounding helped. An eruption of coughing filled the air.

"Ima," she said, and hurried to the sink to pour a glass of water, "what happened?"

"My breathing got stuck," her voice still choked, stuttering. She took a few sips of water.

"What do you mean, 'got stuck'?"

"It got stuck, while I was breathing, all of a sudden the air wouldn't come out." The color had returned to her face. "It's lucky you were here. What's that noise?"

Teeteeteeteet came the angry sound of protest from the open line in the living room.

"Ooh, Ilanit," Ori said and ran to the living room. She replaced the ivory-colored receiver and then lifted it again, sticking a finger into the dial, hesitating over calling back.

"*Jinn*," her mother said, "do you know where Asher is? He promised to help me with the shopping but he's late."

"Ah, I forgot, Asher . . . " Ori said and didn't complete the sentence. Ofra appeared in the doorway—a draught, a whirl-wind of movement. "Asher'll be late, he's got practice," she announced.

"What practice?"

"Practice," Ofra repeated. "Basketball. Josh the sports teach-er's getting a team together."

"How do you know?" Ori asked.

"How do I know?" Ofra looked at her scathingly.

"He didn't say anything about practice," their mother said. "It's not like Asher. He's a responsible child."

"He's not a child anymore," Ofra said.

"He asked me to tell you at school, but I forgot." Ori said.

"I don't know where your head is these days," their mother said, "why are they making a team at school all of a sudden?"

"Pchhh," Ofra said, "it's that Josh and Judy with their ideas. Putting Netivot on the map or something. They found them-selves the right place, *balad jua*."

"Don't you call Netivot that," their mother said with sud-den anger, getting up sluggishly and stretching. "D'you hear me? I've told you a thousand times you've got no respect for anything."

"Why, what did I say?" Ofra retorted, her voice rising too. "What do you think? Everyone calls this place *balad jua*."

"What's *balad . . . jua*?" Ori interjected, and the word '*jua*' with its difficult gutturals, she posed as a question, seeking confirmation she'd pronounced it correctly.

"The village of the starving," Ofra replied.

Their mother gave her an angry look and sighed, "*Ayma*," the air was expelled from her lips, a cloud of vapor, and was interrupted by a loud whistle that came through the door that Ofra had left open when she came in.

"I'm going out," Ofra said in response.

"Why? Is it you they're whistling for? Who's whistling for you like that?" their mother said and with long strides strode out onto the verandah with Ofra and Ori in her wake.

Now it was Ori's turn to catch her breath. The radiance of May—although the day was sinking into dusk, and its glow at this hour had been borrowed from summertime—lay like a thick cloud over the street. The light intensified, the asphalt gleamed. The houses were afire with soft flames and the roof tiles with a halo of gushing, flowing lava. The ancient margosas in the park and the strike of evening coming slyly like a sudden upheaval, the neighborhood cisterns—cracked cisterns, two boys lounging, tall and brown, full of insolence and as burned as a shadow. To see better, Ori went to the end of the verandah, as far as the rail set into the low wall, but their mother's voice stopped her.

"Why are you whistling like that, eh?" she called out to the boys, who responded with shameless laughter. "You don't want to mess with me," she continued, "this is a respectable house and my daughter's a respectable girl. Why are you whistling at her?"

"I-ma," Ofra protested through clenched teeth.

Their mother turned to her, her night braids veined with gray lay on her face and she parted them with her hands, combing them back with her fingers.

"Don't give me 'Ima'," and she went right back to reprimanding the boys. "Get out of here, d'you hear me?"

"We're waiting for Ofra," the one on the right ventured.

"You've nothing to wait for. Ofra's not leaving the house tonight."

"What are you talking about?" Ofra burst out.

"You get inside this minute."

"What do you think I am, three years old?"

"You're my daughter till you're eighteen and you'll do what I tell you. Now get inside."

"No I won't."

Their mother turned to look at her. Ori had never seen such resolve in her face—the eyes wide, two daggers, the nostrils flaring and trembling and grating on the silence as they breathed and the lips stretched, so stretched. "I told you to get inside this minute."

Ofra walked to the door with mechanically. Their mother didn't even glance after her but shifted her attention, an intense, feverish shaft of light, back to the boys.

"Don't you dare show your faces here again. You," she said to the one on the right, the spokesman, the giggler, "I know you. You're Zaguri the butcher's son, and you," she said, moving to the one on the left, "you're Marima's grandson. Don't think I've got no way of finding you."

———

Ori went to Ilanit's house. Fearfully, she asked her mother's permission to go out, and her mother asked sharply, "Where to?"

"To Ilanit's. Our call was cut off because of what happened before." she replied.

Her mother moved her head indecisively, too proud to admit that she'd behaved arbitrarily with Ofra—what had sparked her anger so much; so they'd whistled. Big deal—and Ori took advantage of the benefit of her doubt.

Ilanit saw her coming and got up to meet her. She was sitting on the sidewalk and, wads of absorbent cotton between her fingers, lacquering her nails by the light of the streetlight.

"Say, why did you hang up on me?" she yelled at her.

Ori delayed her reply until she was sufficiently close to answer her in her usual tone of voice. "I heard a noise from the kitchen. It scared me so I dropped the phone and ran to check what had happened. A cat got in and knocked over a plate. By the time I got back you'd hung up. Then Ofra came home from school and made my life a misery."

"I thought you'd hung up because of what happened with Sigal," Ilanit said and sat down on the sidewalk again next to the open vial of nail polish and the tightly closed bottle of acetone.

"Well, why are you standing? Sit down," she told Ori a moment later.

"What was that thing with Sigal really all about?" Ori asked, and remained standing.

"Nothing, a game. Just for laughs."

Ori looked at her in silence.

"So, what, are you pissed about it? It's only Sigal. It took you time to get back to normal and now you've started going crazy again."

"What?"

"Have you heard what happened with Gvinush?"

"What did you say?"

"Her parents grounded her for a month after school, because her whole report card was only satisfucktory, except for PE. Judy's nuts about her."

Ilanit's ruse worked, but not as she'd intended. The word 'satisfucktory', their pet term, angered Ori for no apparent reason. The word, in all its special overweeningness, its absurd attempt to soften the significance of failure, was suddenly revealed to Ori.

"Satisfucktory," she spat the word and its foul taste out.

"Yeah, her whole report card. She'll be lucky if she goes up next year," Ilanit said with no little Schadenfreude in which longing verging on admiration was clearly evident.

"I'm sick and tired of hearing about that Gvinush," Ori said.

"Sit down," Ilanit told her, "and I'll put polish on your nails."

She sank down onto the sidewalk, not because Ilanit had asked her to—a pain had shot through her stomach. A memento from the afternoon. Ilanit took her hand but she pulled it away.

"I don't want nail polish," she protested.

"Whatever," Ilanit replied. She pulled the wads of absorbent cotton from between her fingers and laid them on the sidewalk. Then she held her fingers up to the light and examined her work. "I love this blue with the gold flecks," she said, moving closer to Ori and displaying her hand. "Admit it, it's great."

A flicker of gold lingering on blue water, where did she know that combination from? Ah, yes, the description of the eastern approaches to the Kingdom of Spring in the Ariella books. She felt a pang of yearning, it had been a few days since she'd read them, and the distance, being outside them, seemed like a cut to her. The fifth volume was on her bedside table. She had to get back. She stood up in one movement.

"I'm going," she said, "I forgot the English homework."

"*B'zat*, whatever," Ilanit said.

"See you tomorrow."

"Hold it. I forgot to tell you the most important thing."

"What?" she asked impatiently.

"Aliza Edri's having a birthday party tomorrow night. She told me to invite you."

"How come she's inviting me?"

"She said you're okay because of what you did to Sigal today."

"Will Gvinush be there?"

"No, I told you. She's grounded. She's not allowed out and in any case her brother Dakar's real mad at her. If she goes to the party, she's dead."

"I'll think about it."

"Listen, Ori, if you're not going, neither am I."

"I said I'll think about it."

She went to the party, perhaps because she felt indebted to Ilanit. Maybe, she thought, Ilanit had fought for her. Who knows, maybe then, when she'd seen her sitting with Gvinush, she'd taken her side? She had always been weak and needed the support of other girls. She was terrified she'd be ostracized and that fear governed her every move. That's why she'd stuck to Ori all through elementary school, because there was something hard and sharp and unsubmitting in Ori, which had gained force since her two-month muteness. She was the only one who had dared rebel against and act insolently towards Gvinush. But not Ilanit, not her. And now she had the chance, perhaps, of reconciling the poles of her world, Gvinush's tyranny and Ori's iron will.

Aliza Edri lived at the bottom of her street. The soft wooly darkness was pierced by the streetlights. She was thankful for the hint of its chill. She liked her pre-summer clothes more than the others, light on her body and concealing the flesh. She liked that, yes, the narrow space of the concealment. She passed a hand over the long-sleeved reddish silk blouse that had been bought for her bat-mitzvah, and touched the denim dress, that was also a present, the embroidered pocket on its upper part covering her chest, and the shapeless patches sewn randomly onto the lower part. In her ears she wore Ofra's pearl earrings. When she came to ask for them, dressed and ready, her hair combed and pulled tight, gleaming from innumerable combings, Ofra turned up her nose and said, "God knows where you got your dress sense from, it's definitely not from me."

The music flowed from Aliza's house, which was built somewhat strangely, higher than the road with a staircase leading to it at the front, but to get into the backyard you had to go down another, steep staircase leading from the back door. It seemed to her that notes were pouring down on her from the dimly lit windows. She recognized the song, Madonna's "Into the Groove." Aliza idolized Madonna, and this worship was a bone of contention between her and her mistress Gvinush, who was mad about Cyndi Lauper, and if it hadn't been for her older brother Dakar, who guarded her zealously, at the Purim party she would have dyed her hair like the singer's. So Ilanit told her.

She climbed the steps, said a quick hello to Aliza's parents who were sitting in the vestibule, a sort of wide verandah enclosed with blinds, and crossed the house that she hadn't visited since severing relations with Gvinush, and went down into the yard.

The yard was planted with pomegranate and lemon trees alternately, the base of their trunks encircled with neatly arranged stones, and a carpet of lawn between them. Amongst the branches burned small points of light, giving off a weak brightness, like shining clips in thick hair. Tangled in the web of light bodies moved, and although they were hidden in the partial darkness, Ori knew what their appearance would be like, pure and sublime, like suns washed with milk, silver from Tarshish and gold from Uphaz, the work of a craftsman and the hands of a silversmith, and blue and crimson are their garments, and the hair beautifully coiffed and the lips glistening and tight and the eyes saying: come with us, we are simple, easy to attain, we have no secrets, there is no darkness in us. Ori tried to identify some of them, squinting to locate Ilanit, Aliza, standing stiffly in embarrassment.

"Ori," Aliza's voice came to her, cloyingly jovial, "It's great you came."

What's great got to do with it, Ori wondered, and Aliza grabbed her elbow and pulled her into the yard, pointing out the tables covered with paper and the drinks and disposable cups. "There's lots to eat," she said, "my mother's been cooking specially."

The music changed. "Voyage Voyage," which the kids in the class dubbed in Arabic, "*Shwayeh Shwayeh*," "Slowly Slowly", and the singer—"Eraserhead", was now playing. Ori, surprised by the welcome, handed her the present she held in her right hand. Her calf muscles began trembling. Aliza took the present and vanished, and Ilanit popped up.

"How long've you been here?" Ori asked.

"Oh, I just got here, at eight on the dot, like we arranged," Ilanit replied.

Ori studied her. Ilanit was dressed to the nines, wearing something similar to what she'd worn for her bat-mitzvah party. A blue tee shirt, its collar cut, a gaudy blouse revealing thin shoulders, another peroxided streak in her hair, lipstick, purple tights hugging narrow hips and legs like two twigs, and fingernails gleaming with the polish from yesterday.

Ori looked at the yard: a curtain of lace on which were embroidered elaborate movements and light and shadow of distant lands, of a marketplace and its hubbub. Where had that come to her from? She didn't know, just as she didn't know how she'd pluck up the courage to cross the meter of no man's land between the steps and the party, even with Ilanit's help. And with that thought her skin started burning. She clenched her fist so as not to scratch or touch it.

"So what do we do?" she asked with an effort.

"What d'you mean? Eat, drink, talk, dance," Ilanit replied. "Walk around. I'll be back in a sec." And she shoved her onto the grass, forcing her into this night. And she was in the yard but the burning of her skin only intensified. They surrounded her on all sides—familiar faces from school, from higher classes, laughter and chatter, the boys bunched together on one side, the girls on the other. Only two or three couples dared to dance in the middle of the yard, and one boy exaggerated his movements, deprecating them, earning the right to move his body by the force of ludicrousness, laughing. She recognized him: Noam Ohana, and now he nodded at her as he danced, opening his arms. She ignored him and walked falteringly to the drinks table, the straps of her sandals catching in the grass. As she poured herself a glass of grapefruit juice, the cup unsteady in her hand and the juice overflowing onto the paper table covering, she heard her old name breaking through the tumult and the end of "Voyage Voyage". By the time she identified the voice, the third or fourth time it spoke her old name, the opening notes of a song she didn't know were already thundering out. No, she told herself, it's not possible, and her eyes darted here and there searching for Ilanit, the bitch.

But her look found the girl calling her name, Gvinush bearing down on her with a crooked, contemptuous smile on her face. She was wearing a green crepe dress whose neckline clung to her body as reedy as a boy's, the body already maturing and changing into the body of a young woman, and its skirt was short, knee-length, its hem stiffened. Over her shoulders, a blue shawl. Her yellow braids were coiled atop her head, a tower of hair, a chignon the girls called a "cox". Her eyelids were painted turquoise, framed by Rimmel. "Flora the mute," she said, "aren't you ashamed to show your face here?" and she closed in on her with long strides. Strange, how corporeal, with size and volume, the song became, like a shoal of eels in the dark waters of the deeps. The loudspeakers screamed, the words illuminating electric shocks.

Her search for Ilanit became feverish. Where is she? Where? "Recognize this from somewhere?" Gvinush asked. Dangling from her finger was a sort of swinging pendulum. No, not a pendulum, a small plastic bag tied with string.

"What is it?" she asked, taking a step back, her hand feeling for the cup of juice on the table. Her throat was dry.

Gvinush took another step towards her, her hand holding out the bag.

She realized what was in it.

A curl of dark hair.

The confusion that engulfed her was replaced by rage. She felt it rising, bursting out from her navel and flaming together with the pain emanating from her skin. Where's that Ilanit, the traitorous bitch, where is she? Her muscles reacted with the sudden strength she found. Her body, inclined backwards and pressed against the drinks table, suddenly tensed and she leapt forward, shoving Gvinush aside and navigating her body between partygoers. Their glances flew at her but she crossed the edge of the lawn, and her impetus carried her up the steps, at the bottom of which Ilanit was standing giggling with Noam Ohana, a kind of vinous deepness flooding her cheeks.

It was then her anger dissipated, as if Ilanit standing there, and the flattering chirping she uttered, were sufficient to explain everything: the effort, the deceit, the exploitation of shared memories, the betrayal. She pitied her, she pitied her, pure and simple. But not only at that moment—realization dawned on her clearly—she'd pitied her all through their childhood, for her desire to belong, to become assimilated, for her horror of missing out on events and the important rumors, for her loneliness in her parents' home, to whom she'd been born when they were almost old and after their other children were grown up; her mother had had her when she was forty-two, a real medical miracle, and her father was even older. They were no longer as strong as they had been, they could hardly speak Hebrew and belonged to a different generation, which in the eyes of the kids from her class, was ancient and remote. And that was how Ilanit was perceived, an odd remnant whose speech, from time to time, was peppered with unconventional words in Moroccan and French, that evoked mockery and animosity—"Grandma", they used to call her, until she dropped the foreign words in second grade and learned, under duress, which of her parents' words had filtered down into the children's new language, and those that gave her away.

———

Ori didn't know how she'd be able to go to school next day. Not because she feared Gvinush and her minions, that now included Ilanit, but because of Sigal's presence, a tensile mass of insult and shame in the left-hand row of desks, and at recess hiding in one of the crannies in the limestone hill with only Ophir for company, circling around her with his typical restlessness, and then vanishing and reappearing by Ori, transfixing her with an accusing look. When she got back home her mother questioned her about why she'd come home so early, and she replied, "A lousy party," and immediately asked, "d'you know anything about the Danino family?"

"Rabbi Danino?"

"Yes."

"Poor things. Not everybody has good fortune."

She herself knew very little. She had never shown any interest in Sigal and so she hadn't come across any scraps of information and kept it. Sigal's father was a rabbi and she had a lot of brothers and sisters. They lived near Netivot's industrial zone, in the neglected neighborhoods, as Gvinush had once referred to them, the neglected neighborhoods.

Ofra was at home too, her grounding having been extended to the whole week due her father's intervention, who had come home late, exhausted from his evening shift, to find his wife and eldest daughter arguing in choked voices. Ofra was sitting in the living room watching television. It seemed that despite her anger she'd overheard them, because she suddenly broke into their conversation.

"Why, what good fortune have we got?" she said insolently, "We've got no money, if it wasn't for your parents we wouldn't have this house either, and you and Abba work like dogs. You'd think we're not living in *balad ju'a*."

"You don't know how to be thankful for anything," their mother said, "at least you've got food on the table and clothes to wear."

"Yeah, sure, and what clothes. I've got to save every shekel and do babysitting to buy new sandals and Asher goes to work to buy himself a bed."

"*Ewa*, you're exaggerating. I buy you new clothes every holiday and make meals for you and cook meat. Don't make a mountain out of a molehill, Ofra."

"And the Danino family," Ori said gently, suddenly tired of the constant bickering, "haven't they got food on the table?"

"They've got food alright, lots of it," Ofra replied, "Because her mother helps in the Baba Sali's courtyard and every evening she takes home all the leftover food that people bring, and she gets from the women who make couscous and bake cakes there. That's what they eat, and that's why the whole family are such fatsos. But get with it, it, Ori, open your eyes a bit."

"They're very poor," their mother said, "and it's true, they're taken care of, but they're in a far worse state than most people in this town."

"Why don't they give them money?" Ori asked.

"Who'll give them money? The government?"

"Yes, the government."

"Sometimes I don't know if you're just stupid or plain naive," Ofra said, and their mother sighed.

The conversation didn't improve her mood. In her room she tried to read the fifth Ariella book. The tension was at its height. The crown prince of the Kingdom of Winter had disappeared, and from all corners of the four kingdoms came rumors of the destruction he was wreaking, while Ariella felt that her powers were waning, as if molten iron had been poured into her head, and she and Pereh were racing against time to solve the riddle and find whoever was guilty of the prince's apparent doings. But Ori's thoughts incessantly turned back to Sigal, and all her efforts to lose herself in the pages of the book came to naught.

And she didn't feel any better next morning when Sigal, who was late for the first period, handed Elisheva a note. Sigal remained impervious to her pleading looks through two lessons. At mid-morning recess she packed her things, put her pencil case and notebooks into her bag with the same meticulousness and gravity that accompanied all her movements, and went home.

The first lesson after recess was PE, and Ori didn't think twice. She, too, packed her things into her bag and took out her notebook, which she had decided to take to school every day to keep it out of Ofra's hands. Then she kicked her bag under the desk and followed Sigal out. Sigal was walking with her head bowed, her body bent, not noticing what was going on around her, and all the while Ori kept a safe distance behind her.

The scenery didn't vary much as they left the streets near the school that were familiar to Ori. Single-story houses in front of which grew weeds and dried-up poincianas, were only slightly less cared for than those in her own neighborhood, and the iron fences around them, their paint was peeling just a bit less than in her street. And yet despite the minor differences, a feeling of neglect was evident; the light was more parching and the groundsel pods suddenly broke off and whirled in the air and hit the fence rails and fell to the asphalt and frightened the sparrows, forming waves of ash. This is a different kind of beauty, Ori thought.

Sigal's house stood at the end of the street, beyond it a wild wilderness; a field of thistles and doum trees called *nabuq*, and barriers of prickly pears called *sabras*. Sigal went inside and Ori stayed outside, trying to pluck up her courage. What would she say to her? Why had she come here? Then she heard Sigal from the depths of the house, "All right, I'm going out." She waited until her outline would be visible in the doorway, but Sigal didn't appear.

After a few moments Ori went to the door and knocked. Nobody answered. She banged again, harder. Someone's footsteps rustled towards the door and it opened. Facing her was a fat man wearing a black hat, his beard gray and sparse and his features bulbous. She recognized him: Rabbi Danino. He visited their house quite often to talk to her father, and for some reason was in charge of distributing the Passover *haroseth* to the members of his synagogue. He looked at her with dim eyes, weighing her up.

"Whose daughter are you?" he asked.

"I . . . I'm Elhayani's daughter . . . I've come for Sigal . . . We're in the same class."

He went on examining her skeptically.

"Could you call Sigal?" she asked, and became irritated.

"She's out."

"I didn't see her come out and I've been waiting for her here for about ten minutes."

He nodded. "She's in the backyard."

Ori was silent.

"You can go around," he said, pointing with a swollen red finger to the path that wound around the right-hand side of the house.

"Is it all right?"

He nodded again.

"Thank you," Ori said, and added, "Rabbi." The addition made her feel stupid, so she turned around and strode quickly along the path.

She couldn't see Sigal in the field. She couldn't see a soul, just her and a few hidden partridges peeping out, and the wild vegetation and the wild oat stalks that came up to her knees. But a second look revealed another well-trodden path that wound between the prickly pears and close to the thorns of the doum trees. Hesitantly, she put one foot on it, then the other, and started along it. After a minute's walk the path suddenly ended. She circled a wide-branched doum tree and came to a small barrier—not exactly a barrier, but concrete blocks laid one atop the other to form an unstable wall. Balls of paper had been stuffed into the spaces between the blocks. Ori pulled one out and straightened it. It was a note with the words, "Frog, I'm sorry I threw a stone at you and if you could you'd throw it back at me. Sigal."

What's this nonsense, Ori wondered as she gave the note the respect it deserved and put it back. She took another one and read, "I had a bad thought today. I wanted Rimona Peretz to die. I'm sorry. Sigal." And another one, "If I'd been a better student Bonni wouldn't have gone crazy. I'm sorry. Sigal." Ori pulled out note after note, her curiosity aroused, and read dozens of expressions of regret and remorse for things Sigal had done, or had only thought about. Written in one was, "When Flora-Ori Elhayani cut off my hair I cursed her that both her arms would be broken. I'm sorry. Sigal."

Ori felt how the dull blade of steel that had pierced her chest was now being sharpened and honed. She started crying and didn't know why. Not out of compassion. The tremendous loneliness hit her, and she realized that she, too, unconsciously, had become loneliness's subject. She forced herself away from the wall and told herself to leave; but there was still one note she hadn't read. It was stuck in the bottom of the wall. She bent down, pulled out the ball of paper and straightened it out. This one was different from the others. It said, "Say not,

I am a child: for thou shalt go to all that I shall send thee, and whatsoever I command thee thou shalt speak."

Ori stared at the words. Her tears finished, dried up, and the fire ignited on her skin at last night's party again licked it, the fine hairs that had already sprouted near her wrist, each and every cell. The walls of her heart moaned. Pain ripped at her belly. Until her ears picked up the sound of footsteps trampling the undergrowth, and she quickly regained her composure; she stuffed the scrap of paper into her pocket and turned towards the path. Sigal appeared close to the doum trees.

"What are you doing here?" she demanded.

FIVE

Blood

SHE DIDN'T KNOW WHAT TO DO in the face of Sigal's tense posture. It seemed that the doum trees and the prickly pears, and the partridges that also gathered to listen, were crowding in on her, and her back was against Sigal's wall. Although Sigal had just emerged from behind the tree, she could have been watching her and waiting for the right moment to surprise her. The scrap of paper with the foreign words, clenched in the hand in her pocket, ignited like a little sun and she crumpled it forcefully to suppress the flames bursting and licking from it. In her other, damp, hand she held her notebook.

"What are you doing here?" Sigal asked again.

"I . . . I was looking for you . . . your father . . . he told me . . . "

"You followed me from school."

"Yes," Ori said, her voice fading into wretchedness.

"Why?"

"I wanted to apologize . . . for that day and also . . . "

"For cutting off my hair, you mean?"

"Yes. Me and Ilanit had this game, and I had to . . . "

"Had to what?" Sigal asked, and she stared at her, speechless.

"You know," Sigal said, "I thought you'd changed. After you hadn't spoken for a while and all your friends had left you. I thought that maybe . . . maybe you understood what . . . what it's like being on the outside."

Again the sound of footsteps from the path was heard, and a rustling from the tree, and Ophir Shriki appeared, all hyped up.

"So this is where you are," he said.

"What's going on?" Sigal said, "You've all decided to follow me today?"

"Why'd you go?" Ophir asked the question that Ori wanted to ask, but she shrank from it.

"What's it got to do with you?"

"It's because of Judy," Ophir averred.

Yes, Ori thought, Judy. In the last PE lesson she'd decided to teach them the basic rules of basketball and ordered the girls to dribble the ball the length of the gym. Sigal started off together with Gvinush and Aliza and was left behind. She'd just made it to the middle of the court when they'd got back to the starting point, while the next group of girls waited impatiently for her to cover the remaining distance to them. Judy stopped her and Sigal stood bowed in the middle of the gym, transfixed by the looks of all the girls. Judy wondered aloud, in her heavy American accent, "Sigal, I don't understand. Who's doing the bouncing, you the ball, or the ball you?"

Now Sigal nodded to Ophir, who said, "So you're playing hooky."

Ori's body was freed of its paralysis. She said, "The three of us are."

"No," Sigal replied, "I had permission to leave. You're playing hooky."

"Right," Ophir said and looked at his watch, his nose and mouth twitching to the left. "There's not enough time to get back."

Ori shrugged. "We can stay here."

They stayed, but not next to the wall of blocks. Sigal led them deep into the field to an old Arab orchard—a low, broken stone wall and fig, olive and terebinth trees growing wild, breaking the shackles on their growth, and a thin layer of dust stood in the air, and the spring, although it was about to die, enlivened the air. Sigal took out a blanket from between the stones of the wall and spread it for them. At first they sat on it, listening to the stillness and remaining silent too, and then—first Ophir—lay down on it and gazed at the viscous blue dripping through the foliage. And there, beneath a fig tree and beneath a thick terebinth, their breaths conjoined, their chests rising and falling, indifferent pistons, rhythmically rising and falling together. Until it got late and Ophir leapt to his feet—how had he managed to remain tranquil for so long, Ori wondered—and said, "Okay, we've got to get back," and Sigal protested, so distant, so that Ori didn't know if she'd understood her, "You don't have to." But Ophir had reached the path with Ori behind him, and Sigal called after her, "Wait a minute, Ori."

"Yes," Ori said, "I didn't get the chance to tell you. I'm really sorry."

"No, not that," Sigal said, "what's that notebook you've got in your hand?"

"Ah," Ori replied, "just a notebook."

Ophir was already on the road, but at the gate of the house Ori turned to Sigal who was looking at them both and asked, "What's your phone number?" And Sigal replied, "We haven't got a phone at home. They disconnected it." Ori asked, "D'you know where I live?" and Sigal answered, "In the Makor Haim neighborhood," and Ori suggested, "Why don't you come over this evening?" and Sigal nodded.

When she and Ophir got back to school, right into recess, their stay outside was clearly evident, not only in their clothing and hair which bore broken brambles and straw and strings of dust, but also in their distant look. Gvinush's eye caught them as they came through the hole in the fence right to the foot of the limestone hill, and followed them until they reached the steps leading to the junior high building, but she said nothing, she just scrutinized them with a look of surprise on her face, and on the face of Aliza, the angel standing to her right. Ilanit's face, who was also standing nearby, took on a different expression, of sharp wonderment and guessing, and her nose and nostrils that now narrowed highlighted her teeth, endowing her with the appearance of a small rodent.

———

She and Sigal were sitting somewhat embarrassedly in her yard, talking awkwardly and taking tiny bites from the slices of peach and plum that Ori had prepared. A sort of cold excitement hung over them; the sun was setting, and the rows of houses in the western neighborhoods gnawed at its light. Only its uniform aura—a white-hot metal surface on which were burned the mulberry and bitter orange trees, and the corrugated iron shed, and the thick hedge with its rough twigs and strange leaves—preserved the day. Her mother came out and said, "There's some boy at the door asking for you."

"Who?" Ori asked.

"I didn't ask."

"What does he look like?"

"He's kind of short with blue eyes and he can't stand still for a second. He's on a bike."

She and Sigal looked at one another and burst out laughing. "It's all right," Ori said, "tell him to come in."

Her mother nodded and went back inside, and although she hadn't asked him his name earlier, now he was inside her house she didn't hold back, and by the time they reached the yard she'd managed to question him about his parents—his father was a minor political activist in the Likud Party, and

120

his mother a kindergarten teacher. With unprecedented speed, in the short distance between the front and back doors, her mother had even managed to uncover a nebulous family tie of marriage, between her father's uncle and his mother's grand-mother, and happily told the two girls about it before leaving the three to themselves.

Ophir remained standing, shifting his weight from one foot to the other and his right hand grasping the strap of the school-bag on his back. "So what are you doing?' he asked.

"Nothing," Ori replied, "just talking."

"D'you feel like doing something?"

"Like what, for instance?" Sigal asked.

"Dunno. Maybe go for a walk. I go walking a lot." Sigal shook her head.

"We can play 'Treasure Hunt'. I'll draw a map."

"I haven't got the strength," Ori said.

"Then what? You're going to sit here and talk?"

"Yes," Sigal replied.

"Bo-o-o-ring," Ophir said.

"Look, nobody forced you to come," Ori said.

"Have you heard anything about Bonni?"

"No, nothing," Sigal replied, "and I've been trying to find out. I asked Elisheva this morning and she said he's . . . " Her voice broke and she fell silent.

"My sister said he's in a closed ward."

"A convalescent home for mental patients," Ophir said.

"So why are you asking if you already know?" Ori said.

"I thought maybe something new had happened." He sat down on a chair next to Ori, took a slice of peach from the plate on the table, and asked, "Can I wash this?"

"Why?" Ori wondered.

"I can't stand plums, and maybe the taste of plums has stuck to the peach."

"I'll get you another peach," Ori said and went inside. When she came back into the yard carrying a small plate containing peach slices, she saw that Ophir was rummaging in his bag. He straightened up and took out a book. She put the plate in front of him. "What's the book?" Sigal asked, and in reply Ophir held it out to her.

Ori bent over her and looked at it too. Small, rectangular, a hardcover inscribed with a black helix. Its title, in sensuous purple lettering, was "Hypnosis".

"Idolatry," Sigal muttered and handed it to Ori.

"What are you talking about?" Ophir protested, "Right at the beginning it says it's all scientific."

Ori inspected the introduction. For some minutes she wandered between the lines. When she spoke to Sigal, her voice was numb, thickened.

"Ophir's right," she said, "it says here that it's been scientifically proved. They don't know how hypnosis works, but they use it"—she went back to the book to find the precise wording—"in psy-cho-log-ical therapy."

Sigal seemed skeptical. Ori went back to the book. "Say," she asked, "where'd you get it?"

"The municipal library."

"But it's from the reading room. You're not allowed to take books out of there."

"I know."

"Then how?"

"I . . . " he flushed. He looked at Sigal who grasped, before he finished the sentence, what he was going to say, and her lips tightened, narrowed, and her thick eyebrows rose, her whole face reproof. "I," he went on, "pinched it."

"What?" Ori said.

"Yeah, sometimes I . . . " he started drumming on his knees nervously with both hands.

"Why?"

"Because they don't let you take books out. They just sit there on the shelves. Nobody even reads them. I know, I go there a lot." He fell silent and took a deep, noisy breath.

"So you steal."

"Not exactly. I take them and take them back. Without the librarian knowing."

"That's not right," Sigal said, "it's still stealing."

"But why? It doesn't hurt anybody."

"That's not the point. You're taking something that's not yours. Thou shalt not steal."

"But what if I found it in the street? It's the same thing."

Ori opened the book again. The fact that it had been taken, that someone had taken the trouble to plan how to get it out of the library under the noses of the women responsible for it, added splendor to it, mantled it in rarity. In the contents was written, 'Suggestion'. The word aroused her curiosity. She opened the book at page 23 and read. Sigal's and Ophir's pointless arguing became a murmur. She sailed on the words and it seemed to her that she understood their meaning. She closed the book. "We've got to try it," she said, cutting their argument short.

"Try what?" Ophir asked.

"Hypnotizing someone."

"No," Sigal said, "hypnotism's for the Gentiles, it's idolatry."

"Come on, enough of that nonsense," Ophir said, "it's like a scientific experiment. Like that time Bonni showed us electrolysis in class, remember? And like at the beginning of the year, when we were in the lab at school and we put a piece of potassium into water and it ignited?"

Sigal looked at them with a pair of severe brown velvet eyes laced with gold, from Ori to Ophir and back. "It's like a scientific experiment?" she asked.

"I'm sure," Ori said, catching her look, "that if what happened hadn't happened, Bonni would have taught us about hypnosis."

From the side she saw Ophir biting his lip, quelling a smile.

"I don't know," Sigal said.

"There's nothing to know," Ori said, "we've decided. But I want to read a bit to understand how this method really works. We can try tomorrow."

"I can't tomorrow," Ophir said.

"Why not?" Sigal asked. "Are you going to steal more books?"

"Stop it," Ophir said, "I've got something on."

"What?" Ori asked.

"Something," he replied.

"Then maybe the day after?" Sigal asked.

"We can meet at my house, at seven. My parents will be out," Ophir said and looked at his digital watch whose black plastic strap seemed too thick on his skinny wrist. "They're showing a repeat of 'Folktales' soon," he added, "do you watch it?"

"Sometimes," Ori replied, "but I don't really like the storyteller's dog."

"What else do you watch?"

"Sometimes I watch 'Lace' with Ofra on Fridays."

"But those three girls are a bit boring."

"How d'you know?"

"I watched it once," Ophir said, and then asked Sigal, who was uncomfortably quiet, "What about you, what d'you like?"

"I don't know," she replied, "I'm not allowed to watch television. It's idolatry."

"Idolatry, idolatry," Ophir said, "enough with the idolatry already. It's only television."

"I can't," Sigal whispered, "ever since my father's been going to the Shas college, he's become stricter."

124

"What's Shas?" Ori asked.

"I don't really know," Sigal replied. "They're some kind of new religious Jews. They wear black suits. My father's started too. They've got a yeshiva round here. Remember that kid who was in our class at the beginning of the year?"

"Who, Dror Biton?" Ophir asked.

"Yes," Sigal replied, "well now he's in their yeshiva."

"So what are we doing," Ophir asked, "television?"

"I told you I can't."

"You can," Ori said firmly, and didn't know where the power that suddenly filled her had come from, from where the so-cutting imperative had appeared. And Sigal nodded and followed them into the house.

—

She and Sigal were early. Ophir lived in the Or Hayyim neighborhood and the route from Sigal's house took her past Ori's house. Sigal had this tendency towards earliness. At school she was always in her place five minutes before the bell. On the way she said to Ori, "I'm still scared about this," and Ori, who was carrying the book in a small shoulder bag she'd borrowed from Ofra without her knowledge, replied, "About what, hypnosis?"

"Yes," she replied, "I asked my father about idolatry and he started talking about hell. He's never talked like that, you know? He's always talked about the Garden of Eden and the leviathan and the wild ox and the light that's kept for the righteous. But now, since he's been with Shas, he talks about hell and sinners and the four types of capital punishment and all that. I heard my mother saying that some of the women from the synagogue who sit in the women's section and hear his sermons have started complaining. And some of the men too."

"So why don't they say something to him?"

"Because my father's the rabbi. And not only that, the men in the synagogue like what he says about the government and discrimination. They've started coming to talk to him on Saturday evenings, and sometimes I listen to them."

"We don't talk about that in our house," Ori said. "Just once Ofra tried to say something and my father shut her up."

They were standing outside Ophir's house. There wasn't a gate, just an opening in the tall fence over which a vine climbed. "We're early," Ori said as they walked through it. The house had two stories.

Sigal knocked on the compressed wood door that was decorated with squares of opaque glass. The chirping of birds answered them from inside and then they heard Ophir calling, "Just a minute."

He opened the door, flushed and sweating, wearing a robe. Underneath it, Ori noticed, he was wearing tight-fitting pants similar to tights. Odd, she thought and glanced at Sigal to see if she'd noticed too, but her face gave nothing away.

"You're really early," Ophir said, "I was just going to take a shower."

"Ah," Ori said, and Sigal lowered her head.

"But it's okay. You can sit here in the living room," he said.

He sat them down on a yellow leather couch and served them Sprite. They stared at the TV screen as Tom and Jerry ran round it in circles; Jerry was fleeing Tom who was brandishing a weapon, an electric saw. At one stage their running became so fast that the tables were turned, or something like that. Ori couldn't follow the action because the sound was muted, and music coming from the stairs up to the second floor captured her attention. A radio was blaring. She managed to identify one of the songs, Culture Club's "Do You Really Want to Hurt Me."

Ophir came back washed and wearing jeans and a tee shirt. "Let's go upstairs," he said and led them up. The music intensified. The blaring radio was up there, on a stand in an extensive space that probably served as a seating area. But the carpet was rolled up and the cushions on which guests were supposed to sit were piled against the wall. The floor was bare.

"I'm sorry," Ophir said, "I didn't manage to tidy up. You were half an hour early."

"How did you hear us with this noise?" Sigal asked.

Ophir turned the volume down on the radio. He smiled and pointed at a light bulb fixed high on one of the walls.

"It flashes when someone presses the doorbell. I'm very often by myself up here and don't hear the bell," he answered.

"Why don't you hear it? Because of the music?" Ori asked.

Ophir stared at her in embarrassment, turned to the carpet and started to unroll it. Ori went to help him, taking one edge and ordering him to take the other. Sigal went to the cushions and spread them on the carpet in a circle. When Ori and Ophir finished unrolling it, the three of them sat down facing one another. "You ready?" Ori asked.

Ophir nodded automatically, eagerly, and Sigal, slowly and skeptically, followed suit.

"Okay," Ori said, "I've read the chapters on how to hypnotize a few times. First of all we've got to decide who to hypnotize."

"Not me," Sigal said, "I won't."

Ophir's leg trembled and his nose twitched. "I'll volunteer," he said.

"No good," Ori said, "it'll be hard to hypnotize you. You can't sit still for a second."

"So who?" Ophir asked.

"That's the problem, because you and Sigal don't know how to hypnotize."

"But neither do you," Ophir said, "you've just read the book."

"Right," Ori replied, "but the book explains that a hypnotist has got be someone with a strong personality."

"What does that mean?" Sigal asked.

"Someone who can influence other people to do what he wants," Ophir said.

"And who's got the power of persuasion," Ori added.

"Oh," Sigal said, and they all fell silent.

"But maybe we don't need it," Ophir burst out a few seconds later, "maybe I can hypnotize. Maybe I've got a natural talent for it."

"I don't want to take part at all. I'll just watch," Sigal said.

Ori looked at both of them. "It's just an experiment," she said.

"Sure," Ophir said. "So let's try it."

"There are a few methods," Ori said. "We haven't got a pendulum, so it seems to me that the one with the candle will be best."

"What's the one with the candle?" Ophir asked.

"Somebody concentrates on the flame of a candle and that's how you hypnotize him. But you've got to have darkness."

"It'll only be dark in another hour and a half," Ophir said. "We can listen to the radio till then. It's already seven o'clock. Top of the Pops is on soon."

He went over to the radio and raised the volume. But Top of the Pops wasn't on. A woman's caressing voice washed over the room. She said, "Right after the news we'll be hosting a panel of experts in the studio for an open discussion about men, women, and relations between them."

"What's that?" Ophir said grumpily, "it's not the music station." His finger hovered momentarily over the tuning button and he missed the boat because the newscast theme came on, and the three of them tensed involuntarily, and Ophir's finger froze. The newsreader's voice spoke of no real news, either good or bad, but the severity and emphasis of the words forced them to listen. Ophir sat down again and they went on listening even after the short newscast had ended, and a song was played. A woman singer sang, "Until evening falls, rain, listen to the women waiting at the window," and Ori saw Ophir humming the tune and moving to its rhythm, his eyes closed and his hands drumming on his crossed knees.

"D'you listen to the radio a lot?" she asked when the song ended.

"Yes, for the past year," he answered.

"What for?" Sigal asked, "what's interesting in it?"

"I like music and they talk about important things happening in the world."

"Like what, for instance?"

"The groups they've got in England, and the wars in Africa, and all kinds of things in Germany and Russia. And in the States."

"Why's that important?" Sigal asked.

Ophir shrugged. "It's important," he said.

"But it's got nothing to do with us," Sigal said.

"It has," Ophir said, "it affects us too."

"How?" Sigal persisted.

Something, her irritated and itching nape, called her, and she detached herself from Ophir and Sigal's voices. On the radio two women were having a discussion in a light, smiling tone.

One said, "And I truly don't understand why we talk so little about the male climax," and that word, 'climax', came to life before her, a huge stone sculpture of a man called Max scaling a cliff—and she smiled.

The other guest said, "There are two reasons. One is that we are still in thrall to the idea that men don't have to prove anything. And the second is that the male climax is very hard to fake."

"D'you know what just occurred to me?" the other one replied, "That even today, when we say 'climax' and not 'orgasm', we are captive to the idea you mentioned."

"And why is that?" the other one asked.

"Because we accept the idea that for us women, any talk about sex must be clean, prettified, while men's attitude leans towards the animal side of sex, because it's in their nature and they need it, and so they can use dirty words like 'fuck', while we have to be satisfied with 'intercourse'."

Ori was so immersed in the discussion that she didn't realize that the women's voices were filtering through to Ophir and Sigal's conversation and taking over the space like the light from the west darkening the room. The word 'fuck', which was unmistakable, flared up between them.

"What's that? Who talks like that?" Sigal said in alarm, "God help us."

"There's a lot of truth in what you say," the other guest replied from the radio. "I think that before we open our mouths, we must pay attention to the terminology we use and why we chose it. And yet the words 'fuck' and 'come' sound to me . . . "

Sigal leapt up.

"Turn that abomination off," she said, her face flushed and her hands over her ears. "Where's the bathroom?"

Ophir, giggling, pointed to a narrow door. He looked at Ori, and his eyes flashed challengingly. And Ori, who felt that Sigal had robbed her of her response, no, no, more than that, that Sigal's response was ridiculously exaggerated and therefore discouraging, returned his look. From the radio came the voice of the first woman again. She said, "We have to take a commercial break, but first a word from our sponsor." Here the voice was lowered and became caressing, deep, as before, "The program 'Music and Conversation' is sponsored by Soda Extreme, offering you juice extracts in a variety of exotic flavors . . . "

Ori knew the wording by heart, and so did Ophir, who mumbled it together with the announcer. It was unavoidable. It was one of the best-known advertisements. It appeared in the *Ma'ariv Lanoar* youth magazine and before *Tossesss* and *Loop the Loop*. Soda Extreme was a national hit: a home appliance for making sparkling water in extraordinary flavors—not cola, Sprite, orangeade, but juices in coconut and mango and strawberry-banana and mandarin and mint flavors. The finale of the commercial was clever: 'Soda Extreme—The World in Your Glass'. But this time as the announcer read it, perhaps under the influence of the impassioned studio discussion, she made a slip of the tongue and signed off the commercial with the words, 'Soda Extreme—The World in Your Ass'.

Ori and Ophir stared at one another, refusing to believe what they'd just heard. Ophir broke the silence. A brief, uncontrolled snort that rolled with a jerky sound, a kind of bubbling in the throat, and then he burst into laughter, no, bleating, that rose from both of them, and they gave themselves up to it, a minute, two minutes, who knows, until Ori raised her eyes and saw Sigal standing in the toilet doorway, her figure outlined against the light behind her, and in the gloom cast by the late hour she was unable to see her expression, but her frozen stance, her hands smoothing her skirt, left no room for doubt—she'd heard it too. Ori fell silent, but Ophir pointed a finger at Sigal, waggled it and yelled, "Soda Extreme—The World . . . " and roared with laughter, and Ori joined his laughter, and Sigal, too, she saw, thawed a little, and took a hesitant step towards them, and Ophir, amid his thunderous laughter, signaled her to come closer and then put his hand on his stomach and sprawled on the carpet. His laughter infected Sigal, first with a gentle gargling, then a tolling of bells, and Ori thought that this was the first time she'd heard her laugh, and the tolling of the bells heightened until it became a floodtide and Sigal reached them and flopped down beside them.

Darkness had floated into the room as they laughed, and every time one of them fell silent, another would say, "Soda Extreme," and their laughter was renewed. In the end Ophir got up and touched the light switch on the wall and Ori saw that Ophir and Sigal's eyes glistened with tears and even in the corner of her own she could feel dampness.

"I'm dying of thirst," Ophir said, and a clear note came from Sigal's lips, and Ophir said, "No, really. I'll get something to drink and a candle."

They stood the candle in a candlestick in the middle of the carpet. Sigal said it could be dangerous and Ophir said he'd take care that nothing happened while he hypnotized Ori. Ori showed him the text in the book and made herself more comfortable on the cushions. She focused on the candle's flame, on the tremor that passed through it, and on its fragile golden nimbus. She slowly sensed the warmth radiating from it and moving over her skin.

"Pay attention to the candle's flame. It is the only source of light in the room." Ophir's voice was rough and hoarse from time to time. "Pay attention to how it moves and twists, how its light spreads and floods the entire space around you. The light is yellow and orange and vast. There is nothing except for it. You are starting to fall towards its source, into the candle's flame. The flame is an abyss, a bottomless pit. You are falling. Let my voice guide you. You can hear no other voice. You are beginning to feel the voice. It has physical dimensions. You can touch it. It is like a rope on which you are hanging over the abyss. And the rope is carefully lowering you and turning into a staircase descending to the bottom of the flame. You feel its heat. It is soft and pleasant and draws you to it. You are staring to descend. Your eyelids are becoming heavy. With each step you descend they are heavier and heavier. Your breathing is becoming deeper and steadier, with each step you are breathing more deeply. You are descending. I am with you as you descend. With each step you are sinking deeper into a dream in which you are still awake, and only my voice exists in it. You are listening only to it. I am starting to count the remaining steps: ten, nine . . . "

Ori tried to listen to Ophir, she endeavored to feel what the book said that the subject—that's what the book said the hypnotized person is called—was supposed to feel, but because of that her thoughts wandered. It's not happening, she told herself, by now my consciousness should be floating like a swimmer in the tranquil water of a lake, that's how the book described the present stage, maybe at the end of the count.

In her head she counted the steps with Ophir, "eight, seven . . . " no, nothing's happening, "six, five, four," well, it was clear that the experiment wouldn't succeed, "three, two," it's Ophir's fault, he's a rotten hypnotist, "one," and she opened her eyes.

A few seconds elapsed until her focus returned and she could see Ophir's face in the faint light of the candle's flame. Ophir's finger was laid over his lips and with his right hand he pointed to the side. Sigal was sprawled on the cushions, her chest rising and falling and her eyes closed. Ophir leant towards Ori and whispered, "It looks like she got hypnotized instead of you."

Ori suppressed a cry of astonishment. She whispered back, "How could that have happened?" and Ophir shook his head.

"Tell her to do something," Ori whispered.

"Like what?"

"I don't know, lift her hand."

"Okay," Ophir said. "Sigal, when you hear the word"—and he fell silent. Ori whispered, "Seltzer", and the corner of his mouth twitched—"When you hear the word 'seltzer'," he said in an authoritative voice, "your right hand will rise into the air."

Ori couldn't hold back and said, "Seltzer." Sigal's body didn't move. Ophir ordered her, "Seltzer!" and Sigal's right hand moved, seeming to hover in the air detached from her body by a will of its own.

"Let's try something else, maybe stick a pin into her," Ori urged him.

"Oh, come on. I've got another idea," Ophir whispered, and to Sigal he said, "Sigal, in a few seconds I'm going to read you something from the book and I want you to remember it. When I finish reading I'll count to ten. When I get to ten you'll wake up and then, when I ask you to, you'll recite what I read. Oh, and apart from that, you'll feel better than you've ever felt. I'm starting."

He opened the book at the first page and began reading.

"Modern science stands helpless and shamefaced before the phenomenon of hypnosis. While there can be no doubt regarding the existence and the extent of the reality and necessity of hypnosis, not one brain researcher or neurologist has a rational explanation for it. It seems that the key to understanding the phenomenon of hypnosis is inextricably linked with questions regarding consciousness that have been asked since the dawn of history, and which remain unanswered today. What is consciousness? What is cognition? With what tools are we, as human creatures, prepared to absorb the reality around us? Is consciousness the consequence of purely biological and mechanical activity, or rather, as various mystics and clerics claim, it derives from an unknown source beyond the ken of our brain? It often seems that these questions, like Escher's maze woodcuts, embody an element that makes them impossible. When asking about consciousness we are using the very means we are studying, consciousness itself . . . "

The excerpt Ophir read twisted onward, replete with terms and expressions whose meaning evaded Ori, and she stopped listening to the content and only followed his straining face and the beads of sweat that began forming on his forehead. And when he concluded the reading with the count she turned her attention to Sigal, whose eyelids had begun fluttering and on whose lips a smile appeared, and it gradually spread as the interval between her breaths shortened.

"Good morning," Sigal said as she stretched pleasurably.

"How'd you feel?" Ophir asked.

"Better than I've ever felt," Sigal replied mechanically.

"D'you remember what happened?" Ori asked.

"What happened when?"

"Well, now, you . . . "

"Fell asleep," Ophir completed the sentence.

"Really?"

"Yes."

"Let's see if it worked," Ori demanded eagerly.

"If what worked?" Sigal asked.

"Sigal," Ophir said, "I'm going to read you a sentence and you complete it, all right?"

"What kind of a sentence?"

"Listen, okay? Here goes," and Ophir cleared his throat and stole a glance at Ori who nodded encouragingly. He lowered his eyes to the first page. "Modern science stands helpless and shamefaced before the phenomenon of hypnosis," he read and Sigal recited smoothly and monotonically, "While there can be no doubt regarding the existence and the extent of the reality and necessity of hypnosis, not one brain researcher or neurologist has a rational explanation for it."

Ori leaned over Ophir's shoulder to better see the words. Word by word, with exemplary accuracy, Sigal recited the first page in its entirety. When she finished, Sigal smiled, an indulgent expression on her face, and said, "What was that?"

"We did it," Ophir said, "you were hypnotized."

"What nonsense," Sigal said, and Ophir, Ori saw, was about to answer her, so she laid her hand on his arm and said, "He was only kidding, you just dozed off."

———

A new wave of excitement hit the school: the Gemara teacher was sick and was replaced by Principal Tuitto, because in the principal's view advanced religious studies—Mishnah for the girls and Gemara for the boys—were the most important lessons in the school. They were also the only subjects in which students could take five matriculation units in the theoretical track. Even the vocational track students, in which boys and girls were also separated into metalwork and domestic science respectively, were compelled to take these subjects.

In the Gemara lesson held in the afternoon in Room 3 on the second floor, the giant outline of Principal Tuitto bent over the teacher's desk. He called the roll. When he got to Ofer Sabbah's name, Ofer answered, "Yes, Tuitto, I'm here."

"What did you call me?" the principal asked.

"Tuitto," Ofer repeated, and a murmur spread through the class. The boys, most of whom were sweaty from the previous lesson, PE, and charged with nervous energy, shifted from side to side, making their chairs move and their desks squeak. Asher—it was Asher's class, and he told her the story in full— held his nose firmly, another student broke wind and Asher said, "He farted." And it was clear that principal Tuitto knew what had happened, which destroyed any degree of mercy in him, if he'd ever possessed such a thing, and he responded with a heavier than usual hand; there was nothing he hated more than disrespect from his students. It was forbidden to address him by name—Yoram, not even his surname, Tuitto, but 'Principal' and only 'Principal'.

"Stand up," he told Ofer.

"Why?" Ofer asked, and somebody sitting next to Asher whispered, "Why Oh Why."

"I told you to stand up," the principal hissed.

Ofer stood up with mocking demonstrativeness. The principal was unimpressed. "Into the corner," he said through clenched teeth.

"What corner?" Ofer grumbled, "What is this, first grade?"

"Into the corner. Don't argue. And stand facing the wall," the principal said. And Ofer strode daintily towards enjoyment.

Halfway through the lesson, as the principal diligently lectured them on the four kinds of keepers and their obligation to a person who entrusted something to their safekeeping, a bundle or a beast, and on his tongue rolled the expression, "it died in its way"—which Ori liked so much when she heard the story, and she repeated it, "it died in its way", and Asher gave her a puzzled look before he went on—Ofer called from the corner, "Principal, Sir, I've got to go to the bathroom." The principal cut him off, saying only, "Control yourself," and went back to his lecture.

"But I can't hold it in," Ofer said and turned to the class, holding his thighs together to demonstrate the urgency of the matter, and the boys laughed.

"I said control yourself," the principal said uninterestedly. "Now who's behaving like a first-grader?"

Ofer turned his back to the class. A minute later the class heard the sound of a stream of liquid pervading the principal's words, playing havoc with his definition of an unpaid keeper.

Again laughter, a thunderous outburst of uncontrolled laughter, and all eyes shifted to Ofer's back, which now relaxed from the pleasure of voiding, and to the puddle of yellow urine that had collected at his feet. The principal's last sentence, "A hired keeper, on the other hand, is obliged . . . " remained suspended in the air, and he looked silently at Ofer, who judging by the movements of his hands, was retying the cord in the sweat pants he was wearing.

"Animal, that's what you are, an animal." The principal's words came out without warning, in a roar, and he leapt forward. In a flash he was at Ofer's side, tugging his ear while shouting, "Beast, beast," and leading him out of the room and into the corridor, with the whole amused class in their wake. Someone even yelled, "Way to go, Sabbah!" while Ofer himself was screaming with pain, "Aiee, take your hands off me, you sonofabitch!" When he told the story, Asher of course didn't say the word "bitch". He never cursed. He said, "you sonof . . . and so on," but the metallic, filthy word embodied in "and so on" was revealed in Ori's mind.

When the principal and his sore-eared student reached the stairs at the end of the corridor, Ofer's protests were cut short, because Tuitto pushed him towards the stairs and his feet got tangled. He tripped and rolled down to the landing, where he lay groaning, his right arm broken.

And that's it.

That's how Asher ended the story, 'And that's it.' The usual darkness returned to his cheeks. The pallor evaporated with the force of renewed activity of veins, and the black gold of his eyes dilated and again filled them with unconcerned gentleness. When Ori bumped into him by chance in the middle of the uproar of recess, he was evidently angry and frightened. Actually, she didn't bump into him. The bristling on her nape led her to behind the gym. Asher's feet were sunk into a woven carpet of morning glory and dandelions. So were Judy's, who was standing beneath the sorrowful foliage of a pepper tree and talking to him with wide gestures, in a sharp whisper. She didn't hear what was said. She just peeked and moved away towards the synagogue, waiting for Asher to show up. Judy didn't follow him. She evidently went into the gym through the back door. Ori made like she was just leaning against the synagogue wall, and when Asher came past walking quickly she called him, as if surprised to see him. He stammered something, spoke her name. Then he asked, "Did you hear what happened with Tuitto and Ofer Sabbah?"

She, who had already heard fragments of the story, replied, "Not exactly," and was happy that he'd raised the subject.

A week later they were told that Principal Tuitto was leaving the school and would be replaced by a new principal, Avshalom Baruch. Barely two days passed and rumors were already flying about this Baruch and his hard-line management of a school in Ofakim. At their school there was a rule about wearing school uniform, but no one enforced it. It was enough to wear any kind of blue shirt. Not with Baruch, they whispered in the schoolyard during recess, not with him. Girls' jewelry was out: no earrings, one bracelet, and don't even mention the ankle bracelets worn by the girls in the senior classes. Only school uniform that would be inspected at morning assembly. Plain long denim skirts for the girls, jeans for the boys. Black, white or gray sneakers. Lace-up shoes. No more thongs. No more peroxided or dyed hair, no more hairdos. Hair loose, a ponytail or braids, and for the boys—a short haircut and knitted yarmulke, not the velvet or white ones of the kind kept in the synagogue for festivals.

Ofra repeated the new rules to Ori every evening. And every evening there was another, more horrendous one. In the course of that day, for instance, the idea came up of making the tenth-grade and upward boys wear the small, fringed prayer shawl under their shirts, and by the day's end Ofra told Ori about it aloud, as if it were already a fait accompli. And Ori, to appease her, responded with astonishment, disgust, as if she hadn't heard the rumors herself.

"What a cheek," Ofra said. You and Asher I can understand, but me? In any case I'm not allowed out in the evenings. So now I've got to go to school with these rules? I'm never going to dye my hair back to black."

"But what will you do?" Ori asked.

"Don't worry about me," Ofra said resolutely, "I always find a way. I'm not one of those who suffer in silence."

Too true, Ori thought, and Ofra said, "Don't look at me like that, like you're surprised. You don't know what I'm capable of."

Ori sighed and said, "What, for instance?" and Ofra replied, "Like the time me and Asher hung Dakar from a tree."

"Dakar, Gvinush's brother?"

"Yes, yes, her idiot brother. Dakar, pchhh," and that sound, 'pchhh', suddenly uprooted the name 'Dakar' from its natural context, from the person it belonged to, and in her mind's eye Ori could see a spear, the other meaning of the Hebrew name. What an odd name. "Why's he called Dakar anyway?" she asked.

"After some submarine that disappeared."

"What submarine?"

"Don't you know anything? A navy submarine. The year he was born a submarine disappeared, like the sea swallowed it. They didn't find a trace of it. They thought that the Egyptians or Jordanians had sunk it. What a stupid name, eh? But it suits him."

"Why?"

"Because he's screwed up. Did you know that he remembers the names of all the kids that were murdered or killed in accidents off by heart?"

"Where does he know them from?"

"From TV, that's where."

"But . . . what children?"

"Tslil Shelach and Nava Elimelech and Oron Yarden and all those kids from the accident at the Habonim junction, about thirty were killed in that accident."

Ori stared at her uncomprehendingly.

"The Habonim junction?" Ofra said. "The bus that got stuck on the railway crossing?" and Ori continued staring at her and Ofra knocked on her head with her knuckles and said, "Hello, anybody home?"

"Stop it," Ori said. "So why did you hang him on a tree?"

"When I was your age, that Dakar decided to get in my face. Every day when I left the house he'd be waiting at the end of the street with a cane and hit me on the back. I wouldn't see him, he'd hide in a different place every day. I'd get to the end of the street and suddenly I'd feel my back burning."

"What . . . why did he do it?"

"How do I know? I told you he's screwed up."

"So what happened?"

"After a few days I'd had enough. D'you know the wood behind school?"

"Yes."

"Well, I arranged with Asher to come to my school after school and he'd get Dakar to go there with him and I waited with a rope by the tree we'd chosen. The moment they got there I gave Asher the signal we'd agreed on at home and we both jumped him. Asher got his hands and I tied his feet. Then we tied his hands and shoved him against the tree and tied him to it. We got two thick branches and hit him. We left him hanging there till the evening. Then Asher went to his house and told his mother he thought he'd seen Dakar in the wood."

Ori smiled. "And what happened to you?"

"Us? Nothing. Dakar was dead scared of us. He said that two kids he didn't know had grabbed him and tied him up."

Ori looked in shock at Ofra's supercilious smile as the latter stretched out on the couch and reached for the book at its side. "In brief," she said before opening it, "nobody messes with me," and their mother's voice seemed to answer her from the kitchen,

"Ofra, it's your turn to wash dishes this evening."

"Talk of the devil . . . " Ofra muttered.

"Ofra!" their mother shouted hoarsely, and coughed.

"All right, all right, I heard you," Ofra replied.

Their mother came into the living room.

"*Jinn*, it's late," she said, you've got school in the morning,"

Ori replied, "But I wanted to wait up until Abba gets home from work."

Their mother shook her head.

"He'll be a bit late. One of their machines broke down."

So Ori got up unwillingly and went to her room. The seventh and last book in the Ariella series was waiting for her on the bedside table, and it was more sinister than the previous ones. She'd read the first three chapters and couldn't find the strength to get beyond them, so she went back to the beginning. Once more she was faced with a mystery: Many of the inhabitants of the City of Tempest imagined they could see the same figure, an albino man in garments of shining linen, in his hand a long staff of polished iron that spat fire and acrid odors with a roar. Ariella knew what it was right away. A rifle, and the albino was massacring the inhabitants. But they didn't die: anyone hit by a bullet sank into feverish hallucinations and saw deranged scenes. Now she'd reached the end of the third chapter in which Ariella and Pereh were forced to part and go their separate ways into the Four Kingdoms to find a lead to solve the mystery, and once more the book depressed her. She put it down on the bedside table. A gibbous moon was trying to rise, brightening the darkness with a yellowish light. Ori turned onto her side.

———

At first she detected a movement. The foliage of a wide-branched ficus hit by the wind. As she moved closer she saw that from one of its branches, that pointed towards her, a boy was hanging and he was in a kind of harness around his hips and shoulders. It seemed to her that he was swinging, but his distorted face—the eyes wide and cheeks sunken—told her he had been dead for some time, that death had come to him suddenly, terrifyingly. She carried on walking and more ficuses sprang up around her, the body of a boy or girl hanging from them, and faint voices, perhaps the cries of their ghosts, echoed in the distance. She saw a figure fleeing through the trees and took after it in pursuit. Its appearance slowly became clear: the broad back and thin neck, the raven hair woven of trusses of ash, the arms at the sides of its body even as it ran. In all these the fleeing figure resembled that of her father. She called his name and then he was standing before her. It was not her father but Bonni, shaved, wearing a suit, but on his face were different features, the upturned nose and the eyeballs of Josh, two slivers of greenstone. Even the syllables broke on his tongue as they did with Josh, "What's your name, girl?" he asked.

Vainly, she tried to remember. Then, in a flash, she realized that she had never had a name. She told him.

"No one has a name," he told her, "they never had. But when you leave here it will suddenly dawn on you that you recall a name that is yours alone, a life that only you lived. Do not believe."

"Do not believe who?" she asked.

"Open your mouth and put out your tongue," he ordered.

She did as she was told. In his right hand he held a pair of long tongs and in them a piece of parchment, inscribed on both sides. He laid it on her tongue. "Now eat this parchment," and she chewed it without delay. Its taste was of honey, flavorsome. She felt it sliding down her gullet and into her stomach. Then she felt a piercing pain and she knew she had experienced it in the past, in its weaker form, but not like this. The words on the parchment separated in her stomach and began racing around inside it, and with them the pain. She turned to ask the man what she should do, but he had vanished. The forest of hanging children was at her back, and before her a quiet river in the depths of whose dark water the sky was reflected. The pain in her gut intensified, a swarm of hornets buzzed inside her, trying to burst out of her belly. She knew what she must do to rid herself of them. A rock ledge jutted from the bank where she stood, kissing the river's surface. She climbed onto it and bent to the water. She extended a finger from which boiling blood dripped, and letter after letter the sentence was written in blood, "Make you a new heart and a new spirit: for why will ye die, O house of Israel? For I have no pleasure in the death of him that dieth."

Each of the letters shivered, but the surface of the water as taut as the terrible crystal fixed them in their place. She inspected her work with approval, crimson flames flickered in the form of the words. It seemed that the pain in her stomach was receding. She laid a hand on it, rubbed it in a circular movement, and the rock ledge broke off. She fell into the water, which was no longer water, but blood, rivulets of blood washing over her and filling her nose and mouth. She was not afraid. The viscosity and saltiness of the blood told her it was the blood that had spurted from her finger. "How strange," she thought, "drowning in your own blood." And she awoke.

But the blood's stickiness did not vanish with the dream. It stayed with her. A moistness between her thighs, trickling. Frightened, she jumped out of bed and switched on the light. In the middle of the bottom sheet was a large red stain, and further evidence of hornets, the drawn blades of their stings, ripped through her belly. She looked down. Another bloodstain was spreading across the front of her mother's long nightgown that she was wearing. She called out, an incomprehensible jumble of sounds.

Ofra came first, followed by Asher. One look at Ori's night-gown and bed was enough for Ofra. She blocked the doorway in front of Asher, who was trying to peek inside, his voice still wrapped in sleep, but the urgency awakening in him. "Ori, are you all right?" he asked.

Ofra answered for her, "Yes. This isn't for you," and she let their mother in, who had also arrived, her hair in disarray and hiding her face. She closed the door before Ori managed to see if her father was there as well. But he wasn't.

Ofra put her arm around her shoulders and her mother kissed her on the forehead and said, "*Ya binti*", my daughter, with such gentleness.

Ofra added, "I'm sorry. I should have warned you. I didn't imagine it'd happen to you this early. At the rate you're developing I thought you'd have at least another year."

Through the door she dimly heard her father's interrogatory questions and Asher telling him something or other.

———

She stayed awake until dawn, a lake of homogeneous dust, weightless, filled the room. Above it, raucous bunches of the early birds. Ofra had stayed with her after their mother left, explaining what their mother called 'the manner of women,' which was nothing but a series of pains and anxiety, dates that must be circled on the calendar, sanitary pads, expecting the worst. At a certain point Ofra realized that she was impervious to her explanations, perhaps because of the look that darted over the walls and returned to the cover of the book on her bedside table, and she got up and said, "You'd best go to sleep now. Believe me, everything will seem better in the morning."

Ori had no intention of going to sleep. The dream was etched too deeply for her to fall asleep again. Of all its scenes, it was the sight of the letters of boiling blood forming on the water's surface that was the most terrible, and she couldn't block it out. The words she had written reminded her of something. She'd come across two similar sentences in the past. She crouched next to her nightstand and extracted her notebook from the narrow gap between it and the wall, opened at the page on which she'd recorded Bonni's words, beneath which she'd copied the verse from the note she'd taken from Sigal's wall. Verses! That's what those sentences are! How hadn't she made the connection? They had been whispering to her since first grade, at the celebration when they received a Bible, and on rectangles of Bristol board carelessly stuck to the classroom walls, in Torah lessons. But there, there they were only words in a dead language, from another time, and its cold fingers gripped her throat, the throat of every child in the class. But the words in Bonni's verses, Sigal's, and now in the verse from her dream, glowed in her brain like an ember, a murmur of sparks and cinders.

Under the two previous verses she wrote the dream verse, and looked at all three:

"Woe is me, for I am a man of unclean lips, and I dwell in the midst of a people of unclean lips."

"Say not, I am a child: for thou shalt go to all that I shall send thee, and whatsoever I command thee thou shalt speak."

"Make you a new heart and a new spirit: for why will ye die, O house of Israel? For I have no pleasure in the death of him that dieth."

There's some kind of connection between them. They had got to her; not without reason and not by chance. Ever since she heard that terrible voice from the TV. Had that been a dream too? Before she went into their meaning she had to find their source. And she knew who'd be able to tell her. Sigal. Now they'd forged an alliance she'd be able to ask her.

Yes, the alliance. Throughout the days of rehashing Principal Tuitto's exploits and Baruch's edicts that were looming, she'd avoided all contact with Ilanit, and Ilanit quickly averted her eyes whenever they met Ori's. In class, in the corridor, she made herself small and fled, but mainly in PE lessons; in the first minutes of the lesson Judy grasped that something had happened between the two girls, not just some fleeting friction, but a knife had slashed them apart, and when she divided them into pairs she insisted on putting them together, and they behaved coldly towards one another, using brusque sentences. And once, when Gvinush took out of her pocket the little plastic bag with Sigal's stolen curl in it, and fingered it with delight in front of Ori and Sigal and Ophir, Ori saw the tiny smile forming on Ilanit's lips.

But what separated her and Ilanit welded the three of them together. They had their own password. One only had to say "Soda Extreme" and they burst out laughing, especially when that Gvinush, with all her arrogance, brought some small bottles of juice she'd made with the new Soda Extreme appliance her mother had bought. The girls all clustered around her at morning recess—and she, Sigal and Ophir and gone over to find out what the meeting was about—and she made it a real performance, taking out the bottles and lecturing on the different colors and flavors like the host on a TV show. But the moment she blurted the words "Soda Extreme", the three started giggling, at first a stifled chuckle and then bleats of laughter. It was a spasm, not a voluntary action. Their combined laughs had an extraordinary effect—Sigal's tolling bells and Ophir's snorts and the sound of her own laugh; what was its sound? A wheezing motor—the girls turned to look at them, holding their stomachs and their zany laughter. Gvinush's words were cut short and she attempted a piercing look. "Get lost," she said angrily, "who asked you to come? Especially you, Shriki.

You've found two girls who give two hoots about you, or are you a girl yourself?"

Ori answered in his place, laughing and speaking alternately, "Big deal . . . what's that juice you're so . . . proud of . . . way to go . . . what else is new . . . ?"

And Ophir added, "It's just seltzer."

On hearing the last word Sigal stiffened, her body straightened up, her neck straight and her arms folded on her chest. In a mechanical tone she began reciting, "Modern science stands helpless and shamefaced before the phenomenon of hypnosis. While there can be no doubt regarding the existence and the extent of the reality and necessity of hypnosis, not one brain researcher or neurologist has a rational explanation for it. It seems that the key to understanding the phenomenon of hypnosis is inextricably linked with questions regarding consciousness that have been asked since the dawn of history, and which remain unanswered today. What is consciousness? What is cognition?"

The girls stared at her uncomprehendingly. Somebody, perhaps Ilanit, said, "You screwed-up blubberguts, what's that nonsense?" and somebody else—Aliza?—pushed her shoulder: a thin arm sent out from the girls crowded into a single mass. Sigal didn't move, didn't stop her recitation, didn't even acknowledge that she'd heard or even ascribed importance to their response. Her eyes were vacant, her face expressionless. "She's been possessed," said a third girl— the squinty 'Rita North-and South'?—and a fourth choked, perhaps trying to stifle a cry of fright. The fifth banged her chest and a sixth said, "I need the bathroom." Thus the signal was given and the girls took off in all directions, making all kinds of flimsy excuses, leaving Gvinush, boiling with anger, and Aliza and Ilanit, on sentry duty beside her. Gvinush looked at the three. The recitation was over. Sigal smiled happily.

"You, the three jerks," Gvinush said, "your time will come," and she turned her back on them and strode off, mincing exaggeratedly.

Gvinush was right. They were a single unit. The Triumvirate. Odd. When had that expression popped into her mind? After the hypnosis all three had felt the bonds that bound them, but only acknowledged their existence when they heard about Principal Tuitto's dismissal. Not that the dismissal had any effect. It was their way of tallying time. Summer had already started to appear. At first only a gash of the noonday heat of the end of April, and after it a bleeding, overflowing *hamsin*, a momentary but menacing majesty. The acacias flowered in all their yellow force, rustling their sighs. In the evenings the swallows went mad in the sky, tiny machines running out of control. The three of them watched them quite often, the fragmented trajectories they traced in the patches of purpling blue that filtered through the foliage in the old Arab orchard behind Sigal's house. That was their regular meeting place. They met almost every evening, not talking a lot, being there was sufficient, being together, the presence. But it happened, as it had two days earlier, that unconventional ideas arose. For example, Sigal was sitting on a rock, Ori was lying on the blanket in the middle looking upward, Ophir was sitting with his back against the trunk of a terebinth and playing with piece of wood. He said, "I'd like to know what was here a long time ago, what the place looked like."

Sigal looked at him. Since she'd done her public recitation of the first page of the hypnosis book, she'd nursed a grievance against him; not anger, but a hint of complaint was evident in her words. Ophir had apologized. He said it was all a mistake and hadn't meant the word 'seltzer'—and as he uttered the word he put a hand over his mouth to blur its sound—to make her comply. He suggested that he hypnotize her again to cancel the compliance, but Sigal refused and only forbade him to utter the word that was damned for all eternity.

"What d'you mean, 'what was here'?"

"Dunno. People lived here. It belonged to Arabs, no?"

"Perhaps," Sigal replied skeptically, "but Arabs from way back, not from today."

"What's the difference?" Ophir asked.

"That the old Arabs are like the ones in Morocco and Algeria and Iraq, and the ones that lived in Spain at the time of Maimonides and Rabbi Yehuda Halevi. They were gentle and liked the Jews. Not like the Arabs of today that throw rocks and kidnap children and want to drive the Jews into the sea."

"Who told you that?" Ophir asked.

"My father," she replied, "he talks about it a lot."

"I can imagine," Ori interrupted, "that a thousand years ago there was a sultan's palace here and he wore silk turbans. And his wives walked around in robes made of rare cloths, in a thousand colors, and they wore jewelry made of gold and precious stones, rubies, topaz and emeralds. And their robes rustled as they walked. And in the evening they'd come down to the orchard, and there was a little stream here"—Ori was carried away by her words, painting a picture she could see in her mind's eye, a picture borrowed down to the last detail from the description of the palace of the Sovereign of the Desert in the Kingdom of Summer, in the Ariella books—"and the stream flowed in a circle around the orchard, within the wall, around the fig and olive and pomegranate trees, and you could hear the babbling of the water inside the stone, and peacocks roamed freely in the orchard, and brilliant jerboas sparkled in silver cages, and red and blue songbirds, that could sing in human voices, perched on the branches and sang a thousand songs."

Ophir sighed in amazement. Sigal asked, "Where did you get that idea?"

"From a book I read," Ori said, and carried away by the enthusiasm sparked by the scene, she tried to tell them about Ariella, but in her eagerness the details got confused, piled one on the other, unconnected in her mind, and fired onto her tongue. What filled her throat as she tried to restore order to them? She fell silent, and again tried to tell them about Ariella and Pereh, the bond between them, and their oath never to be parted. But then she recalled that in the present book, the seventh, they did part, and that she hadn't read it to the end, for a few days she'd been stuck on the third chapter that ended with . . . "I know," she said suddenly, "we should do what Ariella and Pereh did, and swear a blood oath."

"Eh?" Sigal said.

"Before Ariella and Pereh part, they have a kind of ceremony. They prick themselves and mix their blood in a bowl, Pereh's blood is purple, and then they taste the mixture and Ariella casts a spell that if one of them is in distress, the other, even if he's at the other end of the kingdoms, will hear him and come to his aid."

Ophir and Sigal exchanged glances.

"What d'you say?"

"Er . . . " Sigal said, "it sounds like . . . "

"Idolatry," Ophir said, and snorted.

"Yes."

"But it's not, it's not," Ori insisted. Again that resolve flowed through her and she knew how to imbue her voice with it, to whip them up with its help. "We must," and she repeated the word 'must' several times, bringing down all of Sigal and Ophir's opposition, the latter saying submissively in the end, "But how?"

"You've got to heat a needle over a low flame, a candle or something . . . "

"Not candles again," Sigal protested.

Ori ignored her. "And when the needle's hot," she went on, "you prick your finger. A tiny prick and you squeeze out a drop of blood. We can do it tomorrow night."

Next day Sigal and Ophir tried to get out of it, using any excuse they could think of. But Ori had made up her mind and nothing would change it. In the face of her tight-lipped resolve, her huge eyes sowing terror below the short fringe she'd adopted, and her tiny, tense body, they stammered in the middle of their excuses. Fear beat within them when they got to the old orchard. Ori was already bent over the candle, heating the point of a needle whose eye was wrapped in a scrap of cloth against the heat. She pricked her own finger first to show them how cowardly they were, and then Ophir's, whose excitement made him shake and her to almost miss the finger pad. Sigal looked away as she pricked the skin and squeezed the finger above the first joint to force a drop of thick blood to drop into the small bowl she'd brought. She mixed the blood with her finger and ordered them to put out their tongues. She touched the tip of each of them. The taste of the blood was nauseating, rank. At that moment she knew she would never forget its saltiness and weight in her mouth, as if it were white hot and had seared her palate. Lucky she'd thought of everything. She took out the bottle of juice she'd put into her bag earlier, and a bar of chocolate, one of the latest and best of the Vered Hagalil line, and offered them to Ophir and Sigal. A deep silence surrounded them. Even the swallows had stopped their screeching. Even the brown partridges were mute. The palmate leaves of the fig trees did not rustle.

"Now everyone's got to tell a secret," Ophir suddenly whispered, and Sigal nodded her grave agreement. "A secret," she murmured.

They knelt, hands on knees, backsides on heels, backs straight.

"Remember," Ophir began, "when you came to my house too early that evening and I was all sweaty?"

They nodded.

"You can see I've got this problem that I don't stop moving, right? It started when I was in sixth grade—we didn't know each other then—and it was really bad. I wasn't able to sleep, I couldn't sit still in class. My parents took me to a specialist who treats motor disorders, that's what it's called. He said I've got to do some kind of physical activity, to get the nerves out of my body. That's what my parents told me."

He swallowed his saliva and they waited. They had time. The evening, too, had stopped its progress.

"So I started dancing. I've got a lesson once a week in Beersheba, and every day I dance for an hour. There's a program on the radio that plays the songs I like, and I dance any way I want according to the movements I learn with the group."

"I'd like to see you dance," Ori said, and Sigal followed suit, "So would I," she said, and then after a brief silence, "Now it's my turn."

They looked at her expectantly. She said, "When we met in this field for the first time, there was a wall of blocks there, remember?"

Again they nodded, waiting. Not a sound. Only lips opening and closing, a tongue licking the inside of the mouth.

Sigal continued. "I call that wall 'The Wall of Forgiveness'. If I do something bad, I write a note and put it in the wall. That way God can hear me."

They looked at Ori. She said, and not one of her senses rebelled or protested, "Remember that I didn't speak for about two months?"

Their eyes rested on her gently, checkered velvet and graying sea, calling on her to continue.

"One night in the winter I woke up and turned the TV on, and I heard a voice coming out of it, I can't describe it. It was an amazing voice that gave me the shivers, and it said to me, 'Rise, Ori, my light, for your light has come', and I knew it was calling me by my proper name. That's why I changed my name. Next morning I started talking again."

Sigal tensed slightly, and Ophir's body bent towards her, ready to spring. Until she actually uttered the words she hadn't imagined how they'd lain stifled inside her, breathless, and by voiding herself of them, with the relief of the voiding, something else confounded her, still nameless and fluttering, and Orphir and Sigal felt it too. She knew it beyond doubt by the movements of their limbs and the spark that flamed in the corneas of their eyes—especially in Sigal's eyes, where she saw a question forming. She looked away from them to the world, which even though it encompassed and demarcated her from every direction, it stole to her: it is the world, or a piece of it, that is moving inside her. She suddenly recognized it in all his corporeality, the hardness of the light concealed in the foliage, the crystalline quality of the dust, the delicate fibers of the time eroding her skin. She gasped in astonishment. A breath of wind answered her, extinguishing the candle's flame. And Sigal's attention was drawn to the lumps of wax at its foot.

Ori got up, wrapped the glass bowl in a piece of cloth, the bowl stained with drying blood, and put it on the ground. Ophir selected a big stone and he and Sigal lifted it and dropped it onto the wrapped bowl. Ori undid the cloth, the bowl was shattered. She spread the fragments around the orchard, under the trees and between the stones, in silence. And the three of them made their way home in silence.

———

Ori waited four days until she was ready to speak to Sigal, and when she finally mustered the courage, she couldn't find an opportunity. They came out of the gym from a PE lesson. Sigal limped at her side. In the lesson Judy had decided to teach them to vault over the horse, a kind of high, padded wooden hurdle over which they had to vault. Judy briefly described how it was done: a fast approach run, both hands on the horse, a vault, legs apart, body over the horse, landing. Nothing simpler. She reviewed the girls to choose one for a demonstration, and smiled invitingly at Sigal. Sigal shook her head vigorously from side to side. Judy didn't give in, with words and gestures. Ori stood up and volunteered, but it only strengthened Judy's resolve, and Sigal capitulated. She stood at the staring line, and on Judy's signal started her run, accelerated, reached the horse, and the expected happened. Her arms wouldn't take the weight of her body and she fell sprawled over the horse and rolled off onto the mattresses that awaited her failure. Gvinush let out a scream of joy and jumped up and started clapping and prancing, and Aliza, Ilanit and some other girls joined in. Drily, Judy said, "Well done." Sigal went back to her place next to Ori, favoring one ankle.

As they went down the gym steps at the end of the lesson with Sigal leaning on her, Ori wanted to tell her that she wanted them to meet in the old orchard that evening, just the two of them, but before she could she felt on her nape, not a bristling this time, not a pulling, but the swish of a blade. She swayed.

"Everything all right?" Sigal asked.

"No, something's not all right," Ori hissed through clenched teeth, and again on her nape she felt a blow, the urgency. "Something's happening." She scanned the sides of the schoolyard and there, to her right, in the direction of the soccer field, she saw a crowd of boys from her class. She pointed, and they hurried over, Ori in the lead and Sigal faltering behind her.

They missed the start of the fight so they didn't know for sure who started it, but they had no doubt: Ophir would never have provoked Noam Ohana. They pressed up against the backs of the boys in the tight circle around the adversaries that hid them from the prying eyes of a teacher or a passing adult. Through the gaps between the backs they saw Noam circle Ophir, slap him, and move back. Ophir stood rooted where he was, his eyes downcast.

"Come on, you pussy," Noam taunted him, "hit me back," and another blow and retreat.

"Stop it!" Ori shouted, her voice rebounding from the wall of backs.

The boys started shouting, "We want blood, we want blood," in a rhythmic tribal chant.

Ori tried to get her hands between the boy's bodies to prize them apart and get herself into the arena they had formed.

"Noam, stop it!" she yelled again.

"Too good to answer me, are you?" Noam asked Ophir, "you're only good enough to go to Beersheba every week and dance like some girl?"

Ophir's clenched hands hung at the sides of his body but he raised his head. Noam shouted crudely, "So it's true, you faggot?"

This time Ophir stood up to him and pounced at him, taking him by surprise with an agile, flashing leap. He grabbed Noam's sport shirt. "Enough," he said, "I haven't done anything to you. Leave me alone."

"You dare to lay your hands on me?" Noam spat. He grabbed Ophir round the neck with his left hand, clenched his right fist, jumped in the air, easily freeing himself from Ophir's grip, and hit Ophir in the eye and on the bridge of his nose. Ophir stumbled backward from the force of the blow and fell onto his backside, stunned. Noam gave him no time to regain his senses. He kicked him in the side, pulled him to his feet, grabbed his shoulders and kneed him in the belly, letting him collapse back onto the ground.

Ophir groaned but didn't cry. His glassy, damp eyes saw Ori, but he didn't cry, and his spirit fanned the flames of Noam's anger, as did the boys' chanting that hadn't ceased for a moment, "We want blood, we want blood."

Noam moved around Ophir who was sitting helpless on the ground, knelt behind him and circled his neck with his arm, strangling him.

"Cry, you pussy," he hissed, "cry, you stinking faggot."

Ophir gurgled.

"Stop it!" Ori yelled again, "Stop it! Do something, he's killing him!"

Sigal, standing beside Ori, started crying. "It's a punishment," she wailed, "we're being punished for what we did."

"Shut your mouth!" she yelled at her, all her anger channeled towards her, "Shut your mouth and go get one of the teachers."

Ophir gurgled again. "Cry, butt-fucker," Noam hissed again and punched Ophir on the side of the head.

Something in the boys' bloodlust abated, perhaps it was Ophir's emptying face. Some of them stopped chanting, and murmured. Ori seized her chance and pushed her way into the circle. She ran at Noam and he, not expecting it and bent on throttling Ophir, didn't see her in time. She reached out and scratched his face. He loosened his grip and let Ophir fall. Ori had never seen eyes like these, flooded with anger, blind, as ugly as unhealed wounds. He leapt at her headfirst. It was her good fortune that she was short and his butt, aimed at her belly, hit her shoulder, just grazing it, but its force was sufficient. She fell and Noam went back to Ophir, kicking him in the side again, one kick. Then a shadow fell over him, Josh's heavy figure. He grabbed him and Noam went wild, screeching, "Let me go, let go, I'll tear you apart, you fucker." But Josh lifted him effortlessly and led him away.

Ori hurried to Ophir lying unconscious on the ground. Blood oozed from his nose and covered his face, his eyes were closed. He wasn't moving. "Get up!" she said in her commanding voice, but there was no response. Someone lifted her off him and pulled her away. She managed to see a few teachers, the school nurse, closing in on Ophir and hiding him. A moment later Elisheva Zikri's arm was around her shoulders, and she whispered, "You're going to see the nurse."

"What happened to Ophir?" she asked.

"The ambulance is on the way," she replied.

Sigal joined them weeping, and the girls also gathered round Elisheva. Then she saw Ilanit's look, filled with pure terror. She caught it with a question whose nature she did not know, and Ilanit shifted it to Gvinush who was standing there, calmly observing the uproar.

———

Ori wept in her room and her mother came in to see how she was. Perhaps she'd heard her from the hallway, or perhaps she'd been listening—they hadn't been able to keep Noam's murderous attack on Ophir secret for a minute, certainly not in a small town like Netivot, and although her mother was not among the gossips, she had plenty of talkative neighbors. When Elisheva drove her home after the nurse's checkup, and she walked through the door, her clothes stained with Ophir's blood and she about to faint with each step, her mother was ready with clean clothes and she led her in silence to the shower, and afterwards fed her with Mama Elhayani's pastries, *meringez* and *shbakiya*, the more sugar the better to get her out of her physical and mental weakness. Her mother asked a few questions, but she was reluctant to answer and only mumbled over and over, "What's happened to Ophir?"

"I don't know," her mother replied, "Elisheva said they'd taken him to hospital." But her answer did not stop the flow of mumblings and her repeated question. Her mother took her to her room. "It was too much for you," she told her, "you should rest, we'll know more this evening."

But Ori just stared at the wall on which she could see Ophir's bloody, dirt-streaked face, and she wept.

"Ori," her mother said, and Ori, even with her shocked senses, was moved by her mother's surrender; she had called her by her new name. She sat up in bed and asked, "What's happened to Ophir?" but this time with matter-of-fact urgency.

"I told you," her mother replied, "he's in Soroka Hospital in Beersheba. They'll know more this evening. What happened there?"

"I don't know," Ori replied. A guess was forming in her mind but she ignored it; its time would come. "Noam Ohana went crazy. He attacked Ophir without warning."

"And you were hit, too."

"Yes, I tried to stop it. He was strangling Ophir and the boys just stood there, they didn't do a thing."

"You've got to be careful. I don't know what's happening to this country. We didn't know about things like this when we were children, a boy trying kill another boy. Back home we all lived in peace."

Now that Ori's tears had almost dried, and her sobbing was only faint, she was able to discern the exhaustion surrounding her mother's movements and which made her voice fainter. What's she doing at home at this hour, she wondered, it's early. She should be at the center. "Ima, what about you? What about your tests?"

"The tests are fine, everything's all right."

"But what about what happened to you a few weeks ago, when you couldn't breathe? Did you go to the doctor? Did you ask him?"

Her mother rubbed her head. "Don't you fret yourself with that," she said.

"Does Abba know what happened?"

"Yes, I told him."

"What did he say?"

"What's he got to say? The doctor said everything was fine."

Ori closed her eyes. Without her knowing how, her heart told her that her mother was lying. Perhaps her mother also sensed it in her forced tone of voice; she changed the subject. "Ori, when's the annual school trip?"

"What about it? You won't let me go."

"Next weekend your father and I are going on a night trip to the graves of the sages in the north. Do want to come with us instead?"

"What will I do there? Like two years ago when you took me to the celebration of Rabbi Shimon Bar-Yochai at Mount Meron, and I didn't stop throwing up all night?"

"That was just a virus, or something bad you ate. But this trip is different. There won't be people you don't know. They're all from Netivot, the community center is organizing it."

"I don't feel like going on trips," Ori said.

"Maybe you'll change your mind? Right now you're a bit shocked," her mother said, and the word 'shocked' made her cough and cough again.

The cry, stuck in Ori's windpipe like a shard of glass, was released, and just now, when there was nothing to awaken it. The words crowded into her mouth, "I don't ever want to go on trips and I'm never going back to that school."

"Enough, stop it, honey." Her mother stroked her hair, clearing her throat quietly, "Enough, stop it."

Ori sobbed, a jet of bile bubbled deep in her stomach and rose, erupting onto her tongue, "Why?" she asked, "why's this all happening? What's it for?"

"It's the blood," her mother answered, "nobody can control it. When it comes, it keeps on coming until you do something to shut it off." And as if to prove her point she was attacked by another bout of deep, wet coughing, and she covered her mouth with her hand to hold back the burst of bacteria. But when she took her hand away Ori could see another sudden color on it. Blood.

SIX

Fire

AFTERWARDS THE TIME PASSED in a whirl of oxygen and blurred scenes. Ori wanted to say something to her father, to warn him about her mother's bloody coughing. Her mother, glancing at the crimson streaks on her furrowed palm, had said, "That's what happens when you strain the throat too much, sometimes you hurt it." Ori replied, "Come on, Ima, it looks dangerous to me.," to which her mother responded, "No, the blood came out when I cleared my throat." And Ori fell silent. It was then clear to her that her mother hadn't said a word to her father about the bloody coughing and that it was up to her to tell him.

That evening, before he came home, Ophir's mother called her mother to tell her about his condition. He was in intensive care with a broken rib and mild concussion. He still hadn't regained consciousness and although his vital signs were strong, the doctors were concerned that he might fall into a coma. Ori asked to speak to her, but when she heard Irit's voice as her mother passed her the phone, she burst into tears again, because Irit had said, "I understand you tried to help him, you and Rabbi Danino's daughter."

Sigal came to her house that evening, shamefaced, and they shut themselves up in her room and tried to reconstruct the chain of events, to make some kind of sense of them. Nobody disturbed them. Ori's father was on evening shift and Ofra took advantage of the loophole; she spent the afternoon and early evening hours in the company of her two suitors. It was Asher who'd come up with the word 'suitors', and when Ori heard it, in her mind's eye she saw Ofra's two new boyfriends running around her dressed in suits, groaning and wheezing, and she laughed. She heard Asher and Ofra arguing in the yard and listened to them through her window. But Ofra, that scorpion, had eyes in the back of her head and she went quiet and pointed at the window, and Asher understood and fell silent. Ori didn't fully understand what they were talking about, but it seemed that Ofra was accusing Asher of something and telling him to stop, otherwise she'd have to involve their parents, and Asher told her she was a stinking traitor and that he knew a thing or two about the hidey-hole where she and her two suitors smoked.

Ofra laughed at him and said, "How can you compare us, I'm all for having a good time, but not like that, can't you see? Sometimes you're worse than Ori."

Perhaps it was uttering her name that made her turn her head towards the window and catch Ori's eyes gleaming in the darkness, two spotlights of honey.

She gave the news to Sigal, who nodded and fell onto the bed. There was something contracted in Sigal's body, as if she were trying to reduce it to a single point in space: her arms were folded on her chest and her movements short, restricted, arthritic. Her voice was slightly hoarse as in return she told Ori about what was happening at school. A police car had accompanied the ambulance and the police had taken Noam to the station, together with Josh, who was the teacher in charge, and they spoke to Noam's parents there too. Rumor had it that because of his young age the police's hands were tied, there was nothing they could do. The police waited for his parents, who arrived together with his big sister, the notorious Pnina—and

Sigal whispered, tilting her head slightly, ashamed she was participating in the fecklessness of this world, "Her husband's a junkie"—and they'd caused an uproar in the station. The father blew up when he heard they were thinking about involving a social worker or bringing in a youth probation officer who'd recommend sending Noam for psychological evaluation, for after all, it wasn't every day they came across a scene of such devastating violence. One of the policemen took the raving father outside and warned him he'd find himself under arrest if he didn't calm down. The mother started up with breast-beating and all that. Sigal mentioned that this was the part of the story the girls like best, especially Gvinush and Aliza and Ilanit, who burst into a dance with movements and yelling and exaggeratedly demonstrated Moroccan breast-beating, the women's display of mourning, as they scratch the flesh of their faces with their fingernails, wailing and keening. A policewoman tried to pacify the mother, and Pnina, the elder sister, attacked her and started hitting her, and when another policewoman tried to separate them, Pnina scratched her hands too, deep scratches that bled—"And that one, may her name be erased, she's got a wolf's nails, that one," Sigal said, quoting Aliza—and she raised her voice in complaint, threatening to sue the policewomen for using force.

Ori asked, "And Noam? What did they do with him?"

"They can't do anything until they bring in somebody from welfare. Maybe they'll end up sending him to an institution for juvenile delinquents."

"I want to visit Ophir and I don't know how."

Sigal was silent.

"And they won't let us in while he's still unconscious."

Once again Sigal said, "It's a punishment. A punishment from heaven," and Ori replied, "It's a pity Ophir can't hear you. He would have laughed."

"What's to laugh about? Doesn't it seem strange to you that all of a sudden, a few days after we did that idolatry, Noam attacked Ophir for no reason?"

"I don't know if it was for no reason. Didn't any of the boys say how it started?"

"They did, because they were in such shock. I heard Tiran Vanunu telling some friends of his from the eighth grade. Right through the basketball game they had in PE Noam was teasing Ophir, and Ophir wasn't even playing because he's got permission not to play games in PE, he just sits at the side and watches. Anyway, Noam called him names and the lesson finished and they started leaving, and Noam followed Ophir and gave him little slaps on the back of his head."

"*Kaffot*," Ori said.

"What?"

"Those slaps, they're called '*kaffot*'."

"Whatever," Sigal said.

"What names did he call him?"

"I don't know. I didn't hear. And when Tiran Vanunu saw I was listening he told his friends, Don't talk near her, she's a collaborator, that one."

"Something doesn't add up," Ori said.

"What?"

"When we were standing by that circle of boys, d'you remember what Noam yelled at Ophir?"

"He yelled a lot of stuff at him."

"Yes, but he also said he'd heard that he goes to a dance class in Beersheba."

"So?"

"What so? How did he know?"

"What do you mean?" Sigal asked, her thick eyebrows arching in puzzlement and then falling back into place in comprehension, "Who told him?" she whispered.

"Exactly," Ori said, "who told him?"

"Only the two of us knew."

"Not only us. Somebody else. And I've somehow got a feeling that Gvinush is mixed up in it."

"Why?"

"It's just a feeling. I didn't offer you anything to drink. Want some juice or something?"

"Water," Sigal said, "just a glass of water."

Ori brought a tray with two glasses of orangeade. When she asked her mother, whose face was still gray and furrowed with exhaustion, if she'd remembered to put a bottle of water into the fridge, she answered, "We don't serve water to guests in this house. Take your friend some juice." When Ori was halfway out her mother called after her, "I've made rice and chicken cutlets in tomato sauce for supper, just the way you like it, and ask your friend if she'd like to stay and eat with us." The moment she got back to her room Ori asked her, and Sigal blushed and only took a glass from the tray and took tiny, careful, economical sips from it, just like the rest of her movements.

"Know what I'd like right now?" Ori asked.

"To go to our orchard and meet Ophir there?"

Ori nodded. Talking was hard. The air was still. Not just a summer evening stealing in, but a full blown *hamsin* reserved for this room alone, for the silence that fell between her and Sigal, a silence they tried to break with idle chat, little stories. It seemed to her that the silence would go on forever. It would remain with her even after Sigal left. A terrible stifling. There was no more in it to expand the chest. And she would go out of the room and encounter her mother, and again the ring tightening round the throat, squeezing the lungs, and the searing in the gullet. No. She'd stay awake till her father got home and tell him about her mother. Maybe she should talk to Ofra first, but what would Ofra have done? And what about Asher . . .

Sigal stood up.

"You going already?" Ori asked.

"No, I need the bathroom, can you show me where . . . " Sigal said, greatly embarrassed.

And Ori remained on her own with the silence looming over her, trying to extinguish her breathing. She inhaled and exhaled, like she'd read in the hypnosis book—generally a good way to relax, it said. A pity that Ophir had taken it back to the library the day after their experiment, Sigal had demanded it in the name of some general moral principle, or out of fear. Sigal, Ori thought, and immediately remembered: the notebook.

When Sigal came back, her hands damp and she was rubbing them together, Ori was ready for her. The verses floated to her eyes from the open pages. She held the notebook out to Sigal, and Sigal shot her a confused, inquiring look. Ori shrugged. She studied Sigal as she read the verses standing up, and when she closed the notebook and opened it again at the beginning and read, verse after verse, page after page—how long did her reading take? A few minutes, an hour, all night?

"I don't really understand what I've read," Sigal said when she got to the page with the verses again, "what is it?"

"Just stuff I write."

"But what for?"

"What do you mean, 'what for'?"

"What do they mean?"

"They're just thoughts, words that come into my head."

Sigal went back to the beginning of the notebook and read one of the paragraphs aloud, "The field was completely white, broad and deep, poppies made of snow or lace mingled with floured ears of corn and white harebells, and onto this shimmering whiteness fell moonlight, soft and glistening. I saw this in a dream. At the edge of the field a man was waiting for me whose face I couldn't see and afterwards, when I knew what his name was, he was no longer in the field. He was called Bahamiron and he fled from a land where nobody ever died, and came to Israel to see what it was like when people do."

Ori smiled at her, and Sigal persisted, "But what does it mean?"

"I don't know. I copied the first lines out of book I like, and after them I wrote the words that came into my mind."

Sigal leafed through the notebook and sat down beside Ori. She pointed at the verses. "And these?" she asked.

"I thought you'd know."

"Why?"

"Because they look like verses from the Torah."

Sigal looked at her long and hard and then went back to the notebook. "The first verse," she whispered excitedly, "is what Bonni told you in class before they took him away."

"Yes, but where's it from, what place?"

"Well, it looks like a verse from the Bible. But why would I know exactly where it's from? Because my father's a rabbi?"

"That too. But also because the second verse, I . . . Sigal, I don't know how to tell you this."

"Tell me what?"

"That I . . . your wall with the blocks . . . well, I, I peeked that day I came looking for you and I saw a note with the second verse."

Sigal was stunned. Her face paled. "You looked at the notes?" The hurt in her voice was so apparent that Ori hastily said, "No, of course not, just one, from the bottom, and then you came."

Sigal shook her head and her hair gathered into a ponytail waved back and forth. The movement of her hair was like a white-hot steel wire passing through Ori's veins. And Sigal's eyes, too, on her like two dull flames, they and the golden sparks in them shooting in her agitation. "Honestly," she promised, "I only peeked at one note, with the verse."

But disbelief lay at the depths of Sigal's look and was revealed despite all her efforts to quell it, in the reflection of the moon sinking into the depths of the well. She sprang up and left the room without a word. Ori called after her even when she was in the doorway, and in the hallway, and when she was swallowed up in the darkness cloaking the street. "Wait, I'll walk you home," she shouted at her back as it moved away and was lost: a misty impression flickering somewhere for a split second and vanishing.

———

How had she got herself into this situation again? Once more she was condemned to wander in the limbo between the camps, to plan stratagems of evasion and wooing. Ilanit had cut herself off from the company of Gvinush and Aliza, and it was evident. At recess she walked on her own or with the other girls, Rita and Shoshi and Miri and Anita and Keren and Sima, whom she despised even more than she abhorred Sigal. On more than one occasion she'd said that those girls were nobodies. Ori avoided her look and felt it on her back, fixed on her in class. With a great effort she kept her head turned, her eyes downcast. And as for Sigal, her place in the equation was reversed: she was to Sigal what Ilanit had been to her—chasing after her in vain. It was not how she'd imagined Sigal's reaction. After all, she'd rectified the wrong before Sigal knew about it. She'd let her read her innermost, secret thoughts. She should have been angry at the rudeness, but only a dull, incipient knife sawed at her. She cried for the thousandth time after Sigal had left, furious, and fell asleep on the bed fully clothed, exhausted. That evening she hadn't managed to tell her father about her mother and her coughing, and sleep wiped away the memory of the event, its menace. When she wasn't deep in the last Ariella book, she wracked her brain to find ways of breaking the boycott imposed on her by Sigal.

In the end she found a way out. Three days after the fight Irit Shriki called them and told her that Ophir had regained consciousness—he'd actually come round a day and a half ago and only now she'd bothered to call! Ori was angry for a moment, a small flare-up in her belly that abated immediately, because Irit said that Ophir had asked that she and Sigal visit him, and if they needed a lift—she assumed that her parents didn't have a car and they wouldn't allow them to go by bus— so they could go with her and her husband; her mother would keep an eye on Ophir during the morning, and they'd relieve her, and their parents shouldn't worry, they'd bring them home too. On behalf of both of them Ori told her that there wouldn't be a problem and that she and Sigal had been thinking for two days about how to get to the hospital.

Next morning she left a note on Sigal's desk, "Ophir's awake and we've got a lift to the hospital. Let me know if you want to go. Ori," and at recess Sigal came over to her. "So how are we going?" she asked bluntly.

"With Ophir's parents at four this afternoon, I already told his mother we're coming."

"Okay. Where are they picking us up?"

"Outside my house. Is that okay?"

"Yes," Sigal replied, and walked away.

She was there on time, by their verandah. She didn't come inside or announce her arrival. She waited for Ori to come out into the street. And Ori walked towards her with a smile, but Sigal pursed her lips and looked at her reprovingly.

On the drive to Beersheva, Ophir's parents, a short, fidgety, potbellied man, and a tall, angular woman with large hands and eyes the same dirty blue as Ophir's, questioned her and Sigal delicately and obliquely. Ophir's father asked if they knew why his son had been beaten unconscious at school and where the teachers were at the time. He told them he'd sent a letter to the regional supervisor demanding to know how his office intended to prevent recurrence of such a vicious attack. He'd threatened that if he didn't get some satisfactory answers he'd go to a higher authority.

Irit, on the other hand, wondered aloud why her son had asked to see them both. Ori realized what was behind her question—Irit knew that her son hung out with them and that they'd come to his aid when he was attacked by Noam, but she didn't grasp the complexity of the relationship that had been formed between him and the girls, and that she didn't know how to behave with her and Sigal: as close friends? As strangers she had to learn to get to know, to accept? Both Irit and her husband voiced their puzzlement in a somewhat hesitant tone. They had still to digest the tragedy that had befallen them, and the questions—masses of words and weary tones—were batted around the car's space.

Ori looked out of the window. She started thinking about the possibilities in the word 'south': hot, huts, shot, shut, shout. She watched the scenery as it sped by, resisting their drive. The tamarisks and electricity poles by the roadside swayed from the power of their movement, and the acacias had been destroyed, an expanse of yellowish-brown loess spread before them, spotted with Bedouin encampments, tin shacks, but mainly it was spellbinding in its monotony.

A few birds circled around ramiform bushes, stands of trees—conifers?—Ori couldn't say. They seemed like sad shapes staining the expanse. With a sudden yearning she thought about her two-month silence when the world was painfully lucid, the black heart of an anemone richer than that, a field of stamens, each existing virtually alone. The air was filled with subtleties. And here everything withdrew into a kind of blank uniformity. A graying line of asphalt was drawn between Netivot and Beersheba, and the further south they drove the fewer possible turnoffs became until only Beersheba remained before them, the only choice, no choice.

Ori didn't remember the link, how her thoughts had led her to the road, the scenery, back to the seventh book in the Ariella series. Another tiny shock in the series of shocks in her world. She'd already read the book to the end with rising tension, not because of the mystery but because of Ariella and Pereh's parting. The further apart they went and what was happening to each of them became more complicated, she tensed even more, waiting for the moment at which they would be reunited. She couldn't bear the parting—because of them. When she reached the end of the book, not only was the mystery far from being solved, but Ariella and Pereh didn't meet.

A brief afterword concluded the book, which said that the author, Prospero Juno, "died in unfortunate circumstances", and Ori wondered as she read it, and she herself was surprised by this wondering, if there were circumstances surrounding death that *weren't* unfortunate. Mr. Juno had rented a car on his trip to the United States and it had led him the way of all flesh: in Texas, on his way from California to New York, he fell asleep at the wheel and didn't complete his magnum opus. His wife claimed that he was in the middle of the eighth and final volume of the series, which was to bring it to a brilliant conclusion—'grand finale' was the term that appeared in the afterword, and Ori had to wait until the next day to discover its meaning in a dictionary from the school library.

Ariella lost her way in the marshes of the Kingdom of Spring as she searched for Napoli of Darkness from where the albino emissary of delusion had come. Pereh had been captured by a tribe of sorcerers in the mists of the western reaches of the Kingdom of Summer, they plucked his soul from his body and imprisoned it in a flask of copper, a metal that was usually lethal for his kind. Prospero Juno had been killed in an accident. His body had been found in the dead of night beside his overturned car. The car was empty, and if indeed his typewriter and part of the manuscript of the final volume had been in it, as his wife claimed, then they had been taken together with his soul. Ori remained alone, outside the pages of the book, shocked, waiting.

The car drove into the hospital parking lot. She and Sigal followed Ophir's parents. The fear of the glass guillotine of the doors gnawed at her as they opened before them. As they hurried through the corridors she tried to shut down her senses, blinker her eyes, stop up her nose, her ears, but in vain: fragments of physical torture filtered through to her, her whole skin bowed to the siege, cracking like wax before flames.

Ophir was lying on a bed whose backrest was slightly elevated to enable him to read. His forehead bore a dressing and his chest, too, was bandaged. He tried to lift himself into a sitting position when he saw them, groaned in pain and fell back into a partially supine position. He mother and father kissed his cheeks. Then they turned to an elderly lady, who was also angular with sinewy arms, sitting in a chair beside the bed. His mother went to her and kissed her on both cheeks. His father only nodded at her sullenly and avoided her eyes. She must be his grandmother, Ori thought.

She looked around. It seemed that nothing had changed since she had visited her mother. Only the patients' faces had changed, someone had peeled off the patients' faces during the last shift and stuck on others in their place. In any case most people aren't genuine and were only invented to be used as set decoration. Here it was again: the same gathering around, the same confusion of whispers, groans, and a thunderous and random burst of laughter that sounded detached and awkward in the room. And there is always one patient, a woman or a man, lying on the green sheets on his own, his eyes vacant, staring at the ceiling.

Ori was embarrassed. How could she talk with all these people around? It would have been easier if they were all unknown, but how do you find the balance between the nameless people filling the room and their ears listening to their conversation, and Ophir's parents and grandmother, who knew each other well.

She didn't have time to ponder the question. Ophir's mother said, "Ima, let's go to the cafeteria for a few minutes and get a drink, we'll let the children be alone for a while. And Shimshon, you come too. They need some privacy at their age."

As they left the room she and Sigal asked in unison, "How are you feeling? When are you getting out?" and then fell silent. Something thudded to the floor. The book Ophir had been reading, that had been quickly laid aside when they came in, had fallen. She and Sigal bent down together, banging their heads. "Ow!" Sigal yelled, and straightened up. Ori picked up the book. She looked at its green cover with an ink drawing of a stone fort and other figures. *The Begum's Millions* by Jules Verne.

Ophir gave them a tired smile. "What's up?" he asked. "Great," they again answered in unison, in a similar tone, unwillingly. "What's great? Something's happened between you. Had a fight?" Ophir said, and Ori was surprised by his acumen. But it isn't the first time he's shown it, she thought.

"What makes you think that?" Sigal demanded, and Ori kept quiet.

"Because you haven't looked at one another since you came in."

"So what?" Sigal protested, and then apparently sensed Ori's resentment, and added, "It's all Ori's fault. But I don't want to talk about it."

Ophir looked at Ori wonderingly. "I did something I shouldn't have, but I've already begged her pardon," Ori explained, and turned to Sigal, "I'm really sorry. I didn't mean it. And anyway . . . " but Sigal cut her short with a shrug, "You've got no respect for people. Do unto others as you would have them do unto you."

"Have you two come here to fight?" Ophir asked with a forced laugh that quickly turned into a wheeze. His hand went to his chest. Ori said, "Sigal, I'll do whatever you want, just tell me what."

"We'll see," Sigal said, and turned to Ophir again. "So how d'you feel?"

Ophir told them. The pain in his chest was awful. He had a broken rib and only by a stroke of luck, so the doctors said, had it not punctured a lung. Apart from that, they said that thanks to his young age the rib would knit within two or three weeks, but the real problem wasn't the rib, but that they couldn't yet tell what the outcome of the concussion might be. At the moment he had a slight inter-cranial edema, and they were waiting for the swelling to go down before they did a CT. When he saw that the situation he was describing was riveting them, he went into detail.

The truth is, Ori thought, the details of the report didn't really interest her at least. It was enough for her that Ophir would be home within a week, but Ophir's punctilious explanations, which repeated the doctors' words, dissipated the tension between her and Sigal, and she nodded, and from time to time asked for a clarification, as did Sigal. She was actually thankful for the lecture and before Ophir's fount of information dried up, his parents and grandmother came back.

"Now it's our turn," his mother sang gaily, "so don't tell all your stories," and his father shifted restlessly where he stood. "Maybe you'll leave us alone for a while, sweeties. You can wait in the corridor," she added cloyingly, which all sounded exaggerated to Ori.

They went into the corridor and the air laden with the smell of death assaulted Ori's nostrils. "I don't like it here," she said to Sigal, "I'm going outside."

To her surprise, Sigal followed her. The canopy of evening was woven from the killing blaze of the firmament, the curved blade of the moon at the end of May, the burnished impudence of the army of stars and the deafening clash of its spear- and arrowheads from Beersheba preening itself by the glow of its streetlights and windows, thousands of unnecessary jewels welcoming a beloved, and not knowing who is at the gate, who has come, and for what. What has come.

The thought tapped like an echo. Ori walked towards the bus stop at the front of the hospital, where a floodlight played on it. She was still holding the Jules Verne book. If Ophir could pinch books from the library and take them back after he'd read them, why shouldn't she do the same?

Sigal sat down next to her. Ori opened the book. Its pages were in low-quality dense print. What's the difference, in any case she wasn't taking in anything of what she was reading. And as if to disturb her already weak concentration, Sigal laughed, the sound of bells tinkling in the wind.

Ori looked at her. Sigal was looking to her right. The bench they were sitting on was made of cast concrete and bore graffiti written in correction fluid and marker pens. Ori leant over to see what had attracted her attention. Sigal's finger pointed at an inscription carved into the bench, 'From first grade and all threw school, Rimona and Aliza always rule'.

"It's not them. It's just two girls with the same name. This is Beersheba," Ori said.

"Oh, yes?" Sigal asked.

They jumped up and began searching for similar inscriptions. If Gvinush and Aliza had written it there wasn't even the tiniest chance they'd stop at one. Ori found the second one written in correction fluid on the post with the numbers of the buses that called at the stop. It was written vertically and they had to crane their heads sideways to read it: 'Rimona Peretz and Aliza Edri, queens of the class.'

"I was right," Sigal said, "they destroy everything they touch. Thou shalt not destroy."

"Yes," Ori said, following her lead, "everything."

Thus the alliance was re-forged. The mixing of blood alone was not enough. The root of the evil had to be seen, revealed, to push them into their enduring roles.

"Come on," Ori said, authority restored to her voice, no longer needing to ask, but to order. "There's something we forgot to ask Ophir."

———

The drive back to Netivot passed in a pensive silence. Irit stayed with her son in the hospital, despite the doctor's insistence that the boy could, and perhaps should be left on his own for the night. The hostility between Ophir's father and grandmother filled the car, but anyway she and Sigal had another matter to grapple with. They had stormed back into Ophir's room, she in the lead with Sigal one step behind her, and right away she'd asked, without even a nod at the three pairs of eyes staring at her, "How did Noam know?"

Ophir quickly regained his composure and said, "Later," and she and Sigal went out and wandered up and down the corridor for a long time, until they were called.

The father was in a hurry to get back to Netivot for a party meeting, and the grandmother was tired from her long stay at the hospital. They went inside to say goodbye and stood at his bedside. But this time his mother stayed in the room and Ophir told her with forced tiredness, "Ima, I've got a few things to say to Ori and Sigal," and she looked at them, especially Ori, and asked, "Are you sure?" Ophir nodded eagerly and she looked at them again with a smile that didn't reach her eyes. "Don't tire him out, sweeties," she requested. But Ori didn't give in. She didn't understand why his mother was raising obstacles, and she didn't care. She needed answers, so she said, "Don't worry, Mrs. Shriki," in her firm, cutting tone, and Irit reluctantly did as she asked.

"So how did he know that you go to a dance class?" Sigal asked.

"Except for you two and Josh, nobody else in school knows."

"Why Josh?" Sigal asked.

"Because he's the PE teacher and because I've got activities every evening, my mom asked him for an exemption for me. They had a real set-to when she asked him at the beginning of the year, and he got so mad that in every lesson he checks that I'm there and then sends me to sit on the bench."

"Josh," Ori said. "Josh," Sigal's voice was a weak echo. In the sixth Ariella book Ariella had to find the right note that would enable her and Pereh to enter the caves in the Mountains of Winter to escape a blizzard. The wind moaned and whistled through the crevasses and the tall conifers creaked as they swayed. Then Ariella grasped the secret of getting into the caves: it was not a constant word or note that would move the rocks blocking the entrance, but the correct note that would mediate between all the different kinds of natural music playing all around, and which varied accordingly. Ariella instructed Pereh to pile up three basalt rocks against a tree trunk and strike them at a given moment. Then a wonderful silence fell followed by the renewed sounds of the storm, but they were different.

That is how Ori felt in that blink of an eye: she wasn't in the hospital room but at the foot of a mountain and she was faced by a fateful mystery. The word 'Josh' in her mouth was as heavy as a coin. In one stroke she understood the finely woven web: the pure terror she'd seen in Ilanit's eyes and Gvinush's equanimity. Josh had told Judy and she, for reasons of her own, had decided to share the information with her favorite student, Gvinush, and the latter, seeking revenge against the three of them, had exploited the closeness being formed between Ilanit and Noam, and Ilanit's desire to appease her. She had incited Ilanit—and Ori had already seen her self-abnegation towards Gvinush in the hair episode—to set Noam on Ophir. What could be simpler? She had the perfect means. Ophir had willingly given himself to them. He goes to dance lessons.

She whispered her conclusions to Sigal as they sat down in the back seat of the Shriki family Peugeot, and Sigal nodded. And as Netivot was revealed before them, six streetlights penetrating the darkness, Sigal told her, "You know what? I forgive you for what you did."

"I didn't mean to read . . . "

"It doesn't matter," Sigal said, "because I didn't write the note you took."

Ori looked at her, astonished.

"I don't know where it's from. But if you give me all three verses I'll ask my father."

They got out by Ori's house, and Ori ran inside and got her notebook and walked Sigal home. Sigal's father knew where the verses were taken from. He dictated to them, haughtily: Isaiah chapter 6, verse 5; Jeremiah chapter 1, verse 7; and Ezekiel chapter 18, verses 31 and 32.

Ori went home happy. Two mysteries solved in one day, she told herself, but she waited two days, maybe three, before she opened the Books of the Prophets to check the source of the verses. They only had fully annotated Bibles in their house that the three of them, she and Asher and Ofra, used for their studies, and two of the books, Isaiah and Ezekiel, were in Asher's and Ofra's rooms. If she asked for them Ofra would stick her nose in and wouldn't let her alone. She could sense when Ori was lying. And if she took the books without permission she'd bring an even bigger load of trouble on herself, because in the past two weeks Ofra had become very possessive of her space, and every entry into her room in her absence was a *casus belli*. And yet the urge was pressing. She had to get her hands on the books. Asher was an easier target, she could easily pull the wool over his eyes; but she wouldn't have to, he'd let her have the book without any questions.

But as she stood outside Asher's room she heard muted shouting. Asher said, "But what do you care? Who I go with is my business." And Ofra replied, "You're only fifteen. You're a minor. She's using you. Do you know she can go to jail for what she's doing?" The anger in Asher's voice increased as he replied, "I'm using her too. And you stay out of it." Ofra, too, was heated, "Asher, I'm not arguing with you. If you don't put a stop to it, I will."

"Enough already. Don't you understand that I . . . "

"No! Judy's thirty-something. She's old enough to be your mother. I know that going with her makes you feel like a man, but it's sick. Sick."

Ori's heart sank. The exact meaning of the words wasn't important—going with—it sounded dangerous. Asher and Judy, why would Asher . . .

"I'm giving you two days to end it," Ofra delivered her verdict, "and then I'm going to Abba. I've got no problem with you telling him I smoke and don't do what he says and hang out with Zaguri and Shetreet. Your mental health is more important to me."

Ori stumbled back to her room, stunned. Judy and Asher . . . What's she got to do with him? Their picture, arguing behind the gym, rose before her and nauseated her. How hadn't she suspected . . . she hadn't eaten a thing since lunchtime but her stomach roiled and her gullet burned. No wonder he'd stopped asking about Gvinush. Judy, is she why he disappeared in the evenings? But how did it fit in with basketball practice? And what—no, no, she didn't even want to ask the questions but they formed in her mind despite her protestations, bringing them down: what do they do when they're together? Talk? Laugh? Hold hands? Even though she was alone, shut up in her room, she felt her cheeks flushing and her neck burning and itching.

She went to the bathroom to wash her face, and Ofra, despite the absentmindedness that characterized her, her somewhat sloppy posture, her vacant look, almost collided with her in the hallway and said, "Why've you gone as red as a beetroot? Maybe you caught a rash in the hospital?" and she didn't reply. Something was stuck in her throat and if she opened her mouth who knows what dark beast might spring out.

She had no choice. She focused her attention on the verses. She'd find a Bible in the library. No. No good. The library wouldn't lend her one and she'd have to pinch it; for some reason the idea made her shudder. No. Maybe she'd ask Sigal. No. Sigal wouldn't take it out of her house. Ah, why hadn't she thought of it before? Mama Elhayani. She'd have to make some kind of sacrifice, go visit her one afternoon. And she hated the very idea.

Mama Elhayani was a confused old lady. Over the past two years she'd had difficulty recognizing her granddaughter. She frequently thought she was Ofra, and on other, rarer occasions, that she was her younger sister who'd died of smallpox when she was Ori's present age. She had this habit of probing her body and saying, "What's this, you're all skin and bones. What man will want you?" and she did this when she thought she was Ofra, and enlisted all her knowledge of Hebrew for her. On other occasions she spoke to her in Moroccan, in words that Ori didn't understand, words unlike those that had infiltrated everyday language and were often used by her mother as part of her Hebrew. In Moroccan she spoke at length and her words were sprinkled with tears, perhaps the fact of her sister's death flashed in her brain.

Things hadn't always been like that. When she was younger she'd actually liked going to Mama Elhayani's house. There were guava trees in the front and the slow-flowing days of the summer vacation had been spent in their shade. One summer she and Ilanit had stretched sheets between four adjacent trees, and the dense guava foliage had provided them with shade. They decorated the camp—that's what they called this temporary structure—with paper cutouts and chains and drawings, and swore to live their whole life there, an oath that was broken a few days later when they had an argument over the beauty of Ilanit's paper cutouts. Every September the guavas ripened and their fragrance pervaded the opening of the school year. But halfway through fifth grade the order of things went awry in Mama Elhayani's mind and past and present and wishes for the future became all mixed up.

She put the visit off and one afternoon, without planning it, her feet led her to her grandmother's, who was sitting by the door as if waiting for her. Tea and dry cookies for dunking were there in a flash. They sat at the small kitchen table that was covered with a checkered oilcloth. She smiled and nodded unceasingly as her grandmother embarked on a long peroration in Moroccan, and she quickly gulped her tea and swallowed the cookies. And when Mama Elhayani said, "Ofra, *ya binti*, at long last you smell like a woman," she knew that the visit was over. She quickly went into the living room and pulled out a splendidly bound Bible from among her grandfather's holy books that covered an entire wall, and put it into her schoolbag. She couldn't escape the traditional kissing. Her grandmother kissed her cheeks three and four times, whispering excitedly, "A woman, *ya binti*, you're a woman."

———

It was hard for her to say that she understood anything of what she read in the Books of the Prophets. To be on the safe side she locked her bedroom door and devoured the opening chapters of each book lying down. The verses had a strange music and they tasted crunchy and lumpy on her tongue, like clumps of earth. There was no story in these books, of that she had no doubt. She summed up her impressions in her notebook: "The three prophets were angry men. They wanted to punish everybody, all the sinners. They managed to find lots of words to describe how wicked the Children of Israel were. They probably gave a lot of thought to it. The Prophet Isaiah says, 'Ah, sinful nation, a people laden with iniquity, a seed of evildoers, children that are corrupters: they have forsaken the Lord, they have provoked the Holy One of Israel unto anger, they are gone away backward.' The words sound beautiful at first, until you realize what they mean. The Prophet Jeremiah likes describing destruction. He's got a lot of words, too, 'to root out, and to pull down, and to destroy, and to throw down.' I like Ezekiel best because at least he sees things, all kinds of interesting creatures with wings and four faces and enveloped in flames and *electrum*."

Strange, when she wrote the word '*electrum*' its form seemed different from the flood of white-gray light she imagined spreading inside the walls. No, it was a kind of seared curtain of light, a deep brightness that surrounded the holy creatures, the wheels or animals. Even Ezekiel, with all the beauty he saw, spouted rage similar to that of Isaiah and Jeremiah. He, too, wanted to punish the sinners.

She understood the Prophets. She, too, wanted to punish. She recalled what Sigal had said about Gvinush and Aliza, "they destroy everything they touch". How true. Isaiah gave her the words: destructive girls. They had destroyed Ilanit. Jeremiah showed her the way, because his series of descriptions of destruction ended with the words, 'build and plant'. And Ezekiel's luminous, scorching *electrum* gave her the means. She knew what she must do.

Enticing Ilanit, who wanted her friendship, was easy. The day after the visit she went over to Ori and asked, "Is Ophir okay?"

Ori could see how much guilt there was in the question, but she offered her no help. She just gave her a blank look and walked away. But now she needed Ilanit. Towards evening she called her, as the books whispered in her mind, and apologized for rebuffing her. She had something important to tell her, she said, but it had to be face to face, maybe she could come by her house in the morning and they'd walk to school together, like in the old days?

Ilanit was expecting her excitedly. Her mother reported that she was waiting on the verandah. But Ori was in no hurry to go to her. As they were walking side by side, she told her, "Asher was asking about you."

"No! What? Why? Do you swear?"

"I'm telling you. He heard you singing from the gym door. Were you really singing?"

Ori knew that Ilanit sang, she'd heard her singing for Gvinush and Aliza, and she'd been surprised. She knew all about Ilanit's anxieties and fears and lack of self-confidence in her voice. They'd started with singing lessons in second grade. They'd hated Nira the music teacher from the moment she'd walked into the classroom. Her walk irritated them, the tapping of the heels she wore grated on them. Afterwards they'd said to each other, She's far too beautiful to be a music teacher. She's probably a spy. As she called out Ilanit's name there was venom in her voice. She drew out the 's' in her surname, Blasssco, so that it sounded like the ugliest word there is. Then without further ado, she'd taken some stenciled pages from her bag and ordered Aliza, who was sitting at the front, to hand them out, and she, that pain in the ass, had given them out with great ceremony, as if she'd been entrusted with a wad of bills and was distributing to the rest of them, the beggars, with a supercilious air. The song was called 'The Song of Comradeship'. Nira played a recording of the song a few times and ordered them to repeat the opening lines. As they sang she closed her eyes. When they got to the end of the first verse, she opened her eyes and hissed, "Somebody here is flat."

Silence fell in the classroom.

"Somebody here is flat," Nira repeated, spitting the syllables one by one, "let's go back to the beginning."

They sang, and again Nira's eyes closed and again they opened in rebuke, scanning the desks, "Somebody here is flat, somebody here has got the voice of a donkey." She fell silent for a moment and nodded her head as if in thought. Then she said, "All right, this time just the boys."

The boys sang harmoniously and Nira sighed, "I was sure it was one of the boys, they're the ones that usually sing flat at this age," she said. "Now, only the girls sitting in the right-hand half of the room sing." And the girls sitting in the right-hand half of the room gave voice to the song. Nira covered her ears with her hands as if the singing was painful. "Enough, enough, I've got it, it's someone in this half of the room. Now, only the girls in the right hand row will sing."

They were both gripped by a sudden fear. Ori knew that Ilanit didn't have a musical ear and couldn't sing, and Nira was closing in on her. She was about to divide the class into single desks and point at her, "Here's the girl with the tin ear and the donkey's voice."

Not one child would ever let her forget it. She thought she must act, create a diversion before Ilanit was discovered and castigated. But she sat paralyzed on seeing Ilanit's paling face and Nira's sharp teeth, which she now showed in her sweet smile. Ilanit was among the last eight girls in the class. She was trapped. Before twenty-four pupils she was forced to squawk on her own. Since then she'd only hummed quietly to herself. Perhaps her new friendship with Gvinush had given her confidence, and maybe in the days they hadn't spoken a latent, surprising talent had burst out in her. In any event, Ori had made up her mind to exploit her passion.

"Yes," Ilanit said, "I was singing. But Rimona and Aliza said I was out of tune."

"And you believe them? Asher thinks you've got a great voice. He asked why you don't come over to see me more often."

Ilanit studied her.

"And you know something?" Ori went on, "he's right."

"So what does he want?"

"Come over this afternoon. I've got a great idea for getting you two together."

"I don't . . . I don't know what to say," Ilanit began, and immediately put her arms round Ori and hugged her. "Thank you, you're the best friend in the whole world," she said.

That day she avoided making eye contact with Sigal; she didn't want to involve her. She secretly passed her a note right under Ilanit's nose and promised to explain everything next day. Ilanit didn't leave her side all day, she even came to sit next to her and chatted, told her stories about how disgusting Gvinush and Aliza were, about their selfishness and how they used her, until Elisheva, who'd had enough of her incessant chatter throughout the Bible class, ordered her back to her place. Her excitement didn't even stop when she got to Ori's house in the afternoon. The punishment arena had been meticulously prepared in Asher's room, and Ori led her there.

"This is what Asher's room looks like now," she told her and let Ilanit take it in, "what d'you think?"

"It's nice. It's a pity he took the posters down."

"Ah, he doesn't like them anymore."

"So what . . . "

"Well," Ori said, suddenly nervous, "we've grown apart a bit and I think we weren't . . . "

"Yes, but we're good now."

Ori nodded. She licked her lips. "Look, what I thought was . . . " she said, "but would you like something to drink first?"

"No, no; I'm dying to know what you've planned."

"Well, it's like this, ah . . . Asher thinks you've got a great voice. So I thought, why not record you singing on his tape recorder, and I'll play the cassette for him. Like by chance. I won't tell him we recorded it specially, just that you're practicing for the end-of-year show. I know he'll ask for the cassette. And after he's heard it a few times you come over when he's home, like by chance, and then . . . "

Ilanit looked at her. There was admiration in her eyes. A glassy look. "Ori," she said, "You're a genius, a genius," and again she threw herself at her in a hug.

"Sure you don't want something to drink?"

"No, let's do the recording."

"Okay, but first I need some water and the bathroom," Ori said and hurried out. She really was thirsty, her throat was dry and she had to settle her breathing, quell the spasms in her diaphragm. She hadn't imagined she'd be so tense.

Ilanit waited obediently on Asher's youth bed, stroking the cushions. She'd brought her a glass of water, just to be on the safe side. Pleased, she scanned the trap she'd set. A mole was still burrowing in her chest. "Have you thought about which song you'd like to record?" she asked.

"Yes," Ilanit replied, "Ofra Haza's 'Flash Gordon'. I think it works."

"Here's the microphone," Ori said, handing her the object in her hand.

It wasn't a microphone but the electrical heating element from Asher's aquarium. She remembered his lectures when he'd fitted it up at the end of last year's summer vacation. She'd pestered him to let her help with the fish, and he showed her how to feed them, how much food to sprinkle, how to transfer the fish to a small container when changing the dirty water, and what to do with the heating element when cleaning it. Never, he warned her, remove the element's glass cover while the unit was plugged in, and never, he made her swear, never, under any circumstances, touch the exposed element, whether it was plugged in or not. She examined the element curiously, the whole thing was two thin metal tubes coming out of the plastic base, coiling around and going back into it at right angles to each other.

Now the aquarium in his room was empty and abandoned; all the fish had died during his evening absences. "Why don't you give them to one of your friends," their mother told him each morning he took out another dead fish, "it's a shame. Cruelty to animals." And that afternoon Ori had spread a cloth over the aquarium to hide it, removed the glass cover from the heating element, plugged it into a socket with a switch that she'd also hidden, under the bed. The switch was presently off.

"That's a weird microphone," Ilanit remarked.

"It's one of the latest ones. Like Madonna's. Ofra told Asher to buy it," Ori explained, and Ilanit nodded.

"You ready?" Ori asked, demonstratively placing her finger over the tape recorder's buttons.

"Yes," Ilanit replied. She cleared her throat and bought the element to her lips. Ori waited tensely. She had to be spot on. Hold it, hold it, yes! The element was touching her lips. Now! She hit the switch with her foot.

Everything happened all at once. The element began sizzling and humming and Ilanit's body responded with tremors.

She couldn't cry out because the metal stuck to her lips as it heated up. She managed a few choked sounds and trembled, trembled.

Sparks flew from the socket and hit Ori's bare shin. She hit the switch again with her heel and the room was silent.

The element fell from Ilanit's hand. She collapsed onto the floor, wailing.

"Now you're clean," Ori told her, deaf to the incoherent sounds of weeping. "Without all your lies. The *electrum* has purified your mouth."

"You're mad!" Ilanit screamed, and as she uttered the words the pain that surely seared her lips hit her consciousness, because her voice rose and the last syllable became a wail. She screamed again and stood up, covering her mouth with her hand, and ran, skidding on the rug, steadying herself on the doorknob, and fled.

"What was that?" her mother asked as Ilanit slammed the front door.

"Nothing," Ori replied, "I told her I don't want to be her friend anymore," and she went to disassemble the device she'd built, screw the glass cover back into place, and get rid of the scorched socket.

She took the tape recorder to her own room. It was Ofra's and she was only prepared to lend it to her on one condition: that she paid for it with a story. And if she didn't like the story, she said, she'd find another way of collecting the debt. Ori happily gave her promise. She knew how much Ofra would love the story of her sophisticated revenge. Ofra listened avidly, rarely interrupting. When she told her about the enticement, for instance, how she'd drawn Ilanit in, Ofra muttered, "Like Asher's interested in girls your age," and Ori didn't let on that she knew what she was talking about, she just put on a puzzled look and went on with the story.

When she finished, Ofra laughed aloud. "You'll become a real Elhayani in the end," she said, "it's in the blood. That's all. It's in our nature to be tough guys, to just listen to ourselves." She suddenly sniffed. "What's that stink?" she yelled. But she didn't have to say anything to Ori, because Ori's skin—now the bristling was spreading all over it, quivering waves—told her.

She leapt up and ran to the kitchen. Their mother was there, choking again, banging her chest with her fist, and the freshly slaughtered chicken she had been searing was smoking and stinking. Ori banged her on the back until a racking cough flecked with blood burst out, allowing her to breathe.

"Is everything all right?" Ofra called from the living room. She had distanced herself from their mother since she had set their father against her.

"Yes," she answered, "only the chicken's a bit burnt."

"All right, tell her that I'm just going out onto the verandah. That smell's driving me crazy."

Her mother was weeping, perhaps from the smoke. "Ima," Ori told her, "if you don't tell Abba today . . . "

"No," her mother said, "you listen to me. If we tell him he'll panic and cancel our trip to the graves of the sages tomorrow. And he'll take me for tests in the emergency room instead. It's for my problem that I'm going. I don't trust that Doctor Goldwag."

"But he's not the only doctor, you can go . . . "

"No," her mother cut her short, "Rabbi Danino's wife said the trip will help me, that I'll get a blessing there that will cure me. The Baba Sali's water isn't any good for me. And when your father and I get back you can tell him whatever you like."

"On one condition," Ori said, grimly, "that right now you sign the consent form for the school trip in two weeks time."

SEVEN

Horev

IN THE SMALL HOURS of the night at Amuqa near Safed, close
to the grave of Yonatan Ben-Uziel, Sylvia Elhayani collapsed.
Oh, why are they called 'the small hours' if the order of the
world goes awry in them? Ori knew the precise time. A dagger
turned over inside her and she woke up frightened. The clock
in her room showed 03:25, and the feeling of power that had
flooded her being since punishing Ilanit, turning it into light
and electrified wings, vanished. At dawn their father called
from the hospital in Haifa and she answered. She was awake
and he, his voice angry and rasping, wanted to know why she
wasn't asleep. She didn't know what to do with his question.
She asked, "Is Ima all right?"

"No," he said. "Where's Ofra?"

"Asleep," she answered, "it's still early."

"Then get her up and send her to phone . . . " he said. "No,
until that one wakes up I'll run out of tokens. Tell her to call
this number," and he dictated a number.

Waking Ofra wasn't easy. Ori got tired of shaking her by
the shoulder and yelled into her ear, "Ofra, wake up, Ima's in
hospital!"

Her shouts woke Asher too. The three of them sat at the
kitchen table, exchanging gloomy glances over the glasses of tea
Ofra had made, digesting her brief, dry report. Their mother
had been rushed to hospital in the middle of the night, she'd

lost consciousness, apparently from lack of oxygen, and when she came round she'd coughed up blood; on hearing this detail Ori lowered her head. They had decided to keep her in over the weekend for tests and observation, and their father had put Ofra in charge of the Sabbath preparations.

"But you can't cook if your life depended on it," Asher grumbled.

"There's a chicken Ima koshered and prepared. How hard can that be? You stick it in the oven for a half hour and that's it. We've got Saturday lunch, and I'll think up something for Friday evening, I'll get a recipe book from Persian Rosa."

Ofra's cooking skills were a disaster. For Friday evening she decided to make a dairy meal. Rosa advised her to make a lazy man's pizza—soak slices of *challah* in milk, put them on a tray, smear them with ketchup, sprinkle with canned olives and cover with a layer of yellow cheese. She could make tomato soup with cream, and rice, she suggested, and serve it with a finely diced green salad, with a little olive oil, salt, pepper and cottage cheese. "And believe me, they'll be over the moon."

Ori had listened to their conversation.

At dinner on Friday evening, Asher said—Ofra insisted that he say the blessing over the wine like their father, and he held the wineglass in a shaking hand and mumbled the blessing—"Listen, you've set new records for gross." The baking had not been a success. The yellow cheese had melted but the milk-soaked *challah* remained soggy and stodgy. The rice was burnt—Ofra forgot it on the gas; the soup had turned—Ofra had added sour cream that was well past its sell-by date; the salad was disgusting—Ofra had added the cottage cheese to the vegetables and the lumps of cheese, discolored by their contact with the oil, were bitter to the taste.

They did not speak except for the necessary requests and instructions. A cloud of terror hung over them. The air was explosive. One wrong movement and this machine—which they called home but was only a weave of taut strings about to break, but were orchestrated—would break down completely. Ori felt in her bones that if anything went out of kilter between the three of them, in that other place in the world—where their hearts beat above the hospital bed which each of them had surely imagined, green, sterile, cold, a step away from oblivion—cracks would appear. And the reverse—if anything happened there, then the space between them would be rent, never to be set right.

Asher took off in the middle of the meal, and Ofra called after him, "Asher, remember, I gave you two days."

Ori asked innocently, "Two days for what?"

Ofra answered brusquely, "None of your business, and help me clear the table. What a mess the two of you have left. You eat like animals."

Ofra went out too, after putting the dishes in the sink; an insistent whistle came from the door. Ofra wiped her hands on her apron and took it off. "How do I look?" she asked Ori, and Ori followed her to the door. The two tall boys were standing in front of the verandah, laughing.

Ori remained alone. She read the Bible books again, the three Books of the Prophets, but she was no wiser. She was restive and thought a walk would do her good. Not long ago, on her walks to the old Arab orchard and back, she discovered that movement energized her brain, that after a few minutes of cadenced walking her mind settled, became clear.

There was only a hint of chill in the streets from which the residents of Netivot absented themselves at this hour, the hour of Sabbath Eve dinner. She saw lighted windows, shadows moving in them, she heard the clatter of forks on plates, laughter she heard, singing, arguments and curses.

Her feet led her. She passed Ilanit's house, who hadn't been at school for two days. How had she explained her puffed lips, the burns on them, to her parents? And past that street she went. To where?

She didn't know, she was distracted and tired and only when she left the area of streets she knew, she realized that something else was guiding her footsteps—a thread humming like a string connected to her nape, and bristling spreading from it throughout her, pulling her along. She let it lead her.

On reaching her destination she realized what it was. Could it be possible that all this time she had actually been following Asher? Now she saw him standing at the front door of a single-story house, ringing the bell, and a woman in a robe welcoming him, opening the door for him and hugging him. Even though the woman's hair was wrapped in a towel and blurred her features, Ori recognized her by her figure: Judy.

What courage they both had, she thought. He comes to her house. And where was Josh? She went into the yard and circled the house. The string in her nape became a whip, lashing and cutting. Were the lashes sending her away or drawing her closer, leading her between the scenes? The living room window was open and the drapes, two pieces of white embroidered weave, were open too. She stood on tiptoe and peered inside. She was just tall enough to look over the windowsill and see a couch at right angles to the window. But first came the sounds: from inside the house, which was hidden from her, the clash of skillets and pots. Someone was in the house apart from Judy and Asher, who was sitting beside her, his head on her bosom, as she stroked his hair. Asher was complaining but his voice was soft as he said, "My sister's found out about us somehow."

"What's she found out?" Judy asked.

"I'm not sure," Asher replied, "but she knows enough and she's threatening to tell my father." He stopped, while Judy's fingers combed his hair. Then he said, "My mother's in hospital in Haifa."

"Poor boy," Judy responded in her usual, eager voice that grated with her words, "then you need some pampering."

Asher smiled. Ori couldn't remember when she'd seen him smile that way, tremendous happiness emerging through the cloud of concern over his face.

And then Josh came into view.

Her heart beat faster. The pounding of her body that she felt in several places, a bird fluttering in her throat and beating its wings against her chest and scratching her guts. She must . . . but the thought remained uncompleted. Judy extended an inviting hand to Josh and he took it. What was grating in this scene? Yes, Josh's upper body was naked and it was different from their father's chest who, now and again, especially in summer, went around without a shirt. Their father's chest was smooth and sunken and his skin-covered ribs protruded. Josh had a muscular barrel chest with a fuzz of hair round his nipples—two dark pink rings sunk in a freckled sea—that crossed the length of his belly. He had a small paunch. He sat down on the other side of Asher and stretched out his legs on the coffee table.

Ori's head was spinning, the lighting in the room dimmed. And her fingers, supporting her standing body, curled like talons and dug into the wooden sill, and her calves trembled. She was about to fall. But she had to see, the string governing her movements would keep her upright even if her body betrayed her. Asher straightened up from his partially supine position and sat trapped between the two, still smiling. Josh's arm went around his neck, his hand clasped his jaw, forcing his mouth open. Does it hurt? Ori wondered.

"You beautiful thing," Josh said, his voice thickening, "you beautiful, beautiful thing," and his mouth crushed against Asher's waiting lips.

The doctors still hadn't found out what had gone wrong with Sylvia's body. But not only her body had been damaged. Some element of reality had been cleft, had strayed. Now Ori realized that life hanging by a thread she had imagined was nothing but an illusion. Her parents came home on Sunday afternoon, gathered the three of them in the kitchen, and told them. What was there to tell—their mother is ill, perhaps even critically. The nature of her illness was still unknown to the doctors. At first they thought it was tuberculosis because of her coughing up blood, but in the end they rejected that possibility.

In the next few weeks she would have to undergo a series of tests, and the three of them would have to manage and help out at home. Their father turned to Asher, who since Friday Ori couldn't look at without feeling her cheeks burning, the gray heat of the shock in her belly, the defilement radiating from him.

"Asher," he said, "most of the load will be on you. Your mother isn't able to carry on working at the day center, and I'll be losing time at work. We haven't got any way of bringing in money. I'll talk to the plant manager today and ask him to take you on for evenings at first, until the summer vacation starts."

It was hard to miss the look of satisfaction on Ofra's face as she heard this. In the struggle between her and Asher she held the upper hand, even if she had done nothing to decide it. Asher wouldn't have time to hang out with Judy. And with Josh, Ori reminded herself and was frightened by the thought, Ofra doesn't know it, but Josh is involved too.

Asher protested. He got up from his chair angrily.

"No!" he said, "I've got basketball practice in the evening. And in the summer vacation there's a basketball camp up north. Josh has already arranged for me to go."

"Forget it," their father said tiredly, "and I'm not arguing with you, understand? Maybe next summer."

It seemed that summer had come with her father's very words. It came from the lengthening days of the end of May and the withered licentiousness of the thistles, from their dry, almost dying heads, abandoned to the parching brightness. It burst forth from the clearness of the sky and from the stickiness of Popsicle wrappers, broke out from television programs and from bodies shedding clothes, the lessening of clouds, from birds fleeing the voiding of the wind, and Ori could no longer avoid admitting its presence. She knew all its signs and chose to hold herself back from them. But there was always one afternoon when her refusal was shattered. The asphalt shone, expelling with a roar the pockets of heat it had collected throughout the morning into the still air.

That's what happened at the very moment she left the house and walked to the orchard: summer arrived. The heaviness of the town's weight hastened to her, the twisted, broken network of asphalt, of the streets, the sprawl of the neighborhoods, the scorched trees, the lone flight of a magpie, the air searing the windpipe, taut as a canopy over the tiled roofs and tarred ceilings of the housing projects, and the bright light of early June, the fumes of furnaces blowing in her face.

Sigal was waiting in the orchard, reading under a fig tree. They sat side by side in silence, and the quiet between them was not that quiet, of the first time, when they lay beside Ophir on the blanket, and the world came to their eyes, their breathing. It was a different quiet. A dense mass of charcoal.

Finally, Ori got up to go. "I'm going to be busy for the next few weeks," she said, "and I won't be coming here."

Sigal nodded. Sylvia had collapsed surrounded by people from Netivot. The news of her illness was in the public domain. "Will you be going on the school trip next week?"

"We'll see," Ori said.

And really, what remained besides waiting to see how the schism in the world would heal? She saw Sigal at school, at recess, but no longer in the afternoons, except for once when Ophir came home. They went to visit him, taking small, silly gifts they found in the municipal market, sneaking through the hole in the fence by the limestone hill and circling the stand of eucalyptus. Ophir's broken rib made it hard for him to move, and from time to time a wince of pain replaced the twitching nose, and his face was milkier than usual. But the sparkle returned to his eyes and for one sweet hour Ori forgot the darkness awaiting her at home.

Darkness. Only when her life returned to touch upon the routine—which was her due, for she was still a little girl and the reality owed her that at least, to submit to her desires, to bow her head to the possibility of happiness—only then the word 'darkness' popped into her mind: only when she left the confines of the house, when she was far enough away to compare, to separate darkness from darkness, light from light. The rest of the time she liked staying at home, being with her mother, or alone, with the Bible that she read incessantly.

Her mother had decided to prepare her, and she resigned herself to it. She'd come home from school, change, and go into the kitchen. Every day they cooked something different. Cooking became an urgent, vital need now that Asher was working after school and had a big appetite, and Ofra, who was set free from the moment that Ori took her place, would come home from her roaming as night fell, no less hungry.

Lunches and suppers were eaten in silence. Only the tastes and aromas of the dishes spoke on behalf of the diners. Like all languages, theirs had a hidden syntax and latent wisdom that dictated its logic. Ori came to know that her mother was fully acquainted with the various sciences: the science of spices and the science of time, the science of herbs and the science of boiling and cooling, the science of liquids and the science of solids. And between the rules of these sciences were hidden small beliefs that had nothing at all to do with them, tractates that mapped the world: with which hand you sprinkle salt, and in which direction the knives should point in the cutlery drawer, what is the power of upside-down glasses, and even more.

From the kitchen to the space of the house, what do tilted pictures tell, shoes whose soles face heavenwards, tears in clothes, leaning against doorjambs, objects that fell and were damaged. The space was replete with signs and omens, overt or covert: a cockroach that crossed the house at night could change a life; a careless bird that collided with a windowpane bore a message from the future; a touch that bites the skin like ice could decide perplexity. The sophisticated patterns of growth attested to the course of fate more than the newscasts. Yes, everything had meaning and implications, trifling ceremonies that reformed and healed the universe, or blocked the path of approaching evil.

When her mother went for the tests—Ori didn't know what a series of tortures it would be, but envisioned it; needles and syringes, blood, and lying on bare, freezing metal plates. She immersed herself in the Books of the Prophets. Isaiah, Jeremiah and Ezekiel rapidly wearied her. The Prophets repeated themselves lengthily and possessed a haughtiness that repelled her. On the other hand, and perhaps in their light, stories she knew from her school lessons took on a new life. They weren't the source of test questions, riddles exploited by the teachers to embarrass students in front of their friends, waves of boredom carried from the past on sleepy voices. No. Astonished, she read the stories of Abraham, Isaac and Jacob, and eagerly the history of Moses and Joshua and Samuel and finally reached the Books of Kings, Elijah, the mad-eyed, fanatical prophet who crisscrossed Israel giving auguries and plotting, and slaughtering and resurrecting, and his ambitious disciple, Elisha. And slowly understanding dawned on her:

She wrote in her notebook: "Sometimes I hate Elijah and sometimes I like him. He's not a good person. And he's bad-tempered all the time. Why are those prophets always angry? Why isn't there a story where they're laughing or having fun? Maybe it's the way they are. Not just anyone's chosen to be a prophet, and to be chosen you've got to be a hard person. Like Ofra. Elijah's a bit like her. He thinks he's always right and that everybody's got to do what he says. If they don't, he gets really mad. I hate that. What I like about him is that he stands up for what he wants, and that he's not ungrateful and he helps people too, like that woman in Zarepath whose son died and he brought him back to life. He stretched himself upon him three times (what does 'stretched himself' mean? What for?) But he also slaughtered a lot of people, and told Jezebel that the dogs would eat her corpse. Elisha is nicer than him. He doesn't go shouting at the kings. And he does all kinds of miracles for his disciples, and fixes the water of the river, and finds an axe for somebody, and he raised the Shunamite woman's son from the dead, he dropped everything and ran to her house and lay upon the child (I think that means that he really laid on him or something) and warmed him with his body until the child waxed warm (what does 'waxed warm' mean? I must check!!!) And he did it seven times. The only thing I didn't like in his stories was that he took the bears out of the forest and sent them to kill the little boys who mocked him. What was that in aid of?"

So what, she thought afterwards. She, too, had enjoyed the pleasure of rage and vengeance. But she'd got nothing out of it. There were other aspects of prophecy she still didn't know about. She reread the three verses she'd written in her notebook:

Woe is me, for I am a man of unclean lips, and I dwell in the midst of a people of unclean lips

Say not, I am a child: for thou shalt go to all that I shall send thee, and whatsoever I command thee thou shalt speak

Make you a new heart and a new spirit: for why will ye die, O house of Israel? For I have no pleasure in the death of him that dieth.

———

They joined a riddle of the kind that Ariella was good at solving. And now, as she read the Bible incessantly and was used to its strange language, and dwelling on the meaning of one word or another bothered her less, now she could see the whole being formed from the parts. The verses had been sent to her. They were messages. Three tidings. The first verse marked her, put her feelings into words; the second relieved her fears; and the third, the third told her exactly what she must do.

———

Two days before the school trip she was still undecided about going. The consent form had been signed and handed to Elisheva, and although it had been handed in some weeks late, she didn't complain. Because of the recent events with Noam and Ophir, which had totally shocked her, she said. And when she heard about Sylvia Elhayani's condition—she'd heard by chance, in the grocery store, she noted, setting herself apart from the gossipmongers she constantly condemned in her Bible class—she asked Ori if she was sure about going on the trip. And Ori replied, "It depends. Can I cancel at the last minute?" and Elisheva replied, "If circumstances necessitate it."

That day Netivot was hit by a sandstorm, a cold wind blew off the desert, glass-like and prickly from the grains of sand. The town was filled with yellowish air. The sun, mummified in the haze, was close to disappearing, and the little birds, brown from the summer, fell silent and senseless in the heat. In the middle of a geography lesson Ori was hit by a sudden fear. She stood up and said urgently to Zion the teacher—a pimply man whose watery eyes stared into space as he explained to the seventh grade students about the hiking routes waiting for them on their trip to the southern Negev desert—that she had to leave.

"Wait until recess," he told her, "this lesson is important for our trip."

"It's not to the bathroom," she replied.

"Then where to?"

"I can't sit here. I've got to go."

"Come on," Gvinush said, surprisingly, "let her go. That one's completely freaked out, and she'll only argue with you for an hour."

"No," Zion said, "you'll sit in your place till the end of the lesson."

And she sat, she forced herself to sit if only to rebut Gvinush's accusation, and nervously drummed her fingers on the desktop. Ilanit pinned her with one of the angry looks she'd send in her direction. The burns on her lips were healing, and only her speech was somewhat impaired when she used certain consonants, like 's', 'ts' and 'sh'. With hand signals and tilted head Sigal asked her why she had to go. Ophir had still not come back to school.

The bell released her. She shouldered her bag and hurried out, passing Zion who put out an arm to stop her, but she evaded him and started running, cutting through the desert-laden air and panting. That's how she reached home, without air in her lungs, and that's how she knew she'd find her mother, lying on the couch and fighting for breath, even though the shutters were all closed and the fan was on in the living room, blowing cool air towards her. Her hands were at the base of her neck, on her collar bones.

"I . . . can't . . . breathe," her mother gasped.

"I know," Ori said.

Her test had come. She rubbed her hands together and stood facing her supine mother. "Close your eyes and spread your arms out," she ordered her mother. Her mother, short of breath, complied. Her fluttering eyelids and matted lashes, and her hair stuck to her sweaty skin, highlighted the gray of her face.

Ori took a deep breath. Her hands were warm from the rubbing. She brought them to her mother's chest and she, too, closed her eyes. Then she laid her hands on her chest, imagining her mother's lungs emptying of the infection contaminating them, of all the filth liable to rot the flesh. "Live!" she thought with all her might, "be well! I'm telling you to be well!"

Three times she lay her hands on her and took them off, rubbing them together each time, and on the third time she was answered by the sound of her mother's breathing stopping, and then a dense bout of coughing that made her mother straighten her back, straighten up, put her bare feet down onto the floor. Then she folded, pressing her belly against her knees and coughing, coughing. Blood spurted from her mouth onto the floor, onto Ori's legs, who was standing before her, stunned, until the coughing stopped for a moment, the tiny moment her mother needed to touch her with a trembling hand and shake her out of her paralysis. Ori leapt to the phone to call an ambulance.

———

She didn't miss the school trip. Her mother was hospitalized and her father was staying with her. There was no one to stop her, and she had her own reasons. When she stood in line with the other children at the bus door, Elisheva again asked her if she was doing the right thing, and Ori replied firmly with vigorous nods. Sigal, too, who was sitting next to her, probed her gently and she rebuffed her questions. "I've got to go on this trip," she said.

The bus was swallowed up in the desert.

"Who was the genius that thought up the idea of sending a group of kids south in the heat of summer?" Sigal asked her as she did what the other girls were doing: wetting a shirt and winding it round her head.

Ori didn't even bother getting into the shade and stood in the burning sun, giving herself up to the scorching heat hitting her head. She didn't drink much from her water bottle, just enough to moisten her throat, to wash away the bolus of the *hamsin* stuck in it. As the day went on her senses gradually dulled: as they walked along one of the dry river beds and listened to Zion's tale about the origins of the strawberry tree and its red trunk; when they stopped to rest, and the boys jeered at the girls; when, at sunset, they came to the Bedouin encampment not far from Sdeh Boker.

She watched the children attack the trays of roast meat and rice and the baklava that was served for dessert. She hadn't eaten a thing all day and felt her organs melting from hunger, white hot in this void, floating. On the bus, as they drove from one location to another, a few of the girls, Shirli and Anita and Rita, offered to share their snacks with her—they'd all brought the same, cheese- and barbecue-flavored—she didn't understand why. Perhaps out of compassion or pity. Two feelings whose meaning she did not yet know.

After the meal they erected a tarpaulin in the middle of the encampment to separate the boys from the girls. She opened her sleeping bag next to Sigal, from whom the other girls had moved away. They were by themselves close to the eastern wall of the camp. The teachers slept in their own tent that Zion put up.

She waited until she heard the sound of the soft snoring and the even, regular breathing of the sleep of the just. She possibly fell asleep herself or into a doze. Whatever the case, there was a moment in the middle of that night, as she lay on her back, her eyes open to the darkness of the camp, when she knew she was the only one awake in the entire desert.

She carefully slid out of her sleeping bag and stole to the tent door, parted the flap and went out into the chill of the night. The rattle of the generator that fed the floodlight over the encampment could not overcome the clarity of the silence, the depth of the wilderness. It drowned in them. She started walking, moving away from the encampment, a latent sense showing her the way.

Nobody knew where Mount Horev, the Mount of Desolation, was. With uncharacteristic daring she had inquired of Rabbi Danino about it before the trip, and he had answered her questions in astonishment. God had been revealed to Moses at the foot of Mount Horev in a pillar of fire, and to Elijah in a great wind, an earthquake, in fire and stillness. The name of the mountain is not derived, as numerous commentators hold, from the word 'desolation', for all the mountains in the desert are desolate. Then why, of all the mountains in the desert, is this once called Mount Horev? Because it is shaped like a sword, a *herev*, a word with the same Hebrew root. She assiduously read the description of the route that appears in the Book of Kings. Elijah walked from Beersheba for a whole day, and from there forty days and forty nights, without eating or drinking, until he reached Mount Horev. But she was already in the middle of the wilderness, just a few hours drive from Beersheba, so the distance she still had to cross was shorter. Her journey was shortened. She twisted her bare feet in the sand, in the awful cold, clutching her mother's nightgown around her, which she'd had to soak in bleach to remove the bloodstain of her first period. It's lucky the sleeves are long, she thought, and lucky that the night is so freezing: snakes and scorpions wouldn't venture out in this temperature. Thought followed thought, and she marched.

How long had she walked—how long did it take for lips to crack in the cold; for feet to be cut in the sand; for a frozen body to forget it is freezing. That was how long it took her to get there.

The mountain towered above her. It was shaped like a serrated, flawed blade, its point threatening to slice the firmament. A sword that fell from the hand of an angel in one of the heavenly battles and had fallen to rest on Earth. But there are no wars in heaven, there is eternal peace. Death and sickness are the lot of the inhabitants of Earth, of those dwelling on the face of the earth.

She climbed up the mountain. The light of the stars and the full moon was enough. The incline was gentle. The retama bushes, which afforded her handholds, grew in abundance there. A quarter of the way up the slope she saw the cave entrance, a cleft in the rock more than a cave. She stood on the sandy surface at the entrance. The stench coming from inside was of a rotting corpse mixed with moss, and she didn't dare pass it. She turned her back to it. Under different circumstances she would have had to wait, to see what would happen, what would come to the place. But her strength failed her, her patience snapped. She had not come to receive. Another desire beat inside her: to restore, to return what had been lent to her and which she detested. Two scenes came into her mind: Asher surrounded by Judy and Josh, who were caressing him, and her mother in their living room, coughing and spitting blood onto the floor. What was the point of it all?

She had been deceived. From the very beginning it had all been a lie, since that voice had restored her power of speech.

The itching and bristling, the promise—they had misled her. She had failed. Now she opened her mouth, on the sandy surface at the cave entrance, and before she called out she looked at the palms of her hands: the words appeared clearly on her skin, singing, dancing, whirling. She followed these raging waves, letters convoluting and flowing up her arm and shoulders, until they disappeared, close to her collarbones, under the skin of her neck, and crossed masses of muscle, fat, blood vessels. And there they stopped, pooling.

And she wanted them to be torn from her throat, she wanted to roar aloud.

"Take it!" she shouted, looking at the clean sky gathered above her, "I don't want it. Whatever it is, I don't need it, I don't want it anymore, I don't want it!"

"Take it."

"Take!"

        "I   don't   want   it."

     "Don't want   it."

               "Don't
          you under
             stand?"

"Taaaaaaaaaaaaaaake"

"I
don't
want
it."

The desolate expanses absorbed her shouts, silenced them. But she did not give up. She carried on raising her voice in a lament until she saw a figure wrapped in white, standing in the moonlight, looking at her from the foot of the mountain.

Her shout faded, she waited for the words of the figure.

———

"Ori!" the figure called her name and she recognized the voice. It was Sigal.

"What are you doing by yourself on the dune?" she asked.

Ori looked around her. Her feet were on a hill of sand, and although she was not at a great height she felt dizzy. She lost her balance and stumbled, fell to her knees. Sigal hurried to her and helped her up and steadied her. The day's early brightness dawned, a slash in the horizon, and the expanses were flooded with gold and became as spectral as exposed bones abandoned to the changing seasons. But the frost of the night still lingered in her veins and arteries and she shivered in that cold sunrise, holding on to Sigal.

They went back to the encampment in time for breakfast. Sigal insisted on feeding her and making her drink, and packed her things for her, and led her, stunned, sleepwalking, to the bus. Her listlessness touched the other giggling girls and they called her to come and sit among them. Their images were etched blurred on her consciousness and she was unable to say which of them welcomed her and who grimaced at the gesture in resignation. And there, on the bus, surrounded by students cackling with laughter, the weight of the loss fell upon her and a tiny sob broke deep in her throat; but when she opened her mouth to release it, she emitted the groan of a shot animal, felled in its flight, surprised by the pain and refusing to believe its meaning—the end of the body's battle. She burst into tears, and the other girls wept with her.

And we are put on earth a little space,
That we may learn to bear the beams of love
And these black bodies and this sunburnt face
Is but a cloud, and like a shady grove.
For when our souls have learn'd the heat to bear,
The cloud will vanish, we shall hear His voice . . .

(William Blake, *The Little Black Boy*)

ONE

April

THE WEATHERMAN HAD PROMISED RAIN—what a strange, overcast April—but the slanting slats of the blinds divided the clean, intense blue sky into a series of rectangles. From Ori's fourth-floor apartment, in whose west-facing wall a large window was set—an expanse of polished glass and wood revealing the building tops exposed to Tel Aviv's sea breezes—a beautiful day seemed to be suffusing the air. What time is it? Ori glanced at the wall clock hanging over the door to the kitchen: ten thirty. Late. She was usually awakened by Barak extricating himself from between the sheets, but turned over and stayed in bed for another hour or so.

Beyond the fog of half-sleep enveloping her she'd hear Alma's quiet protests and the deep, cheery chatter as Barak got her ready for kindergarten, and his hushed chiding, "Shh . . . Ima's still asleep," and Alma's muted giggles in response, too muted, almost conscious. And if she hadn't been just four and half years old—a smart little girl, quite the genius—Ori would have even suspected irony on her part. Because in those morning hours the three of them, she and Barak and Alma, were trapped in a game in which she was merely an extra, standing in the wings waiting for her cue, and the lead roles were reserved for them, for Barak and Alma.

Ori would let the bantering voices amusing themselves with familiar, mechanical sentences fade, she'd wait for the sound of the door softly closing and for its echoes to die out, and only then would she pull herself out of bed. But this morning Barak bent over her before he left and kissed her forehead. And when the fluttering touch of his lips left her and the scent of sweet, fresh aftershave, Dolce & Gabbana, which starkly contrasted with his heavy, dark presence, she sank right back into a velvety abyss for an immeasurable time.

She woke up with a start, like a scream uttered in a moment of terror, and for long minutes she didn't know where she was and what she was doing there, in that wide bed, and she looked in bewilderment at the room and its walls. She'd experienced mornings of waking up in this way in her childhood as well. When the so-called "zero hour" class was introduced in her school, when she was in eighth grade, her mother, who could still stand on her feet, would come into her room to wake her up, and she would sit up with a start at her touch, still shrouded in vestiges of a dream scurrying around as a result of her slumber being abruptly interrupted: tense dreams, dreams in which she is late, dreams in which she stares shamefacedly at the exam paper placed in front of her and which still remained blank when the allotted time was up.

She hastily shook herself free of the sheets enshrouding her, got out of bed and washed her face in cold water, which restored some clarity to her, making the blood in her veins flow differently, the flow of the wakeful subjects of the Kingdom of Day. She went to look out of the window. This would be her omen. If the sky was dark and ominous, as it had been last night, she would stay in and work on the article she had promised for the holiday supplement—only a week remained to the deadline—and if it was clear and bright—she'd go out for a walk.

As she looked out she recalled the weatherman's prophecy from yesterday, a false prophecy, like all prophecies. Omens,

214

on the other hand, should not be taken lightly. Still, she was overcome with indecision.

At the time, when she accepted the supplement editor's request to write a personal account entitled "My Journey From Slavery to Freedom", she knew she was making a mistake. The deadline seemed distant, and as she immersed herself in the editor's soft, somewhat faltering voice and manner of speech—frequently stammering, saying something and then reconsidering, unnecessarily twisting his wording, starting a sentence and then departing from it—she imagined how she would spend a free morning facing the computer screen, sipping her coffee as her thoughts formed lucidly and flowed to her fingertips.

Now the deadline was looming and she didn't have even the glimmer of an idea what to write about, and whenever she recalled her commitment she felt a tightness in her chest. I have to sit myself down, she told herself, it'll be easy. Something short, five hundred words, two hours of writing. It had been several weeks since she'd written a word, since her latest youth book, and she didn't feel the urge. But she had an excuse, an opportunity knocking on her door. At three she had to pick up Alma from kindergarten. She had more than four hours, she'd just make a cup of coffee and then switch on the computer. But as her doubts continued to rebel and revolt, she got dressed, brushed her hair roughly, and her hand was on the door handle. She went out of the apartment and started down the stairs.

She absentmindedly checked her mailbox before leaving the building. "Ms. Ori Elhayani", "Mr. Barak Shulman", "Mr. and Mrs. Shulman", bills, invitations, a post-office notification about a package. Nothing special. With the exception of one envelope, which she turned over between her fingers. It was addressed to "Mr. Barak Shulman" and looked like a parking ticket from the Tel Aviv Municipality. Ori thought: strange, why would Barak be getting a parking ticket? He's got a reserved parking slot in their building, and there's a parking lot where he works, and Alma's kindergarten is within the limits of the parking zone sticker Barak had taken the trouble to obtain a year ago. So why would he be getting a parking ticket, where could he have parked? She mused for a few moments, shoved the letters back into the box and started walking towards Meir Park.

April pervaded the park, and there was something preposterous about its splendor. The heavily brachiated ficus trees, and the bowed tamarisks turning green as if in astonishment, and the reproachful eucalyptus trees with their year-round downcast veneer, and the Syrian olive tree, twisted like an arthritic body, and the flowering coral trees with their clusters of reddish globes, and the date palms planted in their native soil, or possibly in the foreign soil of the coastal plain, and the lily pond in the center of the park, petals of lilac and pearl breaking through the green water like little flaming suns, and thickets of multicolored bougainvillea and rosebushes whose cascading abundance burst through the fence surrounding them—it all seemed somehow excessive, unnecessarily festive, splendor that was pointless here, in front of her. All this beauty was wasted at this dead, luminous hour in the park. What was the point of all this growth? And then she thought, and the thought struck her as if for the first time with the force of sudden enlightenment: Passover Seder Night was in two weeks, and she crumpled onto a bench.

A bulbul, whose yellowish down belly caught her eye, attacked a warbler hiding in the branches of a tamarisk, and drove it away. And two crows flew in different directions, calling to one another, or cawing their individual song. Swifts darted across her field of vision, quivering in mid-flight, gathering their wings and plummeting to the ground, spreading their wings and rising into the air just before crashing into it.

Why had she come here? There must be a reason. Once again she was tormented by the thought of the article she had undertaken to write. Her eyes roved her surroundings. The park's regular beggar, clutching a supermarket cart filled to the brim with empty soda cans, looked at her suspiciously from his hiding place in the shadow of the ficus trees. Not far from him a flock of sparrows had congregated on the sand, and a bulbul, she was sure it was the same one she'd seen earlier, stormed into their midst, scattering them in all directions. She bent down and picked up a small stone, and as she was gauging the distance to the bulbul, the beggar, guessing her intentions, leapt towards her waving his arms. The startled bulbul flew off.

Pity. She'd always detested people who harassed her or made a nuisance of themselves. The beggar belonged to this group. Maybe because he was so quick to defend the bulbul. Four and a half years ago, on the day she and Barak moved into their new home, she'd walked through the park on her own on her way to the hardware store, and the same beggar had stared at her. On an impulse she couldn't explain, a blend of guilt and pity, she took a fifty-shekel note out her pocketbook and offered it to him, and he'd responded by spitting at her feet.

Perhaps her pregnancy had scared him, she was due very soon. Since then she'd been wary of him, and from the day Alma could walk she'd kept her away from him too. Whenever they went for a Saturday afternoon stroll in the park, or to the playground in the park's northwestern edge in the late afternoon, she'd keep her eyes on the child to ensure she didn't wander off and go anywhere near him. But Alma, with that heightened sense children possess of guessing their parents' innermost feelings and with the same natural desire to frustrate them, quickly developed disappearing tactics, as if she'd learnt to gauge the weight of her mother's eyes on her back and in moments of respite to evade the boundaries of its reach.

That's what happened yesterday. She and Barak were strolling along the paths, close to one another, and in the heat of the moment—what had been the heat of that moment: the wind soughing through the trees, a cloud briefly obscuring the sunlight, the forgotten scent of jasmine, something of the omens that expand your chest, that make the world more open and expansive than it really is—in the heat of that moment Barak's thick arm slipped around her waist and she, quite naturally, leaned into him and clung to his chest. But only briefly, because in that instant of their embrace Alma dropped out of her sight and she was gripped with panic, a small one, a series of pin-like stabs moving from her solar plexus to her sternum.

"Alma," she whispered.

"She's probably found a friend," Barak said gently, still clasped in her embrace, tightly embracing her.

"No, No." She disengaged herself and started looking around.

Her eyes moved from the crowds thronging the park and congregating on the fenced lawns towards the avenue of ficus trees, striving to penetrate the blanket of shadows spread between the tree trunks, to find the beggar, to make sure Alma hadn't gone in his direction. And there, beneath one of the trees, she spotted him. *Him*, not the beggar, but *him*, Avner, Avner Assoulin, his usual enigmatic expression on his face.

"Ori," she heard Barak calling her, "Alma's here. I told you she'd met a friend."

She turned towards him impatiently—why was he interrupting her—and saw his pointing finger and his erasable features distorted into a smile resembling joy. Like a child, she thought. His other arm was still slightly curved as if treasuring the shape of her body. About forty meters away Alma was huddled with another little girl, who was playing with a small pushcart on the sandy paths of Meir Park. She turned her eyes back to Avner, but he was no longer there. Only the regular beggar smiling to himself, standing beside his overflowing cart, in full sunlight, as he stood now, too, in those drawn-out moments of remembering, like a sentry at the portcullis of an ancient fortress.

Ori stretched out on the bench. The violent bulbul caught her eye again, landing nearby and leaping towards her provokingly. How like Avner to appear like that, like an illusion, almost five years after he disappeared, vanished into thin air. And just as unceremoniously. He hadn't even picked a special day to disappear, a calamitous day that would allow her to rebel, to hurl something at a world whose order had turned against her. No. Not even that.

That morning she'd gone to have her coffee on the balcony, in the November chill. A few minutes after she got out of bed, uncharacteristically early for her, at six-twenty, he got up and followed her out. For about half an hour he stood looking at her in silence. And she guessed at his eyes piercing her back. Her vulnerable nape, struck by dim light, was exposed when she moved her hair aside. Not a single one of the details recorded in his mind escaped her: the journey of her hand clutching the coffee cup from her mouth to the small wicker table and back. The spiraling vapor, the emptying one sip after another, the fierceness of the morning breeze, the city waking up and coming to life, the first buses departing on their long journeys, the clattering of querulous dishes erupting from the windows of neighboring apartments, subdued calls, the shadows of the cypresses stretching across the sidewalk.

Finally, she sensed that he had shaken himself out of his frozen stance. She turned her head towards him with a mute question.

Avner said, "I'd like to get up one morning twenty years from now, to know how all this ends."

"But you got up this morning," she retorted harshly. "That's all you need in order to know what you want."

It was only that evening that she realized how apt her retort had been.

She came home from the accountant's office where she worked as a receptionist. The door to their apartment was open, all his bookshelves empty; for the past few days he'd been busy sorting through their books, putting his on the right of the bookstand and hers—in another section. She'd ignored the obsessiveness with which he'd suddenly been inflicted. The CD stand was desolate as well. At first she thought the apartment had been burgled. But as she clutched the telephone, about to call the police, she began to wonder, what kind of burglar takes only books and CDs. Instead, she called the bookshop where he worked, and the owner, Boaz Zadok, answered and told her that Avner had announced that he wouldn't be coming in again and that he couldn't be reached. Then she found the note he'd left on the fridge.

She stood up and a wave of anger swept through her. Why was she thinking about Avner all of a sudden? She hadn't even loved him, she'd just needed him, the way little children and animals need. No. Not her. She'd never loved anyone in her life. She hurled the small stone she'd been clutching with all her might at the bulbul, which screeched when it struck. An eye for an eye, she laughed to herself, and thought she'd better go back home because only one hour of the morning remained at her disposal, shining and burnished like a new coin. But a cat, which from this distance she was positive had a completely black coat, although she imagined she'd briefly seen a tuft of rust-colored fur on the tip of its swaying tail, crossed the park entrance leading home, and she saw no reason to take any unnecessary risks, not even thinking what kind of risks. There were no fundamental matters on the agenda, matters in which she needed the movement of the world's cogwheels to make the decision for her, give her a hint how they'll fall, a hint as to what she should do. She felt that this day that had begun so futilely, with that dangerously sound sleep, like toxic honey, was not going to end well, and there was no point in availing herself of portentous omens. But she couldn't bring herself to cross the cat's path, so she exited the park at the King George Street entrance. She already knew where she was headed.

———

However, as she stood at the door of the bookshop on Hashmona'im Street, corner of Ehad Ha'am, she noticed that the shop had changed. It had been a while since she'd been there. Almost five years. Only the sign "Or Zarua", still hanging above the door, gave away that the shop was still under the same ownership. Beneath it had been added, "We Also Buy and Sell Secondhand Books" and, faced with this earthly, tangible addition, the name of the shop was again as puzzling to her as it had been the first time she saw it, six years earlier, while strolling aimlessly.

The pairing of the words "Or Zarua" and the selection displayed in the shop window, which was nothing like the uniform stacks of bestsellers in other shops, piqued her curiosity: Kierkegaard's *Fear and Trembling* alongside Dostoyevsky's *Letters From the Underworld* and Wittgenstein's *Philosophical Investigations* and Martin Gardner's illuminated English version of *The Hunting of the Snark*. She went in, and the slender, ascetic, scholarly-looking sales clerk looked at her thoughtfully when she asked about the meaning of the shop's name, and responded with an air of weightiness, "You should ask Boaz, the owner. He likes to answer that question. He's here every Wednesday afternoon."

"Why?" she asked.

"Why what? Why is he here? Are you asking in principle, from a metaphysical standpoint or just an existential one?"

"No," she laughed, although she didn't know if he was joking, "just from a practical point of view. Why specifically on Wednesday afternoon?"

"Oh," he said, and there was a dismissive hint in his voice. "That. He and his brother, Yachin, have five bookshops all over the country. He's the executive director of the Or Zarua chain. He visits a different shop every day."

"And on Fridays?"

"He ceased from work and rested," he said slowly and melodiously, and again she wondered whether he was being humorous. As she left the shop he called after her, "By the way, my name is Avner Assoulin."

On Wednesday she went back to the shop. From the outside she saw the young sales clerk leaning on the counter, speaking to someone. When she entered she saw a short, potbellied man in his late forties, round spectacles on his hooked nose and abundant graying curls bouncing on his head as he moved frenetically between the shelves. When he looked at her, she couldn't understand what he was doing there. She'd just come from Tel-Aviv University where she'd attended a lecture delivered by A.B. Yehoshua at the Bar-Shira Auditorium, and now the renowned Hebrew author was standing right in front of her, arranging books with youthful vigor.

"You came back," said the young clerk. "I knew you would. The first time you came in I could tell you weren't someone who could resist the promise of an intriguing story." He nodded towards the other man. Now she noticed that his uncanny resemblance to A.B. Yehoshua fell apart on the small details—he had a hairy mole on his chin and his skin tone was darker.

"Boaz," said the young clerk, "she wants to know why the shop is called Or Zarua."

Boaz smiled with unconcealed pleasure. "So the young lady wants to know," he said. "What's your name?"

"Ori," she replied.

"All right, Ori. This is what happened. In our childhood, thirty-five years ago, my twin brother Yachin and I took part in the Bible Quiz. We both had a photographic memory and had an advantage because there were two of us. We were able to memorize the Bible. We grew up on a moshav, Geulei Teiman, and we were invited to stay at a hotel for the four days preceding the quiz, which was held in Jerusalem, together with all the other contestants who came from all over the world. During those four days we were taken on tours and to restaurants to take our minds off the quiz. All the contestants went off to enjoy themselves, except for me and my brother Yachin. We walked side by side and memorized the Bible chapter by chapter. Yachin would say, 'Boaz, which book are you up to?' and I'd answer, 'Isaiah. And you?' and he'd answer, 'I'm still on II Kings'. And the other kids would point at us, and say, 'Look at those Zadok brothers, they don't rest for a second.' And I would say, 'Zadok k'tamar yifrach', the righteous shall flourish like the palm tree, and Yachin would respond, 'Or zarua l'zadok', light is sown for the righteous."

At the end of each sentence his voice became gravelly, and withered and died on the last word, "Zadok". Ori waited for him to continue his story, but he resumed arranging books on the shelves. "Did you win?" she asked when she realized the story had come to an end.

Still busy with the books, Boaz shrugged and said, "What difference does it make?" But the young clerk, to whom she turned questioningly, nodded solemnly, his lips clenched, restraining his smile.

223

"So why is the shop called Or Zarua?"

"Because Tamar Yifrach is not a good name for a bookshop," Boaz replied, turning towards her, the same odd expression on his face, the combination of amazement and disdain she had seen on A.B. Yehoshua's face an hour earlier on the stage in the auditorium when the short doctoral student had attacked him acerbically for his political views.

Ori couldn't resist asking him if anyone had ever commented on his uncanny resemblance to the renowned author. Boaz smiled, not at her but at the young clerk, who said in astonishment, "What are you talking about?" and added, "Strange, I can't recall what that A.B. looks like."

Two days later she returned, bringing with her a photograph of the author she'd cut from one of the supplements and waved it in front of him triumphantly, but the young clerk shook his head and again dismissed her with, "What are you talking about?" She left angrily, letting the door slam shut behind her, but his voice reached her, "My name is Avner Assoulin, by the way. I've noticed you don't use it."

Now, late morning on this spring day, looming before her was a different display window, with stacks of old, yellowing volumes, frayed pages inside faded covers. She went into the shop, which at first looked deserted, a home hastily abandoned by its inhabitants, and then she saw a plump woman, half hidden by piles of books, who stared at her openmouthed, but didn't say a word. Ori quickly found the children's books section and scrutinized it, barely breathing, heart racing, not knowing how she would react if she found a copy of one of her books there: with disappointment at the readers' fickleness, or delight that the book had been handed down, and that the shop was merely a halt in its travels. But she found no trace of her books, and she was relieved.

She continued looking around. Stacked on a table in the middle of the shop was a selection of recently published novels by Israeli authors. She picked up one of the books, and turned to the opening paragraph. Yes, just as she'd thought, another blabbering tale of remonstrance written in patronizing, smug, inane Hebrew. And yet, although she recalled in astonishment the praise the critics had heaped on the author—"A magnificent lover of the language", "Brings dormant treasures of the Hebrew language to life" and other such nonsense—she couldn't put the book down, until a warm, raspy voice interrupted her reading.

"Oh, what a distinguished guest, what a distinguished guest!"

She looked up with a start. Boaz's curls were now completely gray, but his expressive face still radiated immense vitality. He smiled, held out his arms invitingly and she collapsed into his embrace.

They stood there embracing for long minutes, and the plump woman stared at them between the stacks of books. Ori finally disengaged herself from him and he muttered appreciatively, "You haven't changed, you still look twenty," adding, "What brings you here?"

"I was in the neighborhood, so I came in to see what's new. What happened?" she asked, her arm tracing an arc around the shop.

"I was just about to make coffee," he said, "come and keep me company."

The small back room, where she had spent many an hour with Avner, was virtually unchanged. The same jerky sliding door, the same stained sink, the same splotchy marble surface, even the same chipped coffee mugs, and she felt her skin crawl. A small table with a groaning, grumbling computer was the only addition to the small room. Boaz pulled a chair from behind the table and tapped his fingers on it. He handed her a cup of grainy, sickly-sweet coffee.

"We're being slaughtered," he said without any preamble, after she'd taken two hesitant sips.

She scrutinized his face silently.

"We're being strangled," he added. "The big chains are wiping us out, and now that each of them is a big publishing house, or two, no one even throws us small shops a bone. We don't get discounted books, we don't get credit lines. Nothing. They're encroaching upon us, Ori, and all so very politely. The distributors from the big publishing houses come here with big smiles, but when I ask them to let me hold a special sale of the best-selling books, they politely tell me that they haven't got approval, as if they don't understand that the implication for me is a death sentence. You'll see, within two years the entire book industry will be based on three big publishing houses, two powerful chains and a few franchises."

His voice shook as he talked, and Ori was surprised by the intensity of emotion blended into it, as if more than five years hadn't elapsed and they were still engaged in their gloomy conversations.

A week after Avner left she had taken to stopping by at the shop on a daily basis. Boaz now had no staff here and was managing the shop himself. Sensing somehow what she needed, he didn't question her, for better or worse, about the departure, but only talked about mundane things, told her anecdotes from his life, in each and every one of them a subtle, hidden allusion to her own distress.

He was the first person she told about the positive response she'd received from the only publishing house she'd sent her manuscript. And when she told him he put his arms around her shoulders—she was startled by his touch, but forced herself to remain still—and said, "You're embarking on a new journey now." His words deteriorated into mumbling as he continued, "The Lord is thy shade upon thy right hand. The sun shall not smite thee by day, nor the moon by night. The Lord shall keep thee from all evil; He shall keep thy soul. The Lord shall guard thy going out and thy coming in, from this time forth and for ever."

They both knew that he was thus releasing her and himself from the burden of the closeness Avner had imposed upon them with his disappearance. As she looked at him delivering his revealing speech about the conduct of the new storm troopers of the local book market, his resemblance to the renowned author surfaced before her eyes, and she wondered if he'd ever guessed that the knowledge that out in the world two mirror images of him were wandering, one biological and the other imagined and random, was what had planted in her the idea for her first youth novel, *Double Doppelgangers*.

"Why are you smiling?" he asked her.

"No reason," she said. "I was thinking that I'd be feeling sorry for any other person, but not for you. You, you're resourceful and you never give up hope."

"You're right on that score," he said, smiling again. "About a year ago I realized what was going to happen and understood where the future lay, second-hand bookshops and internet sales." He pointed to the computer screen behind her. "And I gather there's no need to be concerned about you either. Your last book sold very well."

"I can't complain," she said, lowering her eyes to the cup of coffee clutched and shielded by her hands, to the ring finger of her right hand, which was encircled by a ring. "I'm married, Boaz, and I've got a little girl, four and a half years old."

She raised her eyes to him and knew what she would see: shock, disbelief, surprise. He struggled with his reactions, and she knew he would be defeated even before he did. He asked faintly, "And Avner?"

"What about Avner? What's he got to do with anything?" she yelled. It was all so predictable, as if she hadn't stopped rehearsing this situation, even her yell, that although it had erupted sharply from her mouth, without warning, sounded hollow to her, like a puny execution of a pre-planned gesture. "He disappeared. What am I supposed to do? Wait for him until the End of Days?"

"You know," he said, "if Avner had stayed here things wouldn't have been so difficult for me. He had regular customers who valued his judgment. They'd come in every week and buy what he recommended. Since he left they've vanished one after another."

"I've got a little girl, Boaz," she repeated wearily, "her name's Alma."

———

On the way home she stopped at the supermarket. She usually made do with buying precooked homemade food, but today, with the article breathing down her neck, she decided that it had been weeks since she'd cooked lunch for Alma herself and it was about time. She wandered absentmindedly along the aisles, pushing an empty cart. It was only when she happened to pass the stacks of eggs that she knew what she wanted to make. Sometimes, when her mother didn't feel like cooking lunch or dinner, and it happened frequently that year, she'd concoct her own version of *shakshouka*. First she'd fry crushed garlic cloves and chopped onions. Then she'd add sliced tomatoes, diced red peppers, finely chopped parsley, a little water, and season it with paprika, salt and white pepper, which she called *lebzar*, bring it to the boil and then cook it on a low flame until all the ingredients dissolved into a bubbling, red paste. Then she'd beat some eggs in a bowl and add them to the pot, stirring constantly, and the beaten eggs would spread evenly in the thick sauce forming soft, delicate flakes. The flavor filled Ori's mouth and she recalled that when she came across the phrase "you can't make an omelet without breaking eggs" in one of the *Ariella the Fairy Detective* books she had so loved, what she saw before her eyes was her mother's *shakshouka*, and she'd thought that that was what it was about, and since then in her mind the phrase was always associated with the sight and smell of *shakshouka*. Yes. *Shakshouka*, that's what she'd make for Alma.

She quickly collected the eggs, vegetables and spices she needed and hurried home. But on the third-floor landing, between the end of one staircase and the beginning of the one leading up to her apartment, her strength failed and she burst into tears. It had been a long time since she'd been overcome with this kind of incomprehensible sobbing, like on that annual school trip that had been put off until the summer when she was in seventh grade. The girls were all seated on the back seat of the bus and poked fun at the boys with songs, taking vengeance on them for the scorn they displayed whenever one of the girls dawdled at the end of the column on an interminable hike in one of the dry riverbeds of the southern Negev Desert and held up the entire class. She came to them in tears, and the girls joined her, some perhaps out of mischief, whimpering in high-pitched or coarse voices, sobbing and grief-stricken. But within minutes their forced sobbing turned into real weeping, into a lament, as if the sound of their wailing and distress had awakened a dormant pain, breaching the heavy floodgate blocking its path. She remembered that sobbing in the back seat of the bus on the way home, pure, unadulterated weeping, a profound, liberated lament over something that refused to stop emanating from them, to get lost. That's how she felt right now, standing on the landing, leaning against the black handrail, pouring her sorrow into the iron.

"*Shatya*," she reprimanded herself when the light in the stairwell switched on and the echo of footsteps rose from the first floor. The reprimand broke the spell on her body, releasing it from paralysis. "*Shatya*, what's the matter with you?" she reprimanded herself again. She had also found the expletive *shatya*, fool in Aramaic, in one of the Ariella books and had adopted it when she was fourteen. "*Shatya*," she'd say to herself in disgust when cups and plates slipped from her fingers when she washed the dishes, and "*shatya*"—when she was sent to the grocery shop armed with a shopping list and forgot one of the items or lost some of the change, and "*shatya*"—when she got low marks in exams. But she only ever said it to herself, and no one knew the secret of the word. Four and a half years earlier, when Alma was born, she called her "*shatya*" affectionately when they were alone, but after the first year, afraid that Alma, who gazed at her with her big green eyes with a curiosity she thought was not typical of her years, would understand the meaning of the name, she stopped.

——

That evening, when Barak came home two hours late, the pot of *shakshouka* was full. She had piled some on a plate for herself, but its flavor and texture were nothing like the flavor and texture that had been preserved on her palate. Alma, too, refused to eat any. "Yuck," she said, "Ima, it's disgusting." And Ori ordered hamburgers for them both from a nearby restaurant.

Alma, who was sitting in the living room earnestly leafing through a book—one of the books she had memorized and could follow the words with her finger, adapting the sound of the word in her mouth to its form on the page—was the first to hear the shuffle of feet outside the door, and look up. And she, sitting facing her, occasionally glancing at her over the screen of her laptop, which she had dragged from the study to the living room, tensed after her.

Barak opened the door silently, like an adolescent coming in late from the prom and trying not to wake up his parents, and when he stood awkwardly at the door in his white flannel tracksuit, the top stretched across his round belly, clutching a briefcase and a stuffed plastic bag, Alma leapt up from the couch and ran to him squealing with joy, "Abba!" Barak bent down to take her in his arms, straightened back up and hoisted her into the air to her delighted squeals. When they calmed down from their game, Alma still in his arms, her legs wrapped around his stomach and her arms around his neck, Ori stood up and went up to them.

They looked at her questioningly, father and daughter, dark and pale, as if she owed them explanations. They were so different to one another; Alma so slim, the embodiment of air and gliding, with her big, green, feline eyes and her fair, curly hair, and he, with his broad, doughy face, dark eyes and thick, dark hair, inherited from his Balkanic ancestors who dispersed to Russia and Romania. Where did Alma get her coloring? Neither his relatives, who were all dark, nor her family, who despite being "fair" Moroccans—her sister Ofra's eyes were blue and two of her father's brothers were redheads—resembled Alma's features and coloring in any way.

"Ima," said Alma, "why are you looking at us like that?"

"You're late," said Ori sternly.

Barak shifted his weight from one foot to the other in embarrassment.

"Abba, stop moving," Alma ordered. "I feel like I'm in a boat."

"I signed up for a gym," he said reluctantly. He put Alma down on the floor and stretched his tracksuit over his belly—not quite a paunch: Barak was one of those physical, big-boned men and his belly completed his large, round outline. He added, "I've become a bit of a potato lately with all those hours at the office and my metabolism, I'm not a kid any more." His lips stretched into a thinner-than-thin, sheepish smile that contradicted his words; the same smile that had captivated her heart the second time they met, a private smile that absent-mindedly appears on the face of a young child thinking about his escapades. The smile broke through all the screens of habit that flatten features, through all the masks cast over the face of a person who does not possess charm of his own to justify love. The fidgetiness that had filled her body during the two hours of his delay began to melt away, but she restrained her arm just in time, before it could lightly caress his shoulder, turned on her heel, went back to her laptop, picked it up and turned towards the study.

Barak followed her, and Alma trailed along after him.

"Ori, I should have let you know I was going to be late. But it was a last-minute decision, we were offered this training package at the office and the gym is at the shopping center nearby. So I signed up and bought a tracksuit at Sport Center. And that's it."

"Where's the gym?" Alma demanded. "I want to go too."

"It's all right," said Ori. "Let's just drop it. It's no big deal."

Barak sighed, and Alma persisted, "Do you have to wear white clothes to go there?"

When they lay side by side in bed before falling asleep, the darkness separating them like a honed blade of smoky crystal, she recalled what her mother had said from within her hallucinations in the last month of her life: one woman can bind a man to herself with coffee, and another can untie the bonds if she places a bloodstained knife between the man and the woman as they sleep at night.

"Are you still angry?" Barak asked in a worried tone, again like a child.

"What's to be angry about?"

232

"That I didn't let you know I was going to be late."

"No."

He turned onto his side, facing her, his thick fingers fluttering over her exposed shins, slowly clambering up her thighs, lifting her nightgown. She moved restlessly when he touched her, and then, when he reached her stomach and massaged it, she shoved his hands off her with both hands, "Stop it, Barak, I don't feel like it tonight."

"Come on, just for a bit, come on," his voice was already low and thick.

"No, Barak, I told you . . . "

"Come on, Ori, why are you being like this?"

"I said no," she almost yelled. He moved his hands away and turned over.

Facing his naked back, tense with insult, the memory of the childish smile came back to her, and a spark of pity ignited in her. A few days ago he'd dragged her to a concert at Leyvik House—Piazzolla tangos for accordion and piano—and the pianist was a childhood friend of his, who had perhaps—she'd never asked—also been his first girlfriend when they were teenagers. Neta, the friend, fell onto him at the entrance, as if she'd been laying in wait for him. Ori greeted her with a nod. Neta ignored her.

"You must do me a favor," she said to Barak, "I need someone to turn the score pages while I play," and she showed him the score sheets in a green binder.

Barak looked at the binder hungrily, and then at Ori, as if asking for permission. At their first meeting he'd told her everything, delivering a brief overview of his life, how in his childhood he'd spent hours at the piano and how, when he was thirteen, the tendons in his hands were afflicted with inflammation and he was forced to give up playing. And how fortunate that at the time electronic organs and synthesizers were becoming popular and sophisticated musical instruments, and the soft keys allowed him to go on playing. He even formed a band in high school, at the end of eleventh grade, that didn't last more than six months, and then, after the army—how exciting to be living in times of such changes—the computer era erupted throughout the world, and he was swept up on its waves and quickly substituted one keyboard for another. He was now a well-established computer professional, and it was a good thing he hadn't pursued his playing, he'd told her then, spreading his hands before her, who knew that his virtuoso fingers would become as thick and coarse as a laborer's?

She granted him her permission that evening with two words, "You must."

He went onto the stage with Neta and sat beside her. She observed the delight radiating from the depths of his face as Neta attacked the piano, and the sharp, wounded notes cracked aridly in the still air, dancing around the spiraling melodies emanating from the accordion. From time to time Barak closed his eyes in sheer pleasure. He was obviously very familiar with the piece, although he rarely listened to music at home. But a stylus sang in his heart; his lips muttered, possibly humming the piano score over the clicking of the keys. And there were several minutes—an eternity—during which Neta's playing softened, the tempo slowed down, and their heads inclined towards one another's, their brows almost touching, her red hair illuminating his dark hair like flickering embers in the darkness, and Ori pursed her lips tightly.

That reddish softness seemed to be hovering over his hair now, engulfed in the darkness. She touched the middle vertebra on his spine and whispered, "Barak."

He twisted his back and recoiled from her. "Stop it," he said.

Ori placed four fingers in the depressions between his vertebrae, one finger at a time, strumming his back.

"Ori," he mumbled, "your hands are cold."

He didn't shake her off this time, and she placed a hand on his arm and lifted herself up until her lips were over his right ear. She breathed into it gently, "I'm sorry," although she didn't feel a scintilla of regret, or passion, just that spark of pity, that she couldn't explain, intensified within her.

Barak moved his shoulder, more weakly, less resolutely.

Ori bit his earlobe, then brought her lips to the point where his chin and neck met, and kissed it, feeling the prickles of the short stubble, sticking out her tongue and licking the taste of previous, bitter layers of aftershave, sweat and soap. And Barak, whose passion reignited in an impassioned outburst, tossed her off him and rolled over, his left hand pressing her arms to the headboard, his right arm supporting his weight, lest he crush her as he leaned into her.

Afterwards she lay in the dark, her face to the ceiling. Barak was lying on his side, mumbling his contentment and drowsiness, gradually reconciling, breathing slowly, his arm resting diagonally across her stomach. She wanted to get up, to wash herself, but her limbs were already seized by exhaustion and pleasure. As if responding to her wishes, Barak turned onto his stomach and his arm extended its control over her body. We are never as alone as we'd like to be, she thought heavily: the ghost or spirit of others always haunts us, insinuating itself into the depth of our slumber, yes, even there—we dream as we live, surrounded by a crowd.

January 15, 2002
Dear Ori,
The truth is that I don't know how to begin this letter. I've made several attempts and none seem appropriate. I can't just

write, Hi, it's Sigal Danino, remember me? Of course you remember. And that's precisely what makes this letter strange. I know it would have been much easier for us both if we'd never met. How do you write to someone with whom you've had no contact since you were fifteen?

I don't know if you've heard, but Ophir and I are married now. I hope you have heard, that this doesn't come like a bolt out of the blue, and that you're happy for us. We have a beautiful boy, Sagi. He's two years old, and we're expecting a little girl. We haven't decided on a name yet.

Ophir doesn't know I'm writing to you. A few weeks ago he came home from work with a copy of your book. He's a graphic designer and works at an advertising agency. In case you're wondering what I do, I manage a Blockbuster branch at the mall. It's not a particularly exciting job, but I'm a simple woman, Ori, I never wanted too much out of life, and this job allows me to devote plenty of time to raising Sagi.

As I started telling you before, Ophir went into a bookshop a few weeks ago to buy a present for Sagi. He saw a stack of books in the children and youth section and went to have a look. You should have seen how excited he was when he told me about it. I realized he was restraining himself, that he was trying not to show his excitement, but his eyes shone and he couldn't keep still. Do you remember the problem he had when he was a boy, with the tics and the motor disorders? It sorted itself out, more or less, when he was eighteen. Nowadays he's pretty calm, courteous, as they say. Except when he gets excited. Then all the old tics come back.

He noticed your name on the cover even before he picked up a copy for a closer look. He told me he stood stunned in front of the stack of books, telling himself it couldn't be you, that is, a book that you wrote. He turned it over and discovered that it said on the back of the book that the author was born and raised in Netivot, and then he was sure.

I read the book that evening. What a strange title, Double Doppelgangers. And the book itself is a bit strange. But I wouldn't have expected anything less strange from you. Reading it brought back all at once a piece of my childhood I thought I'd lost. Ophir felt the same, but he wouldn't want me to tell you that.

I liked the book. I liked the protagonist, Tal Krispel. Because his name sounds like the name of a boy I might know and not the name of some plastic kid like "Yaron Zehavi". I could picture him as the Krispel family's boy who lived at the end of our street in Netivot twenty years ago.

But that wasn't the only thing that struck me. I was swept up by the story. The idea of a boy who strays off the path on his way to school and comes to a ghost school, and that this school is a rep- lica of his school in *City of Darkness*, which is just like his town, only empty and dark, I was swept up by it all. I really, really liked it. And the creatures that dwell in *City of Darkness* captivated me. Some made me laugh and others frightened me. It scared me when Tal Krispel starts seeing his previous town through the cracks in the walls and discovers that two doppelgangers have replaced him, not just one, one at home and the other outside the house.

But I do have one serious criticism. I didn't like the way the boy resolves the confusion. Never mind that he realizes that his two doppelgangers have been created from the echoes of his memories, and they were created because he never stood up for himself, always giving in to the wishes of others. And never mind that this leads him to the conclusion that he had never been him- self, but someone else's invention. But when he decides to forget and forget, to erase all his memories until he is left with just one pure memory, in which he was completely himself, I didn't like that. Nor that this is the only way for him to find the way back to our world to confront the two doppelgangers that are gradually destroying his town.

237

But why am I telling you your own story? The thing that's difficult for me with it all is that Tal can't really tell the difference between happy memories and bad ones. For him, every memory in which he wasn't himself is a bad memory. Only the memory in which he insisted on being untarnished by others is a good one, because there he was real.

Afterwards I read a review in the newspaper that said the book toys with the ideas of some French philosopher. I showed Ophir, and he agreed that the critic was so pleased with himself for identifying the connection, that he almost forgot that it was you who wrote the book. But it makes no difference that that philosopher had similar ideas, because I know exactly where that story sprouted from.

At this point you're probably asking yourself why I am writing to you.

There are several reasons. One, I still haven't been able to shake myself free of the guilt feelings I had as a girl. I'm not religious now, although when I was seventeen I considered strengthening and deepening my religion. If not for my relationship with Ophir I would have sunk into it. And I use that word, because that's how I feel, that I would have sunk. I would have had no choice, I would have surrendered to the conditions of my life. Not that the path away from religion was strewn with roses. No. Today I can look at the whole process with acceptance, I can tell myself, it was difficult there, it happened of its own accord there. But at the time, as it was happening? What can I say? Torture. Hell. The first time I didn't wait for six hours to elapse between eating meat and milk I waited for the heavens to open up and for the hand of God to crush me like a cockroach. I had some relapses, I'd say all the old prayers, God, destroy me with Your wrath, crush my body, don't let me get up in the morning with the burden of my sins. I stopped fasting on Yom Kippur only last year. I still find reasons not to light fire on the Sabbath. You know, some mornings I appeal to God, I say to Him, I'm a simple woman and I have no quarrel with You, so let us make an agreement, You won't harm anyone I love, and I won't speak Your name in vain, I'll stop hating you for letting me leave You like this. Then I come to my senses, I tell myself, what this nonsense you're talking, there's nothing up there, and if there is He or She has so much injustice to answer for that it's better they go on hiding. This was Ophir's argument throughout the entire period of my leaving religion. He supported me wholeheartedly. I know that when we were fourteen you already thought he and I were in love. One time, when I came to console you during the summer vacation, after you were told you were being kept back a year, you yelled at me that the perpetual arguments between me and Ophir were a kind of attraction. You were wrong, Ori, and today I don't mind saying it, Ophir was in love with you, until you cut yourself off from us in the ninth grade and moved yourself to Jerusalem.

It took Ophir more than six months to get over you. We tried to contact you and you rejected us, or perhaps the letters we left with your father never reached you. We heard rumors, and you can probably guess what kind of rumors they were, but we didn't believe them, nor could we refute them. Gvinush was pre-occupied with them up to twelfth grade, inventing new ones. She claimed that these were things your neighbors told her. But by that stage no one had any patience for her any more.

So, Ori, what is it that I want to say to you? People change over time, especially during adolescence. For a long time I thought that perhaps we became such different people that we wouldn't understand why we'd been friends in our childhood at all. But then your book came along and proved to me that deep down inside we speak the same language. It was the sign of life I had been waiting for all this time.

I remember how one time in the orchard that year, when your mother was dying, you told me that one day you'd like to live in a new city, where no one you know has known you since the day you were born.

I asked you then what Ophir and I would do if you suddenly disappeared? And you replied, you'll have my doppelganger. You won't know the difference.

And now I am convinced you were mistaken. We didn't find your doppelganger. And the void wasn't filled. I feel your absence. If you ever find the way back from your *City of Darkness*, to where you migrated when you were fifteen, this is my address in Ness Ziona. If the doorbell rings one evening and I open the door and you'll be standing there in the doorway, there'll be no one happier than I. I know Ophir, too, will be wild with joy, though he'd never admit it. But you'll be able see for yourself how excited he is, with all the nose tics and blinking that'll suddenly start.

I miss you,
Sigal

TWO

Water

ONCE, DURING A SPRING similar to this one, years ago, thousands of years ago, Avner pointed at the row of jacaranda trees, which until yesterday evening had stood stark, proudly displaying their outstretched branches, and towards morning had burst into blossom, and said, "When I was a boy . . . "

Ori fluttered her finger over his lips, threatening but not touching, and said, "Shhh . . . have you already forgotten that we decided not to talk about our childhoods?"

That image, which almost felt as if it had been etched in someone else's memory, an observer watching them from afar—she, on the café steps, wearing a simple cotton dress over her tiny figure, just one meter sixty tall and slim, as sharp as seventy blades, leaning forward to place her finger over Avner's brown lips, outlined like a woman's lips, and the jacaranda trees in the background blazing intensely, burning in the April air—surfaced powerfully before her eyes as she sat in front of her computer screen and thought about a subject for her article. She wanted to begin with a childhood memory, to lure the readers, tempt them to read further, and a muttered protest immediately followed, "*Shatya*, remember you promised not to talk about your childhood," and she wanted to retreat, withdraw her hand, but the Ariella books, the pleasure she drew from them, wandering through the City of Tempest and the Kingdoms of the Seasons they unfolded before her, rose up and overwhelmed her; her eyes smarted and she closed them.

Her third encounter with Avner at Or Zarua, too, was strewn with pitfalls. He was lost somewhere between the pages of a book when she came into the shop, and he answered her questions brusquely. Especially the question about the display window and why he had chosen each of the books displayed in it. He looked up and sighed, "Isn't it obvious?" She didn't know what drove her to continue inquiring, she'd never shown much interest in other people, and why would the detached bookseller arouse any curiosity in her?

"What's with all these questions now? Can't you see you're disturbing me?" he said finally.

She pursed her lips and looked at him for several minutes, her eyes slicing into him, piercing. He was slender, almost fragile. His back, possibly from years of stooping over books, was slightly curved, his hair curly, rusty. His face was strewn with freckles, radiating a kind of gentleness, and his eyes uncoordinated, a deficiency that accentuated his fragility, but also spread an aura of seduction through her. And his fingers, which she had been urged to observe earlier, first of all the fingers, are the key, coarse hands, gnarled, grooved, horny, slightly cracked nails, those were the hands she was looking for, a hint of the erupting beast, of primordial masculinity, not like the boyish Avner, with his smooth, slender fingers curved around the book he was reading, flawless fingers, far too clean, unblemished, no taste of blood. She should have left, but she stayed to watch him. What was it that attracted her to him? She kept her distance from men.

"Well, what is it?" he grumbled at last, "If you think we're waxworks you ought to pay, you know."

"Yes," she easily recognized the quote. "And if you think we're alive, you ought to speak."

"What do you want?"

"An opportunity to use your name." She looked at the book cover, which was blank, without a title. "What are you reading?" she asked.

"*Supernature.*"

"I don't know it. What's it about?"

"Why do people always have to ask what a book is about? Isn't it sufficient that it was written?" he answered defiantly.

In her second book, *Beyond the Cities of Darkness*, she wrote about a girl who breaks a promise, and this trivial matter creates a chain reaction in her life and in the lives of three other children who are seemingly unconnected to one another. The book was replete with the traditional elements of legends and fairy tales, children who exchange their entire family fortune for a handful of beans or a pet, children who open a forbidden door at the end of a corridor, children who ask their parents who are departing on a long journey to bring them back a rose, children who pluck out their heart and bury it in the garden in the dark of night. But the story didn't go anywhere, it remained full of loose ends. The bad guys didn't get what was coming to them, and the good guys didn't triumph. At the end, each of the protagonists was faced with a fateful decision. Perhaps due to the success of her first book, she was frequently asked what the book was about and what she was trying to say in it. She responded that she'd merely sought to reproduce a fragment of childhood, with its illusory labyrinths of imagination, she did not even purport to knead it or accord it an artificial form, and why does a book have to address a single specific subject, was it not sufficient that it had been written?

Now, as the memory surfaced, she flinched. That day Avner had spoken through her lips. But then she had responded, "I see you got up on the wrong side of the bed today," and was immediately embarrassed by the cliché. "Sorry," she said, "that sounded bad."

"No, no, I'm the one who should be sorry," he said and closed the book. "You're right, I'm a bit grumpy. This book attempts to provide scientific explanations for supernatural or paranormal phenomena. It also tries to discover the logic behind various occultist teachings."

"Do you believe in it?"

"In what? Scientific explanations?"

"No, occultist teachings, supernatural phenomena."

"I don't like to deny possibilities."

"You have to if you want to keep your sanity," she said, and again regretted her words. But Avner merely emitted a "Pchhh." And it struck her, that sound, "pchhh", at which her family were so adept, five measures of denial and five of contempt, which she'd always thought typified Moroccan immigrants, and of necessity permeated the regular speech of her parents and her sister Ofra, and was the essence of their dialect and perception, ridiculing everything, a talisman against arrogance, against ambition. One "pchhh" was sufficient to cut through any aspiration, and there were other words too: "*b'shala*", which marked the absolute boundaries of good taste, and "*b'zat*", which interrupted anyone whose heart soared and who spoke highfalutin words, "*b'ki alik, ya m'zrub*" that stifled the gallop of arrogance and "*ewa*" that was accompanied by a twist of the lips and nose and meant—stop it, enough, no more, that does it.

She smiled. "Maybe I should go."

"No, no, wait," he glanced at the clock, his cheeks slightly flushed. "Would you have a coffee with me?"

"What, now? In the middle of the day?"

"Yes, I'm in charge of the shop, I can lock up for half an hour or an hour. I'm entitled to a break, aren't I?"

There were three customers in the shop besides her, a woman and a young couple. The girl was reading a book and giggling, and the boy was standing behind her, his arms around her waist, whispering into her ear.

"Hey, you in the travel and recreation section," he called over to them, "television and the internet were invented especially for you. So you don't have to learn about your sexual development from books."

The girl dropped the book and strode quickly out of the shop, the boy hot on her heels, darting embarrassed glances over his shoulder. The third customer carefully placed two books on the counter and took out her pocketbook, a gloating smile on her lips.

Avner turned over the "OPEN" sign on the door and locked it. He indicated the general direction, and she walked beside him. His boyishness was evident in his steps, light and supple.

Pansies cascaded from the planters along the fence that surrounded the terrace of the café where they sat, dazzling in their engineered colors, mouths of black velvet and fiery, scorched scarlet, and the sheet of light smoldered above them, pure, taut and gleaming. Avner talked about the light while they waited to be served, his reserved nature evaporated and the avidity he'd displayed when they first met, returned to him.

"When I was a boy in Haifa," he said, and at first she found his eloquence, as if he were reciting a pre-prepared speech, pleasant, "I planned to write a kind of catalog of types of light and give them names, you know, like the Eskimos and their myriad words for snow. That's the example that all kinds of language experts present when they want to demonstrate the connection between vocabulary and environmental conditions, and I think, when is an Eskimo lobby finally going to rise and protest against their life being turned into an anecdote in the mouths of mediocre poets and uninspired teachers . . . This is always the case with cultures that seem backward to us, all kinds of remote tribes . . . Anyway, I think I'm losing my train of thought. There are so many types of light; the light that's reflected from the sea at different times of day, the terrible whiteness of the hot desert winds, the blazing colors of the evening sky . . . When I think about it, my childhood was a kind of endless summer . . . "

But as he progressed with his speech, she shrank into her seat and could no longer restrain herself.

"I don't like conversations about childhood. There's always a kind of deception about them."

Her voice burst into his speech and Avner stared at her.

"What do you mean when you say deception?" he asked.

"No, deception isn't a good word. Bribery. In childhood memories there's always a kind of bribery."

"I don't understand."

"When people tell each other their childhood stories they try to captivate their hearts somehow . . . these stories create a false sense of familiarity, as if when you tell me your stories I'll feel as if I knew you in a time that was more innocent, innocent of intentions . . . Do you understand?"

Avner nodded.

"And it's an illusion of naturalness, you tell me about the days when you were natural . . . "

"And I'm not natural now?"

"Now you're you, you have intentions and desires you're unaware of . . . and that's how I want to know you. That's how I want us to meet, like two strangers fumbling in the dark."

Avner looked at her silently, perhaps musing over what she'd said, perhaps wondering what kind of nutcase he was getting involved with. He smiled and nodded lightly a few times, but remained silent until their coffee arrived. He took a sip of his latte and said, "In that case we won't talk about childhood. All right? Deal?" and she nodded in relief.

As they walked down the café steps the sky darkened. Without any prior warning April had become wintry, blustery. Avner looked towards Ahad Ha'am Street and started reminiscing, but she silenced him, and he pointed to the trees lining the street.

"You asked about explanations earlier. Well, I always look for disorder in nature and never find it. You look at the plants, the birds, the insects, it seems as though there's no method and no logic, and then one morning towards the end of April, on the very same morning, all these jacaranda trees light up all at once, like programmed lamps, and you realize that once again you've been proved wrong. Everything works like clockwork, there's no loophole or crack you can go through."

And she asked apprehensively, "Go where?"

"I don't know, far from here," he said dismissively.

But she was insistent, "What do you mean you don't know?"

"I don't know. In Haifa, when I was seven . . . "

"We said no childhood, so no childhood."

"Okay, you're right. But you did ask. I have this dream that still recurs. My mother drives me to Haifa Bay and puts me on a ship that sails into the middle of the Mediterranean. I'm put into a bathysphere and lowered into the depths. And in that sphere I live, look at the corals, the eels and the swordfish."

"For the rest of your life?" she asked, and Avner nodded and smiled. He had a misleading smile, did Avner. A foreign face was reflected in it.

———

When she went out to fetch Alma from kindergarten, and had already decided what her article would be about, she saw drops of water collecting on the bathroom ceiling. A leak from the Gershon's apartment, she sighed. She went upstairs and rang the bell. There was no reply. Returning to her apartment she wrote on a piece of paper, "Dear Mr. and Mrs. Gershon, dampness is forming on my bathroom ceiling, apparently one of your water pipes is leaking. Are you aware of this? Are you getting it fixed? Sincerely, Ori Elhayani (Apt. 10)" and then went back to their apartment and stuck the note onto their door.

She was a few minutes late, and knew, in accordance with the custom of the other mothers to wait at the kindergarten gate ten minutes before it closed, that she would find it deserted. Her haste to get there was surely evident in her movements and clothes. Alma was waiting for her impatiently, walking back and forth along the fence.

"Ima," she called to her, "come and get me already."

The kindergarten teacher, Yael—or was it Ze'ela? she couldn't remember which was which; both of them, in their skirts and with their melodious speech, looked like graduates of the Bnei Akiva religious youth movement—smiled at her and said ever-so-sweetly, her restrained resentment clearly evident, "You shouldn't have rushed, we always take an extra half an hour into account for delays," and opened the gate.

Alma put her arms around her hips and clung to her, as if she'd been abandoned for many long hours, and Ori was conscious of the kindergarten teacher's cold look and didn't know if it was a continuation of her words or a reaction to Alma's dramatic gestures.

Alma said, "Ima, remember you promised we'd go to the playground?" and Ori, somewhat embarrassed by Alma's demand, replied in a confident tone, aware of the kindergarten teacher's calculating eyes, "Of course I remember, sweetie," although she could remember no such thing.

She pulled Alma away, and when they were out of earshot, she asked her, "Alma, when did I promise you that?"

Alma scrutinized her with huge, surprised eyes, "Last night, when I was asleeping."

"Alma, I've told you a thousand times, its asleep, not asleeping. And if you were asleep, maybe you dreamt it?"

"No, I was asleeping and you came to kiss me and I got up and you were crying."

"Alma, it's not nice to tell fibs."

"I'm not telling fibs. I never tell fibs. And I cried too and you said we'd go to the playground."

"Honey," she said, bending down to her and caressing her shoulders, "Ima has to finish writing an article. Don't you want to go home and draw? Or watch SpongeBob SquarePants?"

At the mention of SpongeBob SquarePants, her favorite TV program, the infinite reruns of which she could sit and watch for hours at a time, laughing at the escapades of the yellow sponge and his sidekick Patrick, the dim-witted pink starfish, Alma's mouth opened slightly, but only for a moment, she clamped it shut, bared her teeth, shrugged herself out of her grasp, and yelled, "No. You promised. You promised."

"Okay, okay, sweetie." She stood up and, frowning, marched her towards Meir Park.

They got home about an hour later. She was exhausted from sitting on the bench and keeping a constant watchful eye on Alma, and Alma was still full of vitality, in high spirits, excited by the slides and swings, by the stupid net of blue plastic rings that infants her age liked to hang from and shriek gleefully. As soon as she entered the apartment she heard the sound of water, drops striking the enamel bell of the sink.

"What's that?" Alma asked.

"I think I left a tap on in the shower," she said tiredly. "I'll go and turn it off in a minute. Ima has to make herself a cup of coffee. Then we can find something for us to eat."

Alma bounded from the front door to the bathroom, and as Ori trudged to the kitchen she heard Alma break into song, "It's raining, it's pouring, the old man's snoring."

"Alma," she called to her, "it's not a game, leave the tap alone and come here."

But Alma continued with her ditty, which was becoming more and more wild, "Oh, oh, it's raining, I love the rain."

That child is going to make me lose my mind, thought Ori. A sudden rage at her daughter's rebelliousness—which she'd never experienced before, because Alma's stubbornness and rebellious spirit usually made her laugh—assailed her.

"Alma," she yelled harshly, "I told you to leave the tap alone."

"But Ima," Alma shrieked in delight, "it's raining from the ceiling."

Ori came out of the kitchen and looked down the hallway; she saw Alma standing at the door to the study, her cheeks flushed with excitement and her hair damp.

"What have you done to yourself?" Sudden rage spread through her body. "I told you," she continued through clenched teeth as she walked towards Alma, "not to play," she grabbed her arm and shook her, "with the water."

"But Ima," said Alma with the same glee, "it's raining," and she pointed into the study.

Yes. It was raining. A crack had appeared across the entire length of the ceiling, and thin streaks of water were pouring down, becoming increasingly stronger. The floor was covered in a thin layer of water, which was starting to creep out of the doorway like an eager animal. Ori muttered a curse, and Alma held her breath in wonder. Ori's rage abated, evaporating with the blurted curse, and the child didn't have a chance to wonder what had aroused it.

"Alma," she said urgently, "go and fetch the bucket from the laundry room."

Alma obeyed without question, skipping away merrily.

Ori grabbed a squeegee and began sweeping the water towards the drain in the shower. The water continued to gush from the ceiling and cascade to the floor. A bucket won't be enough, she thought as she placed it on the floor.

"Let's go and get some pots, Alma."

Alma nodded excitedly and skipped ahead. They started darting between the kitchen and the study, adding pots to the row Ori arranged on the floor parallel to the crack in the ceiling. The streaks of water dripped into the pots, striking the stainless steel and the Teflon coatings, emitting notes. Each pot according to its size and what it was made of raised its voice in song, a cantankerous, clumsy melody. Alma listened spellbound, and Ori went to the bedroom, returning with a towel and clean clothes. As she toweled her hair, Alma began weaving her voice into the water's music. "It's raining from the ceiling, and the music's . . . " and stopped short. "Ima," she said, "what rhymes with ceiling?"

"Unappealing," said Ori.

Alma giggled, and her body moved in a dance as she sang, "It's raining from the ceiling, and the music's unappealing."

"Yes," Ori added, "very modern music. Your father would have enjoyed it. Alma, go to the living room and change into these clothes. I need to make some phone calls."

Into the melody she was singing over and over Alma squeezed in the question, "Who are you calling, Ima?" and continued chanting her rhyme, "It's raining from the ceiling, and the music's unappealing."

"Mr. Gershon, to tell him to come home and turn off the tap in their apartment, and Abba, who knows where the Gershon's water meter is," Ori replied, not knowing why she bothered, because Alma was completely absorbed in her song and was trying to add words and sentences to it that described what she was doing, "And now I am undressing," she sang.

Mr. Gershon—that was how his number was saved in her cell phone, without his first name which she didn't know, and that was how she addressed him, formally, much to his satisfaction, and he made sure to look after her affairs at the residents' committee—could barely be heard through the interference in his cell phone. He promised to come home right away and take care of the problem. He even directed her, with repeated shouts, in sentences flattened into single words, how to locate the water meter in the building's backyard. But she still called Barak. His cell phone, however, was switched off. She was transferred directly to his voicemail that floridly assured callers that he would surely have answered had it been within his power, but since he is unavailable, and so on and so forth, he humbly requests callers to leave a message. She tried his office number and his secretary answered, in a more businesslike tone than usual, that he was out at a meeting.

"What meeting?" Ori asked.

"Really, Mrs. Shulman," said the secretary, "you don't expect . . . "

"If you're insisting on calling me Mrs.," she cut her off abruptly, "then it's Ms. Elhayani and not Mrs. Shulman. Where's Barak?"

"I told you, in a meeting. He said he wouldn't be coming back to the office today."

"Why is his cell phone switched off? When he's in a meeting he usually puts it on 'silent' in case of emergencies."

The secretary laughed nervously, and the barking sound erupting from the receiver made Ori realize how ridiculous her question was. What's gotten into her?

"Is it an emergency?" asked the secretary.

"No," Ori answered and dropped the receiver into its cradle.

———

The floor in the study was dry, and Alma was engrossed in her drawings in the living room. Nothing could have dragged her away from them. She had drawn as if bewitched since an early age, from the moment she had sufficient control over her finger movements. On her second day at kindergarten Ori had come to pick her up, and as she stood at the entrance the kindergarten teacher, Ze'ela or Yael, had stared at her and asked, "Who do you belong to?" and she'd said, "To Alma." The kindergarten teacher had looked at her suspiciously, but Alma's face lit up when she saw her, and she earnestly trudged up to them.

"I thought . . . " said the kindergarten teacher, choking on her words, "that Alma doesn't have . . . " and lowered her chin and voice, the end of her sentence lost in an unintelligible mumble.

"You thought what?" Ori inquired.

"That she doesn't have . . . well . . . that her father is raising her on his own."

"Where did you get that idea? Did Alma say that?"

"No, it's just that your husband . . . he came here on his own to inquire about the kindergarten, and he brought her on the first two days and picked her up yesterday and . . . here, see for yourself."

The kindergarten teacher turned towards a brown chest of drawers and opened the one with a sticker marked "Alma Shulman". She took out several large sheets of paper and handed them to Ori. Ori looked at them with rising embarrassment. Alma, who already knew how to write a few words, even if she wrote them backwards, in mirror writing, had drawn two recurring figures, one tall and rounded and the other small, adorned with the outline of a dress. Above the tall figure was the word "Abba" and above the other—"Alma". The background of the drawings was rich with detail and varied from one drawing to another, grass, flowers, a house, sky, sun, clouds, stars, a rainbow, mountains. And in each of them the word "Ima" appeared as well, sometimes above a sun with a human face, at others above a cloud sailing above the two figures.

"So you can see why . . . " stammered the kindergarten teacher.

"You thought I didn't exist?" Ori finished her question.

The kindergarten teacher nodded.

Ori said casually, "Alma and her father play this game that Alma has to hide me in one of the details of her drawings and he has to find me. You know how it is with kids, game and reality get mixed up." She thought the kindergarten teacher believed the story she had just made up.

On the way home she asked Alma why she draws her in a sun or cloud or rainbow, and Alma replied, "Because, Ima, that's what you're like," and even when Ori insisted and asked her in a different way, she didn't change her answer, "Ima, that's what you're like." Although Alma hadn't provided a sufficiently clear answer at the time, she realized she'd made a mistake, and this display of sensitivity and understanding that went beyond her years terrified Ori, because from that day Alma made sure to draw both her parents beside her when she was in the kindergarten, but at home as she labored over more elaborate drawings, she reverted to her old ways and obliged Ori to break forth from nature.

As Ori examined her drawings now, she saw that Alma had changed her habit somewhat. In every drawing a girl was standing in the pouring rain. In two of them, in the corner of the page, a human-faced sun was beginning to rise, and Ori mumbled to herself, "What is that intense radiance rising in the window? No, for that is the east and Ori is the sun."

The door opened hesitantly, quietly. Barak was home, late again, in his tracksuit, its glowing whiteness somewhat dulled.

He stood at the door for a few seconds, indecisive, halfway in, halfway out, his lips trying to say something, but remaining silent. Ori didn't say a word either. In the heavy silence she heard one of Alma's crayons fall to the floor and Alma getting up in a rustle of paper. Alma crossed the room towards him with the gravity that frequently enveloped her when she broke away from her drawings, stopped and turned to face Ori.

"Ima, can I tell him?"

"Of course you can tell him, sweetie, it's not a secret."

"What is it Alma?" asked Barak, shutting the door behind him.

"Did your secretary tell you I was looking for you?" asked Ori.

"Yes, but she told me it was nothing, only that you sounded a bit strange on the phone."

"And that wasn't important enough for you to call back?"

"I assumed that if it was important, you'd call again an hour later. Or leave a message."

Alma was fidgeting, her exaggerated movements signaling to them both that the restraint she was forcing upon herself was about to collapse.

"Abba," she shouted, "it rained inside the house!"

Barak looked questioningly into space.

"And I made up a song about the rain," continued Alma and broke into song; she'd forgotten the original melody, so she made up a new one, just as tuneless as its predecessor, "It's raining from the ceiling . . . " and stopped short. "Ima, what are the words of the song?"

"And the music's unappealing," Ori replied, adding, "There was a leak. A pipe burst in the Gershon's apartment. But I've taken care of it."

"I'm sorry," said Barak, "I switched off my cell phone, and you probably tried . . . "

"And the music's unappealing," sang Alma cheerfully.

"Sorrow is a worthless currency from the outset," she said, "and overusing it devalues it even more."

"It's raining from the ceiling," Alma's voice rose and became unruly.

Barak dropped his briefcase and the bag of clothes. With strained affection he said, "You should write a book of all these phrases of yours," and drew closer to her, to embrace her.

She turned her back to him and said, "I've got an article to finish."

"Ori," said Barak, but Alma's triumphant shout, "And the music's unappealing," cut him short.

———

Barak was sitting on the couch in the living room, Alma curled up in his thick arm, its hairs still damp from the shower. He was reading to her from a book she knew by heart, and when Ori walked past them on her way to the kitchen to make another cup of coffee, he looked up at her but didn't stop reading the story, reciting the words from memory. "And the rabbit promised that tomorrow, when the moon was full, he'd leap . . . "

"No, Abba!" Alma protested, "you don't even know how to read. 'And the rabbit said: Tomorrow, when the moon is full, I'll leap through and make a hole in it.'"

Ori smiled to herself grumpily, and Barak remained silent.

"Go on, Abba, go on," Alma urged him.

"Alma," said Ori, "it's time for bed."

"No, Ima, it's not fair. We'll finish the story first."

"Sweetie," Ori insisted, "you've been very active all day and what with all the excitement of the leak . . . "

"Can I tell about the rain at morning circle?" Alma asked enthusiastically.

"Yes," said Ori, and although she was accustomed to the natural perception her daughter displayed regarding secrets and keeping them, she felt angry at her question. "You can, but only on condition that you go to bed now." She held her hand out to her. "Let's go and change into pajamas."

"I'll put her to bed," said Barak.

"Yes," said Alma immediately, "I want Abba."

She let them tear themselves off the couch and stride to Alma's room, Alma humming something to herself, perhaps the song she'd composed, and resumed making her coffee, then went back to the study.

The article was almost finished. She just had to write the concluding paragraph, but now, just as she was about to be rid of it and its threat, she dragged her heels. The sound of laughter came from Alma's room, and she sprawled in her chair, listening to her husband and daughter.

"Now," said Alma beseechingly, "tell me about my name."

It was the final stage of the bedtime ritual, before the goodnight kiss, a new stage that Alma has added to it two months ago. In Ori's view the whole sequence of events that had led to this addition was ludicrous. And it was all because of Amir Peretz, whose name she'd first heard only six years ago when she'd been living with Avner. In those days Amir Peretz was chairman of the Histadrut trade union and he'd called a general strike to protest against new economic edicts, or for improvement in the employment and pay conditions of the workers he represented, she couldn't remember exactly. Only the mountains of refuse piling up in the streets of Tel Aviv due to the strike annoyed her. The stench and the swarms of flies forced her to think about what was going on in the world, to emerge from the fortress that was isolated from the futility of reality she had built with Avner. One night Avner was watching Amir Peretz's speech on television and he laughed, saying to her, "Look what your neighbor is doing."

"My neighbor?" she asked in bewilderment.

"Yes, he's from Sderot, isn't he?"

"So?"

And Avner, with a kind of amused vulgarity, stated, "You southerners have this tactic of being insulted. This garbage strike is just like the boycott of silence you condemn me to when you're offended by something."

The evening after the Labor Party primaries, when Amir Peretz was elected to the party leadership, Barak came home upset and furious from his day's work at the office.

"You wouldn't believe it," he said to her, "they're all stinking racists in this country."

It was strange to see this large, rational computer professional, forgetting his conditioning for a moment, it didn't happen very often. When she'd first met him, in a Tel Aviv bar that had since closed down, she didn't know that she'd want him, so she'd let him talk to his heart's content about his childhood and his plans and aspirations. He was well off. A prattling fool, she decided to herself when he didn't stop talking. As they talked he inquired about her surname, and when she told him, he said, "Ah, I support your struggle."

"What?"

He laughed. "I . . . I support your . . . "

And she looked at him, waiting for an explanation.

"You know, what was done to you Eastern . . . Mizrahi Jews."

She flinched. The whiplash of that word, "Mizrahi", smarted on her skin. But still, she said, "Tell me, where do you think you're living, in what year?"

"But you . . . "

"Yes, my parents are from Morocco."

"The wage differences are just unbelievable and the fact that there's virtually no representation of Mizrahi Jews in the media and politics and the history that's taught in the schools . . . "

Every hackneyed slogan she'd ever heard was crammed into a single sentence he tried to articulate, and she stopped him there.

"It's not your war," she said.

But she was wrong. If ever there was a war he considered worthy it was the one being waged on the social front. And she couldn't understand why. When she was pregnant with Alma, he told her, "She'll have my surname, Shulman, so you should choose a first name for her, you know, one in which you can express . . . " and fell silent.

"Alma," she said.

"*Al-ma ve-lama*, for what reason?" he'd asked, playing on the Hebrew name Alma. And in Alma's room, where the exchange between her and Barak was being reproduced word for word, Alma squealed in delight at the pun and the squeal filtered into Ori's memories and fired them. Always the same question. Always the same squeal.

"Why don't you give her a name, you know, that has a more Mizrahi intonation. For example, name her after your mother . . . "

"Alma is a Hebrew name. And anything Hebrew is first of all Mizrahi," she pronounced, and saw how her answer pleased him and how he enjoyed telling it to Alma, who recited the sentences at bedtime like a periapt against nightmares, a meaningless but effective formula, and Ori hoped it was nothing more than a passing phase in her development. But Alma's eyes shone that evening when Barak came home upset. Ori responded apathetically to his assertion. He went on to tell her that half the people in the office had announced that they wouldn't be voting for Amir. That's what they called him, as if he were a close friend—Amir.

"They're all hypocrites," he told her. "Everybody's making excuses all of a sudden. I don't like Amir's economic position. Amir doesn't have any experience, and all that crap. Even Hazan from my team is starting to sing that tune. And he's a Mizrahi."

He followed her from the study to the living room, talking and talking, inundating the space with a heavy fog. She shut herself off from his gushing words, didn't let him tell her anything, occasionally grasping at a phrase, a combination of syllables that sparkled like stifled stars in the fumes of his words—just to maintain the semblance of a conversation. She didn't know why she was making the effort; Barak loved her unconditionally, even when she didn't display an iota of interest in his affairs.

"Mizrahi," she repeated softly.

He, probably interpreting her feeble tone as scorn, fell onto the couch next to Alma, who was listening inquisitively to the discussion, her eyes moving between her parents, and began his tirade all over again.

"They're all hypocrites. They should at least admit that they don't want to vote for him because they can't conceive of a Mizrahi Jew as a prime minister . . . And I'm damned if I understand you, Ori. You grew up in Netivot, didn't you? How come you don't have a shred of sensitivity to this issue? It's as if you're deaf and blind to what's happening in the country."

She sighed, but didn't respond. Holding these debates over and over was so tedious. It was neverending, and always with the same primeval passion, as if his eyes were only just opening and seeing the world and its order.

Barak went on. "I don't intend for my daughter to grow up in this reality that's whitewashed and called Israeli. We have to tell Alma," he said, and Ori could see Alma straitening up and paying attention at the sound of her name, "about her roots."

"What, am I a tree? Did you find me in a forest?" Alma suddenly shouted.

"What?" asked Ori, bewildered, and then understood. "No, not that kind of roots."

"I want Abba to tell me."

Ori glanced at him, and he told Alma, "Tonight. I'll tell you at bedtime tonight."

And that's what happened. Every few nights Alma demanded the story of her name, the story of her roots. Ori wasn't prepared to play along, and wouldn't tell Barak about her childhood and adolescence in Netivot, not even for the sake of the story he weaved for their daughter. Barak called her father and Ofra—her relationship with them was cool, flimsy—to try and elicit details, and held long conversations with them. It became a regular thing, a telephone conversation every few days. He even went to visit sometimes, taking Alma with him.

As she sat in her study, the sounds in Alma's room gradually abating, she knew how she should conclude her article, and she wrote furiously until it was done. As she completed the final sentence, Barak asked from the doorway, "How's the article coming along?"

"It looks like I'll be working half the night," she lied. "The deadline's tomorrow morning."

He nodded. It seemed as if he wanted to say something more, but changed his mind. She sat in the study, passing the time reading old files, until she heard him whisper "Good night" to her from the bedroom. Then she reread the article, corrected typos, and emailed it to the editor of the supplement with a few words of contrite apology—about exceeding the specified number of words, about deviating from the subject, and in general for daring to send him a hodgepodge of thoughts that hadn't yet matured sufficiently.

She switched off the computer and went to the bedroom. Barak was deep in slumber. She lay down next to him, fully clothed, her back to him, tensely alert to his movements, and that tension remained with her throughout the night.

She dreamt she was awake, or that part of her was awake and watching the other part moving restlessly in its sleep. Just before sunrise she remembered that Avner had promised to take her to visit his family, and she'd traveled to Haifa on her own to wait for him there, until he arrived. The city wasn't as he'd described it: blackened with soot, emanating fumes of iron and desolation. It wasn't even a city. Just an endless field of hibiscus bushes stretching over the side of a mountain and sloping towards the sea, and she stood in it, not knowing where to turn. It started raining and the heads of the bleeding flowers broke off their stems and fell to the ground, until the field was strewn with chalice carcasses, and she thought: falling bird corpses. She didn't know why the flowers laying torn and tattered in water that tasted of iron reminded her of a flock of crushed birds. She turned away from the spectacle, turning her back to the sea.

Her brother Asher stood facing her.

He said, "Ori, you're dreaming about rain. Do you know what Ima says about rain in dreams?—rain in a dream heralds death."

He drew closer to her, sadly, to kiss her forehead, and his kiss was replaced by Barak's fluttering lips and the cloud of Dolce & Gabbana enveloping him, and she woke up.

When Barak left, taking Alma with him, she stayed in bed and thought to herself: what am I supposed to make of that now?

———

March 27, 2004

Dear Ori,

You didn't reply to my previous letter, but I'm writing you another one anyway.

I think I deluded myself. I told Ophir I'd written to you and that I wasn't going to wait for you to reply. But I did wait. I thought, what could be simpler for you than to contact me now that you have my address? For a few weeks I was angry with you for not

262

making the effort. I called your publisher to ask if they'd passed my letter on to you and the girl who answered was very pleasant and said she'd check and even got back to me and assured me that the letter had been delivered.

Then my anger dissipated. I had other worries. My pregnancy with our daughter Re'ut was difficult, with a lot of pain and tests. Ophir decided to leave the advertising agency and open an independent studio. And on top of all that, our son Sagi broke his left collarbone. He built a tower with building blocks at kindergarten and then tried to climb up it. The kindergarten teachers weren't looking and he fell to the ground. I couldn't bring myself to yell at the kindergarten teachers, although I should have.

You ask why? In 1995, after Ophir came out of the army, we went to the States. Ophir was accepted to the dance and choreography program at Julliard. He had a scholarship that covered his tuition. We rented a two-room apartment in Brooklyn and I got a job as a teacher's aide at a kindergarten for Israeli immigrants. They didn't demand much. The parents wanted a Hebrew-speaker looking after their children. I worked there for a year and discovered how complicated it is to control a large number of children. More than five kids and you lose your sanity. There aren't enough eyes to see everything that happens, and believe you me, after a few weeks you sprout additional eyes. But children, and that's part of raising them, get hurt. If they don't fall or get hit by another child, they catch every possible virus. I remember I always used to ask Ophir, who do you think is more dangerous, a three-year-old bully who hits his friends, or a toddler who gets measles? But you probably know yourself. I read in an article in the weekend paper that you have a little girl. Alma, wonderful name. Why don't you bring her over to play with Re'ut? They're the same age and I'm sure they'll get along.

I don't mind saying this anymore, even though pain shoots through me when I say that the year in Brooklyn was the worst year of my life. Ophir's studies were hard. He'd come home in the evenings frustrated and blaming himself for all kinds of things, "I'm not talented enough," "I haven't got what it takes to be really good," and "Now I understand how our parents' lives and ours were screwed when they stuck them in Netivot." He felt that he'd started dancing when he was already too old. Although, as you probably remember, too, he started dancing when he was about twelve, and joined a dance company when he was thirteen and a half. I'd try to encourage him. But he'd just blow up at me and take all his anger and bitterness out on me. Then he'd apologize and say he didn't know what had gotten into him, that they're giving them hell there, that the mental and physical exertion is so great, and the results so meaningless, that it is impossible to avoid depression.

But a few days later the whole thing would start all over again.

I was at a loss. I began to fear the evenings we spent together at home, I'd try to stay at work as late as I possibly could. Ophir's self-esteem was the only thing we ever talked about, and we gradually got fed up with it. For six months we communicated only through angry and apologetic looks. I felt that Ophir hated being closed up in the same place with me, that every time he saw me it reminded him of the abyss he couldn't stop himself falling into.

At the time a new girl came to the kindergarten, Rayne, three years old, and I instantly fell in love with her. There was something frightened and shrunken about her, and despite her age she still wasn't talking in whole sentences, only in word pairs comprising a word in Hebrew and its equivalent in English, or should I say the other way round? When she wanted a drink, she'd say, "mayim water" and sometimes "water mayim". The funniest thing was hearing her ask to go to the bathroom, "pee-pee-pee".

Most of the time she'd sit on the side and watch the other children. The head kindergarten teacher told me that her mother had been killed in a car accident a few months before. Perhaps that's why I fell in love with her. I decided to teach her to speak properly. I'd spend hours with her, repeating sentences in English and Hebrew. I quickly discovered that she had no problem at all articulating whole sentences. She'd repeat my sentences without any difficulty and she'd say them clearly. But somehow she didn't make the connection between saying the sentences and speaking.

Her nanny usually came to pick her up from kindergarten. But one day a young man came. He asked me if I was "Sigal-Violet". To this day I have no idea who told Rayne that my name is short for Sigalit and that sigalit is violet in English. But that's what she called me. The man, Neil, told me she didn't stop saying my name at home.

His appearance reminded me a little of Josh from "Josh and Judy". Sturdy, medium height, with green eyes and a goatee.

I'm sure you can guess the rest.

He somehow convinced himself that I'm the spitting image of his late wife, and the proof was how comfortable his daughter felt with me. He showed me pictures of her. We're both dark, but aside from that there's no resemblance between us.

It's difficult for me to talk about these things. It's difficult for me to write them, Ori, they seem so private and filled with emotions that no one but me can understand. And yet, when I do talk about them, I'm ashamed. You know, sometimes I have to watch all kinds of films that come to my video library and I can't believe the stories they tell. Everything's so familiar and repetitive: love, separation, quarreling, making up. At the time I didn't feel what I feel now, that those scriptwriters who write all the really bad films had decided to gang up on me of all people. Because not only did Neil start showing a romantic interest in me, and I found out that his family is one of the wealthiest in Florida, Ophir tore a tendon in his ankle in the middle of dance class.

They say that dancers and actors sustain injuries when they're stressed, when they feel that they're not in the right place. They stop listening to their body from the inside and force it to move from the outside. I don't know how true this is generally speaking, but it's not a bad explanation for what happened to Ophir. His career was cut short and he decided to come back to Israel.

I didn't want to come back yet. I felt a responsibility towards the kindergarten. I had three months left to work there. And I also had Neil. You know what's funny? I don't have anything to say about Neil. What kind of person he was. I don't think I really knew him. He wasn't in love with me, he was in love with his wife's ghost and that's why he demanded that I behave like her. You know what's even funnier? His late wife was called Rivka. I can just see you now, laughing hysterically.

So why I am telling you all this, you ask? Because Neil asked me to marry him, offered to pay for me to study design, offered me the whole world. And I turned him down. I didn't know what was happening with Ophir, but I missed him. And you. Strange, isn't it? When he proposed to me I asked him for a day to think it over, and I thought about Ophir and about you. I tried to figure out what you'd do in my place, and I remembered your courage, how you saved yourself. I remember when it was announced in class that you were leaving, that you'd been accepted into a boarding school in Jerusalem, that you'd written to the principal. I won't repeat what some of the girls said. By that time you were already far away from all of us. You stayed back a year and did everything you could to distance yourself from Ophir and me. We understood you, we thought it was a delayed reaction of mourning for your mother. That's what Ophir said. You didn't share your plans with anybody. And I remember that my reaction to the announcement was, Great, I'm happy. Because you were becoming extinguished before my very eyes and you refused to accept help. And when we came to offer our condolences you were rude and violent.

I knew what I had to do: ask myself what I truly want.

I asked, and answered myself, as I've probably already written to you, I'm a simple woman and this world that's so full of temptation and opportunity is too powerful for me. If I'm not careful it'll crush me. I can't want things out of life that I'm liable to regret.

I came back to Israel, to Netivot, to help Ophir get out of his depression. Since returning from the States he'd been living in his parents' house and didn't get out of bed. I told him everything, about Neil and my decision.

He didn't respond, didn't react to me, it was as if I wasn't even there. I grabbed his chin and forced him to look at me. Nothing in his eyes, nothing in his face. I'll never forget that emptiness that had taken hold of him.

A lot had happened during the year we were away from Israel. My oldest brother was appointed rabbi of a congregation in Jerusalem and had moved my parents there as well, whose attitude towards me had been cool since I'd given up religion. I don't make a big deal out of it.

Ophir's parents gave us a room in their house and I spent weeks and weeks with his silence. I'd take him out for walks, read to him from the popular science books he liked so much. He just stared at me. One day I remembered that when we were teenagers and argued about religion and God he told me that I should listen to music. Music, he said, is something that comes to you from the outside, but you can only understand it if it's already played inside you. When it is small and ordinary, the music, it is the monsters that chased you in your childhood, hid under your bed and howled and wailed at night. But when it is truly great it comes like a sound from another world. So I started putting on music. He'd curl up on the bed and weep silently. He'd cry for days, Ori, and as I recall it now I'm crying too. His will returned to him slowly and gradually. The first sign that he was recovering was when he agreed to look at himself in the mirror. Before that, every time he stood in front of a mirror he'd be startled. One

267

day I saw him standing in the middle of the room, waving his arms in the air, bending his knees, like the stretching exercises he used to do before practice, then he raised one foot and lost his balance. He didn't notice me watching him. He crumpled to the floor and wept, heartrending sobs. I went to him.

I think that was when things began changing for him. There may have been other things that happened that I didn't see. Maybe it wasn't his first attempt. But that day his recovery process began for us, and it was slow and with frequent regressions. But he made it. We rented an apartment together in Beersheba, and then moved to Ness Ziona. Ophir decided to study graphic design.

Perhaps I shouldn't be burdening you with my story, Ori. But I couldn't help thinking about it when I read your last book, *Beyond the Cities of Darkness*, which came out two weeks ago.

Do you believe that sometimes, when a strong bond is forged between people, especially in childhood, events in their lives continue to touch one another even after they go their separate ways? I do. More than believe. I know for sure. One time I told Ophir as much and he looked at me oddly. He told me that in modern physics there's a phenomenon that's called "quantum entanglement", which describes two particles that have been separated and can influence each other's state from great distances. If this explanation sounds obvious to you, then it's because I'm quoting Ophir word for word.

But obvious or not, perhaps that's what's happening to us, because in your book you describe three children whose lives change when one of the girls breaks a promise. And Ziva, one of the three children, discovers that her ten-year-old sister Sarit, who her parents had never told her about, disappeared a year before she was born. After Sarit's disappearance her parents moved to another city and raised her to be Sarit Number Two, and she doesn't actually know who she is. And that's the journey she embarks on, to find out why she is a replica of another girl.

I held my breath when I got to the chapter in which Ziva finds out. No way, I told myself. True, both your books are about the importance of being who you really are. But I think there's more than that in Ziva's story.

I let Ophir read it. He said that parts of it could easily have been episodes in the TV series "Buffy the Vampire Slayer", which is the greatest compliment he can give anything. Do you know the series? Ophir thinks Buffy is the most important TV series of the decade. I'm not all that crazy about it but I can understand why Ophir is. Buffy is a typical all-American girl and all she wants in life is to be popular. One day she discovers that she's the Slayer and that her role is to fight against the powers of evil, a kind of savior. I think it's a very childish format that's very strong in our culture. Nowadays everybody wants to be chosen and special. That's what Ophir wanted too. Perhaps he hasn't completely given up on his dream.

Two months ago he made me watch episodes from the sixth series. After he exhausted me with his explanations, we sat down to watch. Buffy's friends bring her back from the dead. At the end of the previous series she sacrificed her life to save the world, if I understood correctly. In the first episodes she's a bit bewildered. And I can't blame her, I can't imagine what it's like to come back from the dead. But time passes and she's stuck in her bewilderment. She's surrounded by friends who brought her back to life, but she's not with them. She's distant and impenetrable. She harbors a lot of resentment towards them. I didn't really understand her. I didn't try very hard either. Truth is I found it quite boring. At some point Ophir told me, she reminds me of Ori after her mother died.

I hope you're not offended. Your name comes up in our conversations sometimes, and not only in that context. The comparison with Buffy is not an exception. Because there was a time when that series took over Ophir's life. Everything reminded him of something in it, at work, in the supermarket, in hotels. Even Sagi caught the bug from him. A few days ago we bought him a small hamster and he named it Buffy. He's a sweet boy and so clever. He loves music. He reminds me of Ophir. Since he became himself again his passion for music has grown. He spends hours in front of the computer screen searching the internet for music that no more than a hundred people have heard about, so he says. In time he hopes to find a small pub where he can DJ this music. But he doesn't stand a chance in Ness Ziona. Who knows, maybe he'll find a pub like that in Tel Aviv.

And then will you come and hear him?

Love,

Your partner in quantum entanglement,

Sigal

THREE

Dinner

THE HOSTESS AT THE RESTAURANT, a noble-limbed young woman, without makeup, whose black hair was held by two pins set with blue roses, told them they'd have to wait. "About ten minutes. Your table isn't ready yet," she said, indicating the couches at the entrance.

Ori saw Barak's roving eyes linger for a moment on her retreating back, then moving on to scan the faces in the restaurant. She knew he would be daunted by the elegance of the place, but she still insisted. She'd left him a message on his cell phone, which in recent days he had taken to switching off during parts of his working day, to skip going to the gym and come home early that evening.

"Why?" he asked when he came in.

Alma, who was dancing and skipping around Lital, the babysitter, shouted towards him, "Abba, Abba, I'm so gladdy you're my daddy," and burst into laughter.

"Because it's ages since we've been out just the two of us," she replied.

That was the thought that had passed through her mind that morning. A few days earlier as she lay in bed contemplating the dream that had frightened her and burrowing into her memory, she'd realized that it had been ages since they'd gone out together, gone out, not to some concert a childhood friend of theirs was giving, just the two of them, without Alma running around getting underfoot, forcing her will on the conversation. The last time they'd gone out was the evening after the general election, when the results were published and final. Barak came home from work all exuberance, his face awash with a gentle radiance, and said, "We've got to go out and celebrate."

She agreed, reluctantly, piling up the obstacles: how could they ask Lital at such short notice? And surely the entire Jewish nation would be going out to celebrate and how would they find a restaurant? And how would Alma take it? Because Alma had to be prepared in advance, given advance warning about every separation and evasion. Whenever Barak traveled overseas for work—although since Alma was born he went less frequently, so he said—he had to weave accurate, detailed stories for her in which only Alma's ability to wait, to suffer the burden of time, assured his return home.

Ori tried to protest against these stories. She told herself, this is how stories come into the world about girls going to search for their beloved, walking until their shoes become threadbare, their flesh scarred, west towards the sun and east towards the moon, to extricate them from the clutch of an ugly witch or the spell of a snow queen, their entire faith bound up in patience, surrender, persistence. Oh, how she loathed those women who journey to the ends of the earth to claim their love.

If those tales had been about her it would be she whose animal disguise was thrown into the fire, she who would be snatched up by the north wind in the dead of night and brought to an iron tower to remain in solitude, she whose heart and eye the mirror shard pierced, making her impenetrable, cold, forcing her to play with the jigsaw puzzle made of icicles to form the word "eternity".

On more than one occasion she protested to Barak about the foolishness of his stories. He just laughed and said, "I don't see what's wrong with it." On his last trip, to France, when

Alma was three, she'd sat Alma on her lap and explained to her that Abba was just going to another country, in an airplane, and she demonstrated its flight with a hovering hand and a whistle, and Alma looked up at her and whispered, "But he'll fall into the sea."

That evening, all the way to the modest restaurant, which they went to on foot since it was within walking distance of their apartment, Barak presented his plans for the new government in great detail, as if someone had bothered to ask for his advice. He named the ministers, allocated portfolios and forged alliances and coalitions between them. For Amir he designated the finance portfolio.

"You'll see," he said gaily, "this is going to be the best government we've had here in years, even though the prime minister is a bit of an idiot and only got where he is by sycophancy and brownnosing. The people have spoken. All the analysts are saying that this has been a social vote."

He was especially exuberant about the big right wing party being crushed when he saw its leader's shriveled face on television and the perpetual beads of sweat glistening above his crooked smile.

"The end of the national era," he proclaimed.

She wasn't really listening to him, but at one point she chuckled at a private thought. They were already seated and eating. Perhaps it was the wine that loosened her thinking.

"What's funny?" he asked her.

She looked directly at him with her huge eyes, which hovered unfocused above her wineglass but hadn't lost their power to subdue him. She recalled how Barak had suggested that he call her father to persuade him to vote for the Labor Party. She, already imagining what her father's reaction would be, encouraged him with a kind of malicious glee, and let him find out for himself.

As he talked to her father, the receiver pressed between his ear and shoulder, his head inclined, she watched the astonished expression spread gradually over his face. She was intimately familiar with the views of Moroccan immigrants of her father's generation—they couldn't even conceive that a Moroccan like them was qualified to be prime minister or a social leader. The destruction machine had worked well. All too well. And Barak, at first furious, then crestfallen, resigned himself to the distortion and did not call her father to gloat when the official polls were published on the eve of the election.

"You shouldn't have picked such a fancy restaurant," he said as they sat on the couch.

She guessed at that precise moment when the appearance of the restaurant horrified him: not when they came through the door and he stared in wonder at the two marble pillars bearing crude imitations of Doric capitals, not when they sat in the red-draped lobby and saw the glass- and steel-covered veranda encircled by rosebushes licking the darkness. No. It was precisely when his gaze fell on the garish crystal chandeliers, the light straining to emanate from them, yet still trapped in chunks upon chunks of gold, cascading sluggishly like heavy inflorescence. She actually felt the thought germinating in his mind and bursting forth to his lips, and the recoiling of his body.

"It's not that fancy," she whispered, "and anyway, we can afford it."

"Just because we can doesn't mean we should," he replied.

She was familiar with his *bon mots*, hackneyed by excessive repetition, which were also bandied about by his mother and father, who also had a kind of attraction towards decency, modesty, a fear of ostentation. On several occasions she'd mocked this outlook of his, which in her opinion held not the slightest bit of ideology or social conscience, and was nothing more than superstition, like her mother's—do not lean against the doorposts of the front door lest the inward flow of good fortune be blocked. Refrain from ostentation, pride, lest the wheel of fortune reverse its direction and crush you as it turns.

She didn't like his parents, although she knew they were very fond of her. Perhaps not necessarily fond—they were grateful to her. She had saved their son from childlessness when they had already given up hope. How come such a successful, wealthy and good-natured man, a real darling, can't find himself a bride? It wasn't as if Barak was shy about matters of the heart. He'd had countless girlfriends. He was just unlucky, that's all. Then along came this little orphan with her iron will, and a litterateur no less, even if she does only write for children—after all, there have to be some shortcomings—and within a few months their boy was fixed up, married, had his own home and a little girl.

Miriam Shulman, Barak's mother, didn't spare her opinions when she came to visit her after Alma was born. She methodically enumerated all his previous girlfriends, each woman and her faults, and did not conceal her admiration for Ori. Even though she articulated it in a cool, detached voice. From her own mother Miriam learnt that it was women who created men's futures, who whilst they can be men of the world and declare wars and destroy the world in their wrath, deep inside their souls they are children, indecisive and insecure and in need of a guiding hand. But why is she standing here prattling, Ori must be exhausted.

Victor, his father, didn't open his mouth and stood at the side of her bed, smiling apologetically. Ori wondered at the silence that had fallen upon him, because he, too, was an indefatigable chatterer. His flushed cheeks, as if he suffered from constant oxygen deficiency or was on the verge of a stroke, resembled a rubber mask. He was a retired driving instructor and was forever wearing out his listeners with tales of traffic disasters and transportation catastrophes.

When the urge took him, he'd take a pen and a sheet of paper and sketch crude maps and diagrams. This is the peculiar junction in Holon and this is the wide thoroughfare, a park on one side and a residential building on the other, which poor Yosseleh, an infant whose parents forgot to pick up from kindergarten, had to cross with the kindergarten teacher's encouragement. From here, pointing at the illustration of the junction, you can't see the "STOP" sign on the far corner, a motorcyclist suddenly appeared, saw the child only at the very last minute and slammed on his brakes, but the rear wheel, which swerved to the front from the impetus of braking, hit the boy and sent him flying, flying isn't the word, it hurled him like a Qassam rocket the length of the street. But his all-time favorite, judging by the number of times he told it, was undoubtedly the story about the elderly man—the vétéran—as he called him, and his Romanian accent was evident in his pronunciation of the foreign word—who went out for a walk one afternoon from the senior citizens home where he lived. The old warhorse walked along La Guardia Street. Walked? Hobbled on his crutches, to be more precise, and at the pedestrian crossing waited for the lights to change. An army jeep stopped next to him, and he, with enthusiasm that put his physical abilities to the test, tried to come to attention and salute, and lost his grip on one of the crutches. His gesture moved the soldiers sitting on the jeep and they honked their horn in response. But lo and behold, the honking was so loud that it upset the elderly man's already frail balance, and he fell to the ground. The soldiers were alarmed and called for an ambulance, what were they thinking those guys, but by the time the ambulance arrived the oldster was already deceased.

These thoughts, these recollections, usually made her treat Barak brusquely. But not this time, this time she held her tongue. They hadn't come here for that. She said to him, "I'm sorry. I wanted us to enjoy ourselves. We can leave if you like."

She infused her words with every possible measure of tenderness, but the harshness of the affront had already seeped into them.

Barak didn't notice. He put his arm around her shoulders and said, "You're right. We can afford it once in a while."

The hostess led them to their table, and Ori sensed Barak's growing discomfort. "Calm down," she whispered into his ear before she took her seat.

"Will you at least tell me the reason?"

"The reason for what? The reason why you should calm down?"

"No," and his arm moved to indicate the restaurant, "the reason why we've come here."

She was accustomed to keeping the reasons for her actions to herself. Even when they affected others around her she didn't feel compelled to explain, to provide reasons, details, and all the more so when the impulse for the action was conceived in a dream. She'd nod or smile inscrutably, knowingly. This time she felt duty-bound to answer Barak, to mumble something in response.

"No special reason. I just thought . . . it would be nice."

The beginnings of a sentence bubbled on Barak's lips, but the waitress interrupted him, and Barak, after briefly reading the menu pointed, as he always did, to the dishes he wanted, not saying their names, as if afraid he would be found wanting if he tried. Ori nodded to the waitress and ordered wine. She just wanted two appetizers and a dessert, she doesn't eat much, she announced, and the waitress responded, "It shows."

When the waitress left, Barak stretched out his arm and gently held Ori's hand, smiling.

"I'm glad we came," he said, adding, "Your father called me today."

"What did he want?"

"To ask if we'll be coming to him for the Passover Seder this year."

"No. No. No. No way. Absolutely not. I don't get it, ever since Alma was born we've been telling him no, and he still persists."

"Of course he persists, you're his daughter, and he hardly ever sees his granddaughter, and then only when I drive over and bring her with me."

"He's got enough new children now, he doesn't need Alma. Or me."

"What are you punishing him for exactly? For remarrying after your mother died? Would you prefer it if he'd remained on his own?"

"Yes," she said sharply, emphatically. "Yes. He already had a family."

"It's got nothing to do with your family and you know it all too well."

"Yes, you've already told me a million times."

"And I'll tell you a million and one times, until it sinks in: there are men who simply cannot be on their own. The very thought of it scares them. From a certain age, being without a woman is like losing a leg or an arm."

"And it's not as if he was around when we were kids. My mother was the only creature whose existence he ever noticed. How could he have done that to her? Thank you so much, really, for waiting until I was fourteen before he started going out with all those Russian women who flooded Sderot."

"He didn't do it to your mother. You know as well as I do that it wasn't your mother he was in love with."

A jeering tone crept into her voice as she said, "What do you mean it wasn't my mother? Who then?"

"Do you remember a few months ago when I came back from my parents, I told you I went into their bedroom to get a towel and discovered that they sleep in separate beds?"

"Yes."

"Do you remember what you said? That your parents had the same arrangement."

Ori lowered her eyes and rubbed her forehead. Strange how she hadn't picked up on that contradiction. She knew that people grow up with facts of life, which they perceive as self-evident, natural, which they don't think about, but not her. She actually . . . And why was she letting Barak's word's permeate her, letting his logic interfere with hers . . . She looked up at him.

"There's no contradiction here," Barak continued, the expression on his face, his flickering irises revealing his surprise that Ori had seen logic of some kind in his arguments. "Your father belongs to a very defined breed of men, men who need that anchor, the knowledge that there is a woman in their life. It all stems from that need, the two children your father now has with Narmina as well. Ofra doesn't care. Why should you?"

She wasn't aware that he'd discussed the subject with Ofra. What exactly had they talked about? About Narmina being only twenty-one when she married their father? About the fact that he met her in a pub where she waitressed and within six months knew that he wanted to set up home and start a new family with her? Did Ofra think that was okay? What else didn't Ori know? Barak made more of an effort to maintain close contact with her family than she did.

He would probably find a common language with Asher as well. But they got married long after Asher went to Chicago and made his home there. He'd hardly called during the past five years. A prick of longing pierced her soul as the waitress came over carrying a silver platter, a novice waiter with flushed cheeks stumbling behind her clutching a bottle of wine.

Ori put her napkin, which had been spread over her lap, on the table and stood up. "I need to go to the bathroom," she said, and instructed the novice waiter to fill her wineglass.

Alva is the name of the heroine in her latest book, *A Map to Getting Lost*. Barak thought the heroine's name was a nod at their daughter's name. What does he know? He read the manuscript and said he'd been swept up by it. She remarked that this was the most personal book she'd written, and he looked at her in surprise, his eyebrows converging on the bridge of his nose. She smiled in response.

Alva's father goes on a business trip in a faraway land, and before he leaves he asks her what she'd like him to bring back for her as a present. She asks for a map. Alva has a passion for maps. Her father returns from his trip exhausted and pale, with a map in his satchel. Not just any map, but a map of the city where they lived, which he found, of all the places in the world, in a remote market in a foreign city. Alva discovers that it is a map to getting lost in a city she thought she knew. It shows buildings and sites and hidden alleys that Alva didn't even know existed. Where the map shows a staircase, there's a fence, the point where, according to the map, a footpath splits away from the main path and leads to a coppice, is where the town hall is situated in the actual city. But if you persevere and follow the map, like Alva and her good friend Vered do, you get lost in one city and find another, a dark and perilous city filled with ghosts and wizards, vibrant with a secret history. Meanwhile, as they explore the new city, her father changes before her very eyes, his gaze dulls and he becomes indifferent to her existence.

Had Barak persisted and grilled her she would have told him why she'd said what she had about the book. But he didn't ask. Now—in front of the mirror in the rest room, as she leaned forward and examined her reflection to see whether her frozen countenance had registered the longing that had begun to burn within her, whether it had left traces—she wondered if her expression gave away the sourness she had felt in her heart at the time.

Her face was without makeup. She took some wet wipes from her bag and cleaned her skin, her eyes, and returned to Barak, who was sprawled in his chair radiating indecision.

He'd ordered liver pâté for his starter, and while she was gone he'd spread it on the toasted baguette that came with it, and left it like that, halfway, ready to eat but untouched, not knowing if Ori would be angry when she returned and found him already chewing. Child, she said to herself, and he smiled apologetically, pleasantly, his stretched lips dissipating the usual gloominess of his face, revealing the space between his teeth.

"Everything all right?" he asked, and she nodded. "So what do you say, about your father?"

"Let me think about it for a day or two," she said, and sat down. She held the stem of her wineglass delicately, and sipped. "Good wine," she commented, and noticed that he'd begun the task of eating, imbibing with a passion, engrossed. She passed her fork over the beef carpaccio she'd ordered, cutting it into strips, tearing it into little pieces and taking a bite, breaking off a hunk of bread, a small one, dipping it into the yogurt dressing from the asparagus, and rolling it over her tongue.

She suddenly wanted him to talk to her, to detach himself from the eating lust, from the pleasure in which he was immersed.

"How's the pâté?" she asked.

Barak's mouth was full. He mumbled, nodding his head up and down.

"Alma's so funny," she said, capturing his attention.

He smiled in encouragement. He finished the toasted baguette and moved to the slices of bread for which he'd saved the fig preserves that were intended to enhance the flavor of the pâté. Barak ate them separately.

"Yesterday evening I heard her squealing in front of the TV. You know what she's like when she gets excited about something. So I went to see what was provoking such a reaction in her. There's this program she's addicted to, SpongeBob SquarePants. Damned if I know why, and I'm supposed to know something about children's minds. Bob is this kind of yellow sponge, a kitchen sponge I guess, who lives under the sea in a pineapple, and he has a friend, a foolish pink starfish called Patrick. In just about every episode SpongeBob and Patrick get into some kind of mischief, driving Squidward, who's a querulous, snobbish, tight-ass squid, crazy. He's the cashier in the restaurant where SpongeBob works too, The Krusty Krab. Are you at all interested?"

"Yes," Barak responded between biting and spreading, "Alma told me a bit, but never in an orderly fashion. I don't think she realizes I don't know the characters at all."

"Children her age don't necessarily understand the difference between their own inner world and that of others. Most of the time she assumes that the consciousness of the people she knows coincides with hers, regardless of how intelligent she is."

"I really do think she's remarkably intelligent."

"Yes, her kindergarten teachers say so too," she said and thought about the past few days, during which, for some reason, she'd been filled with anger at every manifestation of her daughter's unruly personality, something that until then had made her heart overflow.

There was something disturbing in Alma's look all of a sudden; it seemed to Ori that it was penetrating all the screens, and that her secrets—not many or dark ones, but still secrets—were an open book to her. In the presence of a third person, especially with Barak's in the evenings, the flood of affection towards her daughter dulled, and she was tense. It was as if at any moment Alma was liable to blurt out something terrible

282

that would shake everything around her. Not knowing why, her daughter's amusing questions, all of which were about God and death, began to embarrass her, to fill her with fear—but not because she thought it was early, much too early, for such questions. When she was two she looked up from the doll she was busy dismantling, and asked, "Who built the sky?" and Ori had laughed. She also smiled with pleasure when a question multiplied and transformed into a series of sophisticated ones.

Alma would plead with every person she met to tell her their age, and wondered, "Are you bigger than my Abba?" Her other investigations gave away her preoccupation with the age issue. "Ima, who's bigger, you or Abba?" and when answered, she would add, "So is Abba going to die first?" No less amusing to Ori were her ponderings about God's dimensions and powers—"Is God this big?" she'd ask moving her hands apart a little, "Or this big?" spreading her arms to the sides; "Can God beat Sandy?" And when Ori demanded to know who Sandy was, Alma replied, "You know, that cute squirrel. SpongeBob's friend. She's the strongest in Bikini Bottom."

"Go on, you started telling me about SpongeBob . . . " Barak urged her.

The flushed novice waiter removed Barak's plate and the dirty silverware, poured more wine into their glasses, swift as a shadow, elusive.

"Turns out it was a rerun of an episode Alma had already seen and memorized, because before each scene she said, 'Now Squidward will say that he's had enough and leave', and so forth. I sat down to watch with her. The theme of the episode was simple, Squidward is fed up with SpongeBob and Patrick making so much noise and getting into mischief and he runs off to a city where everybody is just like him, deadly boring, gray creatures. There he discovers how bland his existence is without SpongeBob and Patrick, and how much he's changed as a result of being around them, that he's learnt something from them, the value of mischievousness. He begins to hate all the other Squidwards who are just like him. Towards the end of the episode he says to himself, 'A Squidward Paradise! Too much Paradise.' Before he spoke this sentence, I could see Alma growing tense, as if she'd been waiting for it throughout the entire episode, and when he said it in his impassive voice, Alma burst into uproarious laughter. I don't get it. What did she understand?"

Barak mumbled again, engrossed in the entrée the novice waiter had silently slid towards him while she talked. Oh, what's the point, she thought, sipping more wine and nibbling her asparagus.

"Don't you like it?" The waitress who had taken their order appeared out of nowhere and stood next to her.

"I do like it, I'm just not all that hungry."

"It shows," said the waitress with a smile. "But perhaps I can tempt you? Would you like to try something else, we've got . . ."

Ori interrupted her with a gesture, and Barak looked up at her, for a split second, with a hollow look, and went back to his plate. She waited patiently until he'd finished.

"What do you think about the conjectures that Amir Peretz is going to get the defense portfolio?" she asked when he shoved his plate away and made himself comfortable in his chair, gulping his wine.

"What? Where did you hear that?"

"I read it on the internet . . . some political analyst . . . "

"Ah . . . nonsense. Since the content turnover on the internet has become so rapid and the average surfer's boredom threshold has gone up, they let any idiot write, so long as he manages to get surfers to post talkbacks."

"And if it's . . . "

"No ifs and no nothing. There's no room for scenarios here. If Amir takes the defense portfolio he's finished. His mandate is a social one. He's got to have the finance portfolio."

"But this analyst . . . he claimed . . . that most of the objections to Amir Peretz stem from the fact that he's . . . that he doesn't have any ministerial experience and that he doesn't have any defense background and that's the way . . . "

He stared at her suspiciously. "Since when have you been so interested in politics?" he asked.

"I just happened to read it, I was at the computer all day."

"Working on your article?"

"Yes."

"How's it coming along?"

"Final revisions. Proofreading. I finished writing quite late last night. Anyway, it'll be published on Passover Eve."

"Are you happy with the result?"

"Not really. The ideas haven't matured completely."

"You always say that."

"Would you like a dessert?" their original waitress interrupted, the novice waiter hiding behind her, alert to any developments, "We've got . . . "

"Could we have the menus?" asked Ori, and the waitress moved sinuously to the pile at the front of the restaurant. "I've dried her out," Ori muttered to herself. Where did that phrase suddenly appear from? When she and Ofra used to argue, and Ofra hit her with a crushing sentence to which she couldn't respond, emerging triumphant, she'd say, "Ah, you've got nothing to say to that. I've dried you out." The foolish, childish pronouncement now produced in her chest an impulse to burst out laughing. But she stifled it, nipped it in the bud.

Two leather-bound paper tablets were placed in front of them. Barak pointed to a line on his menu. Ori ordered a chocolate and halvah parfait with orange rind. It amused her to fashion the words on her lips and tongue, meaningless words, pointlessly supercilious.

When the poised waitress and her submissive apprentice left them, she noticed that printed at the top of the tablets—what thickness was the paper on which the menus were printed? They were of considerable weight—was the chef's credo. She laughed and showed it to Barak, and he glanced at it and said, "I don't get what's so amusing."

"Every chef's become a poet," she explained. "Listen," and in a voice dripping passion she read, "The luminosity of the waves at twilight, the warmth of the lullabies my mother used to sing to me in my childhood, the ethereal glow of the full moon, the rich scent of dew at daybreak, and the taste of a woman's love; these are the materials from which I concoct my confections." And she signed off with a chuckle.

"It actually sounds very impressive to me, very thoughtful."

"Come on," she urged him and saw the waitress and her acolyte standing over them, ready to serve their desserts, stern expressions on their faces.

Barak coughed. "So . . . what were you saying . . . about Amir . . . "

She shrugged. In any event she'd only read the articles that day and only out of boredom. The suspicious expression returned to his face, or so Ori thought, the slitting eyes and crinkling nose typical of suspicion were evident there, although in the dim lighting of the restaurant she couldn't be sure.

"It's true that in Israel the minister of defense always prospers and the minister of finance, no matter how good he is, is always detested by everyone. But it's a mistake, because Amir's mandate is a social one. The people who gave him their vote did so because they want him to advance the interests of the underprivileged populations and the poor. This election, it marked a substantial change. The public said it's fed up of social issues being shunted aside in favor of defense issues, which is a fallacy that's been sold to it since the establishment of the state. And Amir . . . no, it's unacceptable. Simply unacceptable," Barak said. He picked up the starched white napkin that had been spread over his lap and started crushing and twisting it between his fingers.

"Well, I didn't mean for you to get cross about it . . . "

"What's there to be cross about . . . ? At long last we've got a Mizrahi social leader here, from the right class, who worked his way up from the bottom and knows the population he is representing, and now you're telling me there's talk of him falling into line with the old national perception . . . that he's becoming Ashken . . . " halfway into the word he grasped its inanity and tossed the napkin onto the table. Ori completed it for him.

"Ashkenized?" she asked. Although she tried to quell it, the scorn in her voice seeped out.

"Tell me, what is it with you and this whole issue of Mizrahis and Ashkenazis, rich and poor, veteran Israelis and new ones, why are you so cynical about it all?"

"Do you want me to be angry? Well I'm not angry. I know there was injustice, but when I was growing up it was all a dim and distant echo. I'm trapped. I was born too late to be angry about it all and too early to mock it. So I resort to cynicism."

It was a wonderful lie. So wonderful that she could almost believe it herself. But Barak muttered his disbelief, so she thought; disbelief emanated from his bowed head, and when he raised it she once again discerned the suspicious crinkling of his features. Normally she wouldn't have made the effort, would have dismissed him with a weary look, with a sigh. But this evening, this evening, what was this force that drove her to appear exposed before him, to provoke him into breaching the usual screens. So far the force had only manifested itself in an awkward pain, in pangs of longing, to be known, open, forgiven, desirable. She made an effort.

"It sounds as if I'm mocking, but the truth is I can't take part in this debate . . . It seems inherently flawed . . . Whites and blacks, oppressors and oppressed, it all seems like the thing itself, but what if it's actually only a parable and we're trapped in it. What if we haven't even perceived yet that there's a moral. Maybe we're like children who've been told about the fox who went into the vineyard . . . and instead of asking about the meaning of the story, who the fox is, what the grapes signify, what's the meaning of the fox being stuck in the vineyard, we argue about how many grapes he must have eaten in order to become so fat that he couldn't get out." She breathed heavily and stared at him, locking her eyes onto his.

She'd always loathed the romantic filaments that became entangled in a look. The eyes are a mirror, but not to the soul; a more intricate and complex mirror than others, and yet merely a mirror that reflects to the observer his own reflections and likenesses and the refractions of his desire to see himself reflected. It does not reveal to the observer anything about the observed, but only duplicates the look—in a thousand twists and versions—and returns it to its owner.

That was what she believed. Until she met Avner.

When they returned that afternoon, he and she, to the bookshop, a young woman stopped them. She gently took hold of Ori's hand and Ori looked at her angrily. In those years she couldn't bear any kind of uninvited, unprepared for, physical contact. The woman, her black hair gathered in a tight ponytail, wasn't deterred.

"You have to help me," she said, not pleading, but somehow demanding, and Ori's determination to get rid of her weakened somewhat.

"What do you want?" she asked her.

"I'm making an end-of-year film," she said.

"Yes?" asked Avner. "What about?"

"I don't have a proper script or plot. It's more like a collage of city life. My interpretation of an O. Henry story."

"Which one? *The Voice of the City*?" Avner asked and Ori nodded.

"Yes, do you know it? Cool. Well, there's no talking in the film, it's full of silences, moments of intimacy. Like in the story, where the voice of the city is its silence. That's how I want to capture the spaces where the real encounter happens between people in the city, which always happens without talking, when words are redundant. This way, by means of these mute encounters, I want to direct attention to the silences of the filmed text."

Ori cleared her throat and leveled a cautioning glance at Avner. But Avner was hooked.

"What do you want us to do? Why us?"

"Because I saw you walking side by side and it seems to me that there's a connecting thread between you and that's what I'd like to capture. I want you to stand over there," she said, pointing at a jacaranda tree, whose wild inflorescence threatened to extinguish the sky's brilliance, "and look into each other's eyes while I film."

"And that's it?"

"Yes. That's the film I'm making."

"Let's get out of here," Ori said to Avner, ignoring the girl who was scrutinizing them both, especially her, trying to figure her out, to understand her resistance, which was simple and direct.

That phrase, 'the silences of the text', had become too much of a trend for Ori's taste. In her literary theory course one of her teachers used to say, "You have to listen to the silences in the text," closing his eyes in excitement, as if he was really listening to the subtle silence wafting through the slits in the walls and into the spaces between the words, infiltrating between the students' whispers, until it reached him. Three students, who always sat in the front of the class, would nod and bow their heads, loyal partners in his listening.

Avner was walking towards the tree. "Why are you standing there?" he turned to her and asked, holding his hand out to her. "This, too, is a way of meeting like strangers in the dark."

And she'd walked over to him. They stood in the shadow of the jacaranda, beneath the branches that trembled slightly, shedding petals, purple syllables in an interminable melody of which she was a tiny part, perhaps truly the skipping between one line and another. Their eyes drowned in one another's. And in the depths of his look, as she gazed at his irises, breached the boundary of the cornea and descended through the tunnels of his pupils, something opened up before her. The image that emerged in her mind's eye, perhaps inspired by the shower of petals falling on them, was of a flower in a time-lapse nature film, and she felt a response, and knew that she could linger in that look, like an exhausted traveler, for as long as necessary, so that she wouldn't be sent away. She thought, perhaps that's why the organ of sight is called *oculus* in Latin, because it is a gateway to the occult, to the mysterious. Perhaps that's why if you juxtapose the letters of the Hebrew word for 'eye' you get the root for 'respond'.

As she sat in the restaurant facing Barak, she didn't push the memory from her mind, although early that afternoon, as she was preparing for dinner, she had told herself: no more thoughts about Avner. For more than five years she had pushed him back, filling pages upon pages in an attempt to expel him from her bones. And he, like a terrorist organization, secretly armed himself along the border she had set, crossing it at will and striking.

She'd known that she would fail in one of her actions this evening, because when she'd called the restaurant to book a table she'd glanced at the digital clock on the video recorder and was horrified. It showed 13:13—sinister duality, boding ill, and the ill indeed came. Avner had struck accurately this time. When she'd finished giving Barak her explanation—she'd never been more straightforward and direct—she sought the promise that had been given to her then, generously, not for the purpose of receiving. Barak's eyes struck hers, searching. For several seconds they were flooded with warmth, containing, but were immediately turned away from her.

"What?" Barak asked with an embarrassed smile. "What?"

"Nothing," she said, and thought, perhaps that's why if you juxtapose the letters of the Hebrew word for 'eye' you get the root for 'torture'.

"What else? What's happening with the book?" he continued asking, blind and impervious, and two huge white platters were placed in front of them, in the center of each of which, in the heart of the arid porcelain, a sophisticated structure of colors and textures had been created.

She delayed answering him until they asked for the check and went out to the paved pedestrian mall, into the springtime—darkness, so viscous that it caused shortness of breath. Starkly sculptured clouds nesting in the distant sky. If there were a thousand names for velvet, a thousand manifestations, this night would have been one of its names and one of its manifestations, enveloping limbs, stifling their movement. Perhaps it was the wine, liquid velvet flowing through blood vessels.

A thought passed through Ori's mind, shining like a stranger among other thoughts that bustled and purred. If someone were to look at them now, at her and Barak, walking side by side, Barak with his arm around her waist, had someone been watching them—say, if the drunk sprawled on the bench had lifted his leaden eyelids—would he have been able to see a hidden thread? Was there such a thread connecting her to Barak?

"The book," she said in a slightly choked voice; a hornet buzzed inside her, ascending to her vocal cords, "I understand it's doing well, even very well, but the publisher's marketing manager is cautious, he refrains from making proclamations."

Barak sighed in response, "Ah, there's already the smell of summer in the air," and drew even closer to her, to extract physical contact.

Summer, she thought.

It was summer when Avner suggested that she move in with him.

Tel Aviv was afflicted by a plague of cockroaches. Every evening she had to learn how to face her fear of arthropods in her one-room apartment on Florentine Street. At first, when she caught sight of one of the brown insects crossing her small kitchen, or finding a hiding place, much to her horror, under her bed, she'd freeze in revulsion. Then she bought some bug spray and used it liberally. It was almost enjoyable to watch the vermin scurrying around in frenzy until they stumbled, shuddered and fell still.

One night she woke up and had to go to the bathroom. She switched on the light and saw, despite the fog of sleep that deadened her body, a cockroach scurry and come to a halt at the bathroom door, standing in her way, its feelers quivering and twisting. She retreated towards the sink, under which she kept the bug spray. Her movements suddenly became more lithe and fluid, like those of an experienced hunter, and silent, although she knew insects lacked auditory abilities. She didn't take her eyes off the enemy for a second. It was only when she was clutching the spray can and raised it that she realized, judging by its lightness, that it was empty. She shook it a few times and pressed the plastic top—emitting nothing more than a feeble hiss.

She stood for a few moments facing the cockroach, which remained where it was, following the movement of air with its feelers, she hesitated. The solution was simple: she needed something heavy and the only thing within reach was a book. Her left hand reached for the bookstand, a quick glance and she picked up two volumes bound together with a rubber band. Her right hand groped over the surface next to the sink and found a plastic bag. She wrapped the two volumes, making every effort to avoid making rustling sounds, closed the bag and advanced towards the enemy, who had remained in the same spot. Then, from a height of one and a half meters she dropped the lethal package. The rustling of the plastic bag muffled the sound of destruction.

Then, when she scraped the flattened corpse off the floor with some toilet paper and padded delicately into the bathroom to flush it down the toilet, she examined the volumes she had picked up; they were the two volumes of Céline's *Journey to the End of Night*. "That's a journey you won't be making any more," she muttered to the paper-shrouded cockroach as she tossed it into the toilet, and the sheer absurdity of the whole situation struck her. She started laughing, to herself in the bathroom, in the small hours of the night.

That was the first step in an intricate series of cockroach-hunting expeditions, which held immense pleasure drawn from the perverse joy of watching their death throes. She had to invest rational effort in the choice of deadly weapon: first, not just any book would do—a certain thickness was required to do the job. Second, good taste was also required—exterminating vermin with an anthology of Kafka's stories that includes *The Metamorphosis* would be somehow vulgar, not to mention a blatant display of the sin of simplification, thus, too, with all of Kafka's other works, including *The Trial*. *Angels & Insects* by A. S. Byatt was an extreme case. Additional books were disqualified in advance: *Berlin Alexanderplatz*, for example. What's the connection? If you think about it, the sound of the name "Alexanderplatz" resembles a squashing sound, "*platz*", which could be a good imitation of the sound of the miserable insect's demise. This thought brought in its wake all those jokes that were based on sounds that Asher used to tell in their childhood. "Two birds are flying along, when one suddenly says to the other: 'Watch out, there's a brick walllll!'" or "Two frogs are crossing the road and one says to the other: 'Look, here comes a tru-yuck.'" And the best one—"A kid sticks his head out of the train window and shouts: 'Mom, look at that building-ding-ding-ding, and those rrrrrrrrrailings!'"

She went back to the books. *The Brothers Karamazov* was out of the question. But *Crime and Punishment*, in contrast, ah, that was actually interesting. *Anna Karenina*—God forbid. *The Death of Ivan Ilych*—of course! Those were the best books, whose name, at first glance, acquired a different meaning in the new context she accorded them. *Lolita* wasn't a bad choice due to Nabokov's profound affection for insects. But there were others, better ones. *Invitation to a Beheading*, *A Late Divorce*, *Infiltration*, *Death in Venice*, *The Remains of the Day*, *The Day Lasts More Than a Hundred Years* ("No it doesn't," she whispered to herself), *The Catcher in the Rye* ("although it's not thick enough . . . "), *Under the Volcano*, *Lord of the Flies* ("Um, borderline"), *Wuthering Heights*, *The Last World*, *Past Continuous*, *Critique of Pure Reason*, *The Birth of Tragedy*, *Fear and Trembling* ("thin, too thin, too bad . . . "). She laughed as she sorted the books, stacking them one on top of another. Every time she moved to another apartment she sorted them differently, alphabetically by author, or by title, or by publisher, or by subject. She'd now found a new category, and she wondered if it was a good enough reason to buy books. Still, the best book of all for hunting cockroaches, both in terms of thickness and title—*Gone With the Wind*—she'd never dreamt of buying. There was no other fictional character she loathed more than the tiny-waisted, lackadaisical Scarlett O'Hara, who faints in her mansion when love dissipates.

As the memory passed from her mind, as she leaned against Barak, her heels stumbling on the grooved paving of the pedestrian mall, she again felt that longing, which she'd last felt back then, when Avner had said to her, "come and live with me." She almost told him what had happened to her when she was twelve, when she came home with a gash on her temple; that longing that has no substance or form, and is only a burning flame that can't be captured, because something in its flowing essence, always escapes your grasp, falls out of the mind's reach.

The Gates to Wonderland: Seven Annotations

ORI ELHAYANI

1. THE FIRST GATE

When I was a little girl, ten or eleven years of age, I suffered from terrible tooth decay. My milk teeth refused to fall out and rotted in my mouth, which necessitated innumerable trips to Soroka Hospital in Beersheba and surgical extractions. Sadly, the anesthetics at the doctors' disposal had no noticeable effect. My exposed nerves refused to numb, but extraction was essential. The pain of the extractions was nothing compared to the pain in my inflamed and swollen gums.

I remember with a profound longing the trips with my father and mother, the rapid walk, almost run, down the hospital corridors polished by fluorescent lighting, as cold and exciting as an extinguished heart. With a prick of happiness the clinic appears in my mind's eye: gleaming stainless-steel sinks, tiny forceps and saws glistening with a lust for grasping and cutting, polished, purring drills, thin files, stainless steel tweezers, miniature mirrors, tappers. A picture of bloodstained cotton balls, frozen poppies in snowfields, is painted longingly in my mind.

It was a long time before I understood why. At times of unbearable shooting pain the brain tends to release endomorphins, natural analgesics produced in the pituitary gland and the hypothalamus. The greater the pain, the more of these neurotransmitters are released, creating a sense of euphoria, pleasure. There is documentation on fire survivors whose entire body has been burned achieving orgasm, on masochists whose eyes glaze over when sharpened metal is passed across their flesh, on athletes who strain their limbs to the extreme in order to gain another dose of this natural drug.

Without knowing, my mouth provided me with an opportunity to stand before the first gate to Wonderland. I pressed against it feverishly, holding onto the bars and looking in, yearning to pass through.

———

2. A HISTORY LESSON

Wonderland is a late Western invention. It appeared in the twilight of nineteenth-century Anglo-Saxon civilization, with the invention of childhood. The outlines of the ideal were drawn by British author Lewis Carroll (Charles Dodgson) in two works: *Alice's Adventures in Wonderland* (1865) and *Through the Looking-Glass, and What Alice Found There* (1871). Two additional Wonderlands followed them into the world: L. Frank Baum's Land of Oz (*The Wonderful Wizard of Oz*, 1900) and J. M. Barrie's Neverland (*Peter Pan*, 1904). Since then numerous Wonderlands have been established on the foundations of these four, but all belonged to the twentieth century, to different psychological principles.

I am aware of the surprise this division is liable to evoke in readers' minds. Are the years 1900 and 1904 not included in the twentieth century? Many historians hold that the twentieth century actually began in 1914, with the outbreak of World War One, a traumatic event that generated far-reaching changes in the consciousness of Western man, in his naiveté concerning human nature, in social and in the ways of life. Insofar as Wonderland is concerned, I am inclined to agree. The Wonderlands that were invented after 1914, such as C. S. Lewis's Narnia (*The Lion, the Witch and the Wardrobe*, 1950), are less pure versions, more flawed applications of the Wonderland ideal.

A sweeping argument, some would think; and especially since a certain, primitive form of Wonderland can be found in folktales and ancient cultural sources: fairy kingdoms into which innocent travelers are enticed and cannot find their way back. What about the Garden of Eden? some may well ask; is it not the same as Wonderland in Western civilization?

I do not think so. To support my argument, let us stop standing at the gate. Let us walk in.

———

3. CHILDHOOD

But first, a cautionary word. The most important principle of Wonderland is this: only children can pass through its gates. The fortified wall encircling its borders is the wall of age. Adults cannot see it, sense its existence. For Alice, Dorothy, Wendy and her two brothers, entrance is possible only due to their years. As proof, Barrie writes in *Peter Pan*, "On these magic shores children at play are for ever beaching their coracles. We too have been there; we can still hear the sound of the surf, though we shall land no more."

Furthermore, as adults we often believe that Wonderland is a manifestation of childhood itself, of its essence, and at times childhood appears in our memory as uninterrupted expanses of tranquility and pleasure. We are mistaken. If we remember childhood itself as a Wonderland, why then do we need another Wonderland to which children depart? What is this need for an enclosure within an enclosure, the holy of holies of magical kingdoms? In my youth I came across a version of the Ten Martyrs: The High Priest Rabbi Ishmael Ben-Elisha ascends to the heavenly Merkaba to inquire and ask about the source of the decree issued by the Roman Empire against the People of Israel—the execution of thousands of scholars. Rabbi Ishmael encounters Metatron, or Surya, the Prince of the Presence, and demands to know whether the source of the decree is Divine, in which case it cannot be rescinded. And Metatron replies that he heard an echo behind a curtain screeching, "Ten Sages of Israel will be given to the empire." It was this curtain that intrigued me. I wondered why there, too, in the depths of the heavenly palaces there are partitioning screens and curtains? Why is there a place, even in the exposed heart, to which entry is blocked even to Metatron, not to mention everyone else?

And this place is even more sealed than it is customary to think: it is girls, not boys, who find their way into the original Wonderlands. And these Wonderlands have been prepared for them, they have been woven around them and for them by male authors. Wonderlands have a binding extra-literary construct: an adult man labored over it for a little girl; and they have an intra-literary construct: the extra-literary construct has to have a particular, defined form, the form of an exciting journey. This is where the second principle of Wonderland is revealed: the journey itself does not have a true purpose. The girls visiting it remain untouched, coming out of it just as they entered it, in the same body, with the same consciousness.

L. Frank Baum noted that Alice's travels in Wonderland are random, that they do not have any leading motif or theme; that the reader's interest in them stems from the rapid transition between a profusion of ingenious inventions. He is not captivated by the image of the girl, and does not experience tension regarding her fate. To overcome this difficulty he creates in his Wonderland the appearance of a journey: Dorothy tries to find her way home after a cyclone plucks her out of Kansas and carries her to the Land of Oz. Yet the journey construct he created is forced. It is not clear why Dorothy wants to go back home, we know nothing about her life outside Oz, and moreover, Dorothy doesn't learn anything on her journey. In the annotated edition of *The Wonderful Wizard of Oz*, Michael Patrick Hearn tried to accord to Dorothy's adventure the character of an initiation book. In the concluding chapter of the book, Auntie Em asks Dorothy where she's been, and Dorothy answers "gravely", "The Land of Oz." And Hearn asks, "Why did Baum choose the adverb 'gravely' rather than, say, 'happily'? Here is proof that, for Baum, Dorothy's adventures constituted a kind of traumatic initiation . . . " (*The Annotated Wizard of Oz*). A surprising comment, I have to say, because why does Baum, who took the trouble to present his explicit intentions regarding his book, minimize its true meaning with a pallid word like "gravely"? His declared intention, by his own direct testimony, was to create a "modernized fairy tale, in which the wonderment and joy are retained and the heartaches and nightmares left out". Nothing more need be said.

The adventures of Wendy, the least pleasant of the three, do not leave any mark on her either. Before she came to Neverland, Wendy's destiny was to become a mother, and the reader meets her again as an adult who has fulfilled this purpose, and is precluded from returning to Wonderland. Her youngest daughter, however, is of the right age, and only she can feast her eyes on Peter Pan—the emissary of that Wonderland in our world—and fly to it with him.

Childhood is a long process, filled with ups and downs, of becoming acquainted with three basic elements of adult life— sex, meaning, death. As a child grows he discovers, to his dismay, that these three elements, hovering formless above him, are principles of reality that run counter to the game rules of childhood. Therefore, Wonderland is hidden in the innermost chamber. The menacing elements appear there, but only as parts of a game that are experienced in the present—not as longing for the past or looking towards the future that typify various forms of religious perception, especially with regard to

Paradise, to the two hypothetical paradises: the one preceding life and the one succeeding death. A child can recognize the existence of these components without having to accept them as principles of reality. They are suspended. And that is the most perfect freedom to which any of man's creations can aspire: not repression, but a protecting presence.

———

4. SEX

It is common knowledge that Lewis Carroll, the father of modern Wonderlands, liked little girls. It is well known that among the flock of girls he photographed, and to whom he gave little gifts in the form of letters and *bon mots*, Alice Liddell, the inspiration for the literary Alice, shone like the sun at midnight. We should not condemn a profound and unfulfilled love such as this, for its nature resembles God's love. Terms like pedophilia that are bandied about in the heat of discussions about Lewis, dull one's thinking. Yes, Lewis gave his passions free rein. No, they were not manifested in the flesh, but rather in the spirit— in Wonderland. Barrie, too, was touched by such suspicions. There was considerable talk about his children friends and his relationship with them. Nothing in this respect is known about L. Frank Baum. He was the father of many children. And yet, something drove him to write a Wonderland. Questions concerning his attraction to young girls are inevitable.

That is the extra-literary construct. In itself it is of no interest. What is interesting are the manifestations of passion in the literary works, how sex resonates in them.

In a discussion such as this it is virtually impossible to avoid invoking the spirits of Nabokov and his Lolita. In *Lolita* Nabokov consciously employs the extra-literary construct of Wonderland and turns it into the raw material of his story, the conceptual framework. His Humbert Humbert writes, "She had entered my world, umber and black Humberland, with rash curiosity; she surveyed it with a shrug of amused distaste; and it seemed to me now that she was ready to turn away from it with something akin to plain repulsion. Never did she vibrate under my touch, and a strident 'what d'you think you are doing?' was all I got for my pains. To the wonderland I had to offer, my fool preferred the corniest of movies, the most cloying fudge [. . .]"

But what kind of Wonderland can a man who yearns for the object of his passion, offer?

For the psychotic, uninhibited Humbert the answer is a sexual amusement park, the exhilaration of physical experiences, undisguised, without concealment. The extra-literary construct is presented as is. However, for other creators of Wonderlands the answer is different: the fulfillment of sexual passion must be rejected. The extra-literary construct has to be erased in a series of transformations and take on a different, intra-literary construct. Thus, Wonderland is read like the manifestations of Eros, who is never satisfied but always present. He is transplanted from one object to another; this transplantation is the driving force of the girls' journeys and the source of the pleasure derived from the adventure. There is no sublimation of passion in Wonderland, it is not represented but is tangible because it fails, and it is its failure that enables the girl to continue on her adventures in pursuit of another attempt at fulfillment, like pursuing the glimmer of a deceptive light in a marsh, until she returns to the reality of her life.

The ploy that facilitates this is a brilliant one: the four Wonderlands are presented from the perspective of the girls visiting them, and they are filled with lackadaisical, weak, phony father-figures on whom the girl's fate depends, but towards whom she cannot channel her erotic interests: with Carroll, it was the King of Hearts in Wonderland and the Red King, who is fast asleep, in Through the Looking-Glass; with Barrie— Peter Pan, who is a child himself, and Captain Hook, the ruthless villain whose amputated hand is a symbol of his emasculation; and with Baum—a cowardly lion, a brainless scarecrow, a tin man without a heart and an all-powerful and resourceful wizard who turns out to be an elusive conman. Incidentally, Baum claimed that the inspiration for the wizard's character was he himself.

———

5. MEANING

Barrie names his Wonderlands "Neverlands", and he is the only one of the three authors who tries to describe and define the nature of the lands, "Of course the Neverlands vary a good deal [. . .] but on the whole the Neverlands have a family resemblance, and if they stood still in a row you could say of them that they have each other's nose, and so forth."

The term "family resemblance" was coined by by Ludwig Wittgenstein, one of the greatest philosophers of the twentieth century, in an attempt to indicate the way our mind works when it compiles a repository of different concepts and phenomena into a single category of meaning. When Barrie uses the term "family resemblance", he does not do so from an organized philosophy or coherent conceptual system, nor from a desire to formulate the conditions in which meaning appears, but I believe that Wittgenstein would have welcomed its accurate usage.

In his early writings, Wittgenstein sought to formulate the conditions for a language possessing meaning. The meaning of a sentence, claimed the philosopher, lies in the compatibility between the conceptual image the sentence describes and the state of affairs in the world. Meaninglessness, or nonsense, is created when the conceptual image deviates from the boundaries of the world and the boundaries of the language, which are one and the same. In order enter Wonderland it is necessary to traverse the trenches surrounding our language, to cross over into the meaningless.

Wittgenstein was a great admirer of Carroll. And Carroll, who was a logician and mathematician, was also known for his obsessive preoccupation with brainteasers and nonsense— nonsense stories and poems. Both his Wonderlands owe their existence to these linguistic mechanisms. Neverland and the Land of Oz, too, draw some of their essence from nonsense, from the point where language indicates its boundary, beyond which words lose their meaning and a new meaning has to be found for them in order for them to survive.

Carroll, as is his wont, epitomizes the debate on this issue in a spectacular, clever metaphor. Alice doesn't understand the words of the poem "Jabberwocky" that she reads in Mirrorland. She needs Humpty Dumpty's interpretation. Humpty Dumpty is a pompous creature, bloated with his own self-importance. In a rather scornful tone he declares, "When *I* use a word it means just what I choose it to mean," and assures her that he can explain all the poems that were ever invented. And indeed, with sharpened logic he goes on to break down the words of the first verse of "Jabberwocky" into their component parts and interprets their meaning. But Humpty Dumpty, the master of words and meanings, is nothing more than an egg sitting on a wall that can, at any moment, fall to the ground and shatter, and if that were to happen, all the king's horses and all the king's men wouldn't be able to put him together again.

———

6. DEATH

Death is a component whose presence in Wonderland is the most blatant. A sequential evolution of its appearances can be discerned there. In Carroll's works it emerges in hints of dark humor. At the end of her fall down the rabbit hole, Alice says, "After such a fall as this, I shall think nothing of tumbling down stairs! [. . .] Why, I wouldn't say anything about it, even if I fell off the top of the house." And Carroll adds parenthetically, "Which was very likely true." Martin Gardner, author of *The Annotated Alice*, writes, "William Empson has pointed out that this is the first death joke in the Alice books. There are many more to come." In Mirrorland the jokes become almost crude. Humpty Dumpty tells Alice that had she asked his advice, he would have told her to leave off at age seven. And Alice replies that one can't help growing older. Humpty Dumpty goes on to say, "*One* can't, perhaps, but *two* can. With proper assistance, you might have left off at seven."

In the Land of Oz version, death appears in its full weightiness. Dorothy's arrival in the Land of Oz is attended by the death of the Witch of the East and the Munchkins being freed from her tyranny. And in Neverland, Peter Pan, the boy who took Humpty Dumpty's advice and stopped growing older, says to himself, "To die will be an awfully big adventure."

---

7. THE SECOND GATE

I devoured books from the moment I learnt how to read, when I was six. The first literary Wonderland I entered was not one of the four classics. Its name was *City of Tempest*, created by Prospero Juno. I don't know how familiar present-day readers are with the series *Ariella the Fairy Detective* by Juno. Ariella, the heroine of the books is orphaned and goes to live in the country with her grandmother, who abuses her until she flees for her life and magically arrives in the City of Tempest, which is populated by an assortment of strange creatures. There she discovers her destiny, to serve as seer and revelator for the city's inhabitants, their fairy detective. In her investigations, which lead her to the four Kingdoms of the Seasons surrounding the City of Tempest (there is a fifth kingdom, Napoli of Darkness, that no one, including Ariella, knows where it is and yet are still afraid to enter), she is accompanied by a warrior named Pereh, an immensely powerful monster she saves from death.

I remember how with bated breath I followed the adventures of Ariella and Pereh and the mysteries in which they became entangled. Years later, when I looked for material about the author, who was killed in the middle of the night in Texas en route from California to New York, I discovered to my astonishment the sophisticated game of allusions that formed the basis for the books. Many of the details in the series are based on the Shakespearean play *The Tempest*. First, the name of the author, Prospero, is the name of the protagonist of the play, the Duke of Milan, and Juno is the name of one of the minor spirits serving him. I did not manage to find out whether that was his real name, and whether it was his name that ignited in him his great interest in the play, or whether it was a nom de plume he adopted after he fell in love with the play. In the original English the heroine of the series is called Ariel, the same name as the spirit Prospero rescued from the claws of the witch Sycorax, whose place on the island he inherited. "Pereh" is an unsuccessful attempt to Hebraize "Caliban", Prospero's bonded slave and Sycorax's son. The name "City of Tempest" is a translation of "Tempestville". Napoli, the Kingdom of Darkness, is the city of Prospero's sworn enemy, who joined forces with his brother to dispossess him of his assets and exile him and his daughter, Miranda.

By means of the literary puzzle he devised, Prospero Juno directs us to one of the classical works that augur the modern Wonderlands of Carroll and those who followed. A little girl lives with her father on an island, isolated from the rest of humanity, surrounded by fairies, enchanted spirits and monsters, trapped in frozen time. In the distance looms the inevitable trinity—sex, death, meaning. The revelation will divide her life into "up to now"—consuming longing, and "from now on"—anxious anticipation.

—

April 27, 2006

Dear Ori,

Forgive me for starting my letter in this way: Ophir told me that he read an interview on the internet with Joss Whedon, the creator of *Buffy the Vampire Slayer* (remember? The series I told you he's crazy about in my last letter). In this interview Joss Whedon says that the sixth season of Buffy is the one he likes best, because in it the enemy is life itself. That is, the evil creature against which Buffy and her friends do battle is life's difficulties.

But how do you triumph over life? And what's left when the war's over? No one has the answers to these questions. And that's why, because from the outset there are forces of darkness here that cannot be vanquished, it seems to me that most people don't even know that they're in the midst of a battle. There may even be some people who have triumphed and don't know it. Only someone who's lost knows the outcome.

I'm asking about us, about me and Ophir, about what stage we're at.

Life hasn't been cruel to us. Sagi and Re'ut are healthy and intelligent children. Ophir's studio is doing well, and there's no shortage of work. Ophir can afford to take on only projects he's interested in. I got a promotion. I'm now Blockbuster's South-Central regional manager. In short, I've got no complaints.

But not everyone's as lucky as we are.

We went to Ophir's parents for Passover Seder Night. I heard a terrible story there. Have you been keeping up with what's happening in Netivot? If you've been following Ilanit's life, you probably know that she got married when she was seventeen with a truck driver older than her who got her pregnant. There was talk at school about her wedding for weeks, but that was after your time, and I don't know how much of it you heard.

Two weeks ago Ilanit's eldest daughter went to the police station, semiconscious, and asked the officers to come and help her mother. It turns out that for a long time now Ilanit's husband has been beating her and she's been hiding it because of the shame. She forbade her children to tell anyone about the beatings, even their grandparents. But in the middle of a quarrel that broke out between the parents the eldest daughter ran out of the house and went to the police. When they arrived at their house they found Ilanit on the floor. The other children were locked in one of the rooms, screaming in terror.

It took the police several days to catch up with Ilanit's husband, who had vanished with his truck. Ilanit's arm was broken and she had a fractured femur. A social worker was sent to them. Chances are the younger children will be put into foster care.

I had a lump in my throat when I heard the story. It sounds like something you read in the newspapers, not something that happens to people we know. (I told the story to a colleague at work and she said, I thought things like that always happened with you people in Netivot. She's the type of person who can't admit to themselves that they're prejudiced. Her reaction made me cry. Everything seemed so wretched at that moment.)

I couldn't stay in the living room. I went up to the second floor.

There everything came back to me. The carpet that's usually spread out in the corner was rolled up against the wall, and the color and smell of evening were just like the color and smell of the evenings the three of us spent that spring, when we became friends. I remembered that something strange happened the first evening we met at Ophir's house, but I couldn't remember what it was (Ophir becomes evasive whenever I ask him about that evening). Since then I started feeling somehow more and more comfortable with myself. You could say that was when real life began. Mine at least.

I also thought about the pact we made. How did you manage to persuade Ophir to prick himself? Even as an adult he's still scared of needles, and one time when he scratched himself on a rusty iron fence, I had to beg and plead with him to get an anti-tetanus shot, and in the nurse's office he started trembling when we went in. You can imagine how much effort I have to invest to persuade him to have tests once a year. Sagi inherited his fear of needles and jabs from his father. But he's a child, and he can be tempted with a movie or a computer game. Well, they say a man has to preserve something of a child's spirit.

And Ophir certainly has. You should see the shine in his eyes when he finds new music. A few days ago he finished preparing a podcast. Do you know what that is? Of course you do. I'm asking out of politeness. I read in an article about you that your husband is an executive in a computer company and I'm sure you know all about these innovations. I needed explanations.

I was sitting reading in our living room. Ophir came up to me all excited and told me he'd finished working on his podcast. The whole thing was something of a surprise to me. I knew he'd been working on a personal project, but he kept the details to himself. I asked him what a podcast was and he told me it was a voice or video file that any surfer can upload onto the internet and which other surfers can download or listen to or watch. He uploaded onto his website a collection of songs he'd collated over several months. He told me that for him it was like editing a radio program according to his own personal taste and broadcasting it.

I didn't understand what all the excitement was about. If anyone can upload what they want onto the internet, then it diminishes the accomplishment a bit, doesn't it? Ophir said that the very fact that this is possible completely changes how we consume music. He continued his explanation, but I lost interest. It might fascinate you. I always felt that you and Ophir shared a common language in these things. I'm enclosing the address of his studio's website. On the homepage there's a link to his podcast: www.ophirshriki.co.il.

But the truth is, Ori, that I'm just skirting the issue. Among the memories that started flooding me on Seder Night there was one that made me write to you. When you didn't reply to my last letter, I decided not to write to you again. What's the point, I thought, I derive imaginary comfort from these letters, I'm still waiting for an answer.

And I haven't given up on you. I read *A Map to Getting Lost* as soon as hit the shops. Ophir bought it for me as a gift. I liked your two previous books, but I liked *A Map to Getting Lost* more. I found myself, my experiences, in both of your first books. And in the new one I found you. Although you dealt with these subjects in the previous books, children getting lost, children embarking on a journey to find out who they are, in *A Map to Getting Lost* these subjects become personal.

When I read your interview in the newspaper, I was surprised that the interviewer didn't make any connection at all between your life and the book. He asked you about being a Mizrahi Jew and you answered that when your husband pesters you on the subject you remain silent. What do they expect from people when they ask them that question, that they'll play the role of the angry children who managed to get out of nowhere and won't let anyone forget it? He didn't even get that the children in your three books are going nowhere because there, nowhere, reality isn't yet complete. It can't be grasped. Only nowhere do they have a real chance of being someone new who hasn't been told by anyone who they should be.

Is it all right that I'm writing these things to you? As I was reading your last book I couldn't help seeing you in the heroine of the story.

But I still kept to my promise and didn't write.

Then I read the article you wrote for the holiday supplement about Wonderland.

It was clear to me that you tried to write a dry article. Some of it, especially the whole discussion about meaning and non-sense, kind of went of over my head. I've already told you, and I don't mind repeating it, I'm a simple woman, Ori. I arrive on time and leave on time and I laugh in the right places and cry in the right places. But I don't like being made to feel stupid, and that's what I felt when I read that part. I thought about the word Gvinush would use whenever she didn't understand something— "t'harwid", nonsense. The philosophical part was a bit t'harwid for me. Incidentally, Gvinush lost it a bit after her brother Dakar was killed in that terrorist attack near Afula. It took the police six months to identify the body. Everybody was sure he'd gone off somewhere and no one was looking for him. What was he doing in Afula? After that Gvinush (she shortened her original name and calls herself Rimon now) became all spiritual and divorced her husband, some Dutch TV cameraman, on the grounds that he wasn't Jewish. Imagine. Gvinush! A beautiful woman walking around Netivot in ghalabias with two somewhat scruffy children, all tranquility and smiles.

So what did I want to say? I didn't entirely understand the article. Ophir tried to explain it to me, and even then it seemed like sophistry to me. But I could still sense the feelings you had when you wrote it. I felt that you were taking a big step towards yourself, even bigger than the one you took in your last book. I was happy for you, but for me too. A wave of pride washed over me. It's hard for me to put the reason into words. As if you're writing in two languages, and everybody else only understands one language. But I am fluent in both of them.

I also remembered that I was actually your first reader, when we were twelve. But when you showed me your notebook, with your innermost thoughts, I didn't understand what it was that you were giving me.

Now I think I understand. And it's clear to me that we can't let any more time just pass of its own accord. Every year that goes by takes a piece out of us. That's the reason I'm writing to you, Ori, to tell you that even if the road is long and winding, don't give up. I've put a light on in the window and the house is open and my hand is reaching out.

Yours,
Sigal

FOUR

Singing

THERE WAS A SENSE OF RECKLESSNESS in Tel Aviv that spring. No. Not in Tel Aviv, but in her; it was in her that the air blazed in every direction and in her flesh that flocks of birds squabbled. Ori could no longer lie to herself. The tension had been there before, growing and insidious, but it was only in the past three weeks, since they'd come home from the restaurant, that she had acknowledged its existence. Now the days were like this: something gnawed at her; a shroud of apathy accompanied all Barak's activities, like a hornet buzzing against a windowpane. During the brief exchanges with him a kind of sharp pain sliced through her, as if an ulterior intention was pulsing in the sentences with which he chose to conclude their incidental conversations, as if every such fraction of a second, in which the conversation ended and only empty space remained between them, was a sign that he'd lost interest. She could no longer bear the anguish she felt, so she minimized her already laconic sentences. For a whole week she avoided him, lowering her eyes when he came home, kept her answers brief and businesslike, shrank back from him at night, drawing away as if offended. Nothing touched him. He didn't inquire. Didn't get angry. The flutter of his lips on her forehead, which extricated her from her slumber, became a morning ritual he never missed. That was the extent of his efforts.

But she wanted more. More. What did she want?

It was precisely his offhandedness, which should have satisfied her, that gnawed at her. She found herself thinking about him, imagining conversations between them. When she read her books her train of thought was interrupted and turned to him. When she tried to write, his broad, awkward outline appeared before her and sabotaged the words.

At the end of the seventh day she couldn't stand the tension any longer and turned to him in anger, after Alma was confined in slumber and there was no danger of her trying to drown out their conversation with roaring songs or random dancing filled with skips and spins, "Why don't you talk to me anymore? I feel like you've lost the desire to talk to me."

She saw the furrows forming on his forehead and his eyes scurrying to marshal themselves, wondering what trap was being set for him. He replied with a tenderness blended with caution, "What are you talking about, Ori?"

"About you not being bothered by this silence between us. As if you've lost interest."

"I've noticed that you've been avoiding me. But this isn't the first time it's happened. You have days like that, when you shut yourself off, withdraw. I always thought it was that time of the month. And I understand these moods, I let you take your time and they pass."

"But it's different now."

"How is it different?"

"Never mind," she replied, choking. "You're right."

"I've got to prepare my presentation for tomorrow's meeting," he said, moving towards his study.

"What are you working on?"

"Oh, just a new program to protect data in . . . uhm . . . peer-to-peer software . . . for home computers."

"Peer-to-peer? What's that?"

He was standing, and the few meters between them were strewn with potholes. His back was partly turned to her, the back of his neck tense, in mid-departure. She knew he had no intention of talking to her, but she persisted. Barak turned back towards her.

"What's the matter, Ori, what's with the sudden interest?"

"I'm trying to understand what you do."

"After more than five years of marriage? You've never shown any interest before."

"We should be more involved in each other's worlds. Otherwise . . . " The word fell into the dark space between her and him. It wasn't an abyss, but congealed, vibrating air in which the words stuck, like bullets in jam.

"Maybe we could start that tomorrow," Barak said with resolve, he walked away stiffly and vanished into his study.

She remained standing in the hallway, with the findings of the conversation embedded in viscous mass. It's not going to go away, she thought, like those ballistic boxes in forensic laboratories, she would be able to pull out the slugs one after another and find out which weapon fired them and from which angle.

She heard Alma muttering a faint protest in her sleep. She's too sensitive, that girl, she thought, and went into her room. Alma's face was glistening with perspiration and choking sounds escaped from her throat. Ori sat on the edge of the bed and put her hand on her brow. It was a bit warm. Her daughter's light sleep broke, and she opened her eyes in the dark.

"Who is it?" she asked.

"Shhh . . . " she whispered to her, "it's all right, Alma. You were just having a bad dream."

"No," Alma protested and emitted an odd, whining sequence of syllables. Then she lay for a few minutes, staring into the darkness, her breathing regular, her chest rising and falling slowly, until Ori thought she had fallen asleep again and smoothed her hand over her cheek.

"I dreamt I had a little cat," Alma said, "really cute, like Shauli's little cat. And we went to the playground in the park and Shauli came with his cat as well, and he said, 'What's your cat's name?' and I said, 'Peertopeer'."

"What was the cat's name?"

"Peer-to-peer," Alma repeated, emphasizing each syllable.

"Okay," said Ori.

"And you and Abba were there too. You were looking at the sky and Abba asked you, 'What's the matter?' The sky was dark and then a black peacock suddenly jumped out of the circle on the slide and snatched Shauli's cat. And then Shauli started to cry. He said, 'What am I going to do?' and then Abba told him, 'Now you won't see him again for five years' and you said, 'You'll get another cat.' And then Abba said, 'Tomorrow'."

"So it was a bad dream after all."

"No. It was a good dream, because Shauli said to me, 'Why don't you let me play with your cat.' And I said, 'No. He's all mine.' And then Shauli cried again."

"So it was a bad dream for Shauli," Ori said and tickled Alma.

Alma giggled. "Stop it, Ima," she said. "Go to Abba now. Alma wants to sleep."

"All right," Ori whispered. "Maybe we can do something fun tomorrow when we get back from kindergarten." Alma nodded with a yawn and said, "But remember you promised this time."

Ori waited until Alma's senses switched off and her eyes closed. Then she cried. She wept silently. At first over Alma, out of an unfathomable terror that assailed her; something had gone wrong, some terrible impending fate was coming to claim her daughter. She sensed it in her dreams, and the signs appearing in her nighttime visions were the worst omens of all. There was nothing within her power to protect her from it. Then her mother's image appeared, sitting on the edge of her bed on the nights following the devastating news, a pale ghost gradually fading away before her eyes.

Ori had insisted on going with her parents to hear the results of her mother's tests. She wasn't to be dissuaded. Even her father, the anger in his voice striking her, couldn't break her resolve. She accompanied them. The specialist at the hospital, too, frowned in disapproval as they entered his office. Doctor Gavish, she would never forget his name, his image, his face. A graying, gaunt, long man with sunken cheeks and a sharp chin; thick eyebrows over sky-blue eyes peering menacingly through his spectacles, which slid down his fox-like nose. She and her parents stood in front of his desk and he scrutinized them, weighing them up, their resilience, their preparedness. When he saw her he stated, "These discussions are no place for a little girl." He had a pleasant, caressing voice and an old-Israeli accent, stressed, like Shlomo Artzi's in "Hasamba and the Horse Thieves".

"Discussions?" asked her father.

His face was pallid and fraught. He tensed his lips as he uttered the word, and again she saw the missing upper tooth. The gap pinched her heart. Her father pulled a handkerchief folded into four out of his shirt pocket and dabbed his brow. She clung to her mother's waist and looked straight at the doctor.

"I'm staying," Ori said. Residues of the tyrannical authority she'd had remained in her voice.

Doctor Gavish laughed heartily.

"You won't understand anything anyway. Sit down," he said, indicating two chairs. Her parents obeyed. Without being prompted, she dragged a white-lacquered wooden chair from the corner of the room and sat down next to them.

317

"Mrs. Elhayani," the doctor began, but his eyes lingered on her father crushing his handkerchief between his fingers, and Ori hung onto the caress of his voice: if she refined it, rode it, the demons wouldn't be able to leave his throat and infiltrate the room. "I'll begin with the bottom line," he continued, "my experience has taught me that there is no easy way to say these things." And Ori could see that his eyes were fixed on her father the whole time, that he didn't look into her mother's face. "We've repeated the tests and there's no doubt about it. Believe me, I wish there was. Mrs. Elhayani, you have a rare degenerative lung disease. Tracheal syndrome. I'm sorry to say it's incurable."

Ori didn't have to imagine the meaning of the words because their significance swelled around them, and the fluorescent light seemed to dim. She could taste the darkness in her mouth, bitter, as bitter as medicine. Her father blurted a sob, and her mother clutched his hand even more tightly.

"What does that mean?" he asked.

"The cells in your wife's lungs are dead. Her pneumonia has accelerated the rate of degeneration. A tenth of her lung cells are dead tissue now, and in these degeneration processes the blood vessels are damaged as well. That's the reason for the coughing."

He stood up and walked over to the wall on his right. His hand fumbled at the side of a thick viewer that hung on the wall, probably searching for a switch to light up the board from the inside, and two grayish images with black stains lit up.

"These are X-rays of your wife's lungs," said the doctor, now addressing only her father. "One of them," he pointed to the image on the left with his pen, "was taken on the day she was discharged from the hospital, after she'd recovered from her pneumonia. "And the other"—the pen moved to the image on the right—"was taken a week ago. The deterioration in the condition of the lungs is very worrying."

"What . . ." her father started to say.

"Due to the accelerated death of the cells, your wife is inhaling an increasingly smaller quantity of air. Consequently, all her vital functions will gradually become impaired. She'll be more tired, her thinking will slow down. This disease causes slow suffocation. That is the meaning of its name in Latin, but as early as the Greeks . . ."

Ori stopped listening. The darkness crept into her, through her eyes and nose. And through her mouth. She mustn't touch it with her tongue. But it penetrated the pores of her skin until it filled her, like dark cotton wool. At some point she refocused. Her father stood up and yelled.

"Stop lecturing us and tell us what we can do." Doctor Gavish was taken aback. Her father continued, "Do you think I care what the Romans called this disease and what it's called in different languages? Who do you think you are?"

The doctor continued speaking in the same caressing tone, with the same measured silky softness.

"Modern medicine doesn't have any answers," he said, "I thought if I told you the history of the disease you'd be able to draw some . . ."

"Comfort?" her mother asked, the first words she'd uttered since they'd walked in. "May God forgive you, doctor. How long have I got?"

"There are steroids that can slow down the rate of cell death, and there are treatments that might increase the quantity of oxygen entering your body, like inhalation therapy on a regular basis. But even then . . ." he fell silent, and then his voice finally broke out of the indifference in which it had been immersed. "A year at most," he said.

In the nights that followed Ori would wake up screaming. The darkness she had swallowed in the hospital permeated from her into the world, the moon's crooked toenail stuck in the window and didn't move. Something powerful and ominous was approaching, a beast from one of the pasts, the whole night was its breath on the delicate sheet glass of August. The first time it happened her father rushed into her room and placed his gnarled hand over her eyes, forcing them shut.

"Ori, Ori," he said as he breathed heavily. "Now listen to me, Ori, fear only has as much power as it's given, do you understand me? It doesn't exist. I want you to repeat what I've just said, and that's what you must do whenever you wake up scared in the middle of the night, all right?"

She moved her head a little, his hand pinned her to the bed and she couldn't nod. She muttered over and over, "Fear only has as much power as it's given. It doesn't exist."

A kind of stillness spread through her body and her heart calmed down, stopped trying to break out of her ribs. On subsequent occasions she found her mother sitting on the edge of her bed, as if she'd sensed Ori's distress as soon as it was born and rushed to her room, staying to watch over her until she was overcome with exhaustion.

She came out of Alma's room. She went to the bathroom to brush her teeth, swallowed a valerian capsule and retired to her bed. Her closed eyelids felt heavy. The effect of the valerian wasn't immediate. It took some time until it shredded her thoughts, poured slumber into her limbs. And when Barak lay down beside her, she was already tumbling down the incline of the slumber tunnel, but he put out a moist hand and drew her out of the depths of the earth into which she had descended and they made love absentmindedly. The physical barrier had been crossed, but both of them remained in their solitude, like two drowned people embalmed in the depths of the ocean.

———

The next day, as she went downstairs on her way to fetch Alma from kindergarten, her feet became entangled, and the first foot to step on each of the landings separating each staircase was her left foot. Anger flared up inside her. Today, too, would be unprofitable. "*Shatya*," she whispered to herself as she pushed open the front door of the building.

Alma was waiting at the kindergarten gate, looking thoroughly ashamed. Yael, the kindergarten teacher, stood beside her patting her head, comforting her.

"Good afternoon, Mrs. Elhayani," she said.

"Good Afternoon, Yael," Ori replied.

"Tze'ela, I'm Tze'ela."

"Sorry. What happened to Alma?"

"Alma had to be punished today. Isn't that right, Alma?" Tze'ela said in a saccharine tone that Ori found nauseating.

Why do these kindergarten teachers have to sugarcoat reality? Alma had been punished and it probably hurt her to be separated from the other children. Not that Ori objected entirely to punishment as an educational method, but why wrap the whip in fur? She kneeled in front of her daughter and coaxed her chin up. Traces of tears were evident on her cheeks. The blood vessels around her eyes were swollen with blood. Alma clutched the hem of her dress, an ivory-white dress with a green floral print. Since the day Alma had started displaying refinement in her choice of clothes and shoes and jewelry—and would insist on buying one outfit and not another, and knew every morning precisely which dress she wanted—Ori had let Barak dress the child, thus letting go of another thread of her daughter's life. Now it felt like a mistake. There was a vast disparity between the vitality Alma's presence asserted, with her electrifying, flaming eyes, her hair that wouldn't respond to any hairbrush, her defiant features, and the frail angel in her present attire, in any of the delicate, nauseatingly frilly and ruffled crêpe dresses.

"Punished?" Ori asked Tze'ela.

"Perhaps it would be best if Alma were to tell you." She placed a reassuring hand on her shoulder. "Alma?"

"I pushed Shauli at morning circle," Alma admitted reluctantly.

"And . . . " Tze'ela urged her.

"I insulted other children."

"What did you say to them?" Ori asked.

Alma shrugged and looked at Tze'ela, and Tze'ela said, "Four days ago Alma began making a habit of passing criticism on the other children at the entrance to the kindergarten."

Ori waited for her to explain.

"She stands at the door every morning and as they arrive she tells each child that his shoes are worn or that he's wearing the same shirt he wore yesterday or that his pants are a disgusting color or that he's dirty. She goes into great detail. On the first day we thought it was a game, and so did the other children. On the second day the children began crying and we took Alma aside for a little chat. Yesterday we thought she'd understood, but today she resumed the habit."

"I'll talk to her," said Ori, "it won't happen again."

"Look, it really isn't any of my business . . . " said Tze'ela, "but perhaps . . . sometimes . . . " and she composed herself, "is everything all right at home?"

"Yes," Ori said and pulled Alma behind her. She added in a whisper, "Everything's fine. Alma's been having nightmares recently. She's not sleeping well."

—

The kindergarten wasn't far from the café, and the air, despite the bubbling of the first *hamsins* from the increasing boiling of the days, was pleasant, breezy. Ori preferred to walk.

Alma ran ahead of her, skipping between the bauhinia trees, the mouths of their magnificently colored orchidean flowers—brilliant white and deep purple—gaping at her. Once in a while she stopped and shoved her face among them, or picked green-washed poplar leaves from a tree trunk and tried to blow through them, to whistle.

Barak had shown her how to elicit a sound from the leaves; you fold them in two, gently press one side and stretch it, then bring the other side to your lips and blow. The pressure of the blowing, he'd explained to Alma, makes the edges of the leaf vibrate, creating the sound. Alma couldn't do it, but she didn't give up either, and tried at every opportunity. Barak tried to explain, in vain, that it couldn't be done with just any leaf; that the leaves growing on the trunk at this time of year were hard and thick, as opposed to those growing on the higher branches.

The radiance of the sun was broken by the dense foliage of the ficus trees lining Rothschild Boulevard, and Alma ran towards it. "Alma, wait," Ori called after her, "you don't know where we're going."

But Alma continued running, compelling Ori to walk faster as well. She caught up with the child at the traffic lights. Alma waited impatiently until Ori reached her; her parents had strictly forbidden her to try crossing the road, even though she had already displayed impressive mastery of the colors and meaning of traffic lights. Alma was choking with excitement, she waved her arm towards the center of the boulevard and gave Ori her other hand when the light turned green. Now Ori understood what had captured Alma's attention: a large bird with which she was unfamiliar, its black feathers comprising a myriad of metallic hues, the tassel on its head alternately spreading and closing as it hopped and pecked at the grass growing between the ficus trees.

"What kind of bird is it?" asked Alma, drawing closer to it.

"I've no idea," Ori answered impatiently, "I've never seen anything like it before."

Alma circled around the bird, which peered at her sideways and rolled its eyes. Alma laughed.

"Black peacock," she said.

"What?" asked Ori.

"Black peacock, that's the name of the bird," said Alma and skipped after it. The weight of her landing on the grass sent the bird into the air. "Wait," Alma shouted, "I want to get a feather from you." But the bird continued its ascent. Alma hit the tree trunk in annoyance.

"Alma," said Ori, a spark of anger flaring up in her. She struggled to quell it.

"I wanted a feather," muttered Alma, and her gaze wandered downwards. She suddenly emitted a shrill, ear-splitting yelp. A yelp of supreme joy. Among the contorted, sinewy roots of the ficus, lay a feather, its edges frayed with age, but still a gleaming feather. Alma picked it up and burst into a dance. "Feather, feather," she sang, "I want you and none other."

"Aren't you hungry?" Ori asked, and Alma stopped short. Her face became serious.

"I'm very hungry," she answered.

They crossed to other side of the boulevard, one of Alma's hands clutched tightly in Ori's, the other clutching the feather, stroking her face with it, which she continued doing as they entered Café Migdanot. The rich aroma of chocolate, an aroma with a tangible presence and dimensions, engulfed Alma and she tensed. The hand holding the feather fell to the side of her body.

"Chocolate," she said, her mouth agape. She released herself from Ori's grip. "I want some."

Ori nodded and Alma drew away from her, hurrying towards the glass cabinets displaying slabs of chocolate. Ori watched her from the corner of her eye and gestured with her fingers to the hostess, a table for two. The hostess went up to Alma and knelt beside her. "Nice, isn't it, sweetie? What's your name?"

"Alma," said Alma.

"Do you like chocolate?"

Alma nodded vigorously. "Look," she said to her, "the black peacock left me a feather."

"That was a nice thing for it to do," replied the hostess. "See those pipes?" she pointed to the pipes running close to the ceiling and along the walls, "outside Tel Aviv there's a chocolate mountain, and every day it melts a little and the chocolate flows through the pipes until it reaches us."

Alma tapped the hostess's mouth with her feather.

"I've got a chocolate mountain as well, under my bed. And every night I bend down and bite it. Mmm, delicious."

The hostess smiled at her.

"But I'm sure it's not like here, is it? Here there's all the chocolate you want."

"My Abba's got a chocolate car and a chocolate airplane," said Alma.

The hostess was becoming a bit exasperated. She tried again.

"But you're glad you came to our café. It's delightful."

"It's more fun at the Krusty Krab," declared Alma.

"The Krusty what?" the hostess laughed in bewilderment.

"The Krusty Krab," repeated Alma. She leveled a disappointed gaze at the hostess and abandoned her in favor of Ori, who was looking intently at a huge metal vat in which thick liquid chocolate was being mixed. Alma stood on tiptoe but couldn't see over the edge of the vat. Ori lifted her up.

"Wowww," exclaimed Alma in amazement. "I want you to putting me in there."

"Put, Alma, you say put," Ori corrected her. "And you can't get in. See?" She tapped the glass that covered the vat.

"Your table's ready," said the hostess and led them over to it.

No sooner had they sat down than an excessively friendly waiter swooped down on them. He fussed over Alma.

"What have you got there?" he asked.

"A black peacock feather," Alma replied proudly.

"How did you manage to get hold of a feather like that?" asked the waiter. He was plump and there was something soft in his posture. His round face looked as if it had been spread with pink wax. "Did you know that it's an enchanted bird that appears only once every fifty years, in the spring, and it gives away one of its feathers, and only to someone who has wizardly blood in their veins."

Alma was thrilled. The waiter beamed, blushed, and stole a glance at Ori, making sure she was listening.

"Can a black peacock beat God?" asked Alma.

"The black peacock is a very powerful creature. At one time he was the King of the Birds," replied the waiter, "seventy angels waited on him and he lived in a palace made from mist halfway between the North Star and the Southern Cross. But one night . . . "

"Yes," Alma interrupted him. "But can he beat God?"

"Perhaps we should order," said Ori, "Alma will have the children's meal, pizza and French fries. And bring her lots of ketchup. She loves ketchup. I'll have the Belgian waffle with mixed berries and chocolate sauce, but no whipped cream. And a latte."

"And what about Alma, won't she be wanting something sweet?"

"Later," said Ori.

The waiter hurried away, and Alma said, "Ima, put my feather in your bag," and placed it on the table. Distractedly, Ori stroked the downy aura surrounding the blackness of the feather. She lingered on the softness of its touch, the fine current tingling her fingertips.

The waiter returned, glowing like a light bulb, and placed in front of Alma a large plate, a bowl filled to the brim with ketchup and a glass of pale milkshake. Alma looked from the plate to the waiter and back. She pushed the plate away roughly.

"You've got crooked teeth and a watermelon head," she said to the waiter.

"Alma!" Ori exclaimed. She'd had enough of her daughter's wisecracks, her rudeness. In the middle of Alma's plate there was a slice of toast, decorated as a face. Two cherry-tomato halves served as eyes and two strips of pepper, one green and one red, depicted a nose and mouth. That's the problem, she thought.

"I'm sorry, my daughter detests peppers, of any kind or color." She said to the waiter.

"Oh," said the waiter, "no problem, I'll take them off for you, sweetie."

"No," said Alma furiously, "it's already touched the cheese, I don't want it!"

The waiter smiled at Ori.

"I'll bring you a new one, sweetie." He took her plate and returned a few seconds later.

The nose and mouth on the pizza were now made from tomatoes as well. Alma examined the face up close, sniffed it, and her love of tomatoes triumphed over her suspicion. She stuck her tongue out at the nose on the pizza face.

"What are you doing?" asked Ori, nodding to the waiter who was standing at their table eager to serve.

"I'm licking its nose. Meow, I'm Peertopeer the cat," said Alma, and the waiter laughed affectedly.

A waitress stopped at their table and placed in front of Ori a plate with mounds of fried banana strips and mixed berries in chocolate on a waffle. Alma's pupils widened in wonder.

327

Alma plucked the eye from the pizza face and dunked it into the ketchup. Then she shredded it between her teeth. Her eyes didn't stray from Ori's plate.

"Want some?" Ori asked, and Alma nodded eagerly.

———

Ori knew that the situation was inevitable, but still hoped to evade it, to move out of range of the waiter's sensors and antennae. His devotion was over the top. He stopped at their table every few minutes to ask how they were doing, to make sure everything was to their satisfaction, to see if they needed anything. Even Alma, who enjoyed the attention, answered him curtly when he asked her if she liked the waffle. But he was waiting for them at the door, and when they finished he escorted them out to the street.

"Excuse me," he said to Ori, "you're Ori Elhayani, aren't you? The children and youth writer."

"Yes?" she said, thinking, *children and youth writer*, who uses phrases like this?

"I do a bit of writing myself . . . fantasies for youth, and I'm trying to find out how to send . . . "

Ori had no intention of rescuing him from his discomfiture. She was surprised by the very fact that he'd approached her. That was the advantage of writing for children and youth, her readership was more interested in her books than in her; her characters and plots were more real to it than her life.

"Look . . . what's your name?"

"Michael, Michael Kagan."

"Look, Michael. I don't know what advice to give you. Go into a bookshop. Find some books you think are similar to your writing and write down the names and addresses of the publishing houses that published them, and send them your manuscript. That's what I did."

"But . . . the only books that resemble what I write are your books, and I'd like to hear your opinion."

Alma tugged at Ori's belt.

"Ima, let's go to the playground."

"What is it you're asking me, Michael?"

"If you could give me your email address. I'll send you a few stories. I promise I won't pester you, and anyway you can always block me."

"Ima," Alma shouted, "come on!"

"Okay," Ori said. "On one condition: I'm not promising to answer you."

Michael flipped over his order pad and wrote down the address Ori had just made up; she didn't invent a completely new address, but merely substituted one letter for another.

"Oof," Alma said as he vanished into the restaurant, "what an annoying man."

There weren't many parents and toddlers in the park at that time of the afternoon, and Ori was glad. Crowds of people would have made it difficult for her to keep her eye on Alma as she darted between the swings and slides, squealing glee-fully, more frenetic than usual because of the amount of sugar coursing through her. She appeared and disappeared as if possessed: there she was atop the swaying bridge, and there—at the bottom of the ring ladder, and then standing next to Ori who was sprawled on a bench.

"Ima, come and push me on the swing," Alma said.

"In a minute, let me relax for a minute."

Now Alma was climbing into a blue sphere on the top of the slide, popping her head out of a round window, its outline painted red, and shouting, "Look, Ima, this is where the black peacock came out and snatched Shauli's cat."

Ori wanted to get more details from Alma about her dream and talk to her about her behavior in kindergarten, but she waited for the agitation in Alma's limbs to abate. Then she stood up and walked her to the swing. There, too, when Alma was sitting down calmly, a padded harness keeping her still, she thwarted her intentions. Because Alma said gravely, "You know, I'll be going to Grandpa Ya'akov and Grandma Narmina's house soon?"

"What?" Ori asked, and her hand tightened around the chain of the swing until she felt it cutting into her flesh. "Who told you that?"

"Abba said. He said you said it was all right. Come on, push me."

"Abba told you you're going to Grandma Narmina's?"

"Yes, oof, Ima."

"Look at me," said Ori. Alma turned her head and looked up at her expectantly. Ori noticed that the redness hadn't disappeared from her eyes. But it troubled her for only a fraction of a second. "That's what Abba told you, Grandma Narmina?"

"Yes. I told you. And Grandpa Ya'akov."

Now she understood the meaning of her clumsy descent down the stairs and her leading left foot. Vague curses passed through her mind and she hoped they hadn't breached the barrier of her lips. She pushed Alma with stiff, mechanical movements, her brain refusing to let go of the phrase, Grandma Narmina. Idiot, she said to herself over and over, sonofabitch. She'd show him.

———

In the end her article wasn't published in the Passover Eve supplement. The editor called. In his tortuous manner of speech—she didn't understand why he needed it, because he was delivering good news—he told her that her article was too long for his section, so he'd passed it onto the editor of the special Second Passover Holiday supplement, who'd expressed excitement and willingness to print it.

She received a considerable number of reactions to her article. Not only Sigal wrote to her about it. Other people she knew, people she hadn't imagined read this newspaper, presented her with their impressions. Strange, she never could predict the level of interest the things she wrote would engender. She had published a few essays on children's literature, and there was a virtually inverse proportion between her attitude to the essay, her sense of clearly formulating a new idea, and the interest it gained. It was as if she had to distance herself in order to hit the target. Standing close to the world always blurred it, dulled her thinking about it.

Mr. Gershon smiled at her with his usual cheeriness, but his wife, whom Ori suspected didn't like her very much, insisted and persisted in her old, jagged voice, "I didn't even understand what you were trying to say. Why does the paper print things that people can't read?"

"Perhaps you should write a letter to the editor and suggest that they don't print articles like that." Ori answered with a smile.

"Perhaps I will." Mrs. Gershon said

Ofra read it too. She called, and added to the hostile tone that dominated her voice when she spoke to Ori ever since she'd returned from traveling the world, was fury as well.

"Tell me, Ori, what's this you wrote in the paper about having toothache when you were little. When exactly did that happen? What utter *b'shala*, exaggeration." She said.

Ori was taken aback. She was entirely unprepared for this. To the other accusations—why she'd cancelled on Passover Eve itself, why she hadn't bothered to come to the Mimouna feast Ofra had worked so hard to prepare—she had an answer. But not to this.

"I . . . " she stammered. "It's got nothing to do with reality, you know, literature is the invention of . . . "

331

"And another thing, if I remember correctly, you started reading books when you were older. So how come you write that you've been reading since you were six?"

"But it's literature," Ori repeated and knew how foolish she sounded, "it's like a dream. The facts are unimportant, only the feelings they evoke, what they make you experience. It's all invention . . . "

"I know the difference between invention and reality," Ofra interrupted. "Don't get all high and mighty with me. I may not have gone to university, but I'm not as ignorant or illiterate as you think. When you write something like that, in an article, not a story, people who read it believe that you're telling them something real, something that actually happened. Don't they?"

"Yes," Ori said feebly.

"You're sick," Ofra hissed and hung up.

The editor of the supplement, too, who unlike his colleague spoke in short sentences, called to tell her that the newspaper had received numerous letters about her article, especially from women. Some irate and others complimentary. He went through the main criticisms in a dry tone, which Ori thought concealed amusement, as if publication of the article and the reactions it provoked were a burlesque he had helped stage and was now sitting back in pleasure to watch. Children's literature experts criticized her forced interpretation of the literary works she had written about, and philosophy experts—the license she had taken in her use of *The Philosophical Lexicon*; parents were angry about the contention that the classical children's literature they encourage their children to read is mostly pedophilic; Shakespeare aficionados complained about her erroneous and biased reference to *The Tempest*. He didn't intend to publish all the letters, the editor said, only the interesting ones. In any event he wanted to tell her that there was one letter he thought she'd want to read. She told him she hoped it wasn't a letter from a devoted reader by the name of Mrs. Gershon. He answered that it was actually written by a man.

Only Barak, whose reaction she nervously awaited, didn't say a single word about the article. Maybe it was his way of paying her back, she thought. She saw him pick up the supplement and sit down on the couch in the living room. She was sure he was reading the article, at least she saw the illustration accompanying it—a little girl standing in front of a menacing gate, and the shadow cast by her figure is the long shadow of a man in a hat leaning on a cane—from the corner of her eye as she walked past him.

She could tell he was angry with her. It wasn't the first time. But usually his anger was more general, abstract, surrounding him, enveloping his body like a mantle of fluff for one or two days, then gradually unraveling and detaching from him one layer at a time. Nothing of it found its way into specific action, into a defined object. It wasn't channeled. It didn't sabotage his attitude towards Ori, didn't shut him off to her needs, to her neediness. But not this time. Perhaps she'd gone too far and should have clenched her teeth and dammed her lips. But she couldn't. That phrase, the blade of the words "Grandma Narmina" didn't rust, didn't blunt. It cut at her for a whole week, until she said to Barak on Passover Eve, "I can't bring myself to spend time with my family. But you should go with Alma, she's looking forward to it."

Barak stared at her in disbelief.

"What do you mean you can't bring yourself?" he asked.

"I just can't. I don't have the strength. I'm tired. I'm unhappy."

"Come on, Ori, so what if you don't have the strength. That doesn't come into it."

"I told you, I'm unhappy."

"So what difference does it make where you're unhappy. At least there you'll make a few other people happy."

"No," she said. "I'll just sit there depressed and spoil it for everyone else, and then I'll feel even worse about myself. I'm not going. I've made my decision."

"Fine, then we're not going either."

"Why? You want to go. And they're expecting you."

"They're expecting you too. You've just convinced yourself that you're not welcome."

"It's true. Ofra and my father really don't want me there. Especially Ofra, who's been angry with me since the day I went to boarding school in Jerusalem, but she won't admit it. She and my father have this antiquated concept of family, that no matter what happens, you stay together. I don't believe in it."

"Nonsense," said Barak, "complete and utter nonsense. Unlike you, I take the trouble to speak to your family, and believe me no one has ever said you're not welcome."

"Enough, I've decided not to go because I don't want to feel bad. Don't spoil that for me too."

"I'll spoil it for you and then some." His expression was explosive. "What makes you think you can just do anything you want and you'll be forgiven?"

Ori thought, well, you always do.

Alma ran into the argument, clutching the black peacock feather. She danced an ungainly dance around them, in two circles, tracing the figure eight around them—or perhaps the symbol of infinity—waving the feather and singing at the top of her voice, "Feather, feather, I want you and none other."

Barak caught her up in his arms and she collapsed into him, still singing. There was a hint of malevolence in his voice, Ori didn't doubt that she heard it, "Alma, Ima's decided that we're not going to Grandpa Ya'akov's."

Alma screamed, "No! You promised!"

"You hypocrite. Couldn't you have said we're not going to Grandma Narmina's?" Ori said.

She couldn't decipher the expression on his face—bewilderment? Impatience? Contempt? Alma threw herself onto the floor, pounded it with her tiny fists, and wailed.

On Second Passover Eve he and Alma went to her father's, and the next evening to the Mimouna feast at Ofra's. He didn't tell Ori anything about the events of these two evenings, and she assumed that with that she'd paid for her sin. Now she waited for him to say something about the article. Barak's lips remained sealed. He didn't talk to her, for better or worse. She was entirely attentive towards him. For three days she tensely moved around him in the apartment. Once or twice she found an urgent excuse to call him during the day. She counted five rings before his voicemail assailed her ear with a torrent of metallic words. Finally, fearing that he'd let the memory of the article dissipate, fade, just as spring was gradually fraying, she asked him.

"Oh, I haven't had a chance to read it yet. I hope you've kept the paper, I'll have a look at it sometime." He said reluctantly.

"Alma's eyes are red lately, it comes and goes," she informed him, "I've made an appointment for her to see the doctor tomorrow morning."

And Barak answered absentmindedly, "Really? I hadn't noticed."

———

That evening she shut herself off in her study. In the bottom drawer of the desk, disguised as a draft of one of her stories, she'd kept the note Avner had left on the refrigerator on the day he left. Once again, his words were an angry mob, ready to hurl stones. He wrote:

"Ori, for two months now I've been pondering the possibility of us splitting up, but you've been so withdrawn recently that I find it impossible to hold a conversation with you. The thread of any discussion breaks every few sentences. You're sinking. I'm sorry I have to act this way, to leave surreptitiously. But by doing so it's not only myself that I'm saving. I'm saving you too. I can't give you what you yearn for. Although you won't admit it, you want to surrender, to devote yourself. But not to me. It's not me you want, but someone else, someone you think you'll find through me. For you I am merely a shadow. This conclusion has been echoing in my mind for two months. I've tried to silence it. Unsuccessfully. Winter with its light has made it clear to me that I'm not as patient as I thought. We had some good times. Don't look for me. Goodbye. Avner."

Sonofabitch, she thought to herself, you and your fancy words, always distorting emotions in favor of a polished statement. She crumpled the note between her fingers and tossed the ball of paper into the drawer, accompanying its flight with another curse. Then she spread on the desk the three letters Sigal had sent her. She knew she wouldn't be able to find the energy within herself to reply to her, nor did she want to. The fact that she'd kept the letters and not shredded them as soon as she received them, surprised her. Her eyes wandered over Sigal's words.

I wonder, she thought, what Sigal's voice sounds like nowadays, how she talks. Is she eloquent, does she choke on the calluses in her throat, does she labor over her phrasing, her tongue awkwardly failing her once in a while? Surely in her day-to-day living she doesn't express herself as she does in her letters. The language we speak and the language we write are two entirely different things. Even in people who strive to render them seamless. Each possesses its own experiential status and mandates a different state of consciousness. The belief that they can be identical in any way is erroneous. But that's precisely the problem, the more the error touches upon a more fundamental layer of existence, the more it presents itself as a simpler, more basic truth. The entire history of humanity can be summed up in this . . . Her eyes paused on their way to the bottom of the third letter. She switched on the computer and surfed to Ophir's website.

She skipped the link to the gallery of his works. She felt she had no right to snoop there, even though it had been placed in public view for all to see. She found the link to Ophir's podcast, clicked on "DOWNLOAD" and waited. Even though the internet connection in their apartment, thanks to Barak's occupation, was the fastest on the market, downloading the podcast file took a while because of its size.

When it finished downloading the media player opened up. She put on her headphones and immersed herself in the songs. The collection Ophir had compiled was out of the ordinary. All the songs were performed by male singers, the range of voices vast. A thin, glassy voice opened the collection, followed by a proud, embellished voice, a poignant voice pinched her skin. An air of anguish interlaced them, of regret, of dying love, on the verge of disintegration, surreal, painful childhood landscapes. Virtually all the songs were unknown to her, with the exception of one that scratched at her consciousness, irritating. She had a good ear for music from an early age. From the opening notes she could easily identify songs she'd heard only once. But when she was sixteen she'd realized the disadvantage of her musical ear. In the labyrinth of the music, in its depths, in its small, concealed alcoves, hid memories, the smells and flavors of the circumstances in which she'd heard the songs. Another recipe for memories she had no use for. You had to move on, not linger, not turn back. At eighteen, when she went into the army, she stopped listening to music by choice.

When the podcast came to an end, she listened to it again, and this time she read the list of songs on Ophir's website:

"Ring the Bell", Songs: Ohia

"No Cease Fires", Destroyer

"I See a Darkness", Bonny "Prince" Billy
"Disco Sheets", The Wolf Parade
"For Real", Okkervil River
"We Rule the School", Belle & Sebastian
"Cue the Strings", Low
"Two-Headed Boy Part 1", Neutral Milk Hotel
"Bathysphere", (Smog)
"The Engine Driver", The Decemberists
"Part One", Band of Horses
"He Who Flattened Your Flame is Getting Torched", Danielson
"I Think I Need a New Heart", Magnetic Fields
"Love Love Love", Mountain Goats
"Randy Described Eternity", Built to Spill

———

She'd never heard of the bands performing the songs. It was strange to listen to the diverse male voices, allow them to assail her ears. They didn't have a body behind them, or a face. They came from an imagined space, and there was no image in her mind to attach to them, and they murmured like tongues of fire. Do they actually exist? Had she not recognized the remaining song, eighth in number, she would have thought that this was a sophisticated deception concocted by Ophir. "Two-Headed Boy Part 1" by Neutral Milk Hotel from the "In the Aeroplane Over the Sea" album. Avner used to listen to it devotedly. She remembered the cover: a woman with a tambourine for her head, a young boy beside her, their right hands raised, and beyond them—the sea and two children among the waves, possibly drowning, possibly struggling to swim.

Of all the times this particular album had played on the stereo system in their living room, one time wounded her, collected the

338

scratches of time into the depth of the melody. A few months after she'd moved in with Avner, she lost her job; a secretary in a printer importer's office. It was towards the end of August and summer had its claws firmly embedded in the firmament. She was to blame for losing her job. Instead of typing the letters her boss placed on her desk, she wrote little stories on the computer. That day her boss, David, who was always a morose nervous wreck, walked around the office more irritable than usual. He instructed her to type an urgent letter, and she did, but accidentally printed out one of her stories and handed it to him.

Five minutes later he called her into his office and she could see that his wrath threatened to burst through the boundaries of his body. He clutched the page on which the story had been printed and waved it at her.

"What do you think you're doing? Giving me this trash instead of working? What do you think I am, a welfare office for frustrated writers? I've never read such trash." He tore up the page violently and tossed the pieces into the wastebasket next to his desk. "Forget it," he added, his lips contorting like the edges of a pit in his sweaty face. "You're fired."

She trudged, choked, blinded to Or Zarua. She was almost run over as she crossed Allenby Street. The driver slammed on the brakes at the very last minute, the fender coming to a stop just a fraction of a centimeter from her thighs, and the driver yelled at her in alarm. She couldn't care less.

The bookshop was full of customers preparing well in advance for the deluge of High Holy Days shopping, unknowingly creating another deluge, other crowds. She made her way to the counter. Avner was standing alone at the cash register. There were calls of "Excuse me, is anyone working here?" from every direction. The assistant Boaz had hired for the busy period was off sick. Avner worked the register and hastily gift wrapped the books, which didn't do much for the way they looked. She stood next to him. "I'll take over the wrapping," she said to him, "you look after the cash register."

He glanced at her impatiently and resumed attending to the customers.

"Don't you want to know what I'm doing here in the middle of the day?" she asked him.

"We'll talk about it later."

"That loser David. I accidentally printed out one of my stories and put it on his desk instead of a letter. As if it wasn't bad enough that he fired me, he also trashed the story . . . "

"Ori, really. If you've come here to help, then help, don't disturb . . . "

"Do you want me to leave as well?"

"I don't have time for this now," he said scathingly.

She left a half-wrapped book and went home, where she sat on the couch in the living room, angry, overcome with insult, until Avner walked through the door. But he didn't come over to her; he vanished into the bedroom. A few minutes later he emerged with a book in his hand. He sat facing her and immersed himself in it. She got up and irritably paced the length of the living room.

"You're so unreceptive sometimes," she hurled at him.

"What now?" he asked.

"What now? I told you I've been fired and you're asking what now?"

"You got fired?"

"I told you in the shop."

"I wasn't listening," he said tenderly, like a little boy.

She sat down beside him, letting go of her anger, but when she concluded her account of the day's events—in the course of which she leveled criticism against every single one of the employees at the office—with the words, "That loser David," Avner said in a pensive tone, "Perhaps it was no accident that you printed the story. Maybe you thought that if he read it he'd like you, think that you're not just an ordinary secretary."

"Is that all you've got to say?" She leapt back to her feet. "I don't believe this. How long have you known me? Do you think I care what idiots like David think of my stories?"

She shrouded herself in silence, pursed her lips and bored into him with her eyes. He returned to his book. His face, tense and gloomy, gradually cleared. He raised his head and smiled his alien, disconcerting smile.

"It's not the end of the world," he said to her in a dreamy tone, "we're young and that means we're living in the End of Days. We have no way of truly imagining what the future holds. Only years from now, when the future has already happened, when this whole dark expanse of days and months has been traversed, will we be able to know what we had and didn't understand. Only when our future becomes our past will it truly be ours."

In one of their first conversations he'd mocked her university studies, the fact that she'd sought out teachers to teach her methods of locking her thinking. He told her that he preferred the random knowledge he discovered in books that happen to come to the shop, knowledge that has no regular structure, that is borne on the winds of fate and blows to him in the form of written pages. How she hated him in those moments when he took refuge in his eloquence, in polished turns of phrase, as if he was reading to her from an imaginary book, his eyes lingering in the distance as he spoke to her. She loathed him with all her heart.

"Wait a second," he said to her when he saw her face preparing for battle. He vanished into the kitchen and brought back two glasses and the bottle of wine they had opened a few nights before. There was barely enough wine for two half filled glasses. He raised his glass and clinked it against hers. "Here's to the future," he said, "and to a new job."

She stared at him for a few seconds before taking the glass and raising it to her lips. The wine was sour and seared her throat. She spluttered and started to laugh. Avner put the Neutral Milk Hotel album on the stereo, closed the blinds, darkening the apartment, and stood in the middle of the living room, surrounded by bookshelves and a gentle gloom. The speakers emitted sounds of an acoustic guitar and the coarse, nasal voice of a young vocalist. Avner held his hand out to her. "Shall we dance?" he asked, and grinned.

"This isn't even dance music," she said.

"So what?" Avner replied, "I don't even know how to dance. But for you . . . "

She waited for the first track to end before she stood up and walked towards him. In the second track the vocalist admits his love for Jesus, and as she came into his arms he whispered to her, "You know I love you forever, even when I tell you that you're disturbing me at work."

Once again his words were interlaced with that indifferent tone, and she didn't know if he was joking and quoting or speaking with genuine intention.

When she nestled her chin into the depression in his shoulder, the vocalist vowed to float until he learned to swim, to spit until he learned how to talk. They danced around the apartment, surrounded by acoustic guitars and wind instruments. Every now and then they kissed. Like divers coming up for air they knew the time interval between kisses, how much oxygen they were drawing into their lungs. The body works in mysterious ways. The third time the album played, the words filtered into her and she translated them in her head. One of the songs crept down her spine, gnawing at it, "Oh comely," sang the vocalist, "I will be with you when you lose your breath chasing the only meaningful memory you thought you had left . . . Your father made fetuses with flesh licking ladies while you and your mother were asleep . . . Know all your enemies, we know who our enemies are . . . " and trumpets poured into room and blended, bubbling and gurgling. Avner sang along with the vocalist, descending vampire-like onto her neck, his warm breath a shower of tiny scythes, "Goldaline, my dear, we will fold and freeze together. Far away from here there is sun and spring and green forever . . . Place your body here, let your skin begin to blend itself with mine."

She pressed her body into his, striving to tear down this barrier, which was a body, which was space. She pressed harder and harder. And suddenly they both knew it was evening. What had sprung forth in them in anticipation? What primordial clock calculated the Ends? They came out of their embrace, and showered.

"Why don't we go out? There's a new place on Herzl Street, a bit strange. We probably won't know anyone there." Avner said.

But when they entered, it turned out Avner had been mistaken. In the twilight lighting of the place, which was musty, like a burial cave, and decorated with translucent Indian scarves garishly embroidered in gold, a thickset man came towards them. He was already somewhat intoxicated and the alcohol was evident in his gait. He slapped Avner's shoulder and scrutinized her, his eyes awash with emotion. She wasn't led astray by the warmth emanating from them, she already knew how to read the desire in men's faces, recognized its malignancy beyond the tender mask they adopted. Especially in intoxicated men. Especially in big men, big-boned men like the man in front of her. Their lust for small, slender, ageless women like herself didn't escape her, she knew how their blood gravitated towards them, and their arms reached out to embrace, cradle, perhaps even tear apart. Ay, there's the rub.

And Avner said to her, "Ori, I'd like you to meet my friend, Barak Shulman."

343

FIVE

Burning

AVNER SPOKE BRIEFLY with Barak, catching up. Then he said to her, "I've got to take care of something," and vanished into the back of the bar.

She remained with Barak. The alcohol had loosened his tongue, and a flowing, churning, cascading river of words gushed from his mouth. What didn't he tell her about his childhood, his formative years. The river washed over her glassy skin and flowed on, into the dim expanse. Perhaps shattering fragments of it struck the barman's ears, who refilled his glass twice and nodded with interest every time Barak's moist, flat eyes rested on him in gratitude. It was only when he spoke of his sympathy for the "Mizrahi struggle"—as he apparently called the existential position of anyone who had the misfortune to be born to parents of Arab origin—that he managed to draw a reaction from her. And bewilderment.

What he said didn't fall into line, in her mind, with his occupation, a team leader at a computer company. But she didn't let the issue linger in her thoughts for long. She stared at the chunk of fire embedded in his earlobe, which sparkled whenever he moved, until she realized that it was a piece of metal planted into the flesh; her gaze turned to the slender gold strap of his watch, a feminine daintiness in its features and form, which was entangled in the hairs on his thick wrist.

Avner returned. He'd been gone for half an hour. On the way home she reproached him, a gentle reproach disguised in a jocose mantle. "An agent provocateur"—she took pleasure in the sound of the words for some reason and stretched out the syllables—"all of a sudden. One minute you're here, and the next you're gone."

"Some agent provocateur," Avner chuckled, "if my girl-friend manages to blow my cover on my very first mission. Did you suffer?"

"You mean that Barak Shulman guy? Actually I did a bit. He drove me crazy. Especially with all his talk about Mizrahis and Ashkenazis. Who's got the energy for those discussions any more?"

She didn't ask how well he and Barak knew each other. Avner had numerous friends and acquaintances. Some were from his past; had been in elementary or high school with him, served in the army with him, migrated with him to Tel Aviv. They appeared out of the blue and Avner spent a few weeks in their company, and then they would vanish just as suddenly as they had appeared. At first she'd ask Avner what had happened to that one, and where do you know that one from, but Avner was evasive and would say, "Oh, that one, he left Tel Aviv." "And he's a total idiot. A fascist." And frequently, "You think you know people, and then you discover their taste in books." Perhaps if she had displayed greater interest in people she would have wondered about this characteristic of his. But she had no friends, male or female.

One time Avner asked her about it, why she was so quick to relinquish human company, why she took such pains to remain alone. She replied that she wished she knew how to be alone. That was the problem, she was never alone.

"Alone is the better of the two types of loneliness," she told him, "because at the end of the day there are only two types.

In the first you're surrounded by people who are blind to your existence. You're lonely because your self-worth is derived from their disregard. In the second you're in the presence of such a vast essence, you touch such an immense presence that knows you and knows exactly who you are, that you don't notice the existence of the people around you. You're lonely because you find no purpose in the interest of others in you. They no longer influence your attitude towards yourself. So you're alone."

She fell silent, and words, the source of which she couldn't recall, skipped onto her tongue and leapt out.

"And the Lord said: Behold, there is a place by Me, and thou shalt stand upon the rock. And it shall come to pass, while My glory passeth by, that I will put thee in a cleft of the rock, and will cover thee with My hand until I have passed by."

"What was that?" Avner asked.

"You know, it's from that story about Moses, when he wants to see God's glory, and God commands him to go into the cleft of the rock. In it he is truly alone, because he's close to such a great and powerful entity that protects him from any harm that may emanate from it. He finds himself in a fragment of the most primordial and authentic reality that exists, without paying the price." She answered, her voice trembling although she didn't know why.

"So what are you actually saying?"

She continued her previous line of thought, as if it hadn't been interrupted.

"When you become attached to people you take the risk of the first type of loneliness, but if you don't, you miss your chances of meeting the right person, through whom you can attain the second type of loneliness."

"But why do you need another person in order to touch that great essence, if it even exists?"

"Because this is a world of human beings, and everything in it is done according to human dimensions. That essence, too, is fulfilled in the form of flesh and blood." She replied. Avner looked at her dubiously, and she explained, "If you're sitting on a riverbank and a spirit comes and carries you to the Throne, or if you're walking along and an angel brandishing a sword stands before you, then you know for sure. But what if in the middle of your life someone comes into your life, equipped with all the signs and omens, how will you know? It's difficult to understand. Hard to grasp. But if you've ever been struck by an immense entity and weren't eradicated and didn't lose your sanity, you're condemned to a life of perpetual doubt."

Avner scrutinized her face, trying to see if she was joking, and when he discovered complete seriousness and said, "So there's still a price to pay." A few seconds later he added cautiously, "But you'll know when you meet the right person," and added, grinning, with growing self-confidence, "I'm the right person, right?"

She didn't answer. Characteristically, she hadn't told him that as early as in her first year at boarding school in Jerusalem, where she'd gone in an attempt to extricate herself from the quagmire of her father's home, she'd realized how pointless it was to form relationships with others. She'd been sitting in the cafeteria with two students. They talked to her, asked about her background, her past, her childhood in Netivot. Images she'd tried to suppress, erase, surfaced against her will. The first man she'd had sex with, when she was fourteen and a half, in a field on the outskirts of Netivot. His name eluded her and only his face stretching over her, groaning in carnal bliss, and his wedding-ringed finger, which he'd pass over her lips, remained with her, like an insane engraving. The pale, lean back of another man she watched receding from her as she lay naked and frozen on a table. She shifted her eyes from the girls and pursed her lips. It was late afternoon and the sun erupted behind the buildings like a wild-eyed warrior. A sweltering waterfall cascaded around them. On the latticed hedge of morning glory, whose hollow calyxes gaped thirstily, a goldfinch fluttered. The cafeteria courtyard hummed. That moment was a knife pressed against her throat. She froze. If she moved, she thought, she would be risking her life. Or worse. It *could* be worse. In the distance she heard a bumblebee, its buzzing shrill, grating and loud, and she knew it was singing its death song. She remained sitting, nodded to the two girls as they got up and left. The bumblebee's song died out as well, succumbing to the power of evening. She knew she would never be able to tolerate the sound of someone seeking her company. It was all washed away in rising nausea.

The night groaned and creaked around them on their way back to their apartment. Not the city, its approaches and gates, but the struggle of autumn to be seen, to breach the fortifications of the heat: the cores of the frozen stars above them would gradually diffuse their chill, and the poplars and chinaberry trees would withdraw into slumber. She wanted to embrace Avner again, as she had earlier that evening. Even if she didn't love him, she'd refused to leave him alone since his eyes had opened to her with a mute promise beneath the jacarandas and she'd felt the flame ignite close to her skin, burning. No. She wouldn't allow it. If there were some loose, frightened cords between them she would not allow them to snap, if they were both already trapped like fish in a net, she didn't want to break free. She leaned onto his shoulder and said, "I don't know where that Barak came from. But I hope you don't have any plans to ask him over."

"No. Don't worry. I carry out meticulous screening before I ask anyone over," he said, and she laughed.

She ran into Barak again fourteen days after Avner disappeared. She carefully counted and calculated in her head: fourteen days are twice seven, that kind of multiple must be an omen. And indeed, on the morning of the fourteenth day she received a positive answer from the publishers. A timid editor called to schedule a meeting with her. In the afternoon she went to see Boaz Zadok to tell him her good news. In the evening she ran into Barak.

She went to the little bar on Herzl Street. Winter was still creeping in between the cracks of March. Tel Aviv's beauty, she thought, is wrought by time. It is revealed fleetingly in the brief interim between seasons.

The little bar's décor hadn't changed. The same dimness, like a cancerous colony on an X-ray image, shrouded it. She sat at a side table, not far from the door opening onto the courtyard. A pleasant breeze brushed against the doorframe, pushed through the doorway like a ruffian, and came in, ruffling the gold-embroidered scarves, swinging the hanging lamps with their feeble lights, and contaminating the air with the cloying scent of jasmine.

Ori gently sipped the glass of ouzo she'd ordered. The sweetish taste of anise tingled on her palate. At first she didn't recognize the man who asked if he could join her and then sat facing her, even though the bar was somewhat deserted. When she didn't respond, he said, "Don't you remember me?" And she shook her head. "You're Ori, aren't you? Avner's girlfriend?"

She nodded in confirmation.

"Where is he?"

She felt paralyzed.

"Is he here?"

She shook her head.

"I see," he said, "only yes or no questions. A binary creature."

She nodded.

"Okay. Are you here on your own?"

She nodded.

349

"Are you still together?"

She shook her head.

"You've split up?"

She suddenly realized that she didn't know the stranger facing her and that she was revealing intimate details of her life. "Who are you?" she asked.

"Oh, so you can speak."

"Well, of course I can."

"I'm Barak. Barak Shulman. Remember me?"

Almost five months had elapsed since the bar incident, but she still retained an impression of Barak. He was completely different to the man she remembered. Not in the mass and size of his body, but in the solidness of his presence. The figure etched in her memory had a black center of gravity and vague, frayed margins. Perhaps the alcoholic fog that had enveloped him had attached to his outlines in her imagination. Now he was more focused, as if re-compacted into human form.

"I remember." She said.

"I'm sorry about that time. The next morning I got up with a terrible headache and the first thing I thought was what a jerk I was." He responded with embarrassment,

She didn't come to his aid; she just looked straight ahead.

"But there were mitigating circumstances," he added. "There was no . . . " A gust of wind blew against one of the lamps above her and light washed over his face, and she saw his hesitant, childish smile spreading, revealing the gap between his teeth. And she silenced him.

"There are always mitigating circumstances," she said.

That night, after an hour of somewhat drowsy small talk, she went with him to his apartment, not because of his smile, and not because the number of days divulged the workings of a higher order that tipped in her favor. No. But because letting go of Avner was beyond her power. Oh, why was it so difficult to let go if that was the natural course of the world? You split up, you always split up. Even before a hand fumbled and reached out to embrace, she'd already planned her departure; the separation preceded the encounter, a shower of silver iodide ions absorbing dust and vapor to produce clouds.

Some people try to forget by immersing themselves in the body, by indulging the flesh. She craved remembrance. When Barak touched her she sought a hint of Avner. If only it were possible to pass her fingers over his skin and pluck residues and deposits from it, the traces of his acquaintance with Avner. If only it were possible to expose a slight resemblance in the movement of limbs, a mold, that had clung to him unawares, an unconscious imitation.

She found nothing of this in Barak's body. Avner was different. He waited for the twitches, to which she had condemned her body when she was fifteen, to thaw out, waited until she was able to respond to his touch, dared to reciprocate with a touch of her own. That cockroach-ridden summer, when he'd asked her to move into his apartment, she'd woken up just before dawn, in the false pre-*hamsin* chill. An insect was entangled in her hair. She screamed and shook her head, and having no choice, she grabbed it and threw it against the wall. In the decimated light, as she watched it lying on its back, its segmented legs flailing in the air, her mouth was suddenly dry. She picked up the copy of *The Star of Redemption* that she'd placed on her bedside table in advance, and crushed it; the juices of its squashed entrails stuck to the cover. Then she called Avner, woke him up, and asked if his offer still stood. Her voice was colored with a tone of urgency, and it rose and became distorted. Avner delayed his response. Perhaps he'd fallen asleep holding the receiver. She embarked on a report of her battle with the cockroach with Rosenzweig's help. Avner chuckled. He said, "Ori has murdered sleep."

351

When she arrived at his apartment with a hastily packed bag, he held out his arms and she evaded his embrace. He retreated into the bedroom and she followed, still stunned. She looked at him sprawled on the bed, not bothering to pull up the thin quilt-cover he used for a blanket. Now she noticed: the upper part of his body was bare, virtually smooth, apart from his freckled shoulders, which were strangely hairy, covered in a kind of thin lacework. He slept in his underwear. For ten minutes she stood scrutinizing him. His breathing filled with the whistle of sleep. Finally, crescents opened below his eyelids, he tiredly patted the empty side of the double bed.

"You coming?" he mumbled.

She curled up beside him. He didn't touch her. At the end of that day, when their bodies again lay side by side, his fingers crept. She said she couldn't, that it's hard for her. She told him she was inexperienced, that she'd only ever been with one man, during her army service, one frenzied night with a random soldier, when she couldn't wait to lose her virginity. Had it hurt? Like hell. Since then she shrinks back. It was a casual lie and she sighed at its conclusion, letting Avner interpret the sigh however he chose.

He responded with a story of his own; of all the heartwarming anecdotes in the life of a bookseller, for some reason he chose to tell her about the time he saw a dead man. A man carrying a suitcase collapsed without prior warning onto the sidewalk. The shopkeeper from the nearby sweetshop came out first. Avner watched her stooping over him, shaking his shoulder and rushing into the store, returning with a glass of water, the contents of which she poured onto his face. Avner came out, joining the small crowd that had already gathered around the body lying face up on the sidewalk. Another shopkeeper said he'd already called for an ambulance, and a passerby said, "There's no need," and pointed. Avner saw a pool of collected water in the man's open eye sockets. Someone in the crowd bewailed, "All the first-aid training I was given in basic training, and for what? I couldn't move, I was paralyzed."

Ori didn't respond, sinking into sleep, and in the haze remembered her mother's face during her final days, imprisoned between an oxygen mask on one side, and the fleecy hospital pillow on the other, the burning of the sun already erased from its skin. She groaned and, with a titanic effort, opened her eyelids. Avner looked at her and smiled. He wasn't tempted to pass his hand over her cheek, didn't pressure her even for a second. He let her dictate the pace. Some nights she couldn't go any further than a kiss, lips pressing against lips, and then nights of lying close to him, of an arm cradling shoulders and a caressing hand, gently exploring, gauging the weight of a breast. When she let him penetrate her, she was dry, her vagina like sandpaper. They tried gently, they tried forcibly. Avner finally withdrew. His penis raw from the friction. Her vagina as tight as a locked jaw. She became alarmed, her face imploring.

"A man desires a woman. But a woman doesn't desire a man. She desires his passion towards her," she said. "Keep burning. Keep wanting me, until I stop being afraid. If you cross this river with me."

By the time she was ready for uninhibited lovemaking, of surrendering to the flesh, to its pleasure, her and Avner's routines were sealed. Every time they made love, it was as if he was exploring her body for the first time; an inexperienced boy, guided only by his fervor, making the crudeness of his mistakes forgivable and their lovemaking exciting in its naivety.

Barak, on the other hand, was skilled. He read her flesh according to a map he had sketched during his explorations of numerous women's bodies, knew what would arouse her, excite her, and she, in her search for Avner's touch perhaps blended unawares in his touch, surrendered to it, surrendered, and perhaps

353

her own flesh sought to free itself from the fetters Avner had left behind, encircling and binding her.

As she sat in her study now, staring at the computer screen, at the twisting, liquid forms the media player displayed as it played Ophir's podcast for the third or fourth time, it was the memory of her first lovemaking with Barak that tore her insides. No. The piercing sensation was merely the result. A viper coiled around her lungs and stomach and, suddenly, as the memory surfaced, it bit her, sending explosive bubbles of venom coursing through her.

She had never wondered about or dwelt on Barak's great skill and how he had acquired it. How long he'd worked on it and with how many women. And yet, how can a man like that be content with one woman for five years? The question stuck in her mind, reproducing parthenogenetically, multiplying over and over again. How can a man like that be content with one woman for five years? How can . . .

"Light the flame," the vocalist sang into her ears. "Light dispelling dark."

That's what happened. Like the time she wanted to light the gas stove in the kitchen and the match had gone out midway. She hadn't bothered to turn off the gas and pulled out another match. As she brought it towards the stove the flame erupted violently and a wave of heat smashed against her face, singeing her eyebrows and burning her skin. That was how she felt at that moment. The extinguished match, the substitute match, the explosion of the blue effulgence of the gas flame and the rush of burning air. All the details that had lain unturned in her consciousness fused into a blazing explosion: Barak coming home late; the clumsy excuse of the gym; the apologetic touch of his lips on her forehead every morning on the one hand, and his new remoteness on the other; the cell phone switched off in the middle of the day. How had she not seen it? The signs had been right in front of her eyes the whole time. Barak was cheating on her.

She whispered the words to herself, to endow them with some meaning, as if putting them into tonal material would give them volume and substance, and she would be able to defeat them, dismiss them. At first she whispered in astonishment, then in disbelief that the anguish attending their articulation didn't evaporate. But why did she feel such piercing pain? She'd been prepared for this possibility since the day she had entwined her destiny with his. No. No. From the day she understood her destiny. And she had been so careful. The viper weighing on her organs struck again. There was no need to wonder who the secret lover was, because she, too, appeared in her mind's eye in a burst of flames: Neta; Neta who had assailed him just before the concert; Neta whose head inclined into the charcoal black of Barak's hair, casting flickers of red into it, while Barak filled up with serenity from the notes produced by her playing fingers. Neta.

———

She woke up before dawn, stiff-limbed on the couch in the living room. The window slats cast strips of gray light onto her face. She forced herself to get up and crawl into bed next to Barak, lest Alma wake up early and find her sprawled on the couch. Barak hadn't noticed her absence, but when she grabbed a corner of the light blanket, his arm fell across her, bathed in a light film of perspiration, and she drew it to her to draw sustenance from its closeness. The dampness of his arm made her bilious. She felt violated.

After the morning rituals, when Barak had set off for his day at the office, a drowsy idea struck the back of her mind. And when she dropped next to Alma in front of the TV, which was tuned into one of the children's channels, and drank her coffee. The idea gelled into a plan. But first there was Alma's appointment with the ophthalmologist. She dressed quickly, carelessly, not choosing her clothes, slipping into the first shirt on the shelf, into tattered jeans. She didn't even bother to brush her hair. But she dressed Alma meticulously, arguing with her about her clothes, the color of her socks, her ponytail holders.

Subsequently they arrived at the clinic at precisely the appointed time. But they still had to wait several minutes before the patient ahead of them came out. Alma immediately leapt to her feet, but the patient shut the door behind him.

"She asked not to be disturbed for now," he whispered to them.

Alma stood impatiently at the door. A moment later she opened it without knocking, stuck her head into the room and called, "Why are you talking on the phone? We're waiting for you."

Ori hurried over to her. Once again a flash of anger flared up in her at her daughter's impudence. But her ears caught fragments of the conversation the doctor was conducting in a bored voice, and she joined Alma's protest.

"Really. You can have those conversations in the evening," she reproved her and considered leaving and coming back another day, asking for a different doctor, because if their appointment had begun with such a discordant tone . . . These doctors! She thought resentfully, how dare they?

But Alma was already enthralled by the instruments in the room. She strode towards a device whose metal arches formed the shape of a skull, and shoved her head into it.

"Young lady," said the doctor in the same bored tone, "these instruments aren't toys." Turning to Ori she demanded, "What's the problem?"

"Her eyes are red," Ori replied. The doctor called Alma over and firmly clasped her chin. Ori felt the clasp of phantom fingers. The possibility of Alma's pain became a tangible pain, presaging even greater agony. Her daughter's entire future life flashed before her eyes: at age seven her arm breaking in a bike accident, the first boy whose closeness would make her soul contract, the bullying in class, wonder at the changes occurring in her body, the bitter rebellion against her friends, her slow death from an as yet undiagnosed and unnamed disease. Oh, the Grim Reaper would descend on them both.

She turned her gaze away from her and the battery of examinations became a blur. The doctor pronounced, "An allergic inflammation. I'm prescribing an antihistamine, two drops in each eye three times a day for a week. And change the child's shampoo."

She gave her the prescription and her attention returned to focus on the telephone receiver.

Alma skipped down the stairs. Although they had been on the fifth floor she insisted on walking down. She arrived at the ground floor, where the pharmacy was situated, exhausted. Ori lay her down on a bench, her head resting on her lap. She passed a hand through her hair, gathering curls between her fingers. Alma was born virtually bald, with a thin tuft on her crown. How she'd waited for her hair to grow, imagining what it would look like, its volume, its sheen. And it wasn't only her tresses that preoccupied her, she thought about her daughter's every contour and feature. She observed them forming with interest. Because during the first two years of raising her, Alma had been the substance. Not only because of the physical closeness, the nursing—to which she put an end when the child was three months old—diaper changes, bathing, and the intoxicating smell of skin and milk; and not because the mute flesh needed her at first, and a short time later she could already discern the budding of her soul—flashes of intelligence in suddenly focused eyes, the strained listening to sound, the mumbles and fragments of first syllables. No. Not because of that loathsome generality, common to all babies, but because she was Alma.

She continued combing the thick hair with her fingers and her nails caught on a bump on her scalp, a scar. Alma groaned. Ori was alarmed for a moment, it was the groan of an animal, and the hair between her fingers turned into fur. She abruptly withdrew her hand and turned to look around the room. An elderly man and a young woman, probably his daughter, were sitting on one of the benches near them.

"Now you'll see why I quarrel with them all the time," the man said, "because they stick the labels on the medication boxes so brutally."

Ori smiled at his pronunciation of the word "brutally", because her father's guttural accent was evident in it. The way the 'r' consonant tore from the vocal cords and struck the roof of the mouth before coming out. When it came on the heels of the 'b' consonant, which exploded on the lips, it created a melody so charming it was impossible to resist or avoid the memory she carried with her.

Once, when she was a little girl, she went to help Asher with the shopping and in her enthusiasm decided to carry the juice bottles. Asher warned her that they would be too heavy, but she picked them up and marched from the shop determinedly, but her determination dissipated after just a few meters. The weight of the bottles had turned her hands into callous lead. She put the bottles down on the sidewalk and waited for Asher. When he arrived with the shopping bags the wife of the grocery shop proprietor walked past them. She said to Ori, "Mind the bottles in case some kid on a bike rides past and fizzulates them. She heard the sound of Asher's laughter behind her. Uncontrolled laughter. He repeated the strange word and its rasping pronunciation, "fizzulate". He then used it whenever he could. She understood very well why it amused him.

The man on the bench persisted with his complaining, "Every time I ask them to let me stick the label on myself, but they always say no."

"I'll ask the head pharmacist to let you," answered the daughter, and Ori discerned the apprehension in her voice. She was attuned to her father, to the anger seething in him.

"She'll say no. These Russians, they understand nothing."

"And what do you understand, you Moroccan? That's why they're behind the counter and you're sitting here."

"Me? I get a salary from the state without lifting a finger. And what do they . . . "

"Why do you always have to quarrel about everything? Why do you have to solve everything with a quarrel?"

"Because that's the way it is. If I don't get angry and don't argue, I don't feel alive."

The exchange broadened her smile. She stroked Alma's hair, the damp curls sticking to her forehead, and asked in a whisper, "How was it at Grandpa's house?"

Alma stuck a finger into her mouth and turned it around on the inside of her cheek. "Nfff," she said.

"Take your finger out of your mouth. How many times have I told you not to stick it in, do you want to throw up?"

Alma pulled out a finger smothered in saliva and wiped it on her skirt.

"So how was it?" Ori urged.

"Nice," Alma said.

"That's it? Just nice?"

"Yes," said Alma. "Nice."

It was uncharacteristic of her daughter to be so succinct and express herself so vaguely. But perhaps she perceived, with the same hidden sense that identified the tension between her parents, that she was treading on thin ice. While Ori wondered whether she should continue investigating, a ringing sounded. Their number appeared on the digital display screen.

———

On a momentary impulse she'd concealed from Barak the parking ticket he'd been sent a few weeks before, and hid it among her papers. The exact location on it, she thought, she needs to check it and its surroundings. There's no doubt Neta lives there, and Barak, on one of his visits, had parked in the area and forgotten to display his parking sticker. She left Alma in the kindergarten, despite her protests and pleas to go home. From there she walked to Soutine Street.

She was actually familiar with the artist's work, but the agglomeration of cement and heavily foliaged trees lining the street named after him, and the intense brilliance of May, like pulsing gold bullion, were completely at odds with his angst-ridden, somber style. What a ludicrous thought, she said to herself, and continued up the street to No. 12. As she stood at the entrance and examined the names on the intercom panel and mailboxes she realized she didn't know Neta's surname. She waited a few minutes and looked around. A fairly affluent area, she noted. She heard the hubbub of Ibn Gvirol Street some distance away, in whose architecture, in the way its different buildings had been attached to one another, interspersed with kiosks and shawarma stands and cafés, there was no trace of the tempos, syntax, poetic ploys of the poet who had granted the street its name, and even less so of his worldview. What did the insensate gregariousness of a May afternoon at the Gan Ha'ir shopping mall have to do with the philosopher who asserted that the knowing part of man is the most important part? The thought contained pricks of anger.

"Can I help you?" asked a small, elderly man leaning against the front door fumbling with his key chain. When he managed to open the door, he held onto its frame and persisted, "Who are you looking for?"

"Ah," she began in confusion, and immediately composed herself, "I've come to see my friend, Neta, but I've forgotten what number her apartment is."

The elderly man scrutinized her suspiciously. "Which family is she from?"

"Neta. A bit taller than me, with red hair. She's a pianist."

"There's no Neta here," said the elderly man and slammed the door behind him.

She remained standing at the door for a few moments. She had to remember Neta's surname. It must have appeared on the concert program. With her eyes closed she tried to evoke the image. The program was printed on yellowish paper. Black lettering. Ori tried to coerce physical presence onto the page. There, it says, Piazzolla, accordion and piano, yes that's the shape of the lettering. Now if she pushed just a bit more—her eyes narrowed and her jaw muscles tensed, pressing rows of teeth onto one another. She opened her eyes. What foolishness. Frustration was already beginning to gnaw at her. But she wasn't going to give up. She'd scan all the buildings on the street. Yes. After all, it wasn't a particularly long street, and she would undoubtedly come across a name on one of the mailboxes that had a familiar ring to it. She returned to the end of the street. She'd start with the building on her right—the even numbers, which are luckier. Two is such a delicate, pleasant number.

Half an hour later she reached the other end of the street, with nothing to show for her efforts. She was hot and sweaty and on the verge of tears. A sense of helplessness swelled up in her, like a pretzel in water, filling her with its dankness.

Perhaps Barak had parked on this street, she thought, but Neta actually lives in another street in the area. She would have to scan them all, from beginning to end. But she paid no heed to her own thought, which was echoless; the kind of empty, feeble thoughts that fall, detached, as soon as they form. She should go home.

But as she crossed Rabin Square she felt the toll of her wanderings. She was lightheaded, she hadn't eaten a thing since last night. And she had to take a break from the noise, from the thoughts clamoring about in her head, like pots and pans stuffed into a kitchen cupboard and the door opening abruptly.

She sat at a table in a café—which also served as a bookshop—overlooking the square. She sat outside, because she knew the two proprietors and although she liked them she didn't have the strength to be cordial to anyone, and even less so to talk about her books or the books of others. She gestured to the waitress and ordered a coffee and croissant, stressing the nasal ending of the name of the pastry. The waitress corrected her with an air of importance, "*korasson*," and Ori smiled at her wearily, mumbling, "The crooked cannot be straightened." She almost expected the waitress to say, "What does that even mean?" All words are monsters clawing in the dark, until someone comes along and attaches them to the world, telling them: from here to here you're valid; you are permitted to say. Beyond that, you have no title and no glory.

The coffee was placed before her. So was the croissant. She fingered it distractedly, lost count of the number of sugar sachets she had emptied into the cup. What did she hope to achieve in her search? Say she'd found Neta's house, did she have solid proof? And what degree of solidity did she require? The apprehension that had begun to permeate her heart and throat was as tangible as it could be. Sooner or later she is always betrayed, turned away from, torn away from. Not only Avner, not only

Barak, her father too. And Ofra. And Asher. They'd all betrayed her. Left her on her own.

Ofra had found a way out in her army service and fell upon it as if she'd found a long-lost treasure. Ori recalled how she'd beamed when she received her first orders, and the sheer joy that glowed from her every movement when she returned from the recruitment center in Beersheba, fully recognizing that her salvation was imminent. She asked to serve in a closed base, far from Netivot, and came home for weekends only occasionally. Within two months she fell in love with Nissim, about whom Ori heard completely by chance. Ofra became increasingly distant from her, or was it she who lost interest? Ori saw Nissim only once after Ofra came out of the army and decided to travel with him to the Far East. She never saw him again. Ofra wandered even further east, to New Zealand, where she met Yaniv, an Israeli like herself. And they came back to Israel to get married.

She'd watched how Asher became hard and dry. The factory job their father had found for him the summer her mother was diagnosed was substituted for another job, as a mechanic's assistant, and another, as a market stall trader. A year later Josh and Judy left Netivot following a dispute with Avshalom Baruch, the new principal, who regarded gym classes as a levy he was obliged to pay the ministry of education rather than an important chapter in adolescent law. He wanted the young boys and girls to spend their afternoons in the fold of the Bnei Akiva religious youth movement—Torah and Work—rather than running around aimlessly in the custom of Gentiles.

Ori watched the innocence of youth evaporate out of Asher in a matter of a few nights. At seventeen Asher was absent from home almost every night, hitchhiking to Beersheba or even Tel Aviv, returning at sunrise, skipping school, and eventually being expelled. At eighteen his eyes were already shrouded in a slate-like veil, and his long, supple limbs, dried up. All traces of tenderness vanished from his face, from the feline movements of his Adam's apple when he swallowed—because he no longer did so with embarrassment, only with affront. Muscles and tendons remained—a tightly wound coil, tough, impervious, as if his image had been cast in basalt and animated. He went into the army and was sent to the armored corps, but broke down in basic training and spent a whole year being AWOL, a deserter and in a military prison. At the end of that year he was discharged due to incompatibility with the IDF, and he went to Canada and from there to the States, to Chicago. Apart from telephone calls to Ofra on the High Holy Days—Rosh Hashanah and Passover—and the chance postcard she received from him, the biting chill of Lake Michigan pinching at the messages they carried, no one heard from him at all. What did he do for a living? She vaguely recalled that Josh and Judy had lived in the Windy City before immigrating to Israel. Had he followed them, had he found them, was he happy?

And their father—she'd never understood how difficult it had been for Ya'akov Elhayani. After his wife died, the factory agreed to let him work only day shifts. He wandered around the house as if it were deserted, his children erased from his memory, or as if the very spaces were nothing more than memories dwelling between the walls, in the rooms and hallways. He lived in it, a memory in which his children were alive, but separate from him, two layers of reality placed one atop the other, and no one but them noticed how distant they were, the purgatory separating them.

Ori knew he'd started drinking in the evenings. She followed him, troubled and craving words, a sentence acknowledging her presence, a sign that he knew he was her father and was committed to protecting her, if not to loving her. At first he drank arrack, surreptitiously, from the bottles in the cherry-wood cabinet in the living room, his eyes darting in all directions, frightened, as he emptied one glass and then another into his mouth and hastily gulped them down.

Later, after Ofra and Asher had left home, he drank openly—vodka for which he paid a lot of money at the grocery shop. The new beverage changed everything. Because in his pursuit of it he discovered the changes undergone in the neighboring town of Sderot, which had taken in waves of new immigrants from the former Soviet Union. They carried with them fragments of their homeland, like seeds that are resistant to climatic change. Small grocery shops carrying Russian merchandise sprouted up in the new neighborhoods that had been built in the town, whose population grew rapidly: sausages and frozen seafood, capsules of snow-covered steppes and black oceans, and cheap vodka with a high alcohol content, and young, shapely, lost women. That was all it took. In Sderot they later called those years the "plague years". Slavic beauty seemingly plucked the older Moroccan men like tender leaves from their homes and their wives' arms, and youth was traded for financial stability and a bed to sleep in.

And her father, who traveled to Sderot every week to replenish his stock of vodka, did not escape this storm either. He was absent on more and more evenings, and would come home in the dead of night with a woman. Ori would lay tensely on her bed, fourteen years of age, and listen to the sound of drunken laughter, the broken guttural chatter and the response of different guttural speech, rounded on its edges, receding.

———

Her coffee was cold. She sensed the absence of its heat when she held it in her hands. How long had she been wandering after her thoughts? She fumbled around in her shoulder bag and pulled out a stained envelope she'd found in their mailbox yesterday. The editor of the supplement in which her article had been published had been true to his word and sent her a letter from a troubled reader. The letter was handwritten, not typed, the lettering large and rounded, crude and disordered, childlike. When she'd opened it her eyes had immediately wandered to the bottom of the page to see who had written it, and she closed it, put it back into the envelope and shoved it back into her bag. She had forgotten its existence almost instantly. And she remembered it now because of a silly detail: her hands around her cup of coffee. The last time she'd done this, Alma had been facing her at Café Migdanot and had asked, her head bowed, her eyes peering up at her, "Ima, are you hugging the coffee?"

At first the letters flickered on the page. She couldn't make them come together to form words, and when they finally did, they were meaningless. She persisted. One syllable at a time, until the language was restored:

It was with great excitement and surprise that I read the article "The Gates of Wonderland" by the author for children and youth Ori Elhayani that you published in your Second Passover issue. With excitement—because the notion of Wonderland is not a common one in our local children's literature and one might even say it is alien to it, hence it is rarely addressed in the Hebrew literary supplements. My excitement was twofold. Not only the rarity of the subject, but the article itself is praiseworthy. It is only seldom that your readers encounter such a well-written, original and comprehensive article.

But I was also very surprised. I consider myself an unofficial expert in English children's literature. The author Elhayani devoted the first part of her article to a book series featuring Ariella the Fairy Detective, ostensibly written by an author who calls himself Prospero Juno. I was surprised to encounter a series

I had never heard of, and my surprise grew even more when I searched for information about it. As far as members of forums all over the web that are devoted to literature for children and youth know, no such book series has ever been published. Even the National Library's database, which by law receives two copies of every book published in this country, has no reference to Juno in its list of authors that have been translated into Hebrew.

Was this a case of artistic license taken by Ms. Elhayani? And if so, would it not be appropriate for her to accept responsibility for it as well?

Sincerely,

Michael Kagan

Tel Aviv

———

The impudent little worm, thought Ori. What was this, revenge for giving him the wrong email address? For blowing him off? She hadn't been taken in by his groveling for a minute. From the moment he'd approached her and Alma's table her eyes had penetrated his obsequious, apologetic appearance. She recognized the hunger burning within him, gnawing at him, craving to burst out, to gain recognition. She discerned in him the yearning of the outsider. Which was why she'd hastily blown him off and closed herself to his request.

She asked for the check and, not waiting for it to arrive, left two twenty-shekel notes on the table, much more than necessary, she knew, but she suddenly felt she had to flee. She walked quickly, her shoulder bag flapping against her waist, at times sliding off her shoulder and down her arm, and she repeatedly pulled it back into place.

The unsightly ficus trees lining Chen Boulevard were replaced by the unsightly ficus trees lining Rothschild Boulevard. The sky was the same sky, brilliant azure sheeting; the light the same light. A cyclist swerved away from her at the last minute when she didn't respond to his rapid and irritating bell ringing.

She immediately spotted Michael's plump outline through the entrance to the café. Her eyes followed him until he turned his head in a kind of flinching twitch, and saw her. He smiled and hurried over to her. "Ms. Elhayani," he said, "what a surprise. And where is the sweet young lady?"

"Kindergarten," she replied, glancing at her watch. Her sense of time had gone awry. She'd almost forgotten about Alma. All right, she sighed, she had two hours left. "And you can call me Ori."

"I tried to email you, but it bounced back. I must have written it down incorrectly."

"And is that why you're writing letters against me to the newspaper?" She asked more aggressively than she'd intended.

The ready smile flickered across Michael's lips, but his face became somewhat downcast.

"I . . . is that why you're here?"

"Yes, the editor forwarded your letter to me and I wanted to understand the meaning of your complaints."

"Maybe we should sit down?" he proposed. The hostess, who had observed their exchange, made her way towards them. Michael whispered something into her ear, and she nodded. He told Ori to follow him to a corner table. On the way he picked up a pitcher of water and two glasses. "Would you like coffee?" he asked.

"No, it's all right. I just had one."

"Look, Ori, first of all, I'm really excited that you came. Second, I'm sorry about the letter. The truth is I wrote and sent it in a moment of anger. Yes, I admit, I was a bit offended by your attitude. And when I couldn't send you an email, and then saw your article in the paper, I was even annoyed."

Ori said, "I don't understand. What's the article got to do with it?"

"It's a bit difficult to explain." He fell silent, then added, "Fantasy, science fiction. Youth literature—those are the books I've been reading since childhood. They . . . " He gazed at her for a few moments, "saved me." He coughed. "Sorry for the pathos." He smiled. A flicker of stretching lips. "I . . . "

"You feel that this field is yours by virtue . . . " began Ori.

His cheeks became flushed and he added enthusiastically, "You understand! I knew you would. Only someone who cares about such books knows this kind of fanaticism. People who read *belles lettres* or detective novels or thrillers or whatever, romantic novels, they don't . . . they have a lesser . . . "

"That's a bit of an exaggeration, isn't it?"

"No," he ruled, "not at all. I'm not saying they don't enjoy it. But for them reading is a kind of leisure-time experience, not an existential necessity. They don't define themselves through the books they read."

"I don't agree."

Michael shrugged. He poured water into the two glasses and avidly gulped his down in an attempt to douse the flames in his cheeks.

"So the letter . . . you wrote it to punish me?" Ori said cautiously.

"No. First of all I liked the article a lot. There were things I didn't understand, like that thing about the Garden of Eden. I mean, I'm guessing you meant that sex, death and meaning don't function in the Garden of Eden as they do in Wonderland, that in the Garden of Eden meaning is transparent, because all things are called by their real names, and there's no sex or death, because discovering either of them means expulsion from the Garden of Eden . . . And I'm not sure . . . but what difference does it make . . . there were some things missing in it, like reference to Alan Moore's comics, you know, *Lost Girls*. There he talks specifically about the characters of Alice, Wendy and Dorothy and about the connection between sexual experiences and Wonderland. And maybe . . . actually, that's it. But as I wrote, I was glad it was published. That's what made me respond."

"But you make a very serious allegation," her voice was colored by affront. It trembled. "You say I'm lying and misleading readers."

"I didn't say you're lying, only that you have every right to invent, you're an author, but you should inform . . . "

"But I didn't invent"—this was becoming ridiculous; why was she defending herself to this infant?—"I wrote about books I read as a girl."

"Ori," said Michael, adding softly, "I don't interfere in the stories a person tells himself in order to live . . . I myself . . . "

"Enough. I can't stand any more of these worn-out clichés. Anyone can spout them like a reflex: stories shape our reality, our life, we exist on the borders of the story, et cetera, et cetera . . . blah, blah, blah."

Michael looked at her. His moon-shaped face became even more rounded in astonishment. His beady gray eyes, two splinters of crushed lead sunken into a doughy face, shone.

"Do you mean to say you didn't invent those books?"

"Of course I didn't. What to you take me for?"

"I don't know how to tell you this, Ori, but if you ask me, your Ariella books never existed."

Ori stood up. Enough. There's a limit to everything. What did she need to get caught up with this flabby megalomaniac for, who secretly fosters a sterile literary envy.

"You're insane," she whispered and turned away from him.

———

May passed. Its gnawing glory, too, broke into the depths of summer. A smoky memory of it remained for Ori: from the Independence Day celebrations—complex formations of fireworks; from Lag B'Omer—the smoke of the bonfire on the beach to which she took Alma, the sparks roaring skyward. Barak was there, and he wasn't there. It seemed that he no longer understood what she wanted, or had become deaf to it. What did she want from him? If she turned to him, to share a new idea she had with him, he pretended to not understand, gazing at her in bewilderment. Only the barbwire of well-established words and actions kept them in their place, like the skeleton of an ancient, forgotten animal. She refused him her body at night. He accepted his punishment in silence. And the flame licked her skin.

At the end of ninth grade she was informed that due to her resounding failure in her exams and her absenteeism she would have to repeat ninth grade. No harm done yet, the principal Avshalom Baruch told her, she was merely being returned to her original age group. He had always been opposed to detaching children from their age group and advancing them into higher grades on the basis of intellectual skills. At a certain age they regress, just as in her case. But if she worked at her studies this year and repeated her achievements of previous years, she would graduate high school at eighteen, just like everybody else. She didn't listen to his flow of words. She'd lost interest in studying, as well as in the books she read and the notebooks in which she wrote.

That year she also drew further and further away from Ophir and Sigal. No, to be more precise, Ophir and Sigal drew dangerously closer to one another. She could literally smell how their scent blended with one another's and became one. The air enveloping their orchard was filled with dark omens. On her way there she would count: seven window frames with peeling paint, eleven crows on the electric wire, nineteen mirror fragments

sparkling between the thistles; and more and more prime numbers greater than five which, since learning of their existence, she
knew harbored evil. Time and again she silently watched them
from a distance, their bodies close to one another, almost touching beneath the canopy of the trees, laughing.

Then the yearning began. What was this yearning? According to the usual false images it should have flooded her, a dam
should have broken inside her and the boundless water of the
river it had held in check, furious like a caged animal, should
have swept right through her. But not so. In the darkness of her
high school days, as she walked down the hallways, learning
who she was not, with absolutely no idea who she was supposed to be, the yearning was a flame blazing against her flesh,
feeding her with heat and maintaining a permanent, languish-
ing sear, a slow, constant burning. She wanted that flame, but
all she attained was the irritated skin. A flickering hot wall surrounded her, keeping her alive and expelling her from life. Not
sweeping like a flood, slashing, consuming.

She didn't remember the name of the first man. He spoke
to her in the street as she was trudging home from school. He
was sitting alone in the entrance to an eatery, at a round alumi-
num table covered with a wine-stained cloth. He said, "Doll,"
or "sweetie," or some other word that functioned as an invitation—and she joined him. He asked her if she was hungry.
He was married. He had a habit of caressing her lips with his
ringed finger as he penetrated her, and of shoving it into her
mouth when he climaxed. They usually had sex in an open
field outside Netivot. The first time they had sex she didn't
expect anything. Too many rumors and myths were bound up
in losing one's virginity. She didn't know them, and even if she
had, would she have recognized the connection between them
and the brief tearing pain she felt, the taste of his finger, dirt
from the field clinging to it, and the coolness of his wedding

ring knocking against her teeth? It wasn't the breaking of the dawn, merely the bursting of a bubble. Could she have gone any deeper, penetrated her barrier of fire?

And how deep is sex. At a young age it may be possible to believe that it is skin deep, and the body is imprisoned within a fragile barrier, a shell to be breached. This belief was bound up in a covetousness she couldn't figure out because she was young, and in the way of the young her philosophical inquiries formed in her mind only vaguely. The question didn't surface in its full gravity, it was translated into a sense that directed her actions.

After the first man came others. All she required from them was a lusting glance from the corner of their eye, the fragment of a naked smile. One wanted to hump her, doggy style, to make her scream. Another to fuck her in the ass. A third ordered her to bite his nipples until they bled and then lick the tiny crimson droplets that glistened on them. "Suck me," the thick arm of the fourth grasped her neck and pushed her down, "swallow it all." He had a large member, the taste of the flesh like rubber; to take her mind off the bile rising in her throat she imagined herself observing from above, her lascivious lips pressing around the head of his penis. The fifth, or perhaps the seventh, inspired by some movie he'd seen, booked a hotel room in Eilat, took her with him all the way there to the blazing heat. In the room he smeared her labia with Beit-Yitzhak confiture, Yad Mordechai honey, Hashahar chocolate spread; "Only the produce of Israel for me," he told her. For three days he suckled her. She focused on the mildewy stains on the lampshades, on the scar etched into the full-length mirror in the room, the chips and soft niches in the bed's wooden headboard. They didn't exchange a single word on the way back.

They all had hair, nails, flat or protruding bellies, they had faces, they were animals, they lived in some manner. But they didn't register in her consciousness. They were nothing but faint ghosts of a flame, an illusion that through them she was touching something.

———

One afternoon, a few days before Shavuot, Barak called and said, "Ori, I think we need to talk."

She, her heart dropping, knew what he wanted to tell her.

"What about?" she answered in forced surprise.

"Not on the phone. My parents are coming to Tel Aviv this evening. They want to take Alma out to a restaurant. I told them it was okay. It'll give us time this evening."

"But what's the urgency all of a sudden?"

"I've just come out of a meeting," he said, "a big computer company from Australia has bought one of our developments and I have to go there in mid-June to train them. They've got several branches, so it'll be a long trip. Three weeks."

"But . . . "

"No buts. I couldn't get out of it," he hurried to explain. "You know that in the past year I've managed to get out of all the trips and courses. But not this time. Like I said, it's a big company. They want someone senior to oversee the adaptation of the software to their needs." Ori didn't respond. Barak added, "So, we'll talk this evening?"

The living room walls closed in. She answered him in a faint voice and let the cordless phone drop onto the couch, to switch off as it fell.

All the way to Alma's kindergarten the words "we need to talk" crawled and bored into her brain. She informed Alma that her grandparents would be coming to take her out that evening, and Alma jumped up and down in excitement. When they got home in the afternoon she left Alma to her own devices and put the disk on which she'd burned Ophir's podcast into the stereo in the living room. During the first track, "Ring the Bell", something calmed in her. The singer's thin voice cut the air. Like a honed string. She liked the lines of the song in which he declared, "I know serpents will cross universes to circle around our necks. I know hounds will cross universes to circle around our feet. I know they're close. Step by step one's beside me to kill me or to guide me. Why wouldn't I be trying to figure which one out." There was great comfort in hearing tormented male voices around the house.

Alma, who was engrossed in her drawings, raised her head and said, "Oh, Ima, what are those songs?"

"Don't you like them?"

"No." said Alma, and returned to her coloring pens. Her tongue sticking out to lick the corner of her mouth in concentration.

Ori glanced at the drawing forming on the paper. Alma had again drawn a little girl next to a large, round-limbed man. She no doubt intended to draw the two walking hand in hand, but the man's hand was drawn like a clenched mass on the girl's arm, and the fingers of her hand were taut. Ori waited for her to give a face and name to one of the celestial bodies or the clouds. Alma, however, took a lot of trouble with the features of the two figures, then put the drawing aside and said, "Do you want to know what book Aunty Ofra gave me?"

"Book? When did she give you a book?"

"You know, once, when Abba took me there."

"At the Mimouna?"

Alma was already halfway to her room and didn't respond. She returned clutching a brown book, flame-spouting demons leaping from it to Ori's eyes. "Look," said Alma gaily, "it's a grownup book. It doesn't even have any pictures at all."

Ori recognized the coarse leather binding and the gold embossment. *Chumash*, The Five Books of Moses. With commentaries. A closer look revealed: The Book of Exodus. How come Ofra had given Alma a *Chumash*? And with commentaries? What's with those people in Netivot? Alma handed the book to her with both hands. She took it and opened it. A note in Ofra's handwriting was stuck to the inside cover: "Ori, I hope this helps. I remember when you were a little girl and were going through difficult times these books helped you."

Ori bit her lip until the taste of blood filled her mouth. She returned the book to Alma. "Put it back in your room." But Alma lost her grip on it. It slipped from her hands and fell to the floor, wide open, like a glowing ember, like a torch. She bent down to pick it up, and from the bound pages, like a flash of lightning, she couldn't help reading, "And the Lord said: Behold, there is a place by Me, and thou shalt stand upon the rock. And it shall come to pass, while My glory passeth by, that I will put thee in a cleft of the rock, and will cover thee with My hand until I have passed by."

The skin on her face became taut as parchment stretched over her skull, and she could feel every one of her teeth in her mouth, clearly sensing their odor and the air-filled gaps between them. She froze where she stood, stiffly bent over the book, drawn forcefully by its pull—until Alma bent down, slammed the book shut and picked it up. The child stood up and walked away from Ori along the hallway leading to her room, stretching gloomily, endlessly towards a dark horizon; and only Alma's smiling sidelong glance struck contrarily, burning and consuming.

When Barak came home Ori greeted him with a nod and Alma fell onto him. Ori asked him to take her down to his parents and not let them come up. She said, "They're already playing a bigger role in this decision than they should."

He stared at her in bewilderment and began to protest, but the buzz of the intercom interrupted his objections. He took Alma's hand and went out with her.

When he returned she was waiting for him on the couch. Her windpipe was parched. The uniform of the business world, which he was still wearing—a blue cotton shirt, black pants and a striped tie—alienated him from the domestic living room, she thought. As if he were an uninvited guest. The fabricated evenings he spent at the gym couldn't contribute to his figure, of course. On the contrary, it seemed to her that he'd gained a little weight. Perhaps because he was sweating; there's a subconscious tendency to ascribe sweating to body weight, she thought.

He sat down beside her, his finger reaching out to caress her chin interrupting the flow of her thoughts. She moved away from him mechanically. "What did you want to talk about?" she asked.

He nodded. "Ori," he said, "you've no doubt noticed what's been happening to us recently. We're tense. You're walking around with an angry face all the time, and I, too, haven't exactly been a saint. I'm getting tired of it and I'm not behaving like an adult. I let myself be offended, and I shouldn't. I can see how the tension between us is affecting Alma. I gather from her kindergarten teacher that she's become a bit violent . . . "

Ori sat facing him, paralyzed.

"So I've given it a lot of thought," he continued, "and I've reached the conclusion . . . "

The flame licking her skin trembled, diminished, a faint strip of fire, sighing in an icy draught. She had no doubt. This was the moment when Kay starts lecturing Gerda on the advantages of the intellect in *The Snow Queen*. After Avner had disappeared she'd translated the book for herself, from the English edition of Andersen's fairy tales, because of that awful section she'd memorized day and night for two whole weeks until it became a natural continuation of her own thoughts: "Now his games were very different from what they used to be. They became more sensible. When the snow was flying about one wintry day, he brought a large magnifying glass out of doors and spread the tail of his blue coat to let the snowflakes fall on it. 'Now look through the glass,' he told Gerda. Each snowflake seemed much larger, and looked like a magnificent flower or a ten-pointed star. It was marvelous to look at. 'Look, how artistic!' said Kay. 'They are much more interesting to look at than real flowers, for they are absolutely perfect. There isn't a flaw in them, until they start melting.' A little while later Kay came down with his big gloves on his hands and his sled on his back. Right in Gerda's ear he bawled out, 'I've been given permission to play in the big square where the other boys are!' and away he ran."

Every woman has to experience that moment at least once in her life; strange that it was a man who captured it, and in a children's story no less.

"So what do you think?" Barak asked. His sheepish expression floating in front of her eyes.

"What do I think?"

"Weren't you listening to my suggestion?"

"You suggested something?"

"Tell me, what's been going on with you for the past two months?"

"What's been going on with me?"

"Come on, you know exactly what I'm talking about."

"No, I don't know. Why don't you tell me, because clearly you can see something I can't."

He sighed her name.

"I always knew there was a part of you that that was out of bounds to everybody, including me, and I accepted it. I thought that when Alma was born that part would dissolve. I was right, for the first two years. You were so at peace, so content. You were with Alma. You were with me. I hoped it would last. But I was wrong. That part was merely hiding, it hadn't disappeared, and I watched as it returned . . . I said to myself, all right, I'll accept that too, that part will accompany us for the rest of our lives. I don't know why I didn't fight . . . Maybe because I assumed that it was that which enabled you to write the stories you write . . . what makes you the person you are, the person I . . . " He fell silent, searching for a word. "Want . . . " he said and smiled, perhaps in irony. "But now it seems as if that part is taking over, it's your whole world, you shut yourself off in your own universe . . . I don't even know where you are any more, there or here, with us. Sometimes it takes me time to realize that when you're talking to me it's not me you're talking to, but to some avatar of me in the world you've fled to . . . "

"Would you rather continue apportioning blame, or repeat what you said?" She interrupted him brusquely.

Barak shrank angrily into his seat. Sweat erupted from every exposed pore on his skin. He wiped his hands on his pants and she watched the fleeting stains absorbing into the depths of the fabric, the expanding circles under his arms. The sight pinched her heart—so human—but only for a moment, she wasn't about to let this wave of pity weaken her.

Barak broke the silence. "Ori, listen to me. I'll repeat what I said, in brief."

He spread the fingers of his left hand, and with the forefinger of his right hand listed his main arguments with a tap, from pinky to thumb.

"We're not as close as we used to be." Tap.

"Alma is suffering." Tap.

"Just after she was born we were happy." Tap.

"I know our love is not lost, it is merely hiding and we need to find a way to rediscover it." Tap.

"I think we need another child." Tap.

The sound produced by his finger tapping his thumb clamored loudly inside her. This was not the blow she had anticipated. How dare he? She thought at that moment, is that how he wants to atone for his treachery, to resurrect their marriage by artificial

379

means? Had he given himself a scare and split up with Neta, or perhaps she'd left him. One way or another he was crawling back to her, atoning for his sins against her. A family man. Her anger was so immense, so wild and crushing and destroying all reason, that the question flew off her tongue unchecked.

"Do you really think that under our present circumstances we should even be talking about another child?"

Again that bewildered gaze from him.

"What circumstances? We're financially stable. Neither of us is getting any younger. We've had a good experience with Alma. We never agreed to stop at one child . . . "

She'd had enough of the masquerade, and of his self-righteous face, radiating tenderness and sympathy. She leapt to her feet.

"Enough of this," she yelled. "What makes you think I'd want to have another child with you? So that in two years you'll be bored and cheat on me with another woman?"

"Another woman? What do you mean?"

"I assume you won't be going back to Neta," she said scornfully.

"Neta? What's she got to do with anything?"

"Don't play the innocent. I know you don't go to the gym in the evenings. That you go to meet her after work, in her apartment on Soutine Street."

"Neta lives in Kfar Azar," Barak whispered.

"Kfar Azar?"

"Kfar Azar."

"So who lives in Soutine Street?"

"No one lives in Soutine Street. How do you know about Soutine Street anyway?"

"From the parking ticket you got a month ago."

"What parking ticket?"

"A parking ticket, what difference does it make now. You never saw it."

"I got a parking ticket and you hid it from me?"

"Yes. I thought to myself, what is Barak doing in Soutine Street?"

Barak appraised her sorrowfully. He lowered his eyes.

"Soutine Street is where my group meets."

Ori folded her arms across her chest. Group? How many more fabrications would he try to sell her? People caught in a lie tend to entangle themselves in more lies instead of coming clean. A familiar pattern. Predictable. He disappointed her.

"I didn't think you'd understand," Barak continued. "That's why I didn't tell you. There's this group that formed a few months ago in a social and welfare forum on the internet, after Amir's victory in the elections for the Labor Party leadership. We meet in an apartment on Soutine Street that belongs to Assaf Dinar, who's a member of the group, and we discuss these issues. What needs to be done."

Emptiness. Ori's stomach felt empty. A mountain shifted to reveal an abyss. No. A herd of buffalo fled south, following the heat of the sun and the splendor of the soil, leaving a trampled land in its wake. She started yelling.

"Assaf Dinar? Assaf Dinar? Could there be a more capitalist name than that? And you, an executive in a computer company . . . bourgeois to the bone . . . thinking what needs to be done . . . really . . . I've never heard of such an initiative . . . "

Tears gathered in the corners of her eyes from her laughter. It was the best, most liberating joke anyone had ever told her. Such folly. Stupidity. Foolishness. A group to discuss social and welfare issues. She burst into hysterical laughter, gushing laughter, coarse, vulgar, uninhibited. And Barak watched her. When her laughter finally stopped shaking her inner creatures, she didn't know what to say to him.

Barak got up from the couch and disappeared into his study.

SIX

Parents

ORI DARED TO BELIEVE that they would survive the summer. If they got past the hurdles of the insatiable light and the heat of July and August—and even resolutely dragged their bodies under the furnace-like coils of razor wire of those months—they had a hope. Where did she find the strength? She waited until Barak's anger faded and one night, two days before Shavuot, she went into his study to where he would withdraw from the moment Alma had been put to bed, and stood naked before him.

Yes. She was conscious of the ludicrousness of the situation—a cheap 1980s remake exaggerating a trashy 1940s film noir. But she was so tired of the calculations upon calculations that filled her mind—who'd be the first to break the silence, who was stronger, needier, prouder—until in a momentary flare-up she'd gone into the bathroom, showered, and put on a diaphanous nightgown. She peeped from the doorway to make sure that Alma hadn't awakened by chance and was walking half asleep down the hallway, then she shuffled into Barak's study.

He looked at her wonderingly, fragments of anger still flickering in the brown pupils of his eyes. For ninety whole agonizing seconds—her mental clock counted, counted—she stood before him, and then shrugged off the shoulder straps of her nightgown with an anger she had no strength to resist, and pulled it down to her waist. The neck was not wide enough and her movements, which she thought were sensual, seductive and even provocative, were accompanied by the sound of tearing. She tried to force the nightgown to fall to the floor where it would encircle her ankles like a sort of cloud from which she could step daintily, with feline suppleness, but the sheer fabric—which by now was nothing but a shapeless knot—wrapped itself around her knees, hobbling her.

Seeing Barak's hardening face—he was completely motionless, his fingers hanging frozen over the keyboard—she lost her power of speech.

"If you want another child, why don't we start right now?" She said with great effort. Her throat was dry and her voice shook, lacking the smoothness and depth needed to pronounce the question.

No. Barak's expression hadn't hardened, she suddenly realized, he was trying hard not to laugh, quite successfully too—until she blurted out the question. A long bark of laughter escaped his lips. He coughed.

"Tell me," he said.

He turned back to stare at the computer screen. She freed herself from the bonds of the torn fabric and ran naked, hurt, into the bedroom. There she sprawled on the bed. She covered her body and head with the thin sheet and lay there curled up, blowing the warm air from her lungs into the space she'd created. Her eyes were open, but the world around her was dark.

Barak came to her in the end. His falling body shook the double mattress and the movement of her body from the shock of his opened the floodgates of her tears.

"Ori," he said, and laid his hand on her shoulder. "Ori, Ori," he repeated with a sigh.

"Go away."

"Ori."

"I told you to go away."

His hand lingered and then withdrew. Barak did as she said.

What kind of a man is Barak, she thought, what kind of a person? Because he'd loved her from the start, admired her—and she had needed him—she had never dwelt on the question. It was strange that after five years it now came to her with all its force. You live with a man and he's recorded in your consciousness like a rumor, comes to you like an echo, like a message from a distant land . . .

Wrapped up in the blanket the urge to understand arose, to embrace it all, his dreams and fears. The moment he had discovered the happiness concealed in her body: lying in his room in the afternoon, flooded with pleasure, dreaming of an older woman who'd snatched him—Linda Carter, Samantha Fox, Farrah Fawcett—and used him for her pleasure. Here, she tells him, touch my breast with a finger and then with your tongue, feel. The boring dreams of young boys. But she wanted to be there with her whole being flooded with the desire for another body. The adrenalin rush before a math test, the eyelids heavy at midday in a civics lesson. The shame hitting at age fourteen in the gym. The first movies. The excitement of playing music, the first record he'd been given. TV series. The taste of a lemon popsicle in the summer. The school basketball court on winter days, with late winter clouds gathering above it, getting in five more minutes of play before it starts raining, and when it does rain to stubbornly continue, get soaked to the skin. Smalltime gambling at Purim. Fancy dress. Bragging to friends about conquests, uncontrollable longings, stories from boot camp. What else?

How infinite a person's life becomes from the moment we discover an interest in it, and how negligible, she thought bitterly. Where is the person who is Barak? Where? Every second Israeli boy has the same memories, exactly the same used past. This detail, the division into single events, there's no gain in them. You must probe the whole, the joining, its making of Barak Shulman.

So who is Barak Shulman? How can she understand his nature? People have open desires and hidden passions, and in the tension between these two poles lies the key to who they are. So what did Barak want? What do men want? Money, power, sex, status—in any order.

Barak had plenty of all four, he only had to reach out and take. It was impossible to give him more of what there already was, and everything he gave was out of pure generosity, because he didn't give out of need but rather in distracted magnanimity, casual squandering. He didn't yearn. There was no disparity between him and reality. How do you grasp people who haven't got a hole in their being? What projection do you grab? How do you bend them to your will?

With a great effort she recalled a childhood story he'd told her offhandedly, dismissing it as a trifling anecdote. She imagined him, a chubby boy, dreamily chewing on the end of his pencil as he thought about the next sentence he'd put down in his beautiful handwriting. He was nine or ten and had discovered he had a real talent for Hebrew calligraphy. He'd write splendid titles on his notebooks, design chapter headings in cursive lettering. His homeroom teacher discovered this when she took the class's notebooks home to inspect them. She enthused so much that she decided to adopt him. She turned him into a one boy decorations committee. During recesses, in return for exemption from homework, he had to draw placards with sayings: "Waste to the Bin" and "The Greatest Conqueror Conquers Himself"; "The Contented Person is Always Rich Enough"; "The Wise Man Learns From All Men", et cetera. That hackneyed series of virtues.

The other kids hated him. Every time one of his placards was put up and the teacher presented his work emblazoned on it, the hatred increased. At first they mocked him, made mean comments when they passed him, afterwards they shoved him around in the schoolyard. One morning he came into class and all his placards had been thrown to the floor, torn to shreds, like hacked-off limbs strewn around, "Conquers", "Rich", "From All". He stifled his weeping. That day he decided he would no longer do what the teacher asked. He intentionally worsened his handwriting, made it crude, illegible.

After he told her the story she looked at him, puzzled, waiting for him to tell her why he'd told her such a banal, whining story, but he, apparently, interpreted her look differently. "Don't worry," he told her, "I didn't take it badly. It's what led me to music and later to computers. Because I decided to find something I'm good at and that others would respect me for."

Is that a key? Could human creatures have such simple keys? And if so, is that the crack she's looking for, between whose jagged edges she could insert her fingers and widen her control over Barak? Barak was looking for some kind of recognition of his talent, of what preoccupies him, demands his all. Like his social interest. If only she'd been attentive and not derided and not interpreted his desire to rectify social injustices as the whimsy of a wealthy bourgeois. Because it was clear that his interest lay deeper. He'd lied to her, invented a feeble schedule so he could get away in the evenings and join that group of his.

How impervious she'd been, she hadn't even detected the change in him. He'd matured. What troubled him was no longer the old story of discrimination, the simplistic separation of Mizrahi and Ashkenazi Jews, the ethnic struggle. Following Amir Peretz and his hopes for a new social order had heralded a development she'd missed. He categorically saw the man as a savior, a hero of the working class who had compelled him to take a long look at himself.

Ori, if she wanted to hold on to Barak, she had to find a way of becoming a serious partner in this world of his—not in initiated conversations, staged meals, but with alertness, curiosity—because this thing occupied a central place in his life, or at least had become a barrier erected between them.

Get up, she ordered herself, get up *shatya*, you fool. How long are you going to lie here in the dark like the last of the oppressed poets, wallowing in ashes. Get up, *shatya*, get up.

And she got up, shook off the sheet, dried her tears and got dressed.

Barak was waiting in the living room, the embarrassed smile on his face, his fingers drumming on the arm of the chair.

"I'm getting myself a glass of wine," she said, "want one?"

He nodded and she went into the kitchen. When she came back with two glasses of wine she saw that he'd moved to the couch, and she sat down there too, some distance away.

"So?" he asked, forced offhandedness in his voice.

"So nothing. When are you going away?"

"A few days after Shavuot. On the seventh."

She thought for a moment. "The middle of next week," she said and tapped her teeth on the rim of her wineglass.

"Uhuh," he said.

They were silent.

She shifted restively.

"I read your article," Barak said. "It's good."

"Just 'good'?"

"Come on, Ori, you know what I think of you. Have you got to hear it each time anew, about everything you write?"

"Just this time."

"It's beautifully written," he muttered reluctantly.

Ori smiled.

"But?"

"But . . . " and he was silent. Again, "But . . . " and he closed his mouth. His face—in its pulling, the severity of the lips, the skin suddenly pored—was like his father's rubber mask. And he blurted, "Everything you write is always beautiful in my eyes, your language, your command of words, they're things that can make a difference, arouse others, make them take a stance. Especially here in this country, today, with all the . . . I simply don't understand why you're wasting your talent on nonsense. No, not nonsense, God forbid, delusions and imaginings."

"All right," she said drily, "now tell me about this thing with your group."

"Are you sure you want to hear?"

"I'm sure, I'm sure. You just gave me your honest opinion. We must be candid with each other. Otherwise . . . what difference does otherwise make . . . if something's preoccupying you, I want to know."

"Assaf Dinar," he said, and looked at her challengingly. Now she wasn't laughing. Not only that, now she couldn't even understand what had made her laugh earlier. Wordplay on the Hebrew 'he collected a dinar', is the lowest form of humor. "Assaf Dinar is the manager of the Rosh Ha'ayin branch of Bank Hapoalim. Two years ago he was an investment manager at a Tel Aviv branch, then he was promoted and transferred. After six months there, when he realized what was happening and how ruthless Israeli capitalism is grinding the disadvantaged down . . . "

"Hold it," Ori interrupted him, "ruthless capitalism? The disadvantaged? Since when have you been using terminology like that?"

"If you carry on like this I'm liable to start feeling that you're really listening," he said with the thinnest of bitterness, and immediately added in an apologetic tone. "Okay, I suppose I adopted it from reading about a million messages in the forum and all kinds of articles on the internet."

She filled her mouth with wine, concentrating on the taste, and Barak continued.

"I'll give you one small example. It's a bit silly, but it gets the point over. Think about the banks' commission system that was introduced two or more years ago. Every time somebody draws money from an ATM he pays commission. Now think that for somebody who's got money that isn't a problem, with each withdrawal he takes out more cash, let's say five hundred shekels. But the guy who hasn't can only take out fifty shekels each time. That means that on each withdrawal the poor guy pays ten times more than the wealthy guy. And that's only the start."

She said, "Dante placed lenders charging interest and usurers in the third circle of the seventh level of hell."

"What?"

"Dante Alighieri, the great Florentine poet in the Middle Ages. Haven't you heard of him? Okay, in the first part of his poetic magnum opus, *The Divine Comedy*, he tells of his journey into the Inferno. He passes from level to level and sees the sinners and their punishments. The deeper the level, the worse the sin. So from Dante's viewpoint lending money and charging interest is a very grave sin . . . it's a sin that breaks the Divine commandment, 'By the sweat of thy brow shalt thou eat bread'. In other words, so Dante understood it, man must live by what he does, whether it's art or farming or a craft, and whoever uses money to gain more money is committing a grave transgression."

Barak didn't reply. She looked at him, embarrassed.

"They're lying on burning ground, or more precisely, hopping on it."

"Who?" Barak asked impatiently.

"Dante's usurers. Throughout the seventh level it rains fire and brimstone, and in the third circle the ground burns as well, and they've got to escape the flames and the ground."

"What a sick idea. But the punishment's not the issue, it's how to correct the system." She felt rebuked. Barak went on, "In short, Assaf Dinar, after all the fat cat clients he'd had, suddenly started to constantly come across people down on their luck who knocked on his office door and cried, literally cried. People with no collateral who, if they didn't get a loan from the bank, wouldn't be able to feed their children. That broke him. He began reading the society and welfare forum and then started to respond as well. At some point he contacted me through the messenger, after reading messages I'd posted when Amir won the elections for the Labor Party leadership. We met, he told me his story and we decided to found a group of people who cared about what the new Israeli economy is doing to society."

Ori studied him for a long time. How far away he'd moved. How he'd grown up. Anger began welling in her.

"But what good will talk do?" She forced herself to ask.

"Ah, we're not going to stop at talk. We're planning to establish a body, a non-profit organization, to initiate actions and protest, maybe even organize conferences calling for parliamentary bills. Now Amir Peretz is a minister it will all be easier."

She looked angrily at the half-empty wineglasses.

"More wine?" she asked.

"No, I've got enough in my glass."

She got up, took the two glasses from the table and hurried into the kitchen. She poured the remaining wine into the sink and scrubbed the glasses, focusing on the soap bubbles gathered on her hands. She went back with the washed, still dripping glasses, and the half-empty wine bottle. Barak's arm was stretched across the back of the couch, not leaving her room to recline.

When she poured the wine and straightened up, his arm went around her shoulders. That was Barak: touch was easy and accessible for him. He knew how to heal all the wounds and fractures in one way—touching. Despite the waves of anger still flooding her Ori felt the tendrils of a huge, sweeping gaiety that was out of place, climbing from the depths of her belly to her throat.

In the end Ori was thankful for Barak's business trip. The veneer of conciliation between them was fragile, for her part at least, and she feared it would crack. Together with the gaiety she felt—sham gaiety, separated from the rest of her emotions like a burst bag lying on its side—there was fear in her. She woke up with it and went to sleep with it. When she and Alma said goodbye to Barak at the airport, she felt relief.

On the way back to Tel Aviv Alma repeated to herself the story of the journey, her father had gone to Israel's Mirrorland to bring her a special present. In that land it's winter when it's summer here, and the stars shine backwards and the water flows in a different direction; people walk on the sky there, beneath the sea and the land that float above them. Sometimes you've got to crouch so as not to get a bang on the head from the mountaintops. Ori had made up the story. For the first time in their life together she had helped Barak in his efforts to shield Alma from anxiety.

It was Barak's longest trip in recent years, and Ori suddenly realized how much reality blew onto her through Barak, how much more tangible it was in his presence. People talked around her. A soldier was abducted near Gaza. Qassam rockets rained down on Sderot and the Western Negev. Buildings were hit. The Israeli army moved into the Gaza Strip. Palestinian children died. Close to her ear someone coined the phrase, 'Summer Rain'.

The world's subtleties, on the other hand, did not evade her. The summer got worse, the light turned yellow during the day and orange towards evening, a malleable, amber-like clay thrown onto the walls through the open slats of the living room's west window. The rotting fruit of the ficuses covered the sidewalks in a slippery layer, the hibiscus shrubs thickened and their flowers blushed and then turned white. The bougainvillea calyxes became heavy and sensual, widened in release and glowed. The birds slowly fell silent. The shades of gray on the sparrows' wings deepened, blackened. On the edges of the city, in the unbridled tracts of land, thistles withered.

The passion of summer spread through Alma. She was filled with nervous energy, she hated her television programs, her drawings, books. Every evening she begged Ori to go to the beach. They walked slowly, with towels and drinks and suntan oil, until the jellyfish population increased and was washed up onto Tel Aviv's seashore. A small boy was stung. Ori put an end to going to the beach.

Alma almost drove her crazy, shut up in the apartment. running around, and stretching a piece of elastic between two chairs and jumping over it. Shula Avrahami, who lived in the downstairs apartment, went to Mrs. Gershon to complain about the noise, and they had to go to the children's playground in Meir Park, where Alma's irrepressible energy and Ori's abstractedness combined to bring the child to the verge of dehydration. The emergency room doctor lectured Ori in measured tones about the dangers of dehydration and its prevention, all the while his words were accompanied by accusing glances and Ori found no refuge from them.

If only for that she welcomed Barak's return. She was impatient and eager for the recasting of the solid foundation in her life. But she was disappointed. The man who emerged from the terminal with the stream of passengers was different from the one she'd expected. As usual, Alma saw him first. He was pulling his big case behind him, his head bent. Evening fell behind the glass walls of the hall, a falling veil of dullness, and Barak walked towards it submissively. Alma rushed to him, throwing herself at his legs—"Abba!"—and his grip on the suitcase handle relaxed. The case fell to the floor with a thud and an elderly woman having difficulty with her trolley ran into it and recoiled, cursing.

Barak picked Alma up and she wrapped her legs around his waist and paunch, her arms around his neck, and kissed him hard. Just a thin smile that was actually directed at her, at Ori, flashed across his face. It was dejected, weary. Maybe the long flight, Ori thought, being away from home—for Barak is a man nourished by family life, who flourishes in it—perhaps the reason is even the rapid transition between the two hemispheres, the magnetic fields pulsing at their own rate, jetlag; people aren't made to cross vast distances, evolution hasn't yet caught up with the swiftness of technology. These thoughts continued to whirl around Ori's mind on the way to the car as Barak answered Alma's incessant questions brusquely. Ori drove, and now and then stole a glance at Barak, who was feigning sleep. She knew his sleep well, his fluttering eyelids in the smooth, round face. Now his eyes were tightly shut, his features immersed in thought.

Alma went to bed after much persuasion—her excitement bubbled and overflowed and she wanted to examine all the presents one at a time. Ori tried starting a conversation with Barak, but he said, "I've had an intensive trip. I didn't get a minute's rest. I need a few days to recover."

With a generosity that surprised her, Ori suggested that they accept his mother's invitation and go to his parents in Yavne for the weekend. On the morning of his return his mother had called, and with characteristic ingenuity asked to speak to Alma. As Alma panted into the receiver, asking her grandmother if she knew that her Abba was coming home today,

Miriam Shulman told her that they'd bought an inflatable pool and put it in the yard, and the pool is waiting just for her, for Alma, even though in the meantime they were letting the neighborhood children use it.

"Why don't you come to us for the weekend?" Miriam asked when the receiver was handed back. From Alma's gauging look, that was suddenly serious, Ori guessed that Miriam was up to something.

"We'll see what Barak says," Ori replied.

Alma's demand that they go was not long in coming. She'd also begged her father at the airport. Ori had made up her mind not to give in to this blackmail, but seeing his emptied expression—yes, emptied is the word, she thought, Barak was always so full, not only in size, but in his very presence, steadfast—she relented.

"Okay," Barak said, "it won't do any harm."

———

The lawn in the Shulman family's yard had recently been mown, its tingly smell still stood in the air, assailing the nostrils. In Yavne, too, the sharp evening light of July pierced all the pasts and disassembled them—here the climbing plant that reminded Ori of the hedge her father had tended to hide their yard from the prying eyes of the neighbors, there young poincianas and withered reeds and a tiny palm and a beautifully pruned ficus hedge. Barak lay down on a lounger, sunglasses on his nose, wearing a tee shirt and loose shorts. Unlike his father, he didn't expose his upper body.

Ori thought that from a certain age men should be prohibited from not wearing a shirt. She turned her eyes from Victor Shulman's scrawny chest with its luxuriant white hair that trapped pearls of sweat, and the gold Star of David, back to the book open in front of her. Miriam was fussing around them, going inside and coming out with lemonade, wafers, watermelon. She talked to Alma who was splashing water in all directions by jumping into the pool, over which fine shade netting had been hung. Alma laughed aloud.

"Rest a while," Ori said to Miriam. Not because she was worried about her health, but because of the knowledge that Miriam might hold her indifference to her efforts against her. After all, they had a whole Saturday to get through peacefully.

"Oh, nonsense. Don't worry yourself," Miriam replied from the raised wall of the pool where she was sitting, visibly happy. "Most of the time I don't do anything, and when you finally come for a visit . . . " and then she called to her son, "Barak, have some watermelon. It's the kind you like, I got a particularly firm one without a lot of juice."

Barak nodded and reached out. He took a reluctant bite from the watermelon slice and put it back onto the plate. Miriam frowned but said nothing. After a few minutes she got up from the wall of the pool.

"Ori," she said, "I need your help with something in the kitchen."

Ori took her eyes from the book she was reading, Diana Wynne Jones' *Fire and Hemlock*; two weeks ago she'd found ten of her books at Or Zarua and bought them all on a whim. How had she never come across the works of this writer, who she thought was at least as great as Prospero Juno? The deeper she delved into them the more she discovered a similarity between Wynne Jones and herself, in her she found a kind of distant spiritual sister. This book related to the article she'd written on Wonderland, and she devoured it greedily.

"Is it urgent?" she asked Miriam.

"Yes," Miriam replied and made her way to the door.

Ori looked at her figure and the graying, meticulously cut hair touching her shoulders. In the kitchen Ori asked her, "What would you like me to do?"

"What's the matter with my son?" she asked.

"What do you mean?"

"He's got no appetite. That's not Barak. What's going on with him?"

"He's tired from the trip. Australia's in the southern hemisphere, you know."

Miriam tut-tutted.

"Is everything all right at home?" she inquired.

"It's fine."

Miriam went to the fridge, opened it, shut it, and went back to her place beside Ori, who was following her movements. She leaned against the work surface.

"Alma's already a big girl," she said.

"Yes . . . ?"

"You need something that will inject new life into your relationship." Ori wanted to tell her to mind her own business. She was actually somewhat stunned by the direction the conversation was taking, but before she managed to form a sentence in her mind, Miriam said assertively, "Before he went away Barak told me you were planning another child. What's happening with that?"

"I . . . " Ori began.

"Don't wait too long. It gets harder as time goes by. You know, the biological clock's ticking, as they say."

"Excuse me," Ori said, regaining her composure, "but I think that any decision on having another child should remain between me and my husband."

Miriam retreated, her shoulders sagged as if she'd been dealt a blow.

"I didn't mean to pry," she said, "it's just . . . "

Ori went out of the kitchen and crossed the living room.

396

"Wait, Ori," Miriam said from behind her, "let me explain."
Ori turned to her, arms folded on her chest.

"What's to explain?"

"Victor and I," there was timidity in her voice, and Ori
reminded herself that this woman had been on her side from the
moment they met—so what had sparked anger in her, what was
sparking anger in her recently. Barak. He told his mother about
his indecisions before her asked her opinion. He shut himself off
and left her to her fears, while he mulled over his thoughts. With
an effort she caught the thread of Miriam's words. " . . . and we
always regretted putting our own convenience first. Another
child would have brought joy into our life, back then we didn't
have such a big house, but we would have had more grandchil-
dren now apart from Alma. I miss the time that Barak used to
run through the house laughing. He was such a sweet child and
so happy. And Alma reminds me of him. I think you should be
thinking about another child, Alma doesn't have to grow up on
her own."

Oh, come on, Ori said to herself, what a predictable confession. She went out into the yard. Barak was sprawled on the
lounger, his sunglasses hiding his eyes. Where are the days when
she sensed he anticipated her every movement. He barely nodded as he made out he was listening to the lecture Victor was
giving, again on health and safety, this time on a new law, a law
that would be stricter with crazy drivers and give the traffic cops
the authority to automatically suspend the license of a driver
who jumped a red light. Perhaps, not in the foreseeable future,
some traffic violations would to all intents and purposes be a
crime. Then let's see those madmen doing two hundred kilometers an hour in the middle of the night, once they know their
night out can end in jail.

Her anger at Barak licked at her thoughts throughout dinner,
but she harnessed it then and thus next morning too, when they

split into pairs, she and Miriam in the kitchen making salads, Barak and his father outside, fanning the charcoal. Victor had got up early to cut up the meat and the chicken.

Alma woke up an hour after him and ran naked to the pool. Ori opened her eyes to the white ceiling. Victor's shouts to Alma to go back inside right away and put on a swimsuit, which were accompanied by a horror story about children who swam naked, mingled with her dream in which she was watching Alma standing in the pool, up to her neck in rising water, Miriam whispering behind her back, "If she had a brother or sister, they'd help her get out of there." and Victor pointing at a newborn baby whose head was bleeding, and saying, "This little baby could have gone on living, and now—what kind of life, his skull split like a walnut."

Barak was lying on his back. She studied him: his stubbled cheeks and chin, touched by shadow. His high cheekbones breaking up the chubby roundness of his face. Had he lost weight—she'd read somewhere that people suffering depression look thinner because their eyes are sunken. His lips were slightly open, emitting soft exhalations with a thin night odor on them. She brought her face to his and kissed him on them. Barak turned onto his side, his face in the opposite direction.

As usual, the conversation over lunch turned to politics. His father didn't conceal his dislike of the new government. All the new ministers are dyed-in-the-wool idiots, not to mention that good-for-nothing, the prime minister, he's got the face of a crook, and believe me, we know a crook when we see one. In Romania they would have got rid of him when he was still a young party hack. Victor missed Ariel Sharon, the combination of power and experience that comes with age. True, he didn't always agree with him, on the Lebanon War, for instance, he knew he was misleading the government when they announced the operation. He knew, because you can't fool him, he's recognized cheats and liars from an early age. But the years did something to Sharon, if only he'd had enough courage to get rid of those settler shits, they don't pay taxes and still feel they've got the right to dictate the reality of this country. Who asked them to be there? What kind of a government is this? Why have they made a former chief of the general staff minister of transport? He looks at a road like it's a battlefield. Just see how the level of violence on the roads will increase during his tenure, because his laws will encourage the use of force. That reminds him of the story of the old woman who was driving her big American car on her way home from Tel Aviv to Caesarea late at night. This nice lady is driving along—her whole life is charitable and voluntary work, in the Yad Sarah organization helping the disabled and elderly, in Akim for the mentally handicapped, you name it—in the right lane on the Haifa road. Behind her are two hoodlums, gorillas, honking at her. Why are they honking when the left lane is completely empty? She moves into the left lane and they follow her, she goes back into the right lane and so do they. The old lady sees she's coming to the exit from the main road, by Netanya, and signals she's turning right. The two slobs saw what she was doing and accelerated, overtook her and forced her off the road. What am I telling you? Luckily a patrol car came past otherwise it would have ended with more than shattered windows. So how can a chief of the general staff provide solutions for things like that? Eh? He should have been minister of defense, not that one with the mustache . . .

Ori looked round the table. Barak was staring glassy-eyed at his father. Miriam was occupying herself by cutting a chicken breast into small cubes for Alma, and Alma was immersed in slowly and methodically chewing cherry tomato salad and celery sticks.

She turned her eyes back to Barak. She felt as if a skewer was pushed into the pit of her stomach. She saw the rising tension in his shoulders as his father relented and spoke the name of Amir

Peretz instead of calling him 'that one with the mustache.' She cut Victor's speech short.

"Barak's one of the new minister of defense's great admirers," she said.

Barak looked at her blankly.

"He thinks he'll help him and his friends to advance new social initiatives." She added derisively.

"What do you mean, 'social initiatives'?" Victor asked.

"What, hasn't Barak told you? I thought he told you everything," she said. Miriam raised her head and stared at her. "Barak's a member of a secret group that wants to influence Israel's welfare and social services policies."

She knew what she was doing, she knew full well, but couldn't resist the temptation. Social services, welfare, had with time become four-letter words among the Israeli bourgeoisie. Victor and Miriam could talk forever about justice and modesty, but for them welfare and social services were euphemisms for wasting their money, which they'd earned by hard work and total honesty, on layabouts and freeloaders from development towns and single mothers who'd rather dye their hair than buy schoolbooks for their children.

Miriam started as if bitten by a snake—was 'bitten by a snake' an appropriate expression? Ori had never seen anyone who'd been bitten by a snake.

"Is that true?" she demanded of Barak.

Barak nodded heavily.

"What do you need that for? Haven't you got enough worries? You've just got back worn out from Australia."

"I've got worries. Too many. It's taken me time to realize that they're not the right worries."

"What are you talking about?"

"About the fact that over a million people in this country are not living in dignity, and all we think about is how to buy a better car."

"You're getting carried away, Barak," Victor said, "people who've got no money should go to work. Complaining is always easiest. Do you think that when we came here we had anything? We had to . . . "

"Now's not then," Barak replied, "when you got here there weren't any official mechanisms like there are today, designed to trample the poor. You were poor like everyone else."

"I don't understand what you're saying," Miriam said.

"That Israel's economic and social policies . . . forget it, you wouldn't understand."

Barak stood up. His plate was still full and he moved towards the house. Victor, too, got up and started after him.

"Barak," he called, "what's this bee in your bonnet?"

"Do you understand it?" Miriam asked.

"No," Ori replied.

From the house the voices of Barak and his father could be heard. Barak was talking dully about the blindness of the middle class, and its desire for economic comfort that would enable the ultra-rich to accumulate vast, unreasonable wealth, thus supporting the trampling of classes weaker than them. His father wondered since when had he become such a radical. That was all that interested him: the turning point. As far as he was concerned Barak was a baby who'd been led astray, and Victor, who had experienced the horrors of communism first-hand, so he said, knows those bastards' methods, their brainwashing tricks. He'd been there. He knows. Their ideology is no more than a tool for controlling the masses. Had he met them in Australia? Admit it.

Miriam moved closer to hear better, with Ori a step behind her.

"If you were walking down the street and saw a dog standing on its hind legs and opening a garbage dumpster with its front paws and nosing in the garbage, you'd laugh at its cleverness, right?" Barak said.

"Well, yes," Victor replied.

"And if, fifty meters further on, you saw a homeless person going through a dumpster, you'd be disgusted or at best pity him, wouldn't you?"

"Yes, but I don't see the connection."

"That's what happened to me in Australia," Barak said. "I was walking down a street and that's what I saw. And I suddenly realized that with all my talk, I too, like other people, would prefer to take the dog, not the homeless person, home with me."

There was no point in staying. Even Alma, who'd specialized in inventing ploys to divert adults' attention from their discussions, didn't bother. She went to the pool and rested in it idly. The skin of her hands was wrinkled from soaking in the water.

The debate with Victor energized Barak. On the way back he said to Ori, "You shouldn't have started all that hullabaloo."

Ori delayed her reply until they got home, until the evening, when they were alone. She said to Barak, "You're wrong. I'm glad I told your parents. I've had enough of living with it."

"Living with what, Ori, with what?"

"You know with what."

"With me having a deep interest in things apart from myself and which aren't necessarily connected with my immediate benefit?"

She surveyed him from top to toe. The anger at his mother's questioning, the skewer probing her innards, her loins, her guts, had not disappeared. She could no longer remain indifferent towards Barak. They had moved beyond that. She had let him in. Now she wanted the entrance fee. Let him suffer.

"There's a phenomenon of repentance in married men," she said in as chilly a tone as she could muster, drily, "they have difficulty admitting to themselves that married life and family don't satisfy them, it's apparently connected with guilt feelings. Most of these men grew up in stable homes, with a defined structure,

402

happily married parents even after thirty years of preaching to them about the sanctity of family values."

"I don't think . . . "

"Let me finish, Barak. Repentance is their refuge. Their way of distancing themselves from their commitment without breaking it. All they've done is find a higher vocation in which married life is a necessary structure, but it's a product of lofty ideals, and they just shift from commitment to the individual to commitment to society."

"So you think . . . "

"No, I don't think, I'm sure. You're undergoing a parallel process. You've found a sphere of activity that will alleviate your guilt feelings for rejecting me and Alma."

She had never seen Barak lose his cool, so incensed.

"I don't believe this," he said, raising his voice, "a month ago I told you I wanted another child, and this is what you think of me, that I've found a way of running away from you and Alma?"

"That suggestion was just another attempt at atonement." Ori replied quietly.

"Go to hell," Barak said, "how, tell me how when I talk to you about social justice, helping the weaker strata of society, about reform, you find a way of making it all about you? About my feelings for you? Where did you get such an impossible amount of egotism?"

Ori didn't say another word. Barak angrily paced the living room, circling the small table a few times, his fists clenched, his knuckles white.

———

Twelve days later, she counted, the war in Lebanon began. When she heard the news she felt as if the horror roiling inside her had burst out into the world, to hasten the end.

The evening after their argument Barak informed her, almost incidentally, that he intended to cut his hours at work and devote more time to founding the organization for advancing social initiatives, that would be called "CARE—Concern, Aid, Relief, Empower". All her mind could absorb was, I'm bringing my leaving a step closer.

Hezbollah abducted two soldiers, a woman was killed by a Katyusha rocket in Kiryat Shemona, the air force planes took off, cutting through the clear summer sky and spawning bombs. Then the barrage of Katyushas on the northern settlements, and afterwards flattened villages, collapsed buildings, deserted cities, refugees, fatalities.

Had it not been for Barak's resentment she might have more quickly detected the crack that ran the length of him, like a china doll damaged by a fall. In the first evenings of the war she tried to talk to him, to cut through the haze filling the apartment and reach him. When she went down to buy milk at the grocery store on Tchernichovsky Street, the shopkeeper remarked, after carefully weighing her up, "You look to me like one of those radical lefties who oppose the war," and she left the carton of milk on the counter and walked out. She told Barak about the incident, thinking she was bringing him something, an offering, a sacrifice, an oblation.

"Just Reward," Barak muttered in response, and chuckled bitterly.

"What?" she asked.

"Just Reward. It's what the military operation's called. Who'd believe that name was selected randomly by a computer? It embodies the entire tragedy of Israeli society."

When she didn't reply he said, "You see, the politician who based his platform on improving the conditions of the working class and raising the minimum wage, went to war at the first opportunity."

Ori wanted to say, but I wasn't talking about the war but the insult I felt. Instead, just to annoy him, she repeated the slogan she'd heard in the street.

"But it's a just war. It was forced on us."

Barak chuckled again with the same degree of bitterness.

"Forced on who? On the country with the strongest army in the Middle East? How can a terrorist organization force a war on the state of Israel? The saddest thing of all is that everyone's buying these lies and don't understand what's really happening."

"Stop it," Ori said, "I'm sick and tired of hearing that. You're like a broken record, you talk and talk, but what are you saying?"

He continued lecturing her but she no longer heard him. She had a sudden yearning for Avner's thoughtful silence, his immediate contempt for every hackneyed phrase. She couldn't back down; Avner adhered to the apartment, haunting it like a ghost. He arose before her in each of Barak's steps, his gestures, the words he murmured in his sleep. He wound upwards from the smell of the books she read, flickered on the computer screen. His face, which she had seen back then on that Saturday in Meir Park, popped up and confused her.

In each hour there was a window opening onto the limbo he was in, trapped in a web of time under the ficus and looking right at her. She diligently decoded his facial features. What twisted them into that expression? She identified surprise, shock and fear there. And insult, mainly insult. From the insult small memories continued, which she thought she'd managed to get rid of: Avner reading aloud from an old autobiography and saying, "I prefer these books to all the volumes of *In Search of Lost Time* because they were written out of a pure drive, untainted by artistic pretension," then laughing, and she not knowing if he was speaking contemptuously or was startled by his own words.

More: Avner, overcome by his lust and yearning for contact, twisting himself round her and dancing attendance on her for half days, days. Then, his lust abated, pacing sullen and angry, filled with hatred for his own body. Avner buying her a present and not knowing how to give it to her, suddenly losing the power of speech and stammering, apologizing for the sudden gesture. Avner coming into their apartment with the telephone bill, and the two cartoon characters on the envelope not escaping his irritation, his grumbling, "Really, Plug and Socket. That's real progress since we were kids and couldn't make up our minds about what Wally and Ralph did in their house on Sesame Street. Then we could at least amuse ourselves with the question of who was sticking it to whom. But this, Plug and Socket, what could be more obvious than that?"

Avner in the morning, closing his eyes and praying for the world to end in catastrophe. Once, in a moment of gloom, he said to her, "Come on already, let the hole in the ozone widen, the climate heat up, bring on the new Ice Age, let some engineered killer virus burst out from an improvised laboratory in Russia, let somebody start a nuclear war. I want to see and I'm tired of waiting for the end of the world," he laughed, even then he laughed his enigmatic laugh.

Even Alma's existence, who was on vacation from kindergarten for the whole of July, became blurred. No. Be accurate, she must be accurate. She withdrew from Alma, whose sharp eyes penetrated the depths of her being, stripped her naked. She left her to her own devices. There was a day, she dimly recalled, when Alma had asked her for something, pleaded and yelled; she heard her slamming the fridge door and the doors of the bottom kitchen cupboards in frustration. She went in to check, a carton of milk lay on its side on the floor, a puddle forming from its dripping mouth. Alma licked her lips and fixed her eyes on the puddle, she pointed at it, pleadingly. And Ori answered, "This evening," without listening.

That evening Barak had a fight with her. Alma had complained to him. What had they fought about? She thought of Avner, the fluent sentences leaving his lips like a shoal of tiny goldfish he'd brought up from a hidden depth, slippery and beautiful, sailing through the air to her. She nodded at Barak with a silly smile. For some reason she said, "I'm sorry. It won't happen again."

She didn't fall asleep that night. Not only the choked air of summer hovering over her—something else. Beside her Barak turned over, the sheets wound around his body. Troubled, she got up. She went into the living room and took out another of Diana Wynne Jones' books, *Hexwood*, and opened it. A scrap of yellow paper fluttered from the pages. She examined it. On it was the address of Avner's parents in Haifa. On an impulse she had asked Boaz Zadok for it when she'd bought the books. Perhaps that was why she'd gone to the shop at the outset, and buying the books had only been an excuse. When she asked Boaz if he knew the address, he said he did, that when he'd computerized the staff roster he'd kept Avner's details, hoping he'd come back. At any rate, the information remained buried in the database he'd created. Here, Haim and Nava Assoulin, 24 Yitzhak Elchanan St., Haifa.

When had morning come? She'd read the book throughout the hours of darkness. And it seemed that her spirits had cleared somewhat, that a modicum of lucidity had been restored to her. Now she was jovial with Barak, and he looked at her angrily and went into the bathroom. It doesn't matter. She made coffee for him and laid the table. Made an omelet. She placed the cereal box in the middle, took out jam, butter, milk. Made toast.

Barak sat down opposite her, and Alma, as if she had sensed this possibility of conciliation in her sleep, the edge of happiness, jumped out of bed—Ori heard the padding of her bare feet as she ran down the hallway—and came to them.

Barak's face was still bleak.

"I don't know what happened to me yesterday. It's like I was wiped out." Ori said.

"Wiped out? Starving the child for a whole day? Not feeding her? That's a lot more than 'wiped out'."

"The main thing is that it's behind us," Ori replied with hollow gaiety.

Alma nodded, jam dripping from her mouth.

"Alma, sweetie, we'll go on a trip today, all right?" She said to Alma after Barak had gone to work.

"A trip?" Alma repeated and gave three jumps on the spot. "Where to?"

"We'll drive a bit. Then we'll stop. Have lunch. And maybe we'll go to the movies."

"I want to see 'Cars'," Alma said.

"We'll see," Ori replied vaguely.

Alma insisted on the dress she'd wear, red with a tiny white and yellow floral pattern. Ori thought it too common but didn't argue. She took a lot of trouble doing her daughter's curly hair until it took on some form of falling to her shoulders and back. In a bag she packed a bottle of water, a few snacks.

Alma ran to her room and brought a stupid electronic game that Barak had brought her from Australia. The player had to avoid as many monsters as possible on his way to finding a treasure. He could collect prizes along the way, which gave him power to combat the monsters. But early on Alma had discovered that when the player was devoured by a monster, it made a hiccupping sound, a belching or vomiting sound, depending on the player's situation. The more power he accumulated, the harder he became to digest. Alma would run him into the monsters' jaws and laugh happily when she heard one of the disgusting sounds.

Traffic was heavy on the road to Haifa. To the left the sea was spread out, a giant leaden eye, molten in the July sun. To the right, buildings were replaced by a different landscape, limestone hills—housing projects, entrances to cities on greening slopes. This whole country is the same, Ori thought, the names change but the drabness is similar. Alma was immersed in her game, and now and then her boisterous laughter erupted into the space of the car, drowning out the gentle male voices coming from the loudspeakers. Ori put Ophir's podcast into the CD player. One of the singers sang, "Do something beautiful while you can. Don't be a fool," and she smiled to herself.

The city was almost deserted. Traffic was thin. There was a crater in one of the roads and she circled it cautiously. She found Yitzhak Elchanan Street easily, without having to study the map. It was as if the route had lain inside her, dusty and worn, and risen in her memory from the familiar scenes—the single-story houses built of white stone, sunk into the slope, fenced with rose bushes at the front. She parked at the side and said to Alma, "We're here."

"Where's here, Ima?" Alma looked around.

"Haifa."

"But you said we'd go on a trip."

"This is the trip," Ori said, "come on, now. Afterwards we'll get something to eat and go to a movie, all right?"

They went into No. 24, Ori hurrying, and Alma holding her hand, lagging behind her, her other hand clutching the game, and complaining, "Oof, Ima, I don't want to go there."

"Stop it, behave yourself!" she said sternly, "We've got to make a good impression."

"But I don't want to," Alma whispered.

409

Ori read the inscription on the decorated copper nameplate on the door, 'Haim and Nava Assoulin', and breathed deeply. She rang the bell.

The woman who opened the door, in her fifties, glanced at her briefly and then turned to Alma and fixed her with a penetrating gaze. Alma plucked at Ori's blouse.

"Ima," she whispered, "who's this woman?"

"Nava Assoulin?" Ori inquired.

The woman nodded and sighed.

"You shouldn't have come here," she said, "certainly not at the moment with all the missiles they're firing at us, but don't stand in the doorway, come on in."

Nava's hair, still mainly black, was twisted into a long braid around her head. She had a slight French accent, the words that came from her mouth curled gently at the end, slid into the air, but only that revealed her foreignness. Her speech was as eloquent and punctilious as Avner's. Her eyes were green, large. Her mature body swayed easily, elegantly. She led them into the living room and told them to sit down.

"You're Ori Elhayani," she stated, "I recognized you from the photograph in the newspaper article a few months ago. I've been following you for a long time." She again looked at Alma with unconcealed affection. "You're Alma," she said, running a hand over the child's hair.

When she turned back to Ori, Ori detected a hint of sorrow deep in her eyes, fleeting and immediately vanishing. She didn't ask why they'd come and Ori didn't wonder about it.

"I came to ask about Avner," Ori said, "where he is, what he's doing, whether I can contact him."

"No," the woman answered simply, "you can't."

"How old are you?" Alma asked.

"Sixty-one," Nava replied.

"Ima, is sixty-one more than thirty-five?"

"A lot more, honey, a lot more." Ori said gently,

Alma weighed Nava up and said gravely, "You'll die soon." She switched on her game. Beeps and hiccups filled the air.

Nava laughed briefly and fell silent. Then looked at Ori looked again.

"You shouldn't have brought her," she repeated, "these are unsafe times." She said to Alma, "Ma belle, would you like something to drink? To eat?"

Alma returned her a serious, concentrated look. "Have you got any chocolate?" she asked.

Nava smiled. "Coffee?" she asked Ori.

Ori nodded and got up to follow her into the kitchen.

"Why can't I contact Avner?" she asked. Her tone was too tough, she thought.

"He's not in Israel. He's been in France for three and a half years."

"Three and a half years . . . but I'm sure I saw him in Tel Aviv four months ago, in the park near my apartment."

"What are you doing?" Nava asked, "What can you gain from it?"

"I don't understand. What do you mean?"

Nava gazed at the curved stainless steel body of the electric kettle on which they were both reflected, and between them the bare bulb burning close to the ceiling. Their images were distorted, leaning balefully towards one another around a hub of light, like two ancient goddesses invoking the sun's disk. A cloud formed above the kettle's spout, shaking it. The red light on the handle went out. Silently, Nava poured water into two cups and took out a box of Ferrero Rocher chocolates from one of the cupboards. Ori followed her movements in silence.

They went back into the living room. Alma's eyes lit up at the sight of the chocolate balls wrapped in their golden metallic paper. She snatched one, unwrapped it, stuffed it into her mouth, and immediately reached out for another.

"Alma," Ori said warningly, and she put the ball back into the box as her jaws worked on the one in her mouth. Chocolate-flecked spittle dribbled from the corner of her mouth.

Nava sat in the armchair and looked at Ori, a piercing look. She measured her with a skeptical, grave, judgmental expression. Ori had never imagined that one look could encompass so many expressions. She waited for the verdict.

"The brain," Nava said, "is a deceptive organ."

Ori dimly remembered Avner mentioning, on one of the rare occasions he had broken their agreement never to talk about the past, that his mother's parents had emigrated to France from Morocco in the 1950s, and his mother had immigrated to Israel after their death in the seventies, equipped with degrees in psychology and education she had gained in Paris, and which had served her more than necessary in raising him and Ravit, his younger sister.

A long electronic hiccup broke her train of thought. Alma yelped happily. The chocolate was smeared over her lips and fingers and had stained the game's keys.

"I'm sorry," Ori said. She sipped her coffee. It was bitter. Nava hadn't asked how many sugars she took. "You didn't put sugar in," she noted.

Nava got up again and Ori followed her. But she stopped halfway. On the sideboard there were some family photographs in worked brass frames. One caught her eye. A color photograph of a girl of about ten, with curly, chestnut hair and bold green eyes. That, she thought without knowing why, is what Alma will look like when she's the girl in the photograph's age. Something began rising in her chest.

"That's my younger daughter, Ravit. She lives in France with her husband. Three and a half years ago I sent Avner to live with them. He hasn't been back to Israel since." Nava said.

Ori moved her head slightly. Alma dropped her game onto the couch.

"Can I watch TV?" she asked eagerly, "Have you got the SpongeBob movie?"

"Alma," Ori said, choked, "we're going in a minute. A little patience."

"I'm bored," Alma declared.

"Give me a few minutes," Ori said, and Nava's eyes again captured her attention. "I don't understand what you're saying," Ori whispered to her.

Nava was holding a damp paper towel. She went to Alma and wiped the traces of chocolate from her face and fingers. She caressed her cheek with the back of her hand and kissed her forehead. Alma shook her off, jumped down from the couch and ran to Ori, winding her arms around her legs and burying her face in the hem of her dress.

Nava turned to her and said quietly, forcefully, "Three and a half years ago he came to see me, in total panic. He told me he'd seen you in Tel Aviv, walking arm in arm with an old friend of his and with a little girl about a year old. He didn't have the courage to go up to you. He ran away. The coward. A week later he called me, said he'd lost his appetite, that he wasn't sleeping. That he couldn't stop going to Meir Park in the hope of seeing you again with your husband. I knew he was keeping something from me. I know my son, he doesn't know how to cope with reality, with the guilt that's part of living in this world."

"Do you think he felt guilty because he took off on me?" Ori asked. "That he saw me with Barak and Alma and was jealous?"

Alma peeped out inquiringly from the folds of the dress, and again Nava gave her a long, yearning look.

"You should ask yourself why you came here." She said to Ori.

"I . . . I wanted to see Avner . . . I heard about the Katyushas falling on Haifa, the fatalities, I was suddenly afraid that perhaps . . . that I didn't have many more opportunities to meet him, that tomorrow, the day after, this country might be destroyed, and I wouldn't . . . " Ori stammered in reply.

Nava stopped her with a dismissive gesture.

"Do you believe that? I told you, the brain is a deceptive organ. I believe you saw Avner in the park. But not four months ago, but that day three and a half years ago, when he saw you. You've got to ask yourself why you've come to terms with his appearance only now, why you've decided to introduce him into the logical continuum of your life."

Embarrassment spawning anger. That's what had risen in her earlier.

"I want to speak to Avner," she murmured.

"Ima," Alma called, "when are we going?"

"No," Nava said, "I sent him to France, to live with his sister. I'm a great believer in the healing power of distance."

Ori didn't reply, and Nava, who continued to follow Alma as she hid from her in the folds of Ori's dress, said, "We all make our choices. The price is sometimes silence and hidden torment."

"No," Ori said, "not me." She took Alma's hand and dragged her out, into the street, shocked by the mask of grief that flawed Nava's features.

They got into the car, and Ori, angry and confused, couldn't manage to key in the immobilizer code and turned the ignition key several times. The alarm went off, hooting and breaking the neighborhood's afternoon silence. A middle-aged man came running out of an adjacent house and thumped the car hood.

"Switch the alarm off, you madwoman, d'you want to give somebody a heart attack? Don't we have enough with the Katyusha sirens?"

She felt for the keypad through the veil of her tears, forming a mental picture of digit after digit. Alma stroked her arm.

"Don't cry, Ima. That woman didn't mean to do anything bad to us."

They left Haifa at top speed. Behind them the siren began wailing. Alma turned round to look at the road, to see what all the noise was about. On the radio the announcer read out the names of the towns whose inhabitants should stay in the shelters. Ori's heart was shrouded in mist. They stopped at the Pancake House near Netanya. Alma clapped her hands over the maple syrup and cream, and Ori smiled at her dully. They continued to Tel Aviv, to the Azrieli Center mall. Alma asked to go to the water games area on the third floor, and Ori consented with empty speech and mechanical movements. Afterwards they went to see a movie, not the one Alma wanted, another animated film. Alma clung to her in fright during it and Ori comforted her with remote, indifferent words.

In the evening, when Barak came home, Alma reported excitedly on her day.

"Haifa?" Barak said in disbelief.

Ori was in her study, staring at a new blank document on the computer screen. She had to write something. She still didn't know what. But it was the only way to speak the unvarnished truth. So long as she wanted to.

Barak stormed in, throwing the door open with a bang.

"Haifa?" he yelled. "Are you out of your mind? You took the child to Haifa? What for? To see missiles? To get killed?"

Ori stretched her lips tiredly at him.

"This time you've gone too far," he shouted. "You've got a screw loose. You neglect the child, starve her, and now you endanger her life. That's it. It's over. I can't go on living like this."

A fetid bolus bubbled in Ori's stomach. Her abdominal muscles cramped. She got up from her chair and passed Barak on her way to the bathroom. Barak called after her, "Aren't you even going to answer me?" and added censures and curses. But they didn't register on her antennae and penetrate the storm of insects seething inside her.

As she crouched over the toilet bowl vomiting her heart out, between the palpitations in her chest and the stream of sour bile spewing from her mouth and hitting the porcelain, she heard the front door opening. She tensed and listened. She heard shuffling noises and heavier footsteps and the sound of shushing and whispers, followed by the door closing. The wave hit again and rose from the pit of her stomach. She wailed once. Barak had gone and Alma with him, she realized. Time stood still. All she felt was time standing still. She needed a new heart.

SEVEN

Love

IN THE ISRAELI SUMMER there is a period, from the end of June to early September, that is very similar to the depths of winter in the northern countries. Growth waits under the threat of the frost, deep in ice, or steeped in heat, or sealed in it; tired, preserved greenery. The poinciana petals faded; the ficus and eucalyptus trees arrested; only the fronds of the palms are opulent and the fevered yellow hearts of the frangipani peep out insolently like heather in the snow.

It was in this period that Ori Elhayani moved. The world's loneliness did not trouble her. Since her youth she had been used to wandering through desolate, spacious houses in her quest for ghosts. In the space in which her flame burned she smelt oil and its derivatives from every direction: the streets stank of petroleum, the birds of diesel fuel, and the translucent air of summer was redolent with the odor of raw alcohol. A flammable, carbon diapason lay over Creation.

Every morning she went out. She wore a green cotton dress with a plunging neckline—the moment she'd seen it in the dress shop she'd known it was a dress for days of sorrow— she put on lipstick and sat in a café, a different one each day. She was assailed by a constant thirst that could not be slaked with water. She drank incessantly, but her throat remained cracked. The war swirled around her, spilling over. The heat of the furnaces of the north blew onto her. Among her memories she had nothing to compare it with.

When she was eight and the First Lebanon War broke out, her whole class was rushed to the gym where the order of the day was set out in detail. They were given colored marker pens and told to draw cheery greeting cards for the soldiers in the north. She didn't understand who the cards were being sent to; when she came home from school she'd see her mother standing in the dark kitchen, a small transistor radio murmuring on the work surface, and a hoarse, genderless voice whispering the names of the dead soldiers, like a minute, mute stream of vapor coming from the transistor's extended aerial and crowding into the space of the kitchen.

In the present war, if the dead were crying out, their cry was thrust towards her as a rumble. A throaty whisper coming from Shlomi, Nahariya, Akko and Haifa—perhaps from Nava Assoulin too—from Kafr Kana, Bint Jebail, Maroun a-Ras, and landing on the eardrum.

One evening she was looking through the kitchen window into a boy's room, an Israeli-Chinese boy who'd tried several times to suck up to Alma, even though she behaved standoffishly towards him. A pigeon landed on the windowsill and pecked at the pane, startling her. Then she heard the phone ringing. She hurried to it. Perhaps it's Barak. But only a strange voice, an enthusiastic youngster, came from the receiver. He introduced himself and explained that they—who are *they*, she wondered—are organizing a petition by young writers against the war. He asked if she'd like to join them. She said yes without knowing why, and he asked for her email address. Suspicion rose in her. No way.

"Michael Kagan, is that you?" She barked into the phone.

"No, I told you my name's . . . "

"Michael, you'd better stop harassing me with your letters and insinuations, understand? Or I'm calling the police," she said, and hung up.

The cordless phone was heavy in her hand. She swung it slightly. An inkling of an idea came into her empty mind. Barak hadn't gone far. He could have gone to his parents' home in Yavne or her father's house in Netivot. And Yavne is closer to Tel Aviv, where he worked. That simple deduction traversed the darkness inside her skull like a whip. She slowly dialed his parents' number.

After a few rings Miriam answered with a sleepy "Hello?" But her voice came alive when she recognized Ori's. She said, "Ori, what's happened? Barak and Alma have been here for five days and he won't tell me anything."

"How's Alma?"

"Fine. You know, she's got the pool in the yard so she's *mabsuta*, happy as a sandboy." She incorrectly accented the second syllable, emphasizing the '*ta*', like a knock.

"Put Barak on."

"He doesn't want to speak to you. He warned me that if you call I should tell you that. Anyway, he's gone out with Alma."

"Miriam, I . . . " and her voice choked. She started crying.

"Orinkah," Miriam said gently, "what's happened to you both? What's happened to you?"

Ori hung up.

She looked around questioningly and turned towards the television set that was on Alma's channel. SpongeBob, yellow and frightened, looked out at her from the screen. He was standing in some kind of viscous sea, waiting in a bus station. Bus after bus drove past. He went to the information window to argue and protest, stood in an endless line, and when he reached the front he was told that the last bus had just departed. He emerged into the darkness of the outside, into the emptiness. A good idea, she thought, and closed her own eyes.

Beneath her eyelids, in the lighter darkness, Gadi Blasco was waiting for her. He was Ilanit's elder married brother, and Ilanit, as they grew up, had developed an even deeper abhorrence of Ori. Ori didn't blame her. She'd met him by chance. The house had closed in on her and she went to the factory in the industrial zone where her father worked. She had things to say to him. She reached the factory gate before she'd collected herself and chided herself, *Shatya*, what are you doing here? She stood by the gate for a few moments, looking inside, aware that the guard in his hut was looking at her and wondering whether to call over and ask what she wanted or ignore her until she turned round and left. Maybe she'd wait, she thought, until the bus came out—it was nearly the end of the working day—and flag it down. But she rejected that idea too.

She turned her back on the gate and heard it moving, screeching as it slid open, but continued walking. A banged-up car stopped beside her. The window opened and in the driver's seat she saw Gadi Blasco's face. She recognized him right away. He didn't recognize her, the last time he'd seen her she was ten or eleven. His face was empty, angular, with a curved nose. Small eyes and light skin. A profusion of black, youthful, well-groomed curls bounced on his head. Ilanit had once told her that her brother was so skinny because he was born with a hole in his heart. She hadn't understood the connection.

"Hey," he said, "need a lift?"

She walked round the car and opened the door. Gadi cleaned the seat with a few slaps. In the back seat she saw strewn toys, snack wrappers, a squashed fruit juice bottle.

"You from Netivot?" he asked.

"Yes."

"Where?"

"Makor Haim. Do you work at the factory?"

"No. I'm a welder. I work in a metalwork shop on the other side of the industrial zone. We provide services to the factory. What's your name?"

420

"Ori."

"I'm Gadi. Nice to meet you."

It was a short drive. Her somewhat childlike body, to which breasts and curves had been added, made no impression on him, she could see that. He stole glances at her. When he dropped her at the corner of the street he said, "See you."

Several days later he met her wandering by the school. She'd taken off from a Bible lesson in the afternoon, gone through the hole in the fence to the wood, and crossed it without knowing what she was going to do. She walked the street around the school. Gadi's car pulled up beside her.

"So, Ori," he said, "are we going to keep on meeting like this?" She gave him her most alluring smile and a smile spread over his face. "I'm going to the shop. Join me for a cup of coffee?"

She didn't drink coffee, but she still accepted his invitation. She sat down next to him. He lit a cigarette and offered her one. She refused. They reached the shop. There was another worker there, a man older than Gadi, ungainly and balding. Gadi waved to him and took her into the office. They chatted desultorily. He asked her about school. Afterwards he drove her back to her street and asked if he could pick her up next afternoon. She promised she'd be waiting not far from the school, on the other side of the wood.

The ungainly man, whose name she now knew was Sasson, owned the metalwork shop. The second time she was there he raised a callused thumb to Gadi. Ori ignored it. Gadi chattered, told her about the hole in his heart, about the battery of tests he'd undergone. His words fell onto her like a drizzle of sand from a hole in a sack, grain by grain, a niggling, arousing dripping. Evening fell swiftly, the few autumn days were over and winter was drawing in. Ori smelt the dampness of the earth chilling and waiting. She too was waiting, for Gadi to make his move. She was hungry and tense.

But he didn't touch her. He took her home and a few days later appeared at their meeting place. What's he waiting for, she wondered, why's he talking?

After a week of cautious, chattering pursuit, he took her to the metalwork shop at night. The desk in the middle of the office was bare. He spread a rough, scratchy blanket over it. She undressed without a word and lay on her back. He didn't kiss her. It was brief, disappointing. She wanted more. How deep is sex. There must be something deeper than this. None of the men she'd met had bothered to envelop her with tenderness, to try and seduce her, talk to her. They assumed she was theirs by right. She lay on the desk, illuminated by the faint yellow light of the office. Gadi went outside to take a leak. A yearning was born in her. She got up and dressed quickly, panties and tee shirt. She wanted to feel his closeness, come to him from behind, encircle his body with her arms and lay her head in the hollow between his prominent shoulder blades, not break away. She was already imagining the fragrance of the damp vegetation and the smell of the pieces of rusting iron that had gathered the heat of the day, spotted with the bubbling vapor of urine.

Two men were standing in the darkness outside the shop, whispering. A few seconds of adjusting to the darkness elapsed before she recognized the second man, Sasson.

"I told you I'd screw her in the end. There isn't a girl that doesn't put out. There are men who don't know how to take it." Gadi said.

She retreated into the shop. Took off her panties and tee shirt and lay naked on the desk. Gadi came back inside.

"Get dressed," he told her, "so you don't freeze to death."

"Don't you want to do it again . . . ?"

"Why? What d'you think I am? A machine? Anyway, I've got my heart to think of." He laughed hoarsely.

Afterwards it was impossible to scotch the rumors. There was one extra partner to the act and Netivot is a small town. The rumors circled, preying on her. They reached the school too.

The first to hear them was Gvinush. She had become a girl of breathtaking beauty, and the rumor hardened her heart even more. She bigheartedly spread the information among the girls. When Ori passed they'd call out "*sharmuta*", slut, at her. Boys made indecent proposals to her: to go to the wood with them if she wanted a riding lesson. The circling of the lips was enough to strike at her, "*sharmuta*", the lips sketched with their movement. "*Sharmuta*".

When she couldn't take any more she plucked up her courage and went to the orchard, which she hadn't visited for a long time. Ophir and Sigal had stopped talking to her in the year she'd stayed back a grade, they left her behind like a used article. She didn't feel she had any right to demand anything from them, ask for reasons. It seemed perfectly natural that their figures would get lost among the kids at school, that their appearance would be melted and swallowed up in anonymity. But now she sought consolation, that in memory of warmer days, some kind of special dispensation, familiar faces would appear from the crowd, gentle looks.

From the door of Sigal's house she heard their laughter, and their dangerous closeness filled her nostrils. She forced a smile and moved along the compacted path, around Sigal's wall of forgiveness. She walked noisily, driving the partridges away and rustling through the wild oats. They were waiting for her, two prosecutors. She saw Sigal's lips rounding around that word. There was an expression of disgust in Ophir's eyes.

She didn't protest, she didn't plead, she didn't try and explain herself. She fled. The world was too ridiculous. After the triumphant mockery in Gadi's voice, she couldn't bear physical contact. The very thought of him filled her with terror. She did not

423

have a body, not a semblance of a body, she never would have, she swore to herself. How cruel it was that now, when she had been sufficiently punished, her actions were exacting revenge. All winter, when she went to school and on the way home, in her aimless wandering through the streets of Netivot, that gall filled her mind. Now she awakened to an understanding of her being lost since her mother's death, not knowing where to turn, which road back to take.

It was only at the end of the winter that she found a solution. The sky was cleansed of clouds and limitless. For some reason she took on her walk the weekend paper her father had bought and a plant field guide that in an attack of longing for Ophir and Sigal, she'd stolen from the public library. On the uncultivated land outside Netivot she saw the tortuous track of hogweed in a white carpet spread by its petals on the ground.

In the weekend supplement she read an interview with Shemi Chen from Migdal Ha'emek, the director of a Jerusalem boarding school, who said it was his ambition to integrate boys and girls from the outlying areas into his school based on their abilities and not their education. Education, he said, is another social mechanism enjoyed only by people of means. That Saturday evening she wrote him a long letter, telling him the story of her life since her mother's illness and subsequent death, about the grief in her heart, her increasing disgust with the environment in which she was growing up, the year she was held back a grade, her being lost.

Two weeks later Shemi Chen called excitedly and invited her for an interview. Just before Passover she heard she'd been accepted. She stopped going to school that year. Every day she went to the reading room at the municipal library and read systematically, subject after subject. Now and then she would copy sentences she liked into her notebook. On the first page she wrote: "He who wishes to be saved will pull himself up by his own forelock," and drew two lines under it.

———

There were three wall clocks around the apartment. Ori went from one to the other, removed the batteries from the back, and set the hands to five o'clock. On the way to the car the world's movement began revolving in her favor. She found three five-agora coins, obverse side up. In her car she put Ophir's podcast on to play. As she approached Yavne it was already dusk and the CD digital display showed 35:35. She lay back in the driving seat, playing song after song, until she came to the one before last. One of the singers sang, "Some moments last forever, and some flare out with love love love."

She pulled up by the gate of Miriam and Victor Shulman's house. The sun was still reluctant to set, stuck at the edge of the sky like an insect on a pin. She saw Barak's parked car. She got out of her car and pushed the gate open. The path to the house filled her with terror but she moved along it, crossed it in an eternity, and almost collapsed to the sound of the doorbell.

Miriam opened the door, and Victor, frowning and bare-chested, leaned over her shoulder to see who'd come. He blew through his lips as she came in. Miriam hugged her, saying, "You look awful."

In truth Ori hadn't showered for days. Her hair hung greasily from her head. The edges of the neckline of her green dress were threadbare and the dress itself was layered with coffee stains. With her red lips she surely looked like a survivor of a terrorist bombing weeping vainly for the TV cameras.

Alma ran downstairs from the upper floor and burst into the hall. Her eyes were bloodshot from playing in the pool and her face was sunburnt. Her hair was damp.

"Ima!" she screamed excitedly, "you've come back!" and wrapped her arms around her waist. "What've you brought me?" she asked.

"Myself," Ori replied, and stroked her head. "Where's Abba?"

"In the yard," Alma replied, pulling Ori after her, "come on."

Miriam gave her an encouraging nod.

Barak was sitting in the shady part of the yard, reading a book and sipping lemonade from a glass beaded with condensation.

"Abba," Alma shouted, "Ima's come back!"

He raised his head in surprise and his look fell upon her. She hung back in the entrance, momentarily resisting Alma's tugging and chivvying, then finally submitted. She led, her head bowed, and was ordered to sit in a chair that Alma dragged over and placed beside Barak's. As she obeyed and sat down, she saw Alma pushing a small stool in front of her and sliding it into the space between the two chairs, and then climbing up onto it, cramped between her parents, happy.

They did not speak. The sun set in its own time and none of them started a conversation. Ori didn't know what thoughts were battling inside Barak's head. There was a tumult in her own mind though, thoughts pushing to come out, to come out. She wanted to say, *It's not fair, I thought your love would lead me to a white and quiet place where I'd be able to see things as they are, not the way I see them now, in the depths of a dim mirror.* She wanted to shout, *I thought I'd be given a sign. Do you have a sign to give me, do you have proof?*

But she kept silent. She kept silent.

Alma started singing to herself, wounding the silence with the theme tune of one of the series she watched. Insects swarmed on the mown lawn and the song of the cicadas was borne from afar.

"The governor of the Bank of Israel's announced that all discussions on Israel's welfare policy are to be suspended for at least a year because of the war." Barak finally said.

"I don't follow the news," Ori said, "every time I look on the internet somebody's died."

"This country's got no future. We should fold up the buildings and streets and leave."

"It's not like you to say that."

He looked at her.

"I can't tolerate a state of uncertainty," he said, "and with you, Ori, there's no certainty. When I draw your attention to one thing or another, you always turn your head and look at a third thing. There's always a shadow of somebody else between us."

Alma moved into her arms. "Don't go again, Ima," she called, her lips moving on her skin.

In the dimness of the yard Ori brushed the damp strands of her daughter's hair from her face, from her forehead. Bobby pins, she thought, that's it, bobby pins will impose order on the wild hair, finally give it shape. And for some reason the words 'bobby pins' gave birth to the words 'metal wool combs', the metal combs that flayed the flesh of Rabbi Akiva until he expired . . . No, she told herself, enough, I've got to stop these thoughts. She forced herself to say, not being misled by the alien sound of the words, "I can change. People are capable of changing."

"Really?" Barak replied, "I think that at best they're capable of admitting that they're not living the life they wanted to live."

Again she was silent.

"But that's the calamity of love," Barak went on, "it's like one of those sophisticated brainteasers in game theory. Each side waits for the other to change for it, then comes the moment when each side has to decide whether to give up or accept the fact that the waiting situation itself will turn into love."

"Are we there, at that moment?" she asked.

Barak's fingers fumbled, touched Alma's knee, and she giggled, and then the back of her own hand and her fingers that were gripping the arm of the chair. She thought that the contact would bring with it relief, comfort. It will be the sign, she told herself, I want no more than that, you can abandon the doubt after you abandon the fear. I'm ready.

But there was nothing of this in Barak's touch. The flame that had enveloped her skin in recent months had been extinguished. No. There was nothing but ice, tall masses; arid, frost-sown surfaces; the faces of children turning blue as with their tiny fists they beat against the glazing of frozen water.

———

On the way out of Yavne the car in front of her ran over a careless cat, beheading it under its wheels. In her headlights she saw the supple body, from whose nerves the accumulated electricity still sent out shocks, leaping here and there from the power of death on the road. She braked and waited until the body stopped twitching and came to rest, stilled on the asphalt.

All the way back she tried not to remember Barak's hand touching her, the icy bite on her hand.

She thought about Ofra, sixteen-years-old and walking around Netivot wildly peroxided, tap-tapping in clogs, Ofra in the Makor Haim neighborhood, tsk-tsk-tsk, her jaws masticating gum, who hadn't heard her laughing, and skipping rope to firm up her thighs, and reading dusty books and weeping silently.

Asher came into her mind, almost fifteen in 1984. The air was filled with omens of a holocaust: in Yerucham a two-headed calf was born that shed tears of blood; in Ofakim fish leapt from the ritual bath, heralding approaching doom; a donkey spoke in the Messiah's voice near Dimona. Asher taught her to ride a bike. He took her to the schoolyard in the evening and the fleshy light fell on the two of them. He held the saddle until she was steady and pushed her. She covered a hundred meters before losing her balance and falling off. She lay on the rough paving stones, the bike on top of her, waiting for Asher to come to her aid. But he stood where he was.

A tidal wave of anger rose in her. She thought of Ariella, of that stupid Prospero Juno and his irresponsible driving on the road from California to New York. What demon had possessed him that he decided to drive innumerable kilometers without stopping? Why had he carried the manuscript of the eighth book in his car and not left a backup copy in a safe? Ariella, how had she allowed herself to get lost in the marshes in the east of the Kingdom of Autumn?

At home she sat down in front of the computer screen that had remained on since Barak left, Alma with him. The same blank document came up when she touched the mouse, and the screen saver vanished. The words flew to her fingertips in a rush, burning away the night hours that remained.

When dawn broke, summery and scorching, she read the story. She thought about it for a long time before reaching a decision. She took out a clean sheet of paper and wrote on it in her handwriting, to which she was no longer accustomed. She had to grit her teeth as she meticulously formed the slopes and curves of the letters, the rounded bellies of the 's', the 'b', the 'd', and the 'g'.

Sigal,

People hardly ever write letters nowadays. And you're the only one I know (know?) who perseveres with this lost art. Do you remember me telling you in our childhood about the 'Ariella the Fairy Detective' series of books I so loved? Over the past few

429

weeks I've discovered that a far smaller number of readers than I thought have come across this series. I hope you haven't forgotten.

They say that God created the animals and their names separately, and He gave Man the job of matching them. Man, his hands full of names, ran among the animals, asking: "Lion? Are you the lion? Donkey? Are you the donkey?" He was answered with an unintelligible sound, a bellow or a bray or a grunt or a roar or another voice. In the end, in his despair Man decided to give out the names randomly.

So it's quite possible that the sounds embracing the nature of the name 'lion' are in fact 'donkey', while the true meaning of the chain of consonants and vowels, 'lion', is actually the animal we call 'elephant'. That's language. It gives us a sense of attaining reality, of grasping it, but all the while it's doubtful whether it indicates the right places.

The only way of dealing with this knowledge, I think, is to repress it. But it happens that the senses are so lucid, become painfully sharpened, so that each vein of a leaf, every grain of dust, is unique, and then it is impossible to avoid the certainty that we are living in a mistaken world. I am in such a moment. Everything is clear to me. For years I didn't feel the weight of this clarity. Even its memory had left me.

You can't avoid the mistake but you can pinpoint it. Over the last two months I thought I'd made a mistake of one kind, and last night I realized that it was of a different kind. I had to save myself before I drowned and was lost, pull myself up by my own forelock. I didn't know what the swamp was. I acted on the assumption, which for some reason one makes, that had I made a greater effort in the direction of life, I would have been saved. What nonsense. My mistake was that I blindly chased shadows, that I wanted so much, until I was close to giving up on myself.

I imagine it will be difficult for you to make sense of this since you don't know my history and vagaries in the years since that unfortunate encounter in the orchard. But think about the little girls—the ones whose stories were told and those whose stories were erased with time—who entered Wonderland. They can be Alices, Dorothys, Wendys—women that Wonderland didn't mark, didn't claim for itself. But there are also others who were hurt in their past, and they live their lives with their faces towards the gates of that land, in which once, way back when, they knew the pleasure of an encounter with absolute reality, without blinds, without screens. Isn't that the perfect simile of childhood for us, being in the experience in and of itself?

Those women are waiting for their names to be called, to be let in. But it never happens. Instead they walk beside the walls encircling the land, hoping to find a secret gate, a way in. Sometimes it happens that they find an opening, a cleft in the rock, and they settle into it, wearied by the search, and say, this is the best of possibilities, and they give everything, everything, in order not to know what they know: the cleft is only a temporary refuge, a short-term waiting room. They hold on, and they struggle with all their might as moss spreads over the walls, as jets of steam rise high above the rock, as an avalanche erodes the outline of the mountain ridge.

Tell me you understand. No. Think to yourself, I understand. Don't ask why I'm writing you all this. I need an addressee. For years you were my most devoted and wisest of readers. In your letters I felt that you grasped the essential parts of what I was trying to say in my books. The first letter surprised me. I expected the second, and when the third was delayed and didn't arrive following my book, A Map to Getting Lost, I felt that the book had fallen into rough hands, onto deaf ears. I was very happy to receive your letter when it came.

The latest story I've written is also for you. I append it to this letter. I got the inspiration for it from the last song of Ophir's podcast. Give him my thanks and good wishes. His podcast was like a soothing balm for me.

431

I forgive (if you need forgiveness)
But never yearn,
Ori

She folded the letter, put it and the pages of the story into an envelope, and went to the post office.

On the back of her right hand and her fingers she felt the frostbite left by Barak's touch. She rubbed it against her cheek. The lightness of her husband's Dolce & Gabbana rose into her nostrils. She inhaled it deeply: the fragrance standing in the space of her cleft in the rock.

A few days after her period was late she looked with revulsion at the two bluish lines on the home pregnancy kit she'd bought at the pharmacy. Every morning she went to Or Zarua to check if Boaz Zadok had heard anything about Avner. Every evening, her throat choked, she hung around the door of that bar on Herzl Street. Perhaps Avner would appear through the back door, as had happened that evening; she'd scan the men entering and leaving and every now and then one of them would come over to her. None of them interested her, there wasn't the right man to carry the burden. And then Barak came—had she been waiting for him?—and she went to his apartment with him.

Two weeks later she went to his office at noon, which then was in the Azrieli Towers, to tell him about her pregnancy. They went to a café on the second floor of the Towers and she told him, hesitantly. She wanted him to tell her to abort the fetus, that somebody else should take responsibility for the injustice done to her, but Barak's face lit up in response. He got up and said, "Let's go outside, I can't stay sitting her, I want to jump for joy."

They went out and walked towards Ibn Gvirol Street. It was April, dim and heavy. A mystifying barometric depression that had made its way from Turkey came to a stop above them in Kaplan Street, and torrential rain began falling, ripping the dusty air and filling the cracks in the asphalt. Screaming like a couple of kids they fled into the yard of one of the buildings and took shelter under a corrugated iron roof covering the entrance, they clung together. From his heavy body the sweetness of his aftershave wafted towards her, the essence of spring. She bathed in it. He said, "Marry me."

"I've got to tell you something," she said.

He waited while she cleared her throat.

"When I was twelve," she said, "I came home from school one day with a cut on my temple, trembling all over. I didn't tell anyone what had happened to me that day, not even my parents . . ."

An inviting, supportive smile flitted over Barak's lips. His brown eyes rested on her in total, boundless belief, breaking through the dense aura of the aftershave. She said to herself, No! This can't be. To him she said, "Do you hear?"

"Of course. I'm listening," he said.

"No," she told him, "can you hear it?"

"What?" he asked.

"This quiet. It's stopped raining," she hurried out into the street before him. A soft sun moved towards its zenith and split the clouds. Its light sparkled on the glass towers and chrome of the Azrieli Towers. Ori looked towards them, the bursting brightness hit her eyes, confounding any assessment of distance.

Caliban: [. . .] *the isle is full of noises,*
Sounds, and sweet airs, that give delight, and hurt
not.
Sometimes a thousand twangling instruments
Will hum about mine ears; and sometimes voices
That, if I then had wak'd after long sleep,
Will make me sleep again: and then, in dreaming.
The clouds methought would open [. . .]

Sebastian: [. . .] *Now I will believe*
That there are unicorns; that in Arabia
There is one tree, the phoenix' throne; one phoenix
At this hour reigning there.

William Shakespeare, *The Tempest*
(Act III, Scenes II and III)

Chapter One, in which Pekach Ben-Remaliyahu embarks on a journey

LATE ONE EVENING the princedom's debt collectors came to the hut of Remaliyahu, headman of the fishing village in the south of the Kingdom of Autumn. They hammered on the door until his wife Surah opened it and they burst in, two pug-nosed, thick-bearded men, and a manly woman, bigger and more muscular than her two attendants. Remaliyahu was busy with last year's profit and loss accounts, and every now and again he sighed. According to his father's records there had never been such a bad year in the village's history. The plentiful fish in the Crystal Lakes had dwindled and last year's catch was poor and unfit for trade, either in the big cities or the castles of the kingdom's nobles. Up until ten and a half years ago, the villagers, the fishermen who made their living from the many species of fish from the depths of the Crystal Lakes, had lived well. But no longer.

The debt collectors wasted no time. The two men laid heavy hands on Remaliyahu's shoulders, pressing him into his chair, and the woman unrolled a scroll and read from it: "In accordance with the princely agreement, the entire Kingdom of Autumn, and all the bounty of the land, including its water and air, are the property of the Prince of Autumn, and tenants must pay an annual lease fee. Over the past decade the fees due from the Crystal Lakes fishermen have not been paid to the Prince's treasury. Therefore, we have no alternative but to declare that all the village's assets will be irrevocably repossessed in seven days from today if the fees are not paid, with the addition of an arrears penalty of four hundred green zehorans."

The boy Pekach, Remaliyahu's son, lay on his bed looking listlessly at the window giving on to the Crystal Lakes. In a week's time he would be celebrating his fifteenth birthday, but he had no cause for celebration. In fact, the last celebration linked to Pekach's young life was the Soul Setting Ceremony, a ceremony that every infant, without exception, in the southern part of the Kingdom of Autumn, had to undergo after surviving the first eight days of his life. As the village priest encircled Pekach's head with a circlet of thorns, and was about to utter the spells that would set the child's soul, from its place in the firmament the flame of one of the Kingdom of Autumn's clouds broke away—the clouds that were permanently red as if the glow of sunset was always in them. And the flame fell to earth and licked the infant's body. Surah, Pekach's mother, burst from the crowd and fell upon the infant to shield him from the flame. But the flame was not extinguished. Surah called out to the Gods of Spring and promised she would do anything they asked if only the infant lived. And from the flame came a whisper, saying, "When the boy Pekach is fifteen-years-old, his life will be replaced by another."

And now the date of fulfillment of the prophecy was fast approaching and Pekach felt as if he were paralyzed. All his usual carefree enjoyment of living had abandoned him and he spent his time in bed, deep in thought. There was no point to anything. And that evening, when he heard the hammering on the door of their home, he jumped out of bed in alarm: perhaps his calculations were wrong and the time had come. Tense, the boy crouched at the door of his room. The words held no wonder for him, but the sum demanded by the treasury from his father made him shudder. Four hundred green zehorans? Four hundred zehorans . . . Only once in his life had Pekach seen one zehoran, when he was very small. His father held the pure, round coin in which a greenish mist floated and each time the light endowed it with a different image from the generations of Princes of Autumn. Each zehoran was worth one thousand copper serens, and with one copper seren you could feed a man for a whole day. The debt determined was a fabulous sum. The value of the property of the whole village would not come to one tenth of it. By what right did the prince's debt collectors demand this sum? Rumor had it that a crime committed by the prince had prevented the flow of pure water to the lakes, and brought disaster to the majority of species they sustained. Much grumbling and complaint had been aired on this since Pekach's childhood. Neither supplication to the Gods of Autumn nor vows and oaths had helped, or the attempts to go to the center of the forest where Tarfon, Prince of the Lakes dwelt, to plead with him. No one who had tried had returned. Some of the old women suggested sending an emissary to the distant City of Tempest, to the palace of Ariella the fairy detective, and beg her help. The men dismissed them disdainfully, claiming that Ariella was nothing but a figment of the imagination. And in any case, only a fool would believe that a twelve-year-old girl had the power to solve the problem of the dwindling fish harvest.

After the debt collectors left, Pekach came out of his room and went to his father whose back was bent over the table. Surah, too, came to comfort her husband. But Remaliyahu was inconsolable. "How can we raise four hundred green zehorans within a week?" he shouted, "Only Tarfon, Prince of the Lakes, can conjure up such a sum for us!" And he laughed bitterly.

Without foundation though it might have been, the idea seeped into Pekach's mind and gnawed at it. He went back to his room and pondered. He fell into a deep sleep and had a dream. In his dream he was standing on a rocky pinnacle and a snow-white eagle with a vast wingspan, flew to him; around its neck was a copper chain with a small copper flask hanging from it. Without preliminaries, the eagle said, "Pekach Ben-Remaliyahu, if you seek to save the village, you must go to the lake in the middle of the forest, where Tarfon, Prince of the Lakes dwells, and ensnare him there. Only thus can you compel him to grant your request."

"But how?" Pekach protested, "For it is impossible to cross the forest. Anyone venturing into it is turned into a tree. They say there was a hero who tried crossing the forest by jumping from branch to branch, but the branches skewered him and his flesh was devoured by swarms of bronze beetles."

"Depart, and the way will open before you," said the eagle, spreading its wings.

Pekach woke up. There was no room for doubt or uncertainty. In any case, the life he had known would come to an end in another week, even if he stayed in bed sad and idle. But if he embarked on this journey, at least he would know he had tried to do something useful.

Chapter Two, in which Tarfon is netted and Pekach receives a gift

PEKACH QUICKLY PACKED some provisions, shouldered a roll of fisherman's net, and silently left his parents' hut. It was almost midnight. In the red sky of the Kingdom of Autumn he saw the two mirror moons moving closer to one another. That is how the hours of the night were marked in the Kingdom of Autumn. Two small moons rose on the horizon at both edges of the sky and climbed to their zenith; when they passed each other it was midnight. Close to morning, on completing their orbit, they would vanish below the horizon and the birds would start singing.

Pekach strode quickly along the village paths. No one saw him as he left. The path to the forest was there to see, every child in the village knew it because they were forbidden to set foot on it. Pekach walked along it for a whole day. From a distance he saw the many-branched, broad-leafed trees whose swaying tops endowed them with a tranquil, inviting appearance. It was midnight again. Pekach looked and saw that this time the moons almost touched each other as they passed through the firmament. He had never seen them so close to one another. But on second thought he realized that they had inclined towards each other since the day he was born.

Pekach stood at the entrance to the forest. The path took a natural course between the trees and their dense, latticed foliage glowed in the brightness of the moons until it seemed that the path was leading into a reception room illuminated with a glorious light. What dangers might be lurking in such a radiant and joyful place? Pekach's feet moved of their own volition and in another moment would have trodden on the forest's soil had it not been for a sudden gust of wind in his face that knocked him flat on his back. The white eagle was flapping its vast wings and blocking his way into the forest.

The eagle landed and Pekach knelt before it in awe. "Rise," the eagle ordered, and Pekach did so. "Have no fear," the eagle added, "although we were almost too late. Had your foot stepped onto the soil of the forest, you would have immediately sprouted roots and bark would have covered your whole body."

"So how am I supposed to get to the lake?" Pekach asked.

"Climb onto my back and I'll carry you," the eagle replied.

Pekach climbed onto its back. Its feathers were soft and fine as silk and he was fearful of clutching them lest he damage them. "Hold onto the chain around my neck," the eagle said. Pekach grasped the chain by two copper links as if they were reins, and the eagle took off and soared above the treetops.

The trees below them felt cheated. Their branches reached upwards menacingly, boughs and tendrils whipped the air. One tendril wrapped itself around the eagle's talons, but with a swift peck it freed itself. "Don't be afraid," it said to Pekach, and Pekach replied, "Me? I'm not . . . " and fell silent, for from amongst the treetops came a terrible buzzing and a cloud of bronze beetles rose towards them. Each one was the size of a clenched fist and its entire body bristled with stings and jaws. Pekach held his arms in front of his face in defense. "Fool," the eagle called to him, "keep hold of the chain," and Pekach did so. Then the eagle accelerated and sailed into the cloud of beetles. The beetles flew at them and Pekach felt that his whole body was being stung. But then a strange thing happened: he felt a sting going into him and immediately being withdrawn, or a row of teeth clamping around him and then opening. What was happening?

The eagle and its rider passed through the swarm of beetles and Pekach turned to see if they were in pursuit, but the bronze cloud remained as a mass hovering over the treetops.

"Why didn't they tear us to pieces?" the confused Pekach asked.

"Those beetles are sustained by life force," the eagle replied. "You have life force for six more days, and I don't have any. They had nothing to suck from us."

Now a clearing in the forest was revealed and in it a wide lake, its clear waters gleaming in the light of the two setting moons. The eagle landed on the bank and Pekach climbed down from its back and surveyed his surroundings. The trees lining the center of the forest appeared more bloodthirsty than the ones on its edge. They flexed their branches only slightly menacingly. Pekach looked back at the eagle and saw it had become a stone statue. He touched it with his fingertips: the stone was freezing. He tried to remember the eagle's instructions from his dream. Trap Tarfon? The Prince of the Lakes? But how could a boy not yet fifteen years old hunt such an ancient, powerful and fearsome being like Tarfon?

Exhausted and lost, he lay down at the foot of the statue and fell asleep. His sleep was dark and even, as if someone had covered his head with a tied sack. A shake awakened him. He opened his eyes at once. The white eagle was itself once more and was shaking him with a talon. "Are you well rested?" the eagle asked.

"Yes," Pekach replied, "but what happened to you? Why did you turn into stone?"

"I borrow my power from the moons and turn into stone as they set."

And indeed, the twin moons were now shining above the treetops from opposite sides and were slowly rising towards one another.

"Mark their orbit," the eagle said.

"They move closer to each other every night."

"Exactly," the eagle said, "and once every thousand years the twin moons of the Kingdom of Autumn unite for a few seconds, and it happens on three consecutive nights. Some say they mate, and with the force of their mating the Kingdom of Autumn's flow of water is renewed. With every moment of their unity Tarfon, Prince of the Lakes, is forced to take on the form of a simple fish, and then he can be netted and asked to grant a wish."

"That means," Pekach said, "that I must wait for the moment the moons unite and then I can trap Tarfon? But I've only got six days before my life is changed."

"Tonight is the first night of the three. Ready your net. You must trap him on your own."

Pekach cast his net into the lake and followed the rise of the twin moons. But the closer they came to one another he felt sleep overtaking his eyes and his thoughts wandering. Why was he holding a net in his hands? What exactly was he waiting for? Maybe he'd close his eyes for a minute or two . . .

He suddenly opened them with a start. The moons had already separated and the eagle told him, "You missed your chance. The uniting has already occurred. Tarfon evidently cast a sleeping and distracting spell before the united moons shone on him."

On the second night Pekach sat on the bank waiting for the moment of uniting. But what had taken place on the previous night happened again. His eyes became heavy and his mind wandered. The uniting of the moons passed.

Throughout the third day Pekach laid his plans and when the twin moons shone and the eagle had become flesh and blood once more, Pekach asked it, "Are you affected by Tarfon's spell too?"

The eagle nodded.

"If so," Pekach said, "I've found a solution."

When the moons moved close to one another Pekach told the eagle to lie on its belly and open its beak. He placed the arm holding the net between the upper and lower parts of the beak. The moons commenced their uniting, and the sleeping spell again stole the wakefulness of Pekach and the eagle, but when the bird fell asleep its beak closed on the boy's arm, and the sharp pain brought him to his senses. Pekach tugged his arm and with the force of his tug he fell onto his backside and started to pull in the net. And there, enmeshed in the densely woven twine, flopped a simple fish.

Pekach grabbed the fish he'd caught in both hands. The uniting of the moons had passed and because Tarfon was out of his lake, he remained in the form of a fish and at Pekach's mercy.

The fish opened its mouth and said, "I am Tarfon, Prince of the Crystal Lakes of Autumn. Obey me and put me back into the water immediately!"

Pekach said, "What will you give me? I need four hundred green zehorans to save my village."

"Miserable mortal," Tarfon replied, "you have snared Tarfon the Terrible and all you ask is four hundred green zehorans? I can make you a Prince of Autumn, give you palaces and precious stones . . . " He fell silent for a moment and then said, "I can prolong your life."

Pekach looked at the eagle, but its head was lowered and its eyes closed. "No," he said, "I have come to obtain four hundred zehorans."

"Don't bother me with trifles," Tarfon roared, and the lake's waters raged with the force of his roar.

From behind Pekach the eagle said, "The further away the moons move from each other, Tarfon's fettering will weaken. You must make haste."

"What do you suggest?" Pekach asked, but it was Tarfon who answered. "Pluck a pair of scales from my body," he said in a low, bubbling voice. "If you put them on your shoulders, wings will sprout. If you swallow them, you will be able to speak all the languages of man and beast. If you cover your eyeballs with them, you will see everything that is hidden from mortal eyes."

The fish's body began to swell and Pekach quickly plucked a pair of scales from its body before Tarfon escaped into the lake. But Tarfon did not dive. He stood on his tail on the lake's surface. Now he was as big as a whale and his face was human.

Pekach deliberated. He didn't want wings, for the white eagle would carry him; and what good would knowing all the languages of man and beast be in the short time he had left? But if he could see what was hidden from mortal eyes, perhaps he'd find treasures, and maybe he'd even discover the reason for the dwindling quantity of fish in the Crystal Lakes. He covered his eyeballs with the two scales. He closed his eyes and opened them. The scene he now saw was frightful. Around the trees floated a burning aura and vapor poured from their tops; the copper flask on the eagle's breast pulsed; within Tarfon's fish body innumerable transparent water creatures threshed; and most terrible of all, in the lower part of the sky appeared a black, venomous, burning and bubbling band.

"What's that? What's happened to me?" he asked Tarfon in fright, and he laughed, saying, "Wretched mortals cannot imagine what they will be given, but they still have the gall to ask."

"What's happened to me?" Pekach cried.

"What do you see?"

"I see a black ring around the world, as if the horizon is filled with boiling ink."

"That is only the beginning," Tarfon thundered, "the Four Kingdoms and the City of Tempest are losing their source of life. In the entire universe there is only one creature wise enough to discover the reason for this and prevent this devastation: Ariella, the fairy detective."

"But Ariella's a fairytale, a children's bedtime story," Pekach protested.

"Ariella is real," Tarfon said, and the force of his voice roiled the waters of the lake, "and she is closer than you think. You must go to her. She is lost in the marshes in the east of Autumn."

"But . . . " Pekach said softly, "I have to go back to my village, the princedom's debt collectors . . . "

"If you don't find Ariella in time there won't be a village, fishermen or lakes. There is no telling what will happen if the ring of burning darkness I have seen approaching for years swallows up the kingdoms and the city."

When he finished Tarfon dove into the depths of the lake with a tremendous sound. Pekach went to the white eagle and stroked the feathers on its breast. He had no choice, and there was no point in feeling sorry for himself for having been deceived.

"Can you carry me to the marshes?" he asked, and the eagle lowered its head and let him climb onto its back.

Chapter Three,
in which the White
Eagle tells a story

THE FLIGHT TO THE EASTERN MARSHES was longer and slower than Pekach expected. For two nights they flew, crossing the skies of Autumn tinged with its changing hues of purple, from the pink of dawn to blood-red; they passed over wastes and woodland, bald mountains and steel citadels. As the moons' light waned the eagle was again turned to stone, and as it flamed anew they continued their flight. Pekach was used to sinking into imaginings, and thus he spent all the evenings of the week he had left in his life. In the middle of the night, as they crossed a wasteland and the twin moons—which moved further and further apart each night—began their steep descent, he asked the eagle to tell him the story of Ariella, and the eagle did so.

For thousands of years, the eagle related, Ariella had been the seer and revelator of the City of Tempest, the patron of the city's riddles and mysteries and of the four border kingdoms. But then a spell was cast on her that banished her soul to another world for a dozen years, where she grew up as one of the local girls until she was twelve. During that period the City of Tempest had been hard hit. When Ariella's soul returned to the City of Tempest it seemed that the girl had changed. She found the source of the spell, which was also the source of the city's ruin, and restored things to their former state. But afterwards there were strange happenings in the order of life throughout the kingdoms. Ariella managed to rectify them all, but at the same time she started to suspect that there was even greater ruin coming from Napoli of Darkness, the Fifth Kingdom.

Fifteen years ago a demon in the form of an albino man burst forth from Napoli of Darkness, and with the help of a long iron staff he sowed madness and feverish hallucinations in the minds of the Kingdoms' citizenry. Ariella knew that the time had come to act and uproot this ruin. She and her assistant, Pereh, started following a chain of clues. At a certain point their paths diverged. Ariella's investigation took her to the marshes in the east of the Kingdom of Autumn, the stronghold of the Women of Deceit, while Pereh's route led him into the mists of the west of the Kingdom of Summer, where he was captured by a tribe of sorcerers. The pair did not realize that they had fallen into a carefully laid trap. The Women of Deceit and the sorcerers had joined forces to defeat them, after one Woman of Deceit and a sorcerer had the same vision and concluded that Ariella held the key to either destroying or saving the Kingdoms.

Together they summoned the demon Bahamiron and sent him as bait for Ariella, while spreading a series of false clues to direct the pair's steps. When Ariella reached the eastern marshes of the Kingdom of Autumn, the Women of Deceit were waiting for her and fought her. They overpowered her, introduced a paralyzing toxin into her body, bound her with strong gossamer and hid her in the marshes. Pereh was captured by the sorcerers who dwelt in the western mists of the Kingdom of Summer, and they plucked his soul from his body and imprisoned it in a special flask.

Pekach interrupted the eagle's story: "I don't understand. How did Ariella survive fifteen years of captivity?"

"Ariella possesses unimaginable powers," the eagle replied, and went on with its story.

451

Neither the Women of Deceit nor the Sorcerers of the Mists were aware of the scope of Ariella's powers. Since her return from the other world to her office in the City of Tempest, a split had been created in her. In her soul there were chambers she was unaware of, dormant and dark chambers, cruel and prepared for any sacrifice. When she fought the Women of Deceit she managed to see through all their plans and learned Bahamiron's summoning spell. While still paralyzed by the poison, her powers continued to work. Thus she overcame Bahamiron and ordered him to execute numerous tasks in the Four Kingdoms in preparation for her and Pereh's return.

"Yes?" Pekach asked, "like what?"

"At this moment we are flying to her rescue, for example," the eagle replied.

"Is that part of her plan?"

"Yes," the eagle said, "Ariella was the voice that came from the flame that threatened to kill you while you were still a baby. She reached an agreement with Tarfon that would allow you to live for another fifteen years."

"Why?"

"You'll soon find out."

Pekach saw the glow of the twin moons weakening against the backdrop of the burning band of darkness, which had widened since the first time he saw it. It seemed that he himself was part of a greater plan. The thought shook him before another, more horrifying thought passed through his mind: this was the last day of his life. Next morning the prophecy of the voice in the flame would be fulfilled, Ariella's prophecy.

Chapter Four, in which Ariella is redeemed and Pekach's life is changed

The eagle turned to stone at the entrance to the marshes, not far from a tangle of wild bushes whose tops rustled with thorny tongues bursting from them. Pekach passed the day lying on his back, thinking. When evening came they soared upward and entered the territory of the marshes. The eagle knew where they were going. Pekach looked around as they descended and the eagle's talons touched the ground. No. It was not real ground but a thin layer of earth covered with twisting weeds. Beneath his feet Pekach could feel the trembling of the marsh. A dark mist, like the smoke rising from crematoria, floated in streaks among the gnarled tree trunks whose tops leaned towards the marshland. Here and there the earth seemingly chuckled and blurred figures, dark and winged, flitted from it and hung in the air.

"What do you see?" the white eagle asked.

"I see a thick black mist, twisted trees, and winged figures coming from the earth. Now they're gathering and moving towards us."

"They are the Women of Deceit. They know we have come to save Ariella, but they think we are incapable of seeing them. Stand next to me and look lost, and as soon as you see a yellow-striped figure, whisper a warning to me."

Pekach pretended he had lost his way. He looked here and there while following the figures out of the corner of his eye.

The eagle was right: a figure bigger than the rest, carrying a spear and striped yellow, approached from the eagle's right. When it reached its head, Pekach called, "Now! On your right!"

The eagle stretched its neck and with a snap of its beak caught the figure. It shrieked and its voice restored its realness: a squat woman with bone wings meshed with visible veins, and a taut fleshy web over them. The eagle smashed her to the ground and feverishly began pecking at her belly. Cries of protest came from the other women that quickly became a sorrowful wailing.

"Stop!" the pecked woman screamed. Her belly was holed like a sieve and a yellow fluid seeped from it. "I will give you anything you want."

"I want the ring on your finger," the eagle said.

"Not the ring," the woman sobbed, and as she uttered the word 'ring', Pekach saw the ring shining on the little finger of her left hand.

"Where is the ring, Pekach?" the eagle asked between pecks.

"On the little finger of her left hand," Pekach replied, and without hesitation the eagle, with one swift peck, cut off the little finger. "Take it and put it on," it ordered, and Pekach took the ring from the finger and put it on his own.

The women wept bitterly, but the eagle was merciless. "The boy is now your ruler," it said, "and you must obey him. Take us to Ariella's prison." Pekach nodded as if to back its words, but the women did not stop their lament. "You must order them in your voice," the eagle said, and Pekach called out, "Take me to Ariella!"

Now, all at once the women obeyed. They stopped crying, formed a line and started walking without even glancing at the mutilated body of their former queen.

They quickly came to a tree on whose branches a chill mist like withered blossom had gathered. The line of women came to a stop. The eagle sprang into the air and beat its wings strongly until all the mist was dispersed. The tree's branches were bare and twisted. From the highest branch hung a bluish gossamer thread at whose end was a cocoon made of the same thread. With its beak the eagle snapped the thread and lowered the cocoon to the ground, and then gently pecked at it until a thin young girl of about twelve was revealed. Her dragonfly wings were folded at her sides, and precious stones encircled her brow. Her eyes were closed.

"Order the poison in her body to dissolve," the eagle told Pekach, "the poison will obey the ring."

Pekach brought the ring to Ariella's heart and said commandingly, "Leave this body!" and then turned to the women clustered around them and shouted, "Back to your lairs and never leave them again!" and the women floated away in disarray.

When Pekach turned back to Ariella he saw her eyelids flutter and her eyes open, revealing wonderful purple pupils.

For the rest of the night they talked, Ariella, Pekach and the eagle. Ariella knew everything about their journey, but many unanswered questions remained in Pekach's mind, first and foremost that of his life: why had he been allocated fifteen years? Ariella said gently, "In the morning, when the twin moons go down, we will know more." And for the first time Pekach's heart was pierced by a real dagger of sorrow, for throughout his life he had lived with the fact of his predetermined death, and except for the melancholy that had beset him in this past month, he had gotten used to it. Now something was rebelling inside him, all his nerves and capillaries protested against the knowledge that they would soon shut down. He wanted to shout, to get up and flee. Morning closed in on them rapidly, like an executioner's blade. As the moons began to wane, Ariella caressed his cheek with the back of her hand and said, "I'm sorry, but I had no choice. There is no excuse for what I did to you. I wish I could have found another way."

The twin moons faded and Pekach fell dead on the ground. Ariella placed her hands on his eyes and murmured, "Thou shalt not be afraid for the terror by night; nor for the arrow that flieth by day; nor for the pestilence that walketh in darkness; nor for the destruction that wasteth at noonday." She did not weep.

She looked at the white eagle, which had turned to stone with the waning of the moons, and she waved her hands in a complex series of gestures until a brightness formed around it and it awoke. "Come," she said, and the white eagle hopped to her, bowed its head, and she removed the copper chain from its neck, detached the copper flask and removed the stopper. She brought the flask to Pekach's lips and poured the orange liquid that spurted from it into his mouth. Pekach's limbs convulsed, flailing to the sides and striking the air. Then he leapt to his feet, his eyes wide in terror.

"Pereh," Ariella said. "Welcome back."

Chapter Five, in which Ariella and Pereh depart for Napoli of Darkness

PEREH PROBED HIS NEW BODY for a long time. The absence of his strong muscles was very worrisome for him. "Is this the best body you could find" he grumbled, and then hugged Ariella. "How long has it been?" he asked.

"Fifteen years," Ariella replied. "What do you see?"

Pereh looked around and a cry of astonishment burst from his lips. "I see everything! Everything! What's that ring of darkness burning at the bottom of the firmament?"

"Something is eroding the outlying kingdoms and the City of Tempest," Ariella replied. "We almost managed to follow it but then we fell into the trap laid by the Women of Deceit and the sorcerers."

"And this body?"

"Treat it with care," Ariella said, her voice shaking, "it carried within it a precious, courageous life."

"And what of your promise to break the spell on me?" the white eagle asked.

Only now did Pereh see it. He studied it curiously and finally blurted angrily, "I can see the demonic nature under those feathers. Who are you?"

"I am Bahamiron," the eagle replied.

Pereh's hand went to his belt seeking a knife, and when he found no weapon he tensed, ready to leap at the eagle. Ariella's voice lashed at him: "Don't be a fool, Pereh. Bahamiron is under my protection."

"No!" Pereh protested, "he is the demon that drove the citizens of the kingdoms mad when we set out to hunt . . . "

"I know," Ariella said softly, "but now he is on our side."

"What about your promise?" Bahamiron again demanded.

"Just one more journey," Ariella replied, "we must make haste to Napoli of Darkness. You too. I think you will make the journey better as an eagle."

The eagle crouched before them and they mounted. A violent wind whistled in their ears as it took off. Ariella noted that it was flying south over the marshes, and asked, "Is Napoli of Darkness in the south of the Kingdom of Autumn?"

This surprised her because she had never known where Napoli of Darkness was. Nobody knew. Looking down from a great height over the outlying kingdoms one could see that their geography was unstable, their various parts shrank and expanded in accordance with a hidden logic. A field whose area seemed small at first could run endlessly, high and impassable ridges became green hills, and a traveler in the kingdoms had to rely on an inner sense of travel. So far, as Ariella scanned the kingdoms from a bird's eye view, she had never located Napoli of Darkness.

The eagle replied, "Napoli of Darkness is at the edge of every direction in the kingdoms, so you must constantly follow one direction until it ends, and then you reach Napoli."

And before the eyes of Ariella and Pereh the direction went south and ended. The blood-soaked sky faded until it resembled a grayish rag, and the ground below them also lost its color. When the colorfulness faded and the world was wrung out, exhausted, the eagle said, "We have arrived."

It landed on a lifeless, sandy plateau. "I cannot enter in the form of an eagle," it told Ariella. She and Pereh dismounted and she pressed her forehead to the eagle's and whispered an oath. The eagle turned into a man, his face furrowed by the

458

passing of the years and his white hair was wild. From his right elbow sprouted a long iron staff. He started walking and they followed. Ariella didn't notice exactly when the light faded and the gray landscape around them darkened. At a certain moment they walked among shadows. From every direction came beasts enveloped in darkness, grumbling and bellowing at them. Their outline was blurred, but Ariella and Pereh managed to catch something of their appearance: they resembled animals they knew, but their appearance was exaggerated or distorted, as if someone had tried to knead the image of one animal and endow it with the image of another—to mold a lion from a cow, to soften the outline of a horse and turn it into a she-wolf. The animals circled the three, anger and thunder in their roar.

"What are these creatures?" Pereh asked.

Ariella looked at Bahamiron expecting him to answer, but he said, "You know full well. The darkness of Napoli is also part of your soul that you haven't yet dared to investigate."

Ariella struggled with herself. For a moment she stood planted where she was and then spoke to Pereh: "They are the beasts of the earth," she said, "the first beast created had neither features nor a finished form. It was born in darkness from a cry of despair and fear. And each of these creatures is a different aspect of it, a face and body it takes on to go out into the world."

Pereh looked at them and a flat roar escaped through his teeth.

"They are our problem," Ariella told Bahamiron, "you can leave. You have been a faithful servant and a brave companion, but there is no point in your fighting your own kind for our sake."

"It was not you I served, Ariella," Bahamiron replied, "my role was to bring you here in the end."

"What's this?" Pereh shouted, "Another trap?"

"No, don't be afraid. Even though I am your sworn enemy, the time comes when old enemies must become allies if they want to survive." He opened his arms and the beasts of the earth moved aside, opening a path for them. Ariella and Pereh strode behind Bahamiron. They passed through a rough rock vault and into a dark cleft in the rock whose space was softened by a shaft of light coming from above. "Here is my true master," Bahamiron said, "and now my time with you is over." He turned into a tiny owl and swiftly vanished.

The light intensified. A bearded man, a red cloak fastened around his body and a linen cowl on his head, stood before them. His irises were white, two glowing crystals of salt from whose many facets the light was refracted. In a voice that echoed and was multiplied in the cleft he said, "Welcome to my home, Ariella, Seer and Revelator of the City of Tempest. And welcome Pereh, scion of the Darkness of Napoli."

"Our thanks . . . ?" Ariella replied, and her voice did not echo from the walls.

"Prospero," said the man, "the Red Death and Ruler of the Remote Islands."

"You directed my actions to bring me here," Ariella stated.

"Guilty as charged," Prospero replied.

"What do you want?" Pereh demanded.

"To entrust Ariella with the most closely guarded secret of Napoli of Darkness. To ask her to choose."

"I'm listening," Ariella said.

"It's not that simple," Prospero said, snapping his fingers. "To begin with, I must ascertain that you are worthy."

Chapter Six, in which the tests Ariella must pass are revealed

THE SOUND OF HIS SNAPPING FINGERS struck the rock walls and rebounded from them, shattered into a thousand tiny echoes that multiplied until the entire cleft was one mass of sound, and Ariella covered her ears. The tumult assailed her body and overpowered her. She fell to her knees, her eyes closed. She opened them when the tumult subsided. She could not feel her body. She floated to the top of a hexagonal chamber on whose white walls were inscribed verses in blood in an unknown language. In the middle of the chamber rose two transparent canopies of ice and under each was a frozen body. She recognized them at once. One was her fairy body, with its sophisticated lace wings and the twelve Urim and Thummim stones gleaming around her head. The other was the body in which she had been born on Earth, before she came to the City of Tempest, the body she had left behind by the stump of the oak tree when she fled her grandmother's dread.

Prospero's voice rose from somewhere. "The choice of a body is a choice of a destiny."

Ariella wanted to ask, Is that the choice I must make? But her voice went unheard.

The choice was not particularly complicated. She had already accepted the transition to the City of Tempest, and returning to life on Earth, a world where her dead parents and murderous grandmother had abandoned her was not an alluring prospect. She had not missed that life at all. She discovered that she moved in the direction of her desires. What had been the core of her being hovering in the chamber gained weight and urged her towards the body of the fairy. And now she was again inside it under the canopy of ice, until it was quickly sealed and hid the chamber from her. Within moments the barrier of ice became clear and melted. The temperature also rose sharply. Ariella thawed out and looked around. She was in the heart of a dusty storeroom. On the curved shelves, which seemed about to break, were piled innumerable ceramic figures, some cracked, some new, large and small, swollen and slim, and all in Pereh's new image: a fifteen-year-old boy with dark hair, whose eyes were two pools of wine.

Prospero's voice again filled the chamber: "Take your companion. Good company is worth its weight in gold."

This test, too, was easy. Ariella cocked an ear, sharpened her hearing until only one frequency filtered into it, the frequency of the pounding of the ceramic figures in the storeroom, the frequency of their pulse. Before their parting, she and Pereh had sworn a blood oath and his heartbeat flowed in her arteries. With two fingers she sought the aorta in her neck and learned the beat. Again she listened until she heard a similar beat coming from a shelf in the far corner. She moved to the figure and grasped it. "I'm taking this one!" she shouted. The figure disintegrated in her fingers. A cloud of dust filled her mouth and nose, choking and blinding. She coughed and her eyes watered, and once the bout passed she was in a different place with Pereh at her side. Prospero was standing on a raised podium to which an alabaster stairway led. He gestured her closer, and she took her leave of Pereh with a caress and ascended the stairway.

"Gold and crystal and iron cannot equal it," Prospero said, indicating three goblets—of gold, crystal and iron—arranged on a small wooden table.

"Take the word without which you would be unable to describe life, but with which there is no guarantee that you would wish to live," he added.

Ariella expected to see words inscribed on the goblets, but only flames burned in them: dense red flames in the gold goblet, soft yellow flames in the crystal goblet, and jagged green flames in the iron one.

Ariella enlisted all her senses. A thousand sensitive, slender feelers emerged from her soul and examined the flames. She recognized the flames burning in the gold goblet. They were the tongues of flame of the word 'love'. Apt, she thought, that love should burn in a gold vessel, not because of its rarity but because like gold, its value in human eyes is determined by the propensity of those around them. Love makes a person avaricious. I'm not sure I'd want love in my life.

She told her intellect to look through the flames, every detail of the knowledge it had acquired over thousands of years scanned, assessed and compared them. She recognized the flames burning in the crystal goblet. They were the tongues of fire of the word 'stupidity'. It's only fitting, she thought, that stupidity should burn in a crystal vessel. Not because of its simplicity but because like crystal, it plants the illusion that the world is transparent, lacking dullness. Stupidity makes a person naïve, thinking that what he sees and reality are one and the same. I'm not sure I'd want stupidity in my life.

She could not decipher the flames burning in the iron goblet. She ordered all the means at her disposal to examine the flames, but the word did not reveal itself to her.

"Between love and stupidity and the unknown, I choose the unknown," she told Prospero, who looked at her keenly. She quaffed the contents of the iron goblet and a terrible scream burst from her lips.

"You chose well," Prospero said, "what do you feel?"

"Pain," Ariella replied through clenched lips, "pain."

And truly, every part of her was consumed by excruciating pain. Fire burned her exposed nerves, rough spikes were driven into her eyes, a flight of lances, alternately freezing and white-hot, pierced her skin, cascades of molten lead poured down her back.

Ariella fell to the ground. Pereh rushed to her up the stairway and bent over her, holding her to him. "What have you done to her?" he demanded of Prospero, "Heal her. Take this from her."

"Kiss her lips."

Pereh obeyed. Ariella's lips were feverish and he felt as if he had dipped his own lips into acid. Her body relaxed.

"You have given her sleep, and afterwards—one hour of lucidity."

"Only an hour?" Pereh asked.

"That is what one mortal can offer another, and it makes no difference how ardent his love is—only a respite from torment can be given, not redemption."

"What do you want of us?"

"From you? Nothing. But from Ariella? You will know that when she awakens."

Chapter Seven, in which Ariella learns the secret of all the Wonderlands

"YOU DECEIVED ME," were the first words Ariella uttered when she opened her eyes.

A thin, mocking smile hovered on Prospero's lips. "How can you deceive someone who has been given the right of choice?"

Ariella tried to stand and discovered how weak her body was. Pereh helped her up and she leant on him. "And what now?" she asked, as Pereh held Prospero in a withering look.

"Now—the most closely-kept secret of Napoli of Darkness. Follow me."

Arching from the alabaster podium was a basalt bridge. Ariella and Pereh stumbled across it. Halfway across they saw another rock vault. Prospero crossed it with them following him. Ariella and Pereh let out a cry of horror. At their feet was spread a wide, scorched valley whose slopes had been consumed by fire and were now piles of ash. On the other side they could see the ruins of palaces and fortresses. The slate and marble and precious metals of which they had been built had cracked and melted in the terrible heat and re-hardened into burnt and leaden masses of desolation. The bare, white denuded stone looked like the gaping mouths of black, mortal wounds. On the valley floor, at its heart, a single, a many-branched tree sprouted. Its branches were intertwined until it seemed that a sealed green canopy was stretched over the thick, gnarled trunk. The valley was flooded with orange light whose source was hidden, for the sun did not shine in the smoke-covered sky.

"What is this place?" Ariella asked.

"In ancient times, eons ago, the valley was the dwelling place of the King of Napoli. He lived in a palace overlooking the valley slopes, and in the valley were all the species of flowers, trees, insects, birds, and other animals. It was said that none was happier than the King of Napoli. But one night the king had a dream that troubled his spirit. In the dream he walked through his palace, but the palace was empty. From the mirrors on the walls a girl of about twelve peered out at him. The king wandered through the palace, through the corridors, the rooms and the halls with the purpose of finding the girl, but in vain. He had this dream for three consecutive nights and on the third day he summoned his court wizards and astrologers and ordered them to explain the dream. After sitting and discussing the dream for a whole day, the senior astrologer told him: 'You must ask the girl what she wants.'

"And so it was. On the fourth night the king had the same dream. He ceased his wandering in the throne room and asked the girl peering at him from a big silver mirror what she wanted. To his surprise, she answered him. She is hungry, she said, and she longed for fruit. But, she added, there is no fruit in the world that can satisfy her.

"Once more the king summoned his wizards and astrologers and ordered them to explain the dream. At the end of a day's discussion, the senior astrologer told him that he must gather fruit of all the species known to the court scientists and pile them around his bed. When the girl asked him for fruit he should tell her, reach out and take whatever you wish. And in the king's dream the palace was filled with every kind of fruit of the tree and the earth, and the girl peered out from a medium-sized copper mirror. The king pointed at the fruit and invited her to partake. And as the girl stretched out a thin, serpentine arm from the mirror, the king discovered that his mind was wandering to other dreams.

"But, towards morning the king again found himself in his palace, blackening fruit cores and seeds everywhere. From a small burnished steel shield on the wall the girl was wailing: 'I'm hungry. Only fruit that does not exist will satisfy me.'

"The king awoke from his dream and this time did not need the counsel of his wise men. He summoned the supreme wizard and ordered him to grow in the valley a tree, each of whose branches would bear a nonexistent fruit. On hearing the king's command the wizard's face paled. 'But Your Majesty,' he protested, 'that will require all the magic in Napoli, and that means nullifying all the magical bastions protecting the country.' For there were three terrible enemies threatening Napoli: the Serpent of the River, the Serpent of the Mountain, and the Serpent Fuming in Light, lighter than metal and heavier than a tempest. And these three constantly threatened to destroy it. But the king, seized by madness, did not heed the supreme wizard's warning, and the latter, wretched and dejected, went to obey the king's command and with great magic raised the Perpetual Tree from the soil of the valley.

"The tree blossomed for five days, and at the end of each day the fruit it yielded was collected, impossible, variegated fruit, juicy and fragrant, and placed around the king's bed, and he sank into a dream. In his dream the king fed the girl, but her hunger did not abate and she asked for more and more fruit from the tree.

"And on the morning of the sixth day the mountain on whose slope the king's palace stood shifted, and the water of the rivers roiled and overflowed their banks, and the light was great and strong, boiling and destroying. And the three serpents rose from their lairs and waged war on the king's palace."

Prospero fell silent.

"And then what happened?" Ariella urged him, and Pereh, too, was captivated by the story.

Prospero pointed towards the valley. "That is the result of the war. The total destruction of the royal court, and the end of Napoli's magic. It was neither the wizards nor their spells that overcame the three enormous serpents, but the war. The serpents were wild, unintelligent creatures. They sucked Napoli's springs of magic dry until they were ruined, and brought their own end upon themselves. Only a few of Napoli's inhabitants, those in whose veins magic flows, like Bahamiron and myself—we are all scions of the wizardly line—remained alive. We found a way of surviving."

"What way?" Bahamiron asked with sudden suspicion.

"And what became of the Perpetual Tree?" Ariella asked.

"From the torrents stirred up by the Serpent of the River, and the shaking of the earth by the Serpent of the Mountain, and the boiling of the Serpent of Light, the fruit was scattered far and wide, fired through the barriers of space and time vital for any existence, and in every place a fruit landed, a Wonderland flourished."

"The City of Tempest too?"

"The City of Tempest was the first Wonderland that flourished."

Ariella sank into thought. Her senses and intellect told her that Prospero was telling the truth. When he uttered the words they had the ring of truth, and when she rolled them on her tongue they had the taste of truth.

"What do you want from me?" she asked.

"The Wonderlands are dying," Prospero said. "You have surely felt the dying of the City of Tempest itself, which is why you embarked on this journey."

Ariella nodded her agreement.

"They are dying because the Perpetual Tree is losing its vitality. Bahamiron and I were entrusted with its protection and we have been wracking our brains for eons to find the cause of its deterioration."

He looked at Ariella. She said, "The tree needs a girl because it was born in a dream about a girl, and only a girl can strengthen its substance."

"Yes," Prospero said.

"No!" Pereh shouted, "Ariella . . . No. You mustn't."

"What must I do?" Ariella asked.

Prospero held out his hand and she took it. With her other hand she stroked Pereh's hand. The view of the valley spun around them and steadied. They were standing beneath the Perpetual Tree, under a canopy of leaves. From close up Ariella could see the rot that had spread through the branches and leaf stems.

Once again Ariella's body was wracked with pain and her muscles locked. Prospero and Pereh sensed this, although Ariella ground her teeth and did not utter a sound. Pereh clasped her to his youthful chest and Prospero drew her from him. "Only the tree will ease the pain. It will feed on your torment," he said.

Ariella entered the tree trunk, her wings proudly spread. She sat down cross-legged on the bed of leaves. Gnarled woody cords emerged from the walls of the trunk and pierced Ariella's skin, penetrating her flesh. She groaned and opened her eyes. Pereh was unable to comprehend the expression in them, whether it was astonishment or terror.

"Ariella," Prospero said, "you should have guessed from the start. You are the girl who is all the Wonderlands."

"No," Pereh protested. The sight of Ariella and the tree sucking out her marrow was unbearable. He tried to get inside the trunk, cut the woody cords, rip them from her. Prospero held out his hand and stopped him. "Let it be, Pereh," he said.

And Pereh asked, "Will she be there a long time?"

"Yes. For eternity," Prospero replied.

"Eternity? How long is eternity? I can wait."

Prospero shook his head. "Imagine that once every thousand years a vast metal ball passes through the sky of your native city, and once every thousand years you go up onto the roof and attack it with a feather. You hit it once every thousand years until it is worn away to the size of a pea. For you, and perhaps for me, that seems a long time, but it is nothing but the blink of an eye in the place to which Ariella has gone."

"No! No!" Pereh shouted. "Ariella, get up, get up and return to the City of Tempest with me. We need you. You can't stay inside this tree trunk."

He waited for a long time but to no avail. In the end he turned his back and began making his way back to the City of Tempest. Shoots of grass began sprouting on the valley slopes, spotting the scorched earth, the sky heightened and was cleansed, a wind blew behind him, the rustle of leaves in it twined with the sound of Ariella's laughing voice. She was speaking to him.

"Whether I like it or not," Ariella said to Pereh, "this is my home." and betwixt the boughs dusty birds obscured the embers with their song.

ACKNOWLEDGMENTS

THIS BOOK OWES ITS EXISTENCE to music: each of its chapters was inspired by a song that refused to leave my thoughts. It was the chapter's point of departure, and whenever I didn't know where the plot was going I went back to the song and in it found a thread. I didn't begin writing a chapter before a new song had settled in my mind. The titles of the songs, which are this novel's subliminal technology, can be found in Ophir Shriki's podcast—arranged in the order of the chapters, and traces of them can be found in the chapters themselves. So first of all, a huge thank you to Ma'ayan Cohen for introducing me to the excellent musicians and rock bands over the past decade, for they constitute the lion's share of my musical nourishment.

Quite a few of my friends read the manuscript and made useful comments an d observations. My thanks to Shachar Magen, who urged me to hone the stories of Ori's childhood and adolescence. Thanks to Shlomzion Keinan for elucidating aspects of feminine desire and passion. Thanks to Sahara Blau for encouraging me to expand Ori's boundaries. Thanks to Shva Salhov for in-depth conversations on Hebrew, poetry, Orientalism and Judaism, both in and outside the book. Thanks to Yaron Regev for his questions on the societal location of prophecy in our times.

Very special thanks to Moshe Ron, the Hebrew edition's editor, who accompanied me wisely and with great and accurate insight.

Special thanks to my sisters, Michal Cohen and Avichayil Malka, who unknowingly contributed fragments of stories to the first part of the novel, and to Yasmin Adaf, who read the first draft and drew my attention to Ori and Barak's relationship, the crisis between them, and its resolution.

———

On 28 November 2007, as the book's editing was nearing conclusion, my beloved sister Aviva passed away at the age of forty-three: part of my soul, which up to that moment I had known nothing of its being and emotions and whispers, was ripped out. Aviva endowed me with my reading ethic and gave me my first book (a Sherlock Holmes anthology); she encouraged me to persevere with writing when my first poems aroused revulsion in me, and she motivated me to think again about the works of writers I hastened to dismiss—O. Henry ('You think that the point at the end of *The Voice of the City* is that the hero discovers that the voice of the city is actually its silence. That's a simplistic conclusion. The point is that he can only hear it when he's with his lover') and Jane Austen ('She teaches the reader to be suspicious of any social order and still believe in Man's basic goodness'). Of everything I have written so far, this is her book.

SHIMON ADAF was born in Sderot, Israel, in 1972 to parents of Moroccan origin. He began publishing poetry during his military service. Later, he moved to Tel Aviv and joined a rock band as songwriter and acoustic guitar player. He published three collections of poetry and six novels, for which he won the Ministry of Education Award for Debut book (1996) and the Prime Minister`s Prize (2007). His third collection of poetry *Aviva-No* won the Yehuda Amichai Poetry Award in 2010, and his novel *Mox Nox* won the Sapir Prize (the Israeli equivalent of the Booker Prize) in 2011. He resides in Tel Aviv and teaches Creative writing and literature in Ben Gurion University.